STEELE CITY BLUES

THE THIRD BOOK IN THE HELL'S BELLE SERIES

KAREN GRECO

For Anthony. Always.

CONTENTS

PROLOGUE

"GODDAMN BLOODSUCKERS," I grumbled, slapping at the mosquitos nibbling on the back of my neck.

"Who are you calling 'bloodsucker?'" Frankie asked, giving me a playful shove. Weighed down with over 40 pounds of vampire hunting gear on my five-foot frame, he nearly tipped me into the eight feet of water stagnating below the platform.

Sweat leaked from the small of my back down into my pants, and I pulled awkwardly on the damp waistband. I glanced at Frankie in his leathers; not a bead of sweat on him. In the ripe heat of Orlando in the middle of August, being undead had its benefits.

I wrinkled my nose. "I thought the water they used for the rides was chlorinated. This is a little..."

"Swampy?" Frankie finished for me. "At least they shut the music off at night. Can you imagine if we had to endure that song?" He started humming it. "Iiiiit's a smaaaall world after—"

"Zip it," I said, smacking him in the chest. The last thing I needed was that song on repeat in my head while we searched for the vampire hiding somewhere in the happiest place on earth.

"You know he picked this ride to hide in because of that song, right?" Frankie asked. "Thought we wouldn't have the cobblers to endure that tune."

"The cobblers?"

"Yeah, you know. The balls, as you Yanks like to call 'em," he said, groping at his anatomy like I needed a demonstration. "Nope, the bloke couldn't go hide in the haunted mansion. Had to pick this ode to world peace. The wanker."

The dark labyrinth of tunnels was a perfect spot for an anti-social, undead creature to snatch unsuspecting victims. The happiest place on earth was decidedly unhappy with the fact that a vampire roamed one of its most popular rides, looking for a meal.

The happiest place on earth was lucky the vamp wasn't having much success. No one had died yet, no kid had gotten bit. Only a handful of adults had surfaced with nasty puncture wounds on their necks, which the resort doctors explained away as bug bites. It wasn't an unlikely scenario. There were some weird-ass bugs in Florida.

But when one woman came out with the accusation of vampire, a surge of news crews descended on Orlando. The story went viral, blowing up into an international sensation within hours. The talking heads dismissed the "hysterical" woman's claim. Doctors and ento-mologists were called in to identify the bite marks. The blame was either weird-ass bugs or woman-in-search-of-a-payout, depending on your world-view.

But Blood Ops — the secret government agency dealing with rogue elements of the supernatural population lurking around the United States — knew better. And so did this behemoth corporation.

The Department of Defense didn't even need to bring us in. The happiest place on earth phoned direct. "Classified" was all relative to how many billions were in the bank, I guess.

Frankie started humming that song again — *that song!* — under his breath.

"Shhh," I said, desperate to keep the earworm out. "We need to listen for him."

"I can't help it," he said. "We got here before the ride was shut down. I heard it clear as a bell in the parking lot."

I gave Frankie's arm a sympathetic squeeze, grateful that my human ears were too weak to hear *that song* when we were at least a mile away.

The boats that took enthusiastic theme park-goers through the ride were parked in a row in front of us. It was after 10 p.m., and for the approximately two hours since sundown, Frankie and I were standing at the water's edge, waiting to ambush the illusive vampire on his way out to civilization. There was no way he was sustaining himself with little nips on the audience. He had to leave at some point to feed for real. All the warm bodies in the bustling metropolis of Orlando had to be a lure.

"Maybe we should get in the boat," I whispered. I hoped Frankie didn't notice the excitement thick in my voice. My Aunt Babe had brought me here once, when I was super young. I barely remembered the trip, but it always struck me as one of the happier times of my young, often chaotic life. Not that the chaos was my aunt's fault. What do you do with your not-undead-yet, half-vampire niece? I had too many weird "afflictions" for regular school — preternatural speed and agility, wounds that healed quickly, a taste for bloody-as-hell meat. She had no choice but to leave me with Blood Ops.

I itched to get on a ride, even if it was the one with that blasted song.

Frankie's body shook in silent laughter. "You're a flipping riot, you are."

"I'm not joking, Frankie," I said, gesturing to the boats. "He's nipping at them on the rides. If he won't come to us, maybe we need to go to him."

"Maybe we missed him," Frankie said. He stepped away from the water's edge.

"We've been here since sundown. He's not coming out."

"Where are you going?" Frankie asked, raising his voice. He reached for my arm but just missed as I slid into the first boat.

It rocked back and forth as I adjusted my weight to find my balance. "Come on. I don't want to sit in here all night. I'm turning into a giant mold spore."

"Nina, I am your senior officer..." he started, taking a step away from the water's edge.

"Wait, you're pulling rank?" I asked, then I sucked in my breath as I wondered why Frankie wanted to wait. *On shore.* "You can swim, can't you?"

"Of course I can swim," he snapped.

"So what's the problem?" He didn't answer. "It's an amusement park ride, Frankie." I pointed to the water. "Look, the boats are even on a track."

He raised his chin and pulled himself straight. "Bloody hell, Nina," he swore, putting one foot gingerly in the boat, then the other. He held onto the sides and dropped his ass onto the bench. "I just don't enjoy rides, okay?"

"What's wrong with rides?"

"Amusement parks are preposterous," he said, his hands gripping the boat as it swayed from his movement. "And creepy."

I drummed my nails on the side of the ride. "You are a vampire, Frankie. And you think amusement parks are creepy?"

He shuddered. "There's something about an unmanned mechanical ride moving people that just bothers me, okay?" We sat motionless, in silence. "Bloody hell, Nina, just turn the damn ride on."

I looked at the control panel several feet away. "You're faster then me," I said. "I'll miss the boat."

He leaned his elbows on his thighs. "You have vampire in you. You're fast enough to make it before the boat takes off. So come on then. Let's get this over with, stake this bloody vampire and get back to the hotel."

I grunted to a standing position, stepped off the boat and counted the steps to the control panel. Seventeen. I still didn't believe that my dormant vampire gene could propel me back to the boat fast enough, but Frankie wasn't going to get off his ass.

I examined the control panel and wondered if there was a way to run the ride without the music. *That song* would run in my head for days.

"Just press the red button, Nina," Frankie said impatiently.

I pursed my lips at him and did exactly that. The ride groaned to life, the first bars of *that song* humming along with it. I raced over as the first boat launched, Frankie white knuckling its sides.

My vampire speed propelled my legs faster than the average human, but not fast enough to make it an easy step into the boat. Frankie floated away.

"Make the jump!" Frankie called from his seat. I shook my head. I had been in the field less than three months and didn't trust my body to do certain things. Like make a twenty-foot jump into a moving target.

The boat behind Frankie's was still beside the platform, so I jumped into that one and followed Frankie's ride into the tunnel. I slumped in my seat, my failure over not trying the jump weighing on me. I wanted to call out an apology, but we were almost through the tunnel and we needed to stay alert for this vampire. The faster we nailed his ass, the faster we'd be on a flight back to the Blood Ops base in Nevada. The Orlando humidity was making my hair frizz.

The first room of dancing animatronic children was almost enough to put me off amusement parks. With painted rosy cheeks, their bodies spun in time to *that song* while the pitch black surrounded me. I could barely see Frankie's boat in front of me, and I wondered how he was dealing with the creepy doll children.

A wisp of air tickled the back of my neck, and, goosebumps sprouting, I shivered. My head snapped around searching for something behind me. I was met with empty blackness.

Did the volume just go up on the music?

Sensing a presence beside me, I snapped my head to the left. Nothing. I was about to call out to Frankie, quiet be damned, when I felt two sharp, thin fangs puncture through the skin of my neck.

"Holy shit!" I yelled, pushing on a bony chest before scrambling to my feet. The boat lurched side to side. I dragged the vampire, his teeth no longer attached to my neck, up with me by the front of his shirt. A drop of blood — my blood — was smeared down his chin. "You bit me, you asshole!"

My hand pressed against my neck wound as shock took hold. I'd never been bitten by a vampire before. All I could do was stare at him. Grey crepey skin, bald head, filthy ill-fitting clothes. The vampire was desiccating.

"Just a taste," he said, dragging out the "s" sound like a snake.

"My god, what the hell is wrong with you?"

Using my shock to his advantage, the vampire shoved me back down. Desiccation be damned, he still had a large amount of strength and overpowered me easily.

I struggled against him as the seats of the boat pressed into my back. I pushed at his chest, holding him at arms length, while he snapped his teeth at me. I dragged my leg in and pressed my knee into his sternum, hoping to free a hand so I could grab one of the holstered stakes that pressed into my lower back. Dammit! How was I going to get that out from behind me?

That song continued, louder still, cycling through a different language at each refrain. It burned my eardrums but the vampire hummed along with it.

"Frankie!" I called out, wondering if he'd be willing to jump into the stagnant water, and ruin his leathers, to come help me.

The harder the vampire and I struggled, the harder the boat rocked. My back lifted a few inches off the seat from the movement. I could grab the stake if I timed it just right.

The vampire changed his tactics and grabbed me by the collar of my thin jacket, lifting me up and slamming me back down again. My head lolled over the side of the boat. My hair dangled in the water, its swampy odor filling my nostrils. The vamp pulled me out and dropped me again, jarring my lower back into the side of the boat, my head angled just above the murky water. I gripped his arms, fighting against him to keep my head from going under.

"Frankie!" I barked again, louder. The mix of stage lights and animatronics cast an eerie glow on the ceiling of the ride. The music kept going. The vamp kept humming. The music seemed to have a hold on him, like it was making him mad.

A strong hand clamped down on my forehead, forcing me towards the water. He leaned in, fangs exposed, going for my jugular.

I sucked in a deep breath of air, then went limp under him, submerging my head in the swamp.

I cringed when I felt his fangs sink into me again, gritting my teeth as I felt him suck. I fought against my reaction to struggle and forced myself to let him overtake me. As the seconds ticked on and my body remained limp, he relaxed his hold a bit. The water mercifully muffled *that song* so that I could focus on what I needed to do next. I expelled my air slowly, bubbles barely perceptible on the surface.

I floated my hand around to my back until my fingers brushed up against the wooden stakes. I wrapped my hand around one and slipped the stake out of its holster. The rough wood felt foreign in my grip. I'd never used a stake to kill before. It was always used on a latex dummy, the rubber and plastic a close facsimile of an actual body.

With the vampire chewing on my neck, my training kicked in. I lifted my free hand under his rib cage and pushed up with all my strength, lifting my body out of the water at the same time. I hollered in pain as his teeth ripped away from my neck. Before he could react, I shoved the stake into his heart. His eyes went wide and he dropped on me with a thud.

That song continued as the boat exited the final tunnel.

I shoved the body off and sat up. Soaked through from my shoulders up, my hair dripped and made a puddle on the bottom of the boat. Frankie stood at the cement platform and watched my boat come in.

"What the bloody hell happened to you?" he asked, his eyes widening when he saw the body splayed beside me in the boat.

I ignored the hand he held out to me and jumped out of the boat, grateful to feel dry land under my feet. I marched to the control panel, pulled out another stake from my holster and slammed it into the computer repeatedly until *that song* warbled into silence.

The quiet was bliss.

Frankie looked from me to the staked vamp splayed out in the boat. "You did that on your own?"

"Well *you* didn't help me," I pointed out.

"How was I supposed to know...?" He took my chin and tipped my head, getting a gander at the missing chunk of neck that was beginning to knit back together. "He bit you?"

"I yelled for you..." I rubbed at the chew mark on my neck and wrinkled my nose at the stench from the water rising off my body. "Do you have Neosporin or something? That water is nasty. I don't want the bite to get infected before it heals completely."

"When was the last time you had a tetanus shot? It's healing over fast," he answered. He turned and surveyed the ride. "Funny I didn't hear you. That song, all I heard was *that song*." He shuddered.

"You want to finish him off?" I asked. To kill the vampire true-dead, we needed to cut off his head. Otherwise, if we removed the stake, he'd rise again. "Or do you want me to do it?"

Frankie rubbed at his overgrown black hair, his piercing blue eyes moving back to the vampire. He climbed into the boat and lifted the lifeless body. "Was he desiccated?"

I nodded. It was hard to tell now that he was staked.

"The music affected me. Maybe it made him mental, trapped him here or something. He wasn't feeding except for the few nips."

"So what are you saying? You want to take him in alive?" I asked.

Frankie stepped out of the boat, his feet light on the cement. "Yes, let's see what Dr. O has to say about this," he said, referring to the head of Blood Ops, who was also an ancient Druid priest. If anyone could figure out what *that song* had to do with this vamp losing his marbles, it was Dr. O.

"Fine, but you get to ride with him in the cargo hold," I said, my mind already turning over the number of precautions we'd have to take on the plane, not the least of which was getting another coffin to ship this guy. Frankie wasn't going to share his.

"Your first kill, in a manner of speaking," Frankie said, mussing my hair with his large hands. "Shall we celebrate? Want to give another ride a go? I've heard about this roller coaster, Lighting Mountain or some-such. Was told by Doreen in home office we absolutely had to ride it."

"But you don't like amusement parks," I said.

"But you do." He gave me a small shove towards the exit. "Come on now, I'll snag you a corn dog or something. Maybe we even can try the flume."

1
_____

My 2007 Triumph Bonneville screamed on the downshift, and I lurched forward. The force almost shot me over the handlebars. Frankie's bike engine whirred as he raced to catch up with me.

A bullet whizzed past my ear, the close call more a matter of luck than skill. It was the first near-miss since these clowns started shooting at us three miles back. Now we were coming up on the Thurbers Avenue exit on Interstate 95, and the goal was to lose them on an upcoming curve of the highway.

Mia's long arms snaked around me, hanging on for dear life. She squeezed my midsection *hard*. For a 70-year-old lady, she had one hell of a grip. I hoped the nervous squeeze was from the sudden increased speed and not a bullet, since over a mile ago, I had sworn to her that the idiots chasing us were absolutely, positively, definitely out of bullets.

My bike was a steady 130mph, not even close to top speed. The goons behind us were on those crotch rockets — fast but zero muscle to them. We could lose them once we got past Thurbers, the deadliest stretch of highway in Rhode Island.

Not like it mattered much. Frankie, a vampire, was already dead, so a crash wouldn't kill him. But if I died, I would go from half to full vampire, and honestly, I wasn't up for eternal life right then. Ever since my own mother Leila unexpectedly rose from the dead, killed my aunt and unleashed hell on earth, I wasn't too keen on sticking around forever. The only exception was if I could exterminate as many of these punk-ass vigilantes as possible.

But first things first — getting Mia out of here.

Frankie and I were tasked with getting Mia from the safe house to the airport. Bertrand, the demon mayor of Providence, had hooked us up with a supernatural sympathizer who worked for one of the few airlines still running out of TF Green. The plan was to smuggle Mia onto the last cargo plane flying out that night. It was departing at 11:40 p.m. sharp. Mia would fly to San Diego, where she'd be smuggled to a remote safe house just over the Mexican border. The operation was like an apocalyptic version of the Underground Railroad for witches, vampires and other supernaturals, or supernats, who wanted to live peacefully and discreetly among humans.

As a coven elder whose magic was so strong that it rivaled pretty much all witches, Mia was an important figure among supernats, Leila included. Even when she wasn't practicing, Mia oozed magic. That kind of power put her straight into Mommy Dearest's crosshairs, a very dangerous place to be. Leila would be able to get a read on Mia easily. We needed to get to that plane.

Nice and easy, I pressed on the brakes as the road began to bend. But instead of following my lead and slowing into the curve, Frankie flew past me.

"What the hell are you doing?!" I screamed over the wind, knowing his sensitive vampire hearing would pick up my voice.

Before he could respond, he lost control and his bike went into a skid. His body, still attached to the bike, slid across the asphalt roadway, spinning out of control for a solid 100 feet. The slam of bike and body against the cement barrier boomed through the quiet night.

"Frankie!" I yelled into the wind. My instincts screamed at me to open the throttle, but I forced myself to slow down as I negotiated the dangerous roadway.

When I got through the turn, I stopped the bike in the middle of the freeway. I yanked Mia off the back and sprinted towards Frankie, dragging her after me. If those goons caught up with us, Mia sitting alone on my bike was an easy target.

He was in rough shape, taking a direct hit to the head that left a crack in the huge cement barrier. Blood rushed out of his skull like a geyser. The bike could go up in flames at any second and I wanted to get all of us out of the way. But Frankie's skull was split open, his grey matter oozing onto the ground. The bones were already fusing back together. His noggin knitting shut with his brain bits still on the pavement wouldn't be a good thing. I had to get them back into his head.

Gritting my teeth, I scooped up his brains and tried to push them back into his skull. His head was healing too fast. I couldn't get his grey matter off the pavement fast enough. I reached into my pocket and pulled out an athame. I pulled his blood-soaked hair tight, losing my fingers in its thick darkness. Then, without hesitating, I hacked at the bone to reopen his skull.

"Mia, help me!" I called to the witch. "There, pick that up." I nodded at the brain tissue still on the ground. With one final slam, I re-cracked his cranium. Blood oozed out again. "Shove it in, fast!"

I jammed my fingers into the crack and stretched it out. His skull popped and cracked under the pressure, but it gave way so that we could replace what was missing. Mia, without gagging (bless her witchy soul), picked up Frankie's brain matter and shoved it back into his head. I released my fingers and, quick as can be, his bones knitted back together.

"Well done, Mia!" I said, jumping up to give that heroic witch a hug. I turned just in time to see a gunman walk up behind her and shoot her point blank in the back of the head, execution style. She crumpled to the ground. This time it was chunks of her brain, dark red blood and bits of her broken skull that landed on my booted foot. Unlike Frankie, there was no fixing this one.

Without hesitation, I leapt at the gunman, grabbed his head and gave it a sharp twist. His neck snapped and his body crumpled. I tossed him into the middle of the highway like a rag doll. He landed right in front of two oncoming motorcycles, the remaining members of his posse. They both swerved to avoid his body and dumped their bikes in the chaos, spinning out down the highway.

I ran after them, my living-vampire swiftness getting me there before they could register what happened. I snatched one up by the back of his leather jacket, dragging him along the ground to his buddy. That one I lifted off the ground by his throat.

"What the hell are you, lady?"

That was the one I had by the back of the neck. The one I had by the throat could only wheeze.

"I am no lady," I growled. "I am your executioner."

I tossed them both on the ground and shook out my wrists. A pair of razor sharp blades extended over each hand, my own special weaponized claws.

"You're human, right?" I asked with a smile before plunging a blade into each of their throats simultaneously. I extracted the claws quickly and blood bubbled out of their necks. Between the blood and the expelling air, their throats made a gurgling noise.

"Good god, woman," Frankie said, sneaking up behind me. "Must you always kill in such a vile way? That sound is atrocious."

"How's your head?" I asked, squinting at him. He wasn't listing when he stood. That I could see, at least.

"What are you talking about?" he puzzled. "Come on now, let's clean up your mess."

I wiped the bloody blades against my jeans. "Leave it."

"Are you mad? If we leave this...."

"What? Leila will send her goons out looking for me?" I said, toeing at one of the lifeless bodies. "These were her goons, and they were after Mia, not me."

"Mia?" Frankie looked confused for a minute. "Mia...I can't quite..." His clouded expression went bright with alarm. "Mia! Wait, where is Mia?"

I gave my arms a quick shake. The blades retracted. "They got her, Frankie."

"What do you mean, they got her?" he asked.

I pointed to where Mia lay in the middle of the highway. Her grey hair was black and sticky from the blood pooled around her. "Where was I when all this was happening?"

"You took a nasty bump on the head. You were out for the whole thing."

"Out, like passed out? Vampires don't pass out."

"The ones with traumatic brain injuries do."

Frankie's eyes went wide. "Really? I had a traumatic brain injury? And I'm not a vegetable. Extraordinary."

I wiped my blood stained hands on my ass. "Frankie, we lost Mia. I just executed three of Leila's human henchmen. My jeans are ruined. And I need a goddamn drink. What the hell is so extraordinary about your brain injury?"

His laugh was small and rueful. "Your dad and I used to argue about what would happen to a vampire if the brain was injured. Would we survive? Be vegetative? I figured there had to be something that kept us alive, in a manner of speaking, and there had to be neurons firing in the brain. So I said we'd be veg."

"Well, you can give me the 50 bucks you bet then, since he's not here."

"It wasn't a money wager."

"Bullshit. There was no way you and my dad had this debate without some sort of monetary bet on the table."

Frankie raised an eyebrow.

I was too tired to prod further. "Well, since you're not a vegetable, you can help me roll these two assholes and see exactly who the hell they are."

"What's the point?" Frankie asked. "They *are* human, so most likely they're bounty hunters."

"Yeah and they executed Mia. She wasn't just collateral damage. She was their target."

"Right, and they work for your mom," he said, shrugging.

"Leila," I corrected him. That woman may have birthed me, but she was not my mother. "If they worked for Leila, I want to know who they are, where they live, where they work, who they hang out with. I am sure there are others in their posse tasked with assassinating other witches."

"Good point," he conceded. "Should we call Max?"

I shook my head. No reason to get the FBI involved. Or what was left of it. The Feds now worked for my mother—I mean, Leila. My team, Blood Ops, no longer had the backing of the U.S. government. We were the vigilantes.

"Hey ho!" Frankie called out, digging through a wallet he liberated from one of our attackers. "Got a driver's license on him, out of Connecticut of all places. I think this may be near our roving pack of wolves."

I sighed, remembering the werewolf pack we met just a few weeks ago. It felt like an eternity had passed since. "That's just great. I have zero interest in talking to those pricks again. Werewolves are not exactly team players."

"Keep your friends close, Nina," Frankie reminded me. I stared while he stuffed the dead guy's money in his jacket pocket.

"Frankie, what the hell are you doing? We're searching them, not robbing them."

"Nina, the boys are dead. If they are dead, can I really rob them?"

I opened my mouth to say something, but he cut me off before I took a breath.

"Don't give me crap about dishonoring the dead and all that. It's end times, Nina. Grab the greenbacks while we can."

I didn't argue, especially since I planned on making the same argument for taking their guns. Weapons were in even shorter supply than cash, which was becoming more and more useless anyway. "Find anything else?" I asked, pulling my hands clear of the pockets of the first guy I took down. "This guy was clearly the brains of the operation. He has no identification on him."

"Let's get off the streets then," Frankie said. "Back to the bar?"

"Let's split up though. Something doesn't feel right," I said.

"What do you mean, love?"

"I mean, it feels like we're being watched."

Frankie did a 360-degree turn in the middle of the dark highway.

No one seemed to be around us for miles. "That's paranoia, Nina, and they have pills for that."

I shook my head. "I trust my gut here, Frankie. Someone's been on our tail since yesterday."

"Your mum—" he started and I shot him a look. "Sorry. *Leila*. She's had trackers on us for days."

I shivered, feeling those invisible eyes on me again. "No, it's not her. It's something else. Not sure what."

"So it's your witchy senses tingling?"

I looked down the interstate. The streetlights were out, and most of the houses and high-rise buildings in the distance were dark. The blinds on every window within view were closed tightly.

I nodded. "You stay on the highway. I'll take the back roads and meet you at Babe's."

"Right," Frankie said. "And if one of us doesn't get there in 30 minutes, the other sends out the cavalry."

"You mean Bertrand, don't you?" I asked, growing cold at the mention of his name.

"He's all the cavalry we have at the moment," Frankie said.

That was true. Bertrand was our only lifeline right then, but a demon can't be anything but a demon. That meant he was playing both sides – mine and Leila's – so he'd end up on the winning one. But the winning side was, more often than not, the demon's.

Frankie picked his bike up off the ground and swore at the damage on the left side. "Bloody hell, I don't remember dumping my bike," he muttered before the roar of his engine cut his voice off.

I straddled my bike and started her up, the rumble soothing. I glanced over at Mia, her slight body crumpled in a spreading pool of blood. One more innocent victim in a supernatural genocide. And I failed to protect her.

I kicked my motorcycle into gear and headed to the first exit to take the back roads to Babe's, before the cops got wind of the mess littering the highway.

Welcome to Providence.

2

"FRANKIE HERE YET?" I grumbled to my best friend Darcy when I walked into Babe's on the Sunnyside. I now had sole ownership of the dive bar since Leila burned my Aunt Babe at the stake for being a witch, kicking off this entire mess.

I tossed my road-worn, blood-spattered leather jacket on the bar, ducked under the counter and immediately reached for a bottle of whatever was closest. It happened to be tequila.

"Maybe you should wash your hands first?" Darcy, ever the pragmatist, suggested. She tossed me a bar towel. "Face too." She made a wiping motion up her cheek.

I caught a quick look at my reflection in the mirror behind the bar. Dried blood caked my hands. Blood spatter covered my face, chest and part of my white tank top. It also coated my hair, which was hanging down in sticky clumps. Some of the dried blood looked chunky. Probably bits of brain, given the events of the evening.

I uncorked the bottle with my teeth and took a quick pull, the cheap booze burning a line down my dry throat. I turned the tap on the sink and shoved my entire head under the cool water, washing away the evening's folly. Mia was dead and there was a pileup of bodies on the interstate. Blood and street grime puddled in the sink before swirling down the drain. I wished my memories of Mia's execution could be flushed away just as easily.

The bar regulars — the few that were left — didn't even flinch. With an assist from Casper, the teenaged ghost-witch that inhabited my body from time to time, I had used my rudimentary magic to disguise the bar as a rundown, abandoned shack. To humans, it appeared marked for demolition. But supernats knew better. They knew Babe's as their safe haven, away from pitch-fork wielding humans.

When Leila unmasked my aunt as a witch, she took advantage of the human population's mass hysteria and took over the state-house in a coup. The entire state was under Marshall Law and her human henchmen tasked with hunting down the "new breed of terrorists."

Blood Ops, a top-secret government task force that controlled the supernatural population, was disbanded the minute she tossed the match in Babe's funeral pyre. The head of Blood Ops, Dr. Lachlan O'Malley, was taken into custody and was now sitting in the state's maximum-security prison, nicknamed Steele City. Dr. O, Frankie, Darcy and I no longer had the protection of the United States government.

The irony was, supernatural creatures were perfectly happy in the closet. Witches practiced their magic, vampires found willing blood sources, werewolves whooped it up in the woods. Most of us were content to blend in with the human population. But there was always a bad apple in the bunch, and when a rogue witch caused havoc or a vampire went on a killing spree, Blood Ops was discharged to handle the situation. Whereas before we protected the humans from the likes of us, we now found ourselves protecting our kind from the humans.

When I pulled my head up, water dripped from my hair down my shoulders, soaking my tank top. I grabbed a dry bar towel and gave it a sniff. Smelled clean. "So, Frankie here yet?" I asked again, wiping my face.

Just as Darcy shook her head no, the door to the bar opened. I dropped the towel and reached for the shotgun stashed behind the bar, relaxing my grip when I saw that it was Frankie.

"Hey ho! I see I made it just in time for the wet t-shirt contest."

I scowled as his eyes lingered a second too long on my boobs. "What took you so long?" I traded the shotgun back for a towel and rubbed at my wet hair.

He snatched the tequila bottle from where I left it on the bar. "Stop nagging, woman. I got here quick as I could. You sent me 'round the long way."

He took a pull from the bottle and handed it to me.

"We are taking that bottle out of commission, right?" Darcy asked, horrified by our unsanitary behavior.

"No one gives a shit, Darce," I grumbled.

"Is that so?"

I waved the bottle at the three remaining drunks nursing their booze at the bar. "Am I right?"

They slurred their agreement.

Darcy pulled the bottle out of my vice-like grip. "You've got to snap out of this, Nina," she said. "I love you, and I know it's been really hard, but you have got to make peace with everything."

"Really?" I spat at her. "And how does one make peace with this? You tell me how I can make peace with my aunt being burned at the goddamn stake like it's still freaking 17th-century Salem."

"In Nina's defense," Frankie piped up, "her mum did murder her aunt in an unquestionably barbaric way. Brought me back to the witch burnings from the Middle Ages. Horrible time, that. Are we out of absinthe?"

"And you both are drinking yourself stupid?" Darcy groused, but pulled our last bottle out from under the bar. She shoved it towards Frankie, then dug out a spoon and sugar cubes. "You'll have to get by with a rocks glass. The absinthe ones broke last week."

I slumped against the bar under Darcy's withering gaze. The absinthe glasses shattered when I threw them at a werewolf who came sniffing around at Leila's bidding. Well, at least I'm pretty sure he was sniffing around at Leila's bidding. Darcy wasn't convinced, but I wasn't about to put any faith in a wolf.

Publicly, Leila said she wanted to eradicate the supernatural creatures. Privately, she employed the ones willing to turn on their own. Hell, Leila was passing for a human herself. She was a witch/vampire hybrid, just like me. Her genes mixed with my vampire father's made me even more of a hybrid. But I wasn't undead yet. Rather, I was a living vampire with some vampiric traits. I healed faster, moved faster and, lately, had a hankering for blood.

"No matter," Frankie said, setting up his drink.

"So, was the cargo plane comfortable enough for Mia?" Darcy asked, her attempt to change the subject backfiring spectacularly.

"We lost Mia," Frankie said. His focus on pouring out the green liquid over the sugar cube into the rocks glass never wavered.

"Lost?" Darcy shriveled her nose. "You mean..."

"As in dead," I snapped. "Gun shot. Point blank. In the head."

Darcy gasped. "What happened?"

"I lost my focus when I had to scoop Frankie's brains up off the side of the highway."

"Thanks for that, by the way," Frankie quipped.

"What the hell...you mean you *lost her*?" Darcy started, then softened when I turned my head sharply in her direction. "I'm sorry, Nina."

"What's one more dead witch, right?" I muttered under a sudden crack of thunder that shook the floorboards. A bit of plaster rained down from the ceiling.

Darcy sucked in a breath and gripped the bar, while Frankie glanced up at the newly formed crack, nonplused. He was used to it by now. My voice was flat and my eyes dry, but my frustrations were still funneled through my feral magic. The witch in me hadn't manifested until a few months ago, so my magic was a mess. I took another swallow from the tequila bottle.

"You need to learn to control this," Darcy said, her tone so gentle that the sound of hail pummeling the street nearly drowned her out. "You can't keep screwing with the weather patterns."

"Yeah, Nina, you're making global warming a real thing," Matty said, popping into the bar from the stairway that led to the second floor apartment. Babe's second floor apartment. It was currently occupied by Frankie and me, and whoever else needed a place to crash.

I bristled as my dimwitted cousin swooped in and planted an aggressive kiss on Darcy.

"Don't do that here," I barked when I saw him getting handsy.

Matty paused, his hand halfway up her shirt. "You need to get laid." He tossed his overgrown hair, and rock star entitlement oozed off of him.

Matty was the lead singer in Killing Haley, one of the most buzzed about emo bands in the country. The act gathered even more notoriety after the drummer went all witch-doctor mental on their fans at a Providence show a few months ago, causing the fans to zombie out and cause a riot. Of course, Leila was behind it. And, of course, it was "totally punk rock" and Matty's career skyrocketed.

All this made my cousin damn near insufferable. But he was in love with my best friend, which meant I couldn't stake him.

"Really, you do," he continued, blissfully ignorant of my growing rage. "You are a tense bitch and no one likes to be around you."

I gripped my hands against the wood of the bar. My baby fangs sprouted, sending waves of pain through my jaw as they ripped through my gums. Frankie yanked my arm, holding me back before I tried to rip out Matty's throat. At least the hail stopped. When my vampire buttons were pushed, the magic disappeared.

"Easy there," Frankie soothed, his lanky, muscular form leaning over the bar and into mine. My anger, along with my fangs, receded, but it was replaced by something more unsettling. Frankie's hands on my skin sent electric charges up my body. I tried to shut him out of my head, but it was too late.

When Leila's vampire assassin lover nearly killed me, Frankie linked me to him to keep me alive. The downside of that was we could read each other's feelings. For the sake of our friendship, we kept up mental shields, but sometimes — times like these — they didn't work so well.

Frankie looked down at me, his eyes bright, and whispered, "And if you need to get laid, I'll take one for the team." My knees buckled at the promise that held, but I shrugged myself out of his grip.

"Get away from me," I seethed, hiding my desire behind disgust.

He just snickered and went back to his absinthe.

Casper dropped into my body without any warning, leaving me with a heavy feeling. "Now look who needs to get a room," he quipped.

"Don't you start either," I muttered, shaking out my muscles as my body adjusted to his unexpected presence. The kid needed to wear a cat bell or something. I noticed all eyes in the bar were on me, so I pointed to my head. "Ghost."

I first met Casper when this whole mess started a few months ago. The vampire assassin that tried to off me a knife spelled to drain power from witches, power that the knife could store until it could be transferred to Leila. Casper, a handsome 18-year-old witch who had a promising future ahead of him (including a free ride to neighboring Brown University), was one of his first victims.

Everyone nodded and went back to their alcohol. Except Matty and Darcy. They continued to make out. At least Matty moved his hands to play with her white-blond hair instead of her boobs.

My adrenaline popped and I glanced towards the door, nerves on edge. *We had the address of one of the goons from the highway. Frankie and I could ride out there, scope out his place, maybe see what the neighborhood werewolves were up to...*

"Hate to say it, *chica*, but you could use a valium 'script," Casper said, razzing me out of my daydream. While he rode around in my body, he was privy to my thoughts. Invisible to everyone else, the only way he could communicate was by jumping into my skin. Literally. "We could hit a few pharmacies. There's got to be one that isn't looted yet."

Usually he was respectful of my privacy. Today, not so much.

I brushed at my forehead in displeasure. "What do you know about this?"

"Um, in case you didn't notice, I am a ghost," he huffed.

"A ghost with no one to talk to but me," I muttered, wishing he could go possess someone else. I was the type of witch who had a natural affinity for the dead. That meant I could communicate with spirits. Some would call that a gift, and my gift was a rambunctious teenager who ran his mouth.

"Girl, please," Casper continued. "I was snuffed out by a psychopath. You think I don't understand, but girl I *know*."

"You don't know what loss is like," I shot back at him. The only way through my grief was leaving a pile of dead bodies in my wake.

He rattled inside my head. "I'm still here, haunting the earth, so I *know* I'm dead. How's that for a mind-fuck? Don't you think I feel loss every damn day?"

I crossed my arms and chewed on my lower lip. "I don't know how to do this without Aunt Babe," I admitted, turning my back to the room, keeping my voice low.

"Do what? Magic? We'll figure it out."

"Not the just magic. Just...I don't know, how to live without her," I said, my voice unsteady as I battled back several weeks worth of unshed tears. "She was the closest thing I had to a mother."

"Nina," Casper said, his tone soothing. "You need to live. If you died, you won't really die, so what good will that do you anyway? You want to come back as a *vampira*?"

"Not particularly."

"Then stop going off half-cocked," he replied.

"I just—" I started to argue but he interrupted me.

"You just nothing. I get that you're hurting, but it's time to let that pain go. You want justice. We all do. But there ain't no justice if you're dead."

I puffed out my cheeks. He spoke a hard truth.

"Kind of scary when the voice of reason is an 18-year-old ghost," he added.

"No joke," I said, swiping at my wet eyes with the bar towel. His ego was going to be out of control now.

The front door creaked open and my hand went for the shotgun again. But I dropped it when resident barfly Alfonso poked his head in. His arm was tightly wrapped around his girlfriend Eva. Or at least a figure that was around Eva's height. This person was bundled tight in a dark blanket that made it look like she or he was wearing a burka. Al slammed the door and leaned against it before releasing his grip around his companion's shoulders. She twisted out of the sheet. It was indeed Eva.

"This is bad, Nina," Al started before I could even ask him what was wrong. "It's real bad."

"What's up, Al?" I asked, glancing over at Frankie, who abandoned his drink to gape at Eva's unraveling.

"They tried to snatch her," he said as Eva hyperventilated her way out of the sheet.

"Who did?"

Alfonso pointed towards the street, puncturing the air with a wild finger. "The Goon Squad!" he yelled. "Your mother's Goon Squad!"

"Why the hell did they try to snatch her?" Frankie asked.

Al blinked at him. "Hello? Witch!"

"I know she's a bloody witch." Frankie gritted his teeth as the tension in the bar rose. I felt the wash of emotions tweak at his hunger and wondered when he ate last. "Who sold her out?"

"Neighbors, I guess," Al grumbled. "Knew we should have thrown a spell at those assholes."

"Michael and Kimmie Dorsey," Eva squeaked, kicking the sheet off her feet. "I gave them a tarot reading last year. It wasn't good."

"What wasn't good about it?" I asked, bracing myself for Eva's story as she and Al made their way to join us at the bar.

"The cards said she was cheating," Eva said. "But I mean, I had a sign up that said the tarot was for entertainment purposes only. They didn't *have* to believe me."

"Oh Eva," I said, shaking my head.

"She was fooling around with his best friend because his dick was too small, and somehow that's my fault?" Eva protested.

"Let me guess. You saw Kimmie put a hex on her husband and you offered to remove it?" I asked.

Eva shrugged. She owned a little magic shop in downtown Providence filled with Wiccan kitsch. Before we met her a few months ago, she was a grifter, a con artist, offering to read futures — and remove hexes — all for a hefty sum of money. And she almost always found hexes, which almost always required very expensive removal. The ironic thing was, Eva actually had the gift of divination, so the futures she read were true. The hexes, not so much. Unhappy wives have been known to stray. Didn't need a hex for that.

"Talk about shooting the messenger," Casper quipped.

I rubbed my temples in frustration. "Walk me through what happened, here."

"There's nothing to walk through," said Al, his agitation manifesting in his perpetual motion. "One minute we're, you know...."

"Now there's a visual for you." Casper continued the running commentary that only I could hear.

"...and the next there are three 'roided up goons grabbing at Eva, reading her some sort of bullshit Miranda made expressly for witches."

"How'd you get her away from them?" Frankie asked, failing at hiding his amusement at their being caught in flagrante.

"How do you think?" Al thundered. "I cast a spell."

I tightened my lips. "And the spell did what, Al?"

"How the hell do I know? I didn't wait around to see what happened to them."

I rephrased my question. "What was the spell *supposed* to do, Al?"

"Knock 'em out," he said, his eyes on the floor.

I drummed my fingers on the bar. "For how long, Al?"

"It was a stun spell. I think it was a stun spell. I haven't done one in years! I cast it, they were knocked on their asses, something worked. Now we need to hole up here for a while."

Al was a fellow witch and a close friend of Aunt Babe's. He was also a raging alcoholic who hadn't practiced magic for several decades, not until Leila blew into town. To say his spell work was rusty was an understatement.

"Fine," I said, my voice a little sharper than I meant it to sound. With me and Frankie crashing upstairs, the apartment was already pretty cozy.

"They were human, I assume?"

Al snorted at that. "Yeah. Leila always sends humans."

"There's got to be a reason for that," I said, shaking my head.

"Damned if I can figure out what it is," he added for me. "You got a beer?"

"Kegs were tapped out last night," Darcy said. "The distributor's freaked out by the lack of human ownership of this bar. In short, we are out of beer."

Al grumbled his frustration.

"What about Clown Shoes?" I asked. "I wonder if they'd sell to us."

"That ain't one of them crap breweries is it?" Al asked.

"Crap brewery?" Darcy said. "I thought the beer was quite good."

"Craft," I corrected. "I think he means craft."

"Nope, I meant crap," he stated.

"He thinks craft is crap," I explained.

Darcy smiled at that. "What about money to pay for the beer? Babe's isn't exactly rolling in the cash these days."

I eyed the paltry patronage in front of me. She wasn't wrong. "BYOB — bring your own beer — until further notice, I guess."

Al pulled out a wad of cash. "Nina, could you run to the store for me?"

I rolled my eyes and took at twenty from him. "I'll see what I can find but it's slim pickings out there. Most places were looted."

"Booze is the first to go," Frankie added.

"Bet you're glad you have the place spelled," Darcy said, glancing around. "The bar would probably be burned down by now."

"Yeah, and it took a damn load of work to spell the place to look like it was already looted and partially burned," I added, remembering the three-day ordeal that had Casper and me at each other's throats. But we got it done.

Al got Eva settled onto a barstool. I poured a glass of water and placed it in front of her. "You okay?"

"Oh, thank you, honey," she said, patting my hand. "Yes, just shaken up is all. It's a scary thing to have a bunch of muscle men break down your door and try to snatch you. Thank goodness Al was with me."

"You know, Eva, you could have thrown a spell yourself. You're a crack witch when you put your mind to it."

"I didn't even foresee they were coming. Some great diviner I am," she said, looking into her glass.

"Well, if anyone knows about screwing up spells..." Al said, raising his chin at me.

"Shut up, you old goat," Eva chided him. "Nina's a nice girl, and she just needs a mentor is all, now that..." Eva's voice trailed off and she gave me a sad smile and squeezed my hand again. "I'm sorry, honey. It's not your fault you were never taught properly."

"She never paid attention in Witchcraft 101. That didn't help," Frankie said.

I bit my lip. It wasn't a lie. My Blood Ops training included courses on witchcraft, but since I was a living vamp with no magical inclinations at the time, I skated through those. Hindsight and all that...

"It's all good, Eva," I said. "I am better at the physical stuff. We all need to know our limitations."

Frankie snorted. "Indeed."

I was about to set him straight with a spell Casper and I were practicing, but the door to the bar swung open. For the third time in less than an hour, I snatched the shotgun from under the bar. This time, I leveled it at an interloper.

A tall man strolled into the bar, his face obscured by his Baja hoodie, which was snug around his broad shoulders. I gave the shotgun a pump and aimed it at his midsection.

He held up his hands. "Just looking to wet my whistle, that's all."

My hands began to shake as Casper went into a panic. Trying to control it, my pulse raced as his adrenaline spiked. He pushed himself out of my body, jarring me with a violent enough force that I stumbled forward, lucky that the gun didn't discharge accidentally.

I swore under my breath at the ghost and regained my composure, shotgun still pointed in the direction of the stranger. "You're in the wrong bar, mister. You need to take your business elsewhere."

"I'm certain this is the right one," he said, dropping the hood from his face. "You do have something for whistle wetting, I assume?"

A shock of thick silver hair flowed down the nape of his neck. Under hooded lids, pale green eyes stared down the bar lined with my very few customers. The remnants of a hard life lined his skin. He was old, but this guy looked fierce.

"We don't serve strangers these days," I said. "And you, sir, are a stranger."

"I am no stranger," he snickered. "You hear me, little girl?"

I tilted my head. A strange familiarity filled me at the sound of those five words. But it was Al who stood up and walked to him.

"Well, I'll be damned," Al said, walking a slow circle around the man. "I'm not so sure I'm happy to see you. This isn't the safest city for our kind, you know?"

Al moved between me and the stranger, which rendered my shotgun threat worthless. Not wanting to shoot a hole through Al — not today, anyway — I lowered the shotgun. "You know this guy, Al?"

"Sure as shit, I know him," Al said, crossing his arms over his chest and rocking back on his heels. "And he's either going to be our downfall or our savior, and I'm not sure which."

The stranger's laugh was hearty, tinged with decades of cigarette smoke. He opened his arms and a small smirk spread over his weathered face. "Child, come and give your old granddad a hug."

3

"WELL DON'T JUST STAND THERE like a slack-jawed idiot," the stranger who said he was my grandfather barked. "You going to put that shotgun down or what, girl?"

"Nina," I said. "My name is Nina."

"Your father named you. Never liked it. My choice was Adele."

I leveled a sharp look at Frankie, who didn't hide his smirk. "You say you're my grandfather but I don't know you, stranger."

Al turned to me. "Nina, this is your mother's — Babe's — father."

"Came here all the way from Mexico," the old man added.

"Babe's funeral was weeks ago," I said, not releasing my grip on the gun. "Or, at least, the burial of her remains. We weren't allowed a funeral. Orders of your other daughter."

"That woman is no kin of mine."

"See? That's something you have in common," Al interjected.

Dog started scratching from behind the closed door that led to the upstairs apartment. I cradled the shotgun and ducked under the bar, then moved backwards across the room to the door, not letting the stranger from my sight. My 130-pound hellhound slouched into the bar, stopping by my side so I could give her head a scratch. She stared at the old man and a growl vibrated through her body.

Gramps squinted at her and snarled back. Dog's throaty growl morphed into a whimper. She slithered around my legs and hovered behind me. So much for my noble protector.

"You don't look Mexican," I said, sizing up his light hair and eyes, to say nothing of his towering height and slim build.

"That's because I ain't," he said. "By birth anyway."

Casper's sudden disappearance now made sense. His entire family was from the same area of Mexico that my family was from. And they were scared to death of my grandfather, who had a fearsome reputation across the border. Between Casper's reaction, not to mention Al's uncharacteristic reverence, there was little doubt that he was my *abuelo*. But damn, he was not what I expected. At all.

"How the hell did you become the most feared *brujo* in Mexico if you're a *gringo*?"

"Your ignorance is showing, child," his voice was gruff. He walked over to Frankie and sized him up. "Hand over that bottle, will you, son?"

"These are tough times to go out on the piss, mate. You'll need to find your own bottle," Frankie responded, his eyes darting between the two of us.

"Goddamn limeys," Gramps muttered, then gave a quick flick of his wrist. Frankie clutched his head and doubled over in acute pain.

"What are you doing?!" I yelled, sprinting across the bar to Frankie.

By the time I reached him, Frankie was on the floor, writhing in agony. My grandfather slid into Frankie's seat and took a long pull from the now abandoned tequila bottle.

"Stop the spell!" I yelled as Frankie went into full-on vamp mode. His eyes glowed bright blue and his fangs extended, but he foamed at the mouth and a horrid drowning noise came from the back of his throat. Then the psychic barrier between us collapsed. Searing pain ripped through my head and my ears filled with an unbearable high-pitched sound. Clutching my head, I collapsed on the floor next to Frankie.

"Please!" I whispered, glancing up at Gramps' weathered face.

Another flick of his wrist and we were released from whatever spell the old man had over us. The pain was gone, but the effects lingered.

"Don't underestimate me." He leveled a warning at Frankie. "And don't stand between a thirsty man and a drink."

Frankie and I got to our knees, still panting from the spell. The few regulars still nursing their drinks made brisk work to the exit, deciding to chance it with Leila's goons outside rather than Gramps in the bar.

"Why are you here?" I asked through ragged breaths.

"I'm here to help you pull your sorry excuse for witchcraft out of the shitter."

"You're here to help me," I said with a cold laugh. "I recall a story Babe once told me about how you tried to kill me."

"Your aunt had a flair for the dramatic," he said, snorting. "That was overblown."

"Then you don't deny it?" Frankie asked, his voice low. I watched his eyes take on that eerie vampire glow for barely a moment before it faded. In one graceful movement, Frankie was on his feet.

"Babe brought a baby vampire into the village," Gramps said, lifting his arms in a what-could-I-do gesture. "People were upset. They needed to get out of town."

"I am sure you can understand why Nina wouldn't trust you," Frankie said, holding out his hand to me.

"I don't need your help," I muttered, pulling myself to my feet. I clutched the bar to keep from falling over, my legs still shaky.

"Take that, English," Gramps said behind a roar of laughter. "She's stubborn like her aunt, too."

"I was talking about you," I said. "I don't trust you."

"Trust me, don't trust me," he said with a shrug. "You still need my help."

"I'm doing just fine on my own," I said, lifting my chin.

"Are ya?" he asked. "Weren't you responsible for that little hail shower a few minutes ago? Damn things were the size of grapefruits."

My chin dropped and I stared at the dirty floorboards. Dog came over and nuzzled my hand. We both slunk to a barstool farthest from my grandfather. "That was an accident."

"You seem to have an awful lot of those." Gramps pulled out a handful of balled up newspaper clippings from his pocket. "Let's see," he said, smoothing out a piece of paper. "'Tornado Touches Down in Providence,'" he read, tossing it aside and moving on to the next one. "'Record High! Providence Reaches a Tropical 102° in February'"

I opened my mouth to protest but he simply waved his hand at me. Not knowing what spell that hand wave was capable of throwing, I clammed up quick.

"Nope, wait a minute, here comes my favorite," he said. "'Small Monsoon Spotted Over Narragansett Bay'" His voice trailed out, replaced with a booming laugh. "Now, what were you saying about accidents?

My face burned. "I only meant—"

He crumpled up the news clippings and shoved them back into his pocket. "You are an embarrassment of a witch. Babette made you soft, coddled you. I am here to right her wrong."

I drummed my shabby nails on the bar and took several deep breaths to tamp down my rising anger. Frankie slid onto the stool next to me. We both glared at the old man at the end of the bar who was drinking my tequila straight from the bottle.

"You okay?" I asked Frankie, my voice barely above a whisper.

"Pride's scuffed up a bit, but otherwise fine," he replied. "The old timer has some serious power there. You may learn a thing or two."

"Not interested," I hissed.

"Don't be a fool," Frankie responded. "I'm not a fan of his methods, but he's not wrong, you know."

I glanced at my grandfather, who was shooting the shit with Alfonso. It looked like Eva was flirting. "My vampire traits aren't full blown, but they've kept me alive this long," I said to Frankie.

He sighed. "You've never gone up against anyone like Leila."

"Come on, Frankie. She's sending humans to do her dirty work. I bet she's not as strong as we assume."

"Bullets can still kill you," he said, as if I needed a reminder.

"I'll come back though," I deadpanned.

"Coming back is not something you should look forward to," Frankie said, growing more concerned.

"I'm not."

"No, she's not," the old man said, his voice booming across the bar. How did he hear us?

"Dead," the old man began, "She is a vampire. But alive, she is one of us. She is a witch."

"Gramps, or whatever the hell I am supposed to call you, I am a fuck-up of a witch." I winced as I said it, not accustomed to admitting defeat. "You are absolutely right. Hail slammed down from the heavens when I attempted a spell. I turned the Northeast into a tropical rainforest. Yes, I caused a monsoon over the Atlantic Ocean. I am a one-woman natural disaster."

Gramps actually chuckled.

"Nina, you aren't hopeless," Al interjected. "Your grandfather can teach you. He taught Babe."

"Well, until she got all politically correct," the old man said, rolling his eyes.

"I won't do dark magic either," I said, remembering why Babe hightailed it out of Catemaco in the first place. Gramps practiced the dark stuff—magic that required a large price, often a life, for using it. "So you can save your spells. Stop wasting your time and go back to Mexico. Blood Ops can deal with Leila."

"Blood Ops?" he asked. "That don't exist no more. Isn't your leader behind bars?"

"We're working on that," I lied.

"How?" he asked.

"Prison break." I blurted out the first thing that came into my head.

As soon as I said the words, my mouth twisted up in a small smile. Frankie glanced at me, then a look of recognition spread across his face. Of course. A prison break.

"Are you out of your mind?" Al snapped. "What are you going to do? Just stroll right on into Steele City? That's a maximum-security prison that Leila has on lockdown. You're going to get yourselves killed."

"Nah," Frankie said, watching my grandfather swirl the dregs of the booze around the bottom of the bottle. "We've done prison breaks before. Remember that time we broke into Rikers Island by accident?"

I chuckled. "Yeah, we were supposed to be at Sing Sing but confused the two."

"Wasn't prisoner number 95-A-9876 surprised when we tried to stake him?" Frankie guffawed at the memory.

"Hate to pull you away from your reminiscing and all," said Gramps, his voice stern, "but maybe we should talk about the staking of your mother instead of prisoner number whatever."

"Freeing Dr. O is our priority," Frankie said.

"Mommy Dearest runs a very close second," Al chimed in. "Right, Nina?"

"Who says we can't do both?" I asked.

The old man tilted his head, curious. "What'd you have in mind?"

"Leila's got to be holed up in Steele City," I said.

"Why do you think that?" Darcy asked. She and Matty had watched the family reunion unfold quietly. Matty, nonplused by the whole thing, nuzzled at her neck. If he wasn't a Beta-Vamp, I'd worry that he'd bite her. By genetic mutation, Betas lacked the killer instinct, not to mention their fangs weren't sharp enough to break skin.

"Where else can she be? She's rounding up witches and sending them there."

"Blah blah blah... " Matty's voice pitched up in a whine. "All we do is talk and talk and talk about these witches. When are you going to do something about them?"

"This is none of your concern," I said, adjusting my tone as if he were a five-year-old.

"None of *my* concern?" he asked, his eyes widening in mock surprise. "What about Kittie, what she did to me?"

Gramps leaned forward. "So you met Kittie?"

"She broke up the band," Matty said.

"Killing Haley is on hiatus," Darcy said, correcting him.

"Same thing," he mumbled, lower lip jutting out to a pout.

Kittie had infiltrated Matty's band, posing as a manager. Her magical influence had turned the drummer into a psycho witch doctor who created rabid zombies from pounding on his drum set. I shivered as I remembered the snake tattoo that wound itself around Kittie's body. The damn thing moved. On its own. Creepy.

Kittie was part of Leila's massive master plan and, from what I saw of their relationship, Leila was some sort of mother figure to the Goth-looking young witch. A twinge of jealousy shot through me as I remembered Kittie calling me "sis," her voice dripping with sarcasm. I shook it off fast. Babe was more than enough mom for me.

"She's got the darkness, oh yes she does," Gramps continued. "Runs through her blood and straight through that tat of hers."

"See what you're up against," Matty said. "It's like you don't even want to win. What's the big deal about all this dark stuff anyway?"

Gramps clapped his hands together and then extended them, palms out, towards Matty. "Exactly! What is the big deal?"

"The big deal is that dark magic comes at a price," I said. "Every dark spell you throw chips away at your soul."

"So what?" Matty said, ignoring Darcy's shushing sound. "Vampires don't have souls and there's nothing wrong with me."

I considered all the easy retorts to that comment, but bit my lip instead.

"Vampires do have souls, Matty. I know we're all told otherwise, but your soul is why you're able to love." My eyes darted to Darcy and then to Frankie before settling back on my idiot cousin. "I'm not willing to lose my soul."

"Without love, what's the point of living?" Frankie added. "Particularly for an eternity."

I caught my breath as Frankie's emotions leaked into me. Fire moved from my belly down into my pelvis. My body flooded with longing.

"You're all a bunch of bleeding hearts is what you are," Gramps barked. His voice ripped me back to reality. *"Oh, no, I won't have a soul,"* he mocked. *"Oh, no, I won't be able to fall in love.* Bunch of pantywaists, all of you."

Matty leapt to his feet. "Are you out of your mind, you old goat? Love is the reason to get out of bed in the evening. Love is what drives us, all of us. Love makes us..." Matty stalled as Gramps worked him over with icy eyes.

"Love makes you a goddamn idiot," Gramps said.

Matty opened his mouth to argue, but didn't get a word out. One graceful wrist flick on the old man's part and Matty's head twisted about 180 degrees. A sharp crack echoed through the now dead quiet bar. Darcy's shriek shattered the silence as Matty dropped to the floor.

"See what love gets you?" Gramps yelled over her.

Darcy followed Matty to the floor and cradled his head in her lap. That's when I caught a tremble in her lower lip. "Darcy, it's okay. He's not dead," I said. "He'll wake up in a few hours."

She choked back a sob. "I know."

"Breathe deep, Darce," I continued. "Can you hear me?"

She grimaced, so I motioned to Frankie. He had to be ready to pull her out of the bar and fast. A despondent banshee was a dangerous banshee. Once she started wailing, all humans within earshot would drop dead.

I had a soundproof room installed in the basement of the old factory building that I converted to apartments just for this scenario. It was next to a vampire lair well insulated from sunlight. That space was initially meant for Frankie, but then he was spelled by Bertrand, our demon mayor, to walk in sunlight, so Matty lived there now. Darcy crashed in my apartment above him, since I was staying above the bar. If Bertrand ever pulled the demon spell off of Frankie, he and Matty would be roommates.

Yup, these were my friends. Hell, Matty was family.

Darcy made a sort of half-snuffle noise while Frankie crept closer. I rounded on the old man.

"You did this," I hissed, holding up my hand as he opened his mouth to speak. "Fine, he's not dead, we all know that. You just walk in here and snap necks? You are not welcome here."

Gramps smirked. "Nice backbone on you, kid. But that's not the response I wanted." He tossed out a few Latin words that mixed with his Spanish. I was on the floor faster than Matty dropped. My head felt like it was going to explode.

"You can fight this one, kid. Don't give in to the vampire. Fight it."

I gritted my teeth so hard I thought every one of them would shatter. All I could focus on was the searing pain in my head. My fangs pushed out and my body went cold. I glanced around and caught sight of Eva and Al, who inched away from me with measured steps. I was vamping out.

But it kept Darcy from wailing. She left Matty limp on the floor, giving me a wide berth. Frankie was the only one brave enough—and dead enough—to move towards me. But I shook my head at him, worried he'd get hit with this spell too if he came any closer.

I tried to steady my breathing. I tried to ignore the agonizing pain in my head. I tried to focus on throwing a spell. I heard glass shatter from behind the bar, the result of not only my weak casting but also the wrong spell. Pulling my focus back inward, I muttered another incantation. I heard more glass shattering, followed by a trickle of liquid. Al swore under his breath, which told me I broke one of the few remaining bottles of booze. Dammit. Pain sliced its way through my skull as vampire met witch and they warred within me.

"Get in there, Nina. Don't let the vampire win," Gramps shouted like an overzealous boxing coach.

Three's the charm, right? Another incantation worked its way through my labored breath.

A new sear of pain pushed into my body, this time traveling down to my hands. My nails, usually clipped short, sprouted, their rapid growth turning them into talons. I felt my toe nails strain inside my boots. Whatever he was doing was turning me vampire. Nails sprouting to talons was the midway point during the transition.

My body betrayed me, leaving me to squirm on the floor. That's when Casper the Chicken Shit Ghost jumped back into my body. The impact of his belly flop into my solar plexus barely registered to me, although the grunt he gave said he experienced pain.

"Nina, you're vamping out," Casper squeaked, struggling along with me against the transformation.

"You don't say," I grumbled, doubled over.

"I mean, I've never seen you this far gone before," he clarified. "But I mean, damn girl. There's barely any space for me in here."

Only certain witches could see and be possessed by spirits. It was the one witchy thing I did well. Too well, actually. Getting possessed by a spirit that wasn't Casper was kind of a problem. But right now, my body was rejecting Casper. I could feel it squeezing him out.

"Can you fix it?" I asked.

"Don't know," he wheezed. "But I'll try."

He forced himself into my head and my eyes rolled back. I allowed Casper to take total control of my body.

The ghost flinched. "This is some painful shit, Nina. Does this happen every time you vamp out? Because this is no fun."

"Focus. Please," I begged. Since I couldn't get a handle on my vamping, my body slipped in and out of Casper's control.

"Shit, Nina, I feel your heartrate dropping," he called out before starting his spell. His panic was palpable through his rushed incantation.

His words made my pulse spike, my own panic shooting me full of adrenaline. But my heartrate plummeted just as fast as it rose, sending the room spinning. I called out to Frankie, and felt him at my side even before he grabbed onto me. Then everything went black.

4

THE ENTIRE BAR was huddled around me when I came to. Someone—probably Frankie—had moved me from the floor to the top of a table. The smell of stale beer filled my nostrils and induced a wave of nausea. I rolled to my side and puked up bile. Frankie jumped back before it splashed onto his John Varvatos boots. My vampire partner was a bit of a dandy.

"What happened?" I asked, wiping my mouth with the back of my hand.

Gramps sat at the table across from me. He leaned back in his chair, balanced precariously on its two back legs, and guffawed. "I almost turned you into a vampire."

"And you're proud of that?" I snapped. My stomach gurgled while I fought down another wave of sickness. "You proved your point. You're a powerful witch. So what do you want from me?"

"I want to help you."

"Excuse me if I find that hard to believe," I said, treading carefully with my tone. There was no way I'd survive another spell like that.

He crossed his arms. "It's your right not to believe."

Darcy nudged me back down on the table and placed a bar rag soaked in cold water on my forehead. I hoped it was clean.

"Thanks," I grumbled. "You okay?"

Her smile was small but genuine. "I'm okay. Matty woke up. He's upstairs nursing a stiff neck."

"That was fast," I said.

She glanced uneasily at my grandfather. "He helped. Finally."

I propped myself up on my elbows. "How about you guys go check on Matty? I'd like a minute with my...him." My chin jerked towards the old man.

"You sure, Nina?" Al asked. "I don't like the idea of leaving you here." Eva stood by Al's side, nodding her head in agreement.

"Indeed," Frankie chimed in.

"We'll be fine," I lied. Everyone stood their ground. "Jesus, you guys, go! Go check on Matty."

My crew filed upstairs, feet shuffling along the worn wood. Frankie lurked behind the rest, his hesitation apparent in the looks he tossed my way.

"Frankie, you know I'll let you know if I need you," I said. Even if my grandfather figured out we were bound, he wouldn't be able to stop our ability to communicate. Not that Frankie would be much help. With those spells Gramps was throwing, Frankie was as useless as me.

Reluctance was written all over his face, but he headed upstairs, leaving me alone with the black magic witch.

"Where's Casper?" I asked my grandfather as I heard the upstairs door close. "Last I felt him, he was trying to help me fight off that spell. He's not with me now."

I was worried. Ghosts were delicate. If they exerted too much of their energy, their bodies — a sort of plasma that took on their corporeal shape — disintegrated. And it drove them mad. Once the plasma was chewed away, they became poltergeists, ghosts without shape, without conscience, and you did not want to mess with those suckers. I tangled with a few and it wasn't a good time.

Gramps raised his eyebrows. "Your ghost? He's fine. Popped out just before you passed out."

"You can see him?" I asked.

"Of course I can see him. Where do you think you get it from?" He laughed.

A jolt of ice spiked up my spine. "Why are you here?"

"Told you," he said, turning the now empty bottle of tequila around in his hands. "You need to take down your mother."

"But why?"

He dropped the two front legs of the chair to the floor and then leaned forward. "Child, are you that dense?"

"I know about *that* why," I said, pressing my teeth together to keep my temper in check. "I mean, why would you want to destroy your own daughter?"

"She's upsetting the balance," he said with a matter-of-fact tone.

I sat up on the table, swaying a little as I acclimated to my new position. "The balance? You practice dark magic. And you're going to complain about Leila upsetting the balance?"

"See, your aunt brainwashed you too," he grumbled, jumping up. I flinched when he stood, then relaxed—just a bit—when he walked in the opposite direction. I tracked him as he stalked behind the bar to grab a bourbon bottle.

"Babe..." My voice came out in a strained squeak, so I cleared my throat. "Babe didn't brainwash me. She taught me."

"And I'm here to teach you *my* ways, child," he said, folding his tall frame back into the chair, bourbon bottle in hand. "Now, if you listen to me — learn from me — I will give you the tools to defeat your mother."

"Why would you want me to kill your own daughter?"

"Told you. She ain't natural."

"She's my mother," I said, voice shaking. "And I am her not-natural daughter."

"Child, she has not been a mother to you, not once. The woman you say is your mother birthed you for the wrong purpose, and I won't blame you for that."

"Purpose?" I asked.

He ignored me. "Your aunt took you in, raised you as best she could, found someplace safe for you, all against my wishes and the wishes of our coven. That was being a mother. So far as you are concerned, any maternal whatever you had died when Leila lit that funeral pyre."

"What do you mean, 'purpose?'" I repeated, even though he obviously wasn't going to tell me.

"Don't forget, she killed my daughter," his voice softened.

"So you want me to kill your *other* daughter?"

"Blood for blood," he said. "She's no daughter of mine."

I stewed on that for a minute. "I don't get it. Your reputation as a *brujo* is notorious. Why aren't you puffed up with pride at what Leila's doing?"

"No pride here," he said. "Told you, she's unnatural."

He'd reached the end of his patience with me, I could tell. "So what do you expect me to do?"

"Learn."

"Learn? From you?" I snorted.

He nodded, his face unreadable, and a chill spread through me.

"I'm not interested in learning dark magic."

"It's a dangerous way, but it's not a bad way," he said. "Tell you this. You learn, you'll defeat her. I promise you that."

"So how come you can't defeat her? How much can you possibly teach me? You know tons more magic than me."

"Because it needs to be you."

"Why?"

He shook his head. "It's just what I know."

"How?" I challenged.

"The spirits guide us," he said.

My shoulders inched up with each cryptic response. I didn't believe him. Or his spirits. "So we're charging after Leila because of what some ghosts say? No offense, Casper, wherever you are."

Gramps pulled a pipe out of his pocket. "Not just ghosts. Our ghosts, our family."

"So our dead family," I said snarkily, then looked him up and down as he tamped tobacco down with his thumb. Tall, slim, silver-blond hair, calling into question our actual lineage. "Who may or may not be from Mexico."

"You'd do well to take this seriously."

"I don't mean any disrespect, old man, but I don't know you. There is, however, a gentleman who is like a grandfather to me—yes, Dr. O—sitting behind bars with Leila doing who knows what to him. He is my priority right now. And it's not witchcraft that's going to bust him out. It's strength and agility and some good old-fashioned ass-kicking. And Frankie and I have that in spades."

"You go your way then," he said, sparking up the pipe. "I'll wait and see how you and that vampire fare."

The sweet smelling smoke drifted towards me. I breathed in its warmth as it wrapped around the room. My shoulders eased down from where they hunched at my ears. I inhaled again, this time closing my eyes. I felt the smoke work its way through my body, each muscle group giving into the calm the mist carried with it. Following a long exhale, my nausea dissipated.

"What did you just do?" I murmured. Panic rose in my chest for a brief moment, but as I inhaled the smoke again, the anxiety subsided. I felt chill. And that felt good. Damn good.

"Blood magic ain't just for killing, child," he said, blowing out another puff, the wispy white smoke wafting over to me. "It's also for healing."

Maybe it was a trick, but I didn't care. I allowed the smoke to embrace me. Frankie and I had work to do, but I needed to walk into this fight with a strong body and a fresh mind. Running on adrenaline the last few weeks didn't do any of us any favors. After we tangled with those three clowns on the bikes in the middle of the interstate, it was getting downright dangerous.

"Yes, child, breathe it in..." My grandfather's voice soothed and I settled back down onto the table while he walked around me in a circle. I watched the white smoke snake over my body, and then the old man began to chant.

"This is dark magic?" I mumbled while smoke filled my head and I drifted in and out of sleep.

"This is," he said. He stopped his chanting to answer me, and the loss of the rhythmic sound made me sad.

"Keep singing," I said.

He gave my shoulder a squeeze. "Of course, *mi nieta*," he said, and then resumed his chants.

Grandchild. He called me grandchild in Spanish. I had a grandpa. The thought warmed me to my toes. I had a grandpa who would take care of me. Teach me. Love me. I drifted into a restorative sleep, Gramps watching over me.

5

"ARE you out of your bloody gourd?" Frankie whispered, his anger palpable even though his vocal register was low.

"I told you, I'm fine, Frankie," I responded, struggling to keep my voice low too. "I'm good as new. Better than new, actually. Maybe you should let him do it to you."

"Yes, you *are* out of your bloody gourd," he hissed back. "You think I'm going to let that witch spell me with some sort of smoke?"

"I'm telling you, I feel sensational!" I said, jumping to my feet.

Frankie yanked me back down to the dirt. "You're going to get us both caught. How 'sensational' will you feel then?"

I pursed my lips. "Are you mocking me?"

Frankie stared forward, watching the lights of the prison flicker as day turned to twilight. "Would I do that?"

We were in an industrial park across the street from Steele City, the maximum-security prison where Leila horded the witches and, we assumed, Dr. O. There was no industry in this stretch of the park, but there were a whole lot of power lines. Other than that, the area was covered with tall grass, trees and overgrown bushes.

"Yes," I said, digging at the dirt with the toe of my boot. "You are mocking me."

"You are being a fool."

"Maybe we should trust him," I said. "He didn't kill me."

"Is that our baseline for trust now? Someone not killing you? Because Leila didn't kill you either."

"That's not the point," I argued, popping my head over the bush that we crouched behind to get another look at the prison.

"That is exactly the point," he fumed, pushing me back down by the top of my head. "I can't take any chances on losing you, Nina. I won't."

His grip moved to the back of my head and he twined his fingers around my hair. His deep cerulean eyes stared into mine and he dropped his guard. Frankie's desire flooded me. A soft groan slipped out as my own conflicted feelings tested me. I lost my balance and tumbled backwards, my back landing hard on the dirt.

"Don't do that," I grumbled, pushing myself up on my elbows. Frankie shut off his emotional spigot.

"When are we going to deal with this, Nina?" he asked.

"Now's not a good time," I wheezed, still fighting to catch my breath. His feelings had intensified over the past few months. My own feelings for him, well...those were complicated.

"It's never a good time," he muttered.

I jerked my thumb toward the prison. "I promise you that right now is definitely not a good time."

"What's wrong with right now?" he argued. "We're not battling some demented human or saving some witch or whatever. Casper's not here, spooking. It's just us, staring at a prison."

"Surveillance, Frankie. We are doing surveillance to figure out how to get inside."

He pulled a leaf off the bush and tore at it with precision. "I won't let you ignore this, Nina. Not anymore."

I squirmed. "Have you been watching *Dr. Phil* reruns again? He's not a *real* doctor, you know."

"I'm being serious," he said.

I scooted my butt around to face him. "And I am, too. But the only thing that matters is that I've got your back, Frankie. And you've got mine. That's why we're good together."

He flashed me a fangy grin. "We *are* good together. I'm chuffed you think so, too."

Dammit. I had to watch every word that came out of my mouth. "We are great at saving each other's asses. The other stuff, we will deal with later, I promise. But now is not the time."

Frankie got up and stalked to the dark, nondescript van that we commandeered from Chuck, a Beta-Vamp who we saved from a deadly blood supply a few months prior. I let Chuck and his nest of Betas set up camp at an old farmhouse I owned near the Connecticut border. In a few short months, they dug out an underground haven for their nest to live away from daylight. Chuck and his friends were impressive contractors. Full electricity ran from a solar grid (ironic, that) that also offered thermodynamic heating and cooling. Not that vampires generally noticed temperature fluctuations, but Betas were weak, so maybe they did. They'd even installed indoor plumbing. If we survived Leila, and humans accepted vampires, Chuck and his pals had a lucrative future in bunker building.

Frankie flung open the backdoor and pulled out two lineman-climbing belts. I scrambled to my feet and took the one he held out to me. I tugged it, but his grip on the belt was firm. He pulled me off-balance and I landed into him. He caught me, looping one arm around my torso and pulled me into him.

"Soon it will be the time," he whispered in my ear. He scraped his teeth, fangs not quite distended, along the sensitive dip behind my ear. I fought the urge to melt into him, to cross over that line of friendship, a line that grew thinner each time my adrenaline spiked.

A twig snap behind us was enough to break Frankie's spell.

"Am I interrupting something?" FBI Agent Max Deveroux's voice echoed through the quiet night.

The only thing that escaped around the lump in my throat was a "shhhhh."

Frankie's grip on me relaxed with reluctance. "Not interrupting a thing, mate. She tripped. Klutziest woman I've ever encountered."

I turned and met Max's eyes. I'd love to say that he looked at me with passion. Or pain. Or with anything that conveyed some sort of emotion. Instead, his striking blue eyes looked dead. When I met him six months before, I'd never have guessed that his eyes—defined by small lines that crinkled when he laughed—could appear so lifeless. But being turned into a Berserker could do that to a guy.

I snatched the lineman belt from Frankie and wrapped it around my waist. "Just about to check out the view. Why are you here?"

"I was in the neighborhood," Max said. "Delivering something to the prison. Noticed the van. You aren't exactly blending in, you know."

I scowled.

"Think you can smuggle us in?" Frankie asked. "That'd be a spot better than climbing a utility pole."

"They search all cars going in. Even mine. You'd never make it past the first gate."

"Pity that," Frankie said.

"Those are quite the outfits you have on," Max said with a snicker. Even his razzing felt cold.

I tugged at the coveralls. "Utility workers climb poles."

"Too bad no one's interested in fixing the utilities these days," he said, thumping his hand on the pole we were about to climb. "I don't think this is the best plan."

"Are you still mad about being left out of this?" I asked. He blew up on us when he heard that we were planning a stakeout without him. He was so mad, he nearly Berserked. But I could count the people I trusted on one hand, and, right now, Max wasn't one of them, so he was out. Blood Ops had a tenuous relationship with the government at best. To have the FBI involved, even informally, didn't sit well with me.

"No," he said.

A lie. He was here in case the operation all went to shit. But I wasn't sure if he wanted to help us, give us an "I told you so" if the plan failed or haul our asses in.

I nudged him out of the way and wrapped the belt around the

pole. "Just don't Hulk out on us right now. That won't do us any favors."

I started to climb and Frankie followed me up. Max remained with his feet firmly planted on the ground.

"Darcy could equip me with a camera or something!" he called up to us, not concerned with how far his voice carried. "I go in there all the time."

Arms stretched, my muscles flexed and I pulled myself higher up the pole. "We don't need the inside layout. We can find those in the old building plans. We need to figure out how to get in."

"I still could help!" he called up to us.

"You just said you can't smuggle us in," Frankie called down. "So which is it, mate, can you get us in or not?"

I stopped climbing and looked down at Max, frustration etched in the downward pull of his mouth. "No. I can't get you in."

"So up the pole we go," I said, resuming my climb. I tried to keep the mood light so that we didn't set him off.

Max's temper was becoming a liability. Each day that Max lived with that Berserker inside him caused his simmering anger to rise closer to the surface. A battle was being waged between the Berserker and his humanity. Lately, the Berserker seemed to be winning.

"Nice view, by the way," Frankie chirped. He had his head just at my ass. Then he made biting noises. Lovely.

"Shut up," I snarled, suddenly self-conscious of the angle of my behind in my workman's Dickies. Not exactly the most flattering uniform. A quick glance down to Max told me that Frankie's playful antics weren't helping his mood much. There was nothing left between Max and me. After Marcello the vampire assassin interrupted our date, and Max sought a favor from resident demon and Providence mayor Bertrand, whatever spark that was between us fizzled.

My attention refocused on the prison as we reached the top of the pole. Frankie pulled out some ridiculous looking oversized wrench from his back pocket.

"What are you doing?" I asked.

"Getting into character," he said, spinning the wrench expertly in his hand.

"Seriously?"

"We won't look like utility workers without tools," he said.

"Wrenches or not, if anyone looks close, we're screwed," I said. "So let's keep our fingers crossed and be as inconspicuous as possible."

I leveled a look at him and the wrench went back into his pocket. We hung in silence at the top of the pole. Stakeouts were dull things. The prison was one of the only structures with working electricity in the state, and sitting at the top of a pole a mere inch from live wires kept me more alert than the usual car stakeout. But I still caught myself nodding off once in a while.

Prison guards in their Ford pickups arrived for their shift. An old school bus retrofitted to transport prisoners also appeared. I perked up as guards shuffled about 50 witches—hands and legs locked in iron manacles to dull their magic—off the bus and into the jail. I glanced at Frankie, sitting straighter as well, watching the guards manhandle the prisoners. My hands formed fists and I mentally picked off each guard one by one as they struck and shoved the frightened witches. Once they shuffled through the imposing stone walls of the prison, we both settled back into our listless slouches, waiting.

"Do you see that?" I asked, perking up again at the sight of a box truck pulling to the front gate. "Can you make out the words on the side?"

Frankie shook his head, and I felt the pole sway a bit. "Barely. Something about linens. A linen service?"

"Better have clean sheets when plotting the end of the world?"

"She's your mum," Frankie said.

"Stop calling her that."

Frankie whistled down to Max, who napped on the hood of his GMC Suburban. Max lifted to his elbows and turned his face towards us. The dim moonlight cast shadows along his strong features.

"What do you know about linen deliveries?" Frankie stage whispered down.

Max looked up at us, perplexed. "You want to talk about table cloths for a dive bar now?"

"Not for the bar. At the prison. Sheets, towels, that sort of thing," I said, my voice trailing off.

"The prisoners change the linens, I think," Max said. He rubbed at his face, still groggy. "I don't know for sure. She barely lets me past the guardhouse."

"You know, I always thought the mark of a civilized dinner was a cloth napkin," Frankie said, ignoring Max. "Which is why I don't like having dinner with you, the fast-food queen. You've never met a drive-through you didn't like."

"You don't even eat anymore," I retorted, and then called down to Max. "Do you know what other days the linen truck comes out?" My voice was drowned out by the howl of a wolf.

I froze at the sound. It wasn't a natural howl.

"Bullocks," Frankie swore, eyes scanning the landscape for the beast.

"Does Leila have any werewolves on the payroll?" I called down to Max.

He shook his head. "How would I know?"

How indeed. Max was new at this supernatural stuff. Spotting a werewolf that wasn't transformed was hard, even for us veterans.

"If it's a turned werewolf, it'll sniff us out," Frankie said. "Best to shimmy down now, I think."

He unhooked the belt and dropped down, landing on his feet without even a thud. My route to the ground was more traditional. And plodding. When I hit the halfway mark, a Humvee roared through the abandoned lot. Floodlights from the tricked out military vehicle turned the dark spot into the Vegas strip.

The high pitch of an electrified megaphone assaulted my ears before a disembodied voice shouted out his order. "Don't move. Put your hands up."

"Which is it?" I called, dangling on the pole. "Hands up or not moving?"

"Get your ass down to the ground," the voice bellowed.

I inched down the pole at a snail's pace, delaying the inevitable showdown with whomever was at the other end of that bullhorn.

When my feet touched dirt, I turned to find Max and two corrections officers from the prison by the hood of the Humvee, wrapped up in quiet conversation. Max's voice sounded calm as he tried to diffuse the situation.

"What are they saying?" I mumbled to Frankie while unhooking the buckle of the lineman's belt. It dropped from my waist and I held it lose in my right hand, like a whip. Just in case.

"Something about trespassing. Max gave them some story about already checking our credentials. Said he was keeping an eye on us anyway. He's handling it well."

Frankie's jealousy normally didn't allow for such generous praise for Max. Even though whatever happened between Max and me before wasn't likely to reignite anytime soon, Frankie still carried on around him like a scorned lover. And our "whatever happened" didn't go much beyond a date that ended with me accidentally conjuring a tsunami during a psychic battle with my mother's psycho vampire lover. Then the guy took a demon charm for me, which turned him from human to Berserker. A second date never materialized. Shocking, right?

Raucous laughter came from the two military men. One clapped the other's back, and then I heard one of them say something to the effect of "the girl can tie me up with that belt" followed by another lewd comment about my anatomy.

Frankie's eyes glowed, and he exposed his formidable fangs. I pressed my hand against his chest to hold back his advancement and saw that Max had the guy by the collar, feet lifted off the ground. Then Max punched him. The guard flew over the hood of the Humvee and smashed into the windshield. The impact left a crack the shape of Texas in the glass.

I turned to see Max's body buffed up. His thigh muscles exploded through his pants, and his arms and shoulders burst out of his t-shirt.

"Max, no!" I yelled.

The cock of a gun drew my attention to guard number two. He

waved the Glock and backed away, looking between a Hulked out Max, Frankie, whose eyes were still glowing, and me. "What the hell are you people?"

I opened my mouth to try to babble our way out of this but he reached into the Humvee and pulled out the mouthpiece for the radio, gun still leveled at us. Before I could spring forward to get the radio out of his hands and keep myself between him and Berserker Max and Vampire Frankie, he dropped both the mouthpiece and the gun. His hand clawed at his own throat and it sounded like he was aspirating. When he opened his mouth, blood poured out.

"What the hell?" Frankie said, and I noticed he kept space between himself and the guard, whose front was now covered with blood. The scene reminded me of something we encountered a few months back, when Beta-Vamps were given a blood supply tainted with deadly opiates. The end result was a gruesome death of exploding bodies that looked eerily similar to the scenario unfolding in front of us. Frankie was poisoned, but we were able to find a cure before he erupted like the others. I wasn't surprised that he kept his distance here. I did too.

A half-transformed Max, however, stomped towards the car, following the periphery of the brush. I breathed a small sigh of relief that he wasn't fully Berserked. It meant that he was still in control of his cognitive skills and able to recognize his allies. A full-on Berserker was just a dangerous mass of rage. His eyes darted to a cluster of trees in the not-too-far distance and he made a grunt, nodding his head towards the foliage.

The guard who was sprawled on the hood of the Humvee came to. He saw his colleague on the ground, coughing up blood. He sat up. His unsteady movements told me he was still groggy from Max's punch. His gun came out and before I could shout a warning, he shot the choking guard right through the throat. Then he placed the gun in his mouth and pulled the trigger.

The echoes of the two gunshots in succession faded and we were left only with sound of Max's labored breathing as he tried to un-Hulk himself.

"What the hell just happened?" I whispered. My hands shook from the adrenaline. I squeezed them together to stop the tremors.

Max's muscles were about halfway to normal and he pointed into the field. A figure moved from behind a cluster of trees, and the light from the nearly full moon flooded his face. My grandfather.

"What the hell is he doing here?" I asked no one in particular.

Frankie responded anyway. "Saving the day, apparently?"

"You know we would have gotten out of that," I said. "Bullets? I mean, really. We've dodged worse."

Frankie picked up a bullet casing off the ground. His fingers sizzled and he dropped the small piece of metal before it burned into his hand.

"Holy water soaked silver," he said. "We would have survived but that would've hurt like a bastard."

"They would have gotten away," my grandfather said, walking straight into our conversation.

"So they deserved to die?" Max grunted out. He was nearly himself again, his tattered clothes hanging on his slighter frame. "Who the hell are you?"

"Teddy Martinez," Gramps grunted back. "They'da gotten away and told Leila. And since she hasn't rounded your ass up yet, I assume she don't know about you, Berserker. I did you all a favor."

Max rubbed his hand through his hair and looked at me. "Martinez?"

I nodded and flashed a sheepish smile. "Max, meet my grandfather."

"Jesus, how many of you are there?" he asked.

I sat on the bumper of the Humvee and made a conscious choice not to be offended. For someone orphaned as a baby, then left on Blood Ops' doorstep, plenty of long-lost family was crawling out of the woodwork lately. "I'm beginning to ask myself the same question."

"We should talk about this someplace else," Max said, glancing around the still night. "Those gun shots are sure to bring others out here."

"And we do what with the bodies?" Frankie asked.

"Leave 'em," Gramps said.

"But if they find bodies—" I started.

"Murder-suicide," he said. "Maybe they were lovers."

I scratched at my scalp, tense from tonight's action-packed stakeout and the tight braid holding back my unwieldy hair. "*You* murdered them."

Gramps shrugged. "You gotta think about the big picture, Nina. What good would it do Dr. O if you were dead?"

I followed Frankie and Max to our utilitarian van, not bothering to answer. He was right. They would have reported everything to Leila, our plan scuttled. And Leila would have known about Max, a secret we were all desperate to keep.

My grandfather reached for my shoulder, holding me back from the others. He nodded at Max. "That one reeks of demon magic."

"That's because a demon did that to him," I said.

He pushed a hand through his silver hair. "So Bertrand's in town."

I stopped and turned to face him. "Wait. You know Bertrand?"

"I know him. And I know his magic," Gramps said, sniffing at the air.

I took a step to the side, my discomfort at his proximity growing. "So he's a friend of yours?"

"Not friend, exactly."

"But not enemy?"

My grandfather just smiled, and I noticed he was missing a tooth. "Go on with Frankie."

"What about you?" I asked, my eyes trained on a mass of bodies with glowing flashlights. They were crossing the prison parking lot and headed for the deserted street between us and the prison.

"I'll catch up with you later," he said, stepping into the shadows. "I got my own places to be."

6

——————

W<small>HISKEY SOAKED</small> ice clinked into the glass when Al spit out the piece he was sucking. "Linen service? What the hell is that place, the Four Seasons?"

"People need to change their sheets," Eva chimed in. "Leila would let them change their sheets, right?"

"I guess if she's a neat freak," I snapped, rolling my eyes. "Sure, let's add neat freak to the list that includes murderous psychotic witch vampire hybrid."

Frankie reached under the table and gave my knee a squeeze. "Eva, I don't think that Nina can say for sure if Leila would allow the prisoners to change their sheets. Or if she even gives them sheets. Remember, up until a few months ago, Leila was dead. And Nina never knew her."

Eva's face dropped. "Oh jeez, of course. I really stuck my foot in it this time."

"You sure did," Al grumbled.

"It's okay, Eva," I said, watching the cringe slip from her face at my forgiveness. "I know you didn't mean anything by it. I'm going to get a root beer. Anyone want anything?"

I darted to the bar and checked the small fridge under the

counter. Three root beers left. "Hey, Darce, any word on any shipments from our suppliers?"

She pulled her eyes up from the paltry number of the night's receipts in front of her. "We have no suppliers. If I get them on the phone, they yammer on and on about Babe being a witch, and how scared they are to come here."

"How do you even get them to talk to you?"

"I pretend I'm human and tell them there was no way Babe was a witch. That I never once saw her twitch her nose and see something strange happen," she said, not quite meeting my eyes. Still, I understood completely why she did that. It was easier to go along sometimes. She brightened. "Although the Clown Shoes dude said he'd pop by later in the week, maybe. If he can find the place."

"Hallelujah! Beer," Al said, clapping his hands together. "Even if it's that crap. You've been dry for too long."

"We've been out of beer less than 24 hours," I pointed out to the drama king, returning to the table with my soda. "But don't get your hopes up, Al. If the distributor does show up, he still needs to find the place. If he's human, he won't see through the wards."

"Can't you take them down?" he asked. "Not forever. Just for him."

"No."

Al gave me a sour look.

Ignoring him, I took a pull from my soda bottle. The carbonation tickled my nose. "It's not like I have paying customers anyway," I added.

"I pay," he barked.

"You run a tab. That's different."

Darcy propped her chin in her hand. "The bar won't go under, will it?"

"The building is owned free and clear," I said. "And I have enough from my inheritance to cover inventory for a long while." One of the perks of being fathered by a several centuries old vampire was the accumulated wealth that came with his age. Relief flooded Al's face. "That is, if we can get inventory," I added, watching his smile fade fast.

"Can we go back to the linens now?" Frankie asked, glancing at the clock. "It is getting on 4 a.m., and Matty is still upstairs playing video games."

Unlike Frankie, Matty wasn't charmed by Bertrand to handle sunlight, even though his father, my Uncle Tavio, was the demon's right-hand man. A demon charm would kill a Beta-Vamp.

"You can put him in the basement," Darcy suggested.

I pursed my lips. "The last time I did that, he said I'd — and I quote — rue the day."

"You know he didn't mean it," she said.

"Right now, I don't need a rock star level meltdown about something as ridiculous as his beauty rest. What vampire needs beauty rest? There's too much at stake for him to behave like a spoiled brat."

"He's just used to being treated a certain way by the people that surround him. He's lived in a bubble—"

"Shit, Nina, your eyes are getting all glowy again," Al said. That's when I felt my fangs slice into my gums.

"Oh my god, Nina. Are you vamping out on *me*?" Darcy asked.

I gripped the edge of the table and took in a shaky breath. "Darcy, you know I can't control this."

"What set her off?" Eva asked. With my body adjusting to this all out assault from the transformation, she sounded miles away. I shut my eyes and willed my body to behave.

"Matty set her off," Frankie said, his voice kind of echoing through me.

"But he's not even here," Darcy protested.

"The very idea of him sets her off," he clarified.

"She's practically foaming at the mouth," Al interjected.

My eyes snapped open and locked onto Frankie. "Don't panic, love," he said, taking my hand and holding it up. "See? No talons yet."

A familiar pop, centered on my head, broke through the vampiric haze. "Damn, girl." Casper's familiar voice flooded me with relief. "You just can't be without me for more than 24 hours."

I grinned until I felt a sharp fang pierce my lower lip. "Ouch!" I cried out.

Casper's chant filled my head. "*Raíz de mi cuerpo a la tierra, el viento, el fuego, el agua. Yo soy el poder, yo soy el brujo. Por el poder del brujo, suelte el mal en esta mujer."*

Every muscle in my body seized as Casper's spell took hold, ordering the vampire to release its hold. Frankie caught me before I dropped to the floor. Pain seared deep into my bones. The vampire magic rooted in my DNA was fighting Casper's spell. Breath rushed out of me while he repeated it.

"She doesn't look so good," I heard someone say. I think it was Darcy.

Frankie shoved the half-empty bottles and glasses aside and laid me out on the table. Then the convulsions started.

"What do we do?" Eva cried, her voice evidence of her rising panic. "Will the holy water help?"

I heard the jug of holy water that I kept behind the bar slosh closer to me. I released on unnatural shriek as a stream of water splashed out and hit my torso. Pain seared through me while the smell of burning flesh filled my nose.

"Get that poison away from her," Frankie yelled. "She's not demon possessed, woman." I felt him rip at my top, tearing my t-shirt off. The cotton strings ripped through my skin where they'd been embedded as my body healed itself immediately after being scorched from the blessed water.

Casper's voice surged through me as he once again repeated the chant. My body still didn't allow me to react, to beg him to stop. Not that he would. The vampire needed to be brought under control, and that's exactly what his spell was doing.

My body seized once more and then shuddered in blissful release. I winced at the lingering pain from the holy water burn on my stomach as my inner vampire receded.

"You all right?" Frankie asked as he helped me sit up. His understated behavior was betrayed by the mix of worry and relief that flowed from him. He was doing a lousy job blocking our bond, which meant he was rattled.

I pressed my hand against my stomach. The holy water burns still smarted. "Yeah, I'm fine."

"You're totally not fine," Casper scolded, calling out my fib.

"I'm fine," I grumbled again, this time at Casper. The entire room looked at me, puzzled. I pointed to my head.

"Ah," Frankie said. "So our ghost saved the day again, did he? Please convey our thanks. One day I hope to meet him."

That buoyed Casper's spirits so much that I thought he'd forget to harp on me for not controlling my ability to turn. It was short-lived.

"You know, you are just like Max," Casper continued, rubbing salt in the holy water wound. "You are always nagging on him to control his Berserker—"

"I don't nag," I interrupted.

He ignored me. "—and you can't even control your vampire, and you've been this way your whole life."

"You haven't known me my whole life," I grumbled.

"Whatever," he said, forcing my arm to move in a talk-to-the-hand gesture.

I gripped my forearm with my other hand and yanked it back down. I hated it when he took over my body. It set my fangs on edge.

"It hasn't happened like this before," I said, keeping my voice low while everyone around me cleaned up the broken glass and puddle of holy water spreading out on the wood floor.

"And it's getting worse," Casper continued. "You need to figure out your shit, girl. Because I can't follow you all the time to fix these things. Not now, anyway."

He was right. It wasn't safe for him to be darting around while I went off around the city half-cocked. Ghost exorcisms were as regular as getting a Dunkin Donuts coffee to start the day, and just as public. He was only safe at the bar, or at his moms. Before I could respond to him, my grandfather careened in through the front door.

"I felt tremors three miles away," he grumbled. "You nearly started a goddamn earthquake. What the hell happened to you?"

"Nothing," I lied. "And I didn't try any spells."

"Really, you sure?" Gramps asked, his eyes now on Eva and Darcy as they paused their cleanup effort.

"Yes I am sure," I said, leaving it at that.

Frankie shot me a dirty look. "She was vamping out. She can't throw a spell and vamp at the same time. So it couldn't have been her."

Casper harrumphed in my head while Gramps paced around the table, eyeing me with suspicion. "You pushed out the vampire using magic then."

I clutched my torn top over the burn mark on my exposed stomach. The room was silent as my friends watched, anticipating a showdown between Gramps and me.

Casper broke the silence. "The old dude is no joke, Nina."

"I hear you, Spirit, but I don't see your form," my grandfather said while his eyes darted around the room, coming to rest on me. "Is he in your body?"

Casper gasped, but I sat stone-faced.

"Impressive," he said, and his expression told me that he wasn't lying. "Makes me think you aren't such a lost cause after all. If you can handle a spirit in your body, even with the undead part living in you, you are stronger than I thought."

"What are you talking about?" I broke my silence.

"The ghost. He enters and exits at will?" Gramps barely waited for me to nod. "Vampires aren't living. The dead can't inhabit the dead."

"I'm not dead yet," I pointed out.

"Not yet, no," he said in a way that gave me chills. "But even alive you shouldn't be able to tolerate him in your body. Not like this. But you do. That's the witch. And that witch is strong."

I shrugged. I knew it was the witch. But that tolerance thing? Some days I had zero tolerance for Casper. He was a right pain in the ass sometimes.

My grandfather changed gears. "Figured out how you're getting in the prison yet?" His question was met with silence. "Seems to me you could use a witch to get you in there."

"We'll use the linen service," I said, my voice flat.

"So you use the linen service and you get inside, and then what?" he asked. "Do you know where you're going once you get in there? Do you even know what your mother is up to?"

"He has a good point," Al said.

I pressed my hands against my temples and rubbed, my head aching. "Okay, I'll bite. Do you have any idea what she's up to?"

"I think I do," Casper said. His voice caused the pain in my head to turn into a full on throb.

I focused my breathing and ignored the incessant thump at my temples. "What do you think she's doing?"

"According to the coven network—"

I cut him off. "The coven network?"

"I went to my mom's sabbat," he said. "So sue me."

I shook my head, augmenting the pounding. "Next time, let me go with you. You step into an exorcism and that'll be the end of you."

"Tell him about the amateur exorcisms," Al piped up while he dropped paper towels onto the puddle on the floor. "We saw one the other day, remember, Eva?"

Eva nodded. "It was terrible."

"You were busy and I had to keep an eye on her," Casper said. "Make sure she wasn't in any danger."

"Don't do it again," I said, my voice sharp to cover up the pang of guilt that slammed into my gut. I should have thought to check in on his mother, to warn her. Covens really shouldn't be drawing down the moon right now.

"When I was there, I heard them say that some of the witches were released. And they were sick, real sick."

I conveyed this to the room.

"Sick like how?" I asked.

"Like drained," he said. "One of the crones said it reminded her of when her husband had cancer, and he had chemotherapy. They can't eat, can't walk on their own, can barely stay awake. They aren't themselves."

I conveyed this to the room as well.

"What about magic, do they have magic?" Gramps barked.

I repeated Casper's words as they echoed through me. "No. Their magic is gone."

"That's what I thought," the old man said, sitting back in a chair with a sigh. His weathered face looked ancient.

"Would you like to elaborate?" Frankie asked.

"Experiments," Gramps said. "She's draining their magic for experiments."

Darcy's face clouded over. "What do you mean experiments?"

"I mean experiments," the old man snapped. "She wants to build a better beast."

"Better than what?" I asked.

My grandfather's eyes sliced into me. "Better than you."

7

I WAS RUNNING on pure rage, so for the first time in the history of our partnership, Frankie rushed to keep up with me. He trailed me through the lobby of the Biltmore Hotel. Once the shining jewel in the crown of the city of Providence, the Biltmore had fallen into a state of disrepair and disrepute. I stepped over a drugged out hooker and pushed through the plasma goo of a poltergeist. The spelled medallion that protected me from body-jumping spirits was clutched in my left fist. I could walk through them but they couldn't possess me.

"Slow down," Frankie huffed from behind. "Let's talk about this."

"There's nothing to talk about," I said.

"You don't know what the old git meant by that."

"Frankie, he called me a beast. What could I possibly misunderstand?"

"So he hurt your feelings," he scoffed.

"No, he didn't hurt my feelings," I said, not quite telling the truth. I mean, who likes being called a beast if you aren't at the gym? "The point is I am not witch or vampire or hybrid. To him, I am *beast*."

Frankie grabbed my arm and turned me towards him. "I fail to see your point."

"My point," I said as I wrenched my arm from his grip, "is that it sounds like I was made, not born."

"Your being bloody ridiculous," Frankie said, chasing after me again. "Of course you were born. Leila was pregnant, nine months later you popped out. I was there, remember?"

I paused and looked up the sweeping staircase, its former grandeur supplanted by threadbare carpeting and a broken mahogany banister. "Yes, you were there, but Bertrand was there too."

"Nina, please," Frankie pleaded, grabbing my arm. "I'd know—"

"You know nothing!" I said, shaking out of his grip. "You're just pissed that my dad kept this from you. So much for best friend."

Frankie looked like I'd just slapped him. I hesitated for a moment, my harsh words hanging in the air around us. I pressed my lips closed instead of apologizing and stalked up the stairs. Bertrand had some explaining to do.

The staircase was the worst part of the journey through the hotel to get to Bertrand's lair, drawing all manner of ghosts and poltergeists. Some pleaded with me to release them from purgatory. Most were angry and picked fights. I ignored all of them, save for the bellboy who sported the remnants of a shotgun blast to the back of the head.

"Is he in?" I asked him, sensing Frankie a few steps behind me.

The boy curled his lip. "What business do you have with the mayor?"

I squeezed the medallion, its ridged pattern cutting into my skin, and braced myself to push through him. There was a loud thwack sound as my body moved through his plasma ooze.

The ghost reversed direction and pushed through me as well. I felt his body try to anchor onto mine and snickered when he gave up in disgust. His translucent figure popped out of my chest and loomed in front of me once again.

"I need to announce your business," he tried again.

"Bertrand knows what business would bring me here, kid."

"Another bloody ghost," Frankie muttered, matching my strides up the stairs. I glanced at him and saw his eyes glowing just a bit. He wasn't at vamp-out level, but the ghosts were getting to him. That was the thing with poltergeists. Even if you can't see them or consciously feel them, they put everyone in a crappy mood.

Hauntings were dangerous not necessarily because ghosts were dangerous, even malevolent ones. Unhappy spirits that roamed places could weigh heavy on the psyche, causing all sorts of mayhem on the people who spent a lot of time in haunted spots, manifesting in deep depression or fits of rage. The number of ghosts and poltergeists that hung around the Biltmore left an undercurrent of simmering angst through the entire property. That's why there were plenty of bar fights, stabbings and shootings in the hotel and the surrounding blocks.

The Biltmore's ghosts weighed heavy on Frankie's psyche. And for them to do that to the undead, well...they were especially potent.

I switched the medallion to my right hand and took his hand in mine, pressing his palm into the other half of the token. The shared medallion helped ward off whatever psychic tricks the ghosts were playing with him, although I risked being less immune to possession. Nothing was foolproof.

I caught sight of my bellboy friend scurrying towards Bertrand's wing of the hotel. He slammed into the door at considerable force and staggered around the top of the stairs, stunned.

"Interesting," I whispered.

"What is?" Frankie asked. The vamp-out glow in his eyes was fading, the spelled object doing its job.

"I think Bertrand locked the spirits out," I said.

"What do you mean?"

"The bellboy, he can't get in."

"What bellboy?"

"Of course, you don't see the ghosts," I muttered, squeezing Frankie's hand in frustration. "One of the ghosts is a bellboy and he usually flits in and out of Bertrand's wing. But he can't seem to get in there now."

Frankie shuddered. "I always feel the ghost presence lift when we get out of this creepy lobby."

"Yeah, but Bertrand's hallway allowed some ghosts in. Bellboy was one of them. He announces his visitors."

"Maybe they're finally fraying his nerves," Frankie grumbled.

"A ghost besting a demon like Bertrand? Come on," I said.

"Casper gets you riled up," he pointed out.

"You try living with an 18-year-old in your brain and see how you like it," I said. "And I am not a demon. If a ghost is rattling a demon, he's not very good at being demonic."

We stopped at the door leading to Bertrand's wing. I brushed my hand over the oiled wood and a series of sparks followed. "This thing is seriously warded."

Frankie pressed his own hand against the door. "Nothing," he said, shaking his head. "It's like he put out a vampire welcome mat."

I glared at him. "Can you push it open, please?"

"You think you can get through it open?" he asked. His face had skeptical written all over it.

"What's the worst that can happen?"

Frankie raised an eyebrow but pushed open the door and gave me a little shove into the threshold. I lamented the bravado of those six words as I stepped into a giant, walk-through Taser. My entire body stiffened. I tried to yell, but only a gurgling noise escaped. This time, Frankie gave me a hard shove and I sprawled onto the floor on the other side of the door.

"What the hell was that?" I barked, pushing myself up and leaning against the wall.

As I caught my breath, Frankie strolled right through like it was nothing. "You want a brush or something?" He grinned at me.

I glared at him. "What?"

"Your hair," Frankie said, motioning with his hand above his head. "It's sticking up all over the place."

Gritting my teeth, I pushed myself up to standing, and smoothed my hair down. Static electricity sparked along my fingers. "Son of a bitch has this place warded to keep out witches and ghosts."

"How'd you make it through then?"

"Not a full witch," I reminded him.

"Neither's your mum," he pointed out.

"My mum also doesn't have a vampire partner to shove her through warded doors," I said, sweeping past him and tucking the medallion safely into my pocket. "Let's move."

My pride was still smarting from the shove and Frankie knew enough not to razz me further. Not now, anyway. He'd be relentless in a day or two.

My step into the anteroom of Bertrand's suite was a cautious one, just in case he had that threshold spelled too. I expected to be met by his usual muscled up vamp bodyguards, but no one was standing sentry in front of Bertrand's office door. In fact, it was wide open, and Bertrand's butter-smooth voice was met by a recognizable gruff one.

"Your wards are shit, Bertrand," Gramps' voice bellowed from inside the office.

My arm sprang out fast in front of Frankie's chest to keep him from walking into the room. Instead, I peered around the doorway. Gramps stood in front of Bertrand's expensive mahogany desk. A half-sneer, half-grin stretched across his wrinkled face. Bertrand's missing goons tripped over each other on their way towards him, only to be thwarted by a simple wrist flick that dropped them to the floor. I stared at their crumpled bodies, awestruck at the power the skinny old man commanded at will.

"Teddy Martinez..." Bertrand's FM radio-smooth voice took the edge off. His dark hair, greying at the temples, set off steely eyes, while his impeccably tailored suit showed off an athletic build. It was no surprise he won the female vote by a landslide. "How did you manage to get out of Mexico?"

My Uncle Tavio's voice came from behind the door. "I'll take care of him, Ami." My dead vampire dad had an undead vampire brother, who was also Bertrand's lackey. I only just found out about him when my life was upended by Leila's psycho boyfriend and his literally infernal knife.

Bertrand stilled my uncle with the wave of a hand. "No need, Tavio."

"Tavio, I haven't seen you since the wedding. You're looking quite undead these days." My grandfather's cold grin told me that he enjoyed egging the old vampire on.

"It would be my pleasure, sir," Tavio said to Bertrand, stepping out from behind the door. His vamped out face carried a profound hatred. His fangs were extended and his brown eyes were like glowing orbs. I'd never seen my uncle in full-on vampire mode, and the danger he radiated caught me off-guard. He was a short, stocky man with silver hair who had Matty, a Beta-Vamp, for a son. Vampire was pretty much where his family resemblance with my dad ended. Until now. Uncle Tavio looked fierce. My face took on a similar expression when I was pissed.

So Tavio didn't like Gramps. And, by all appearances, the feeling was mutual. My eyebrows raised as I soaked in the rising animosity flowing between them. My parents must have had a hell of an eventful wedding.

"Please, Tavio." Bertrand stilled my uncle with the wave of his hand. "You'll get your chance at him. I am interested to learn how this clever witch charmed his way around one of my curses."

"Give a witch a few decades, Bertrand, and a smart one can find his way around curses. Even demonic ones."

"You have even more talent than I realized," Bertrand said, as delight in the game he played with Gramps danced on his face. "You always made me proud, although your impatience proved your downfall time and again."

"What are you doing here?" Tavio asked, his own patience waning.

"I came here to say I told you so," Gramps sneered. "I told you I would break that spell and get out of Mexico and here we are."

My eye twitched at that and I stepped in from the doorway. "What does a demonic spell have to do with you in Mexico?"

Even though Bertrand flashed a smile, his handsome face remained cold. "Nina, so good of you to join us. Your grandfather and I were just catching up. We were once..."

"We weren't anything," Gramps interjected. "You set a spell to keep me trapped in Catemaco. I broke your spell. End of story."

Frankie followed behind me and gave a low whistle. "I've not heard of anyone breaking a demon curse. Certainly not a witch."

Bertrand's easy demeanor cracked for a split second and his eyes flashed red. "Teddy Martinez is a very talented witch. But let's not kid ourselves. That particular curse weakens over time, and I never felt the need to reset it. That's why you were able to crack it."

My grandfather reached into his pocket and pulled out a pack of Faros, a brand of Mexican cigarettes. "Don't rewrite history, Bertrand. I broke your curse." He took one out, placed it in his mouth, and lit the end with just a snap of his fingers, ignoring the fact that Bertrand was seething under the faux-placid expression that he maintained. "And it was as strong as the day you cast it."

"So you were *trapped* in Mexico?" I asked.

"Thirty-odd years. Sound about right?" he asked.

"And you broke the spell? A demon curse?" I pressed him.

Gramps simply grinned and blew a smoke ring in Bertrand's direction, the circle enlarging as it traveled and then broke apart.

"Was that why Babe was in Mexico?" I asked. "To help you break the curse?"

Before Babe was slaughtered by Leila, she was in Mexico for what I thought was a family visit and a little R&R, not to break some demon curse. I remembered Skyping with her and seeing some strange looking men hanging around the internet café. They didn't look shady exactly, but they stood out as odd. Did Bertrand have her followed?

Gramps narrowed his eyes at me but said nothing.

Bertrand simply looked between the two of us. Then he pursed his lips and exhaled his own smoke ring, no cigarette required. It floated across the room and lingered over Gramps' head. Then it dropped down and wrapped around Gramps' neck like a noose. His face turned beet red as the smoke circle squeezed, cutting off his air.

He held up his hands in surrender, but Bertrand didn't make any motion to release the pressure. My grandfather's eyes bulged, like they were ready to pop out of his head. His cigarette fell from his hands and smoldered on the carpet. Watery sounds came from the back of his throat as he ripped unsuccessfully at the smoke circled around his neck.

"Bertrand, stop," I said. I stepped between them to do...I didn't know what. "You two clearly have some sort of beef, I get it. But I think we need him."

"Need him, Ms. Martinez?" Bertrand asked above the awful noises coming from Gramps' throat as the smoke crushed his trachea. "You barely know him. And need I remind you that he tried to kill you when you were a baby? I know your aunt shared that bit of history with you."

"The entire town tried to kill me when I was a baby. They thought I was a vampire."

"You are a vampire," he said.

"No. When I am dead, I'll be a vampire," I pointed out. "Alive, I just have interesting abilities."

Frankie laughed. "That's one way to put it."

I silenced him with a look. "If I have to take down Leila, I have to learn to be a witch. And he needs to teach me."

"So you are ready to embrace your magic?" Bertrand asked, his eyes glinting with amusement.

I shifted my feet. "If that's what you want to call it."

The smoke around my grandfather's throat dissipated. Gramps slumped into his chair, rubbing the rope-like abrasions left on his neck. His eyes were narrow slits, staring at Bertrand in silence. I wondered what he was plotting.

"Excellent news," Bertrand said as he settled behind his oversized ornate desk. "Please have a seat." He motioned to the club chairs across from him. Preferring to keep a wide berth between us, I settled on the couch, sitting on the edge. Frankie sank into the deep comfortable leather beside me.

"Suit yourself," he said before turning to Gramps. "So, my old friend, I see your daughter's return gave you sufficient motivation to break that old curse."

"Daughter?" Gramps spat out, his hand still protecting his neck. "That pox on humanity is no daughter of mine."

Bertrand's laugh was like rich milk chocolate poured over ice cream. "Since when did you care about humanity?"

"You think I am going to stand by while she turns my kind into monsters?"

"Then we have something in common," Bertrand said.

"Since when do you give a damn about the witches?" I interjected. My grandfather gave me a sharp glance and then straightened his posture.

"All matter of supernatural entities are of my concern," Bertrand said, a flicker of annoyance dancing across his chiseled face.

"Since when?" I challenged.

"You'll see she is spirited as your other daughter, Babette," Bertrand cooed. "Pity we lost her."

I fell silent, tears stinging at my eyes. I stared at my boots to keep anyone from noticing.

"Leila will pay for what she did to—"

"Didn't you exile Babette when she took Nina in as a baby?" Bertrand pointed out.

Gramps glanced at me. "I had my reasons. Just like she had hers for taking the baby."

"Love and loyalty, those were her reasons," I said, keeping my eyes trained on the floor. "What were yours?"

Bertrand rubbed his hands together, not bothering to hide his delight at the question I posed to my grandfather. But he interceded anyway. "Perhaps we should let bygones be bygones," he said. "I am sure you both agree that Leila poses a threat to the delicate balance that has kept all of us coexisting with humans for millennia."

"I think that steamer has left the port," Frankie quipped, squeaking against the leather as he leaned forward, elbows on knees.

I nodded in agreement. "That balance is gone. CNN covered the entire thing. Remember?" The national news networks descended upon our tiny state in a few short hours, with Leila's raging bonfire leading most of the broadcasts.

"All the more reason why we need each other," Bertrand said. His grin shot through me like pins.

"Keep your friends close," Frankie muttered to me.

I leaned into him in agreement when the office door opened again. Max stopped dead when he saw us all in the room.

"I didn't know you were throwing a party," he said to Bertrand, hesitating in the threshold.

"I didn't either," Bertrand said, extending his arm out in welcome. "But I'm glad you are here. We could certainly use your expertise."

Max gave a fast shake of his head and then stepped aside. A tall, slim woman skimmed past him, her walk confident considering the height of her heels, which were silent on Bertrand's thick carpet. Even Gramps sat up straighter as she clipped past him and headed straight for the couch. Her tight smile iced over an attractive face.

"Nina Martinez," she said, and her voice carried the same authority as her appearance. "Lovely to finally meet you. You are everything I expected you to be."

She moved the Prada attaché she carried to her left hand and extended her right hand to me. I ignored it, keeping my ass firmly planted on Bertrand's leather couch.

I scowled. "How about leveling the playing field and tell me who the hell you are."

"Of course," she said, her lips edging a grin that did not convey happiness. "I am Mary Jane Colton, the special envoy to Secretary of Defense Elliot Hagel. He sent me."

Frankie stilled beside me as a ball of lead dropped into my stomach. "I'm sorry, Secretary of Defense?"

"We know about Blood Ops, Nina," she said. "Secretary Hagel sent me here to contain the situation."

Bertrand stood and extended his own hand. "Ms. Colton, welcome to Providence. I am—"

"I know exactly who you are, Mayor Bertrand," she interrupted, her voice edged with impatience. "And I expect your full cooperation."

"Of course," he said, covering his anger at her slight with a slick politician's grin. "Anything you need, I will personally see to it that you have."

She nodded, eyeing Gramps, who had slipped from his seat to a corner of the room to blend into the wall. She settled primly into the club chair Gramps abandoned.

She opened her case and pulled out a laptop. Her knee-length skirt rode up as she shifted in her chair to place the empty bag on the floor by her Christian Louboutin shoes, revealing long, lean thighs. Her straight blond hair was set in a neat, low ponytail and extended down the back of her suit jacket to her shoulder blades. The way the dark grey fabric fit her body told me that this was not an off-the-rack purchase. The suit fit her body like it was supposed to, no boxy shoulders or lopsided hems. The woman oozed power. I noticed Max couldn't take his eyes off of her. Nor could Frankie, so I landed a sharp elbow into his middle.

"What can we do for you, Ms. Colton?" Bertrand asked, breaking the uncomfortable silence. His solicitous nature was at odds with the rank smell of sulfur that danced through the air. The demon was rattled.

"Secretary Hagel and our team have managed to turn the news media away from the situation here in Rhode Island," she said, brushing at imaginary lint on her skirt. "They think that the episode a few weeks ago was from a terrorist attack."

"Terrorist attack?" I repeated, raising my eyebrows. "Leila lit my aunt on fire in front of an angry mob. All they needed were pitchforks and we could have been a goddamn Frankenstein reenactment."

"We blamed the behavior on mephedrone poison," she explained. "Terrorists tampered with the water supply."

"Mephedrone? What the hell is that?" Uncle Tavio asked.

"White Magic," Max said.

Uncle Tavio looked confused. I was too.

"M-Cat," he tried again. "Meow Meow?"

"Meow back at you?" I offered with a shrug. Was this some weird flirty thing he was doing? It was like a foreign language.

"Those are street names for bath salts," Max said, his voice heavy with exasperation. "And not the literal kind. You've heard of those, right?"

Frankie looked incredulous. "Bath salts? And the Americans believe you?"

My laugh was hollow. "If it's on T.V. it must be true, right?"

Mary Jane glared at both of us. "It's not outside the realm of possibility."

"Remember that episode in Miami? It made the news a few years ago. That drug turned users into living zombies, chomping on human flesh," Max said, his biceps flexing as he crossed his arms. God, he looked enormous. "Not much of a stretch to explain away the behavior seen here a few weeks ago."

I did remember Miami. The incident happened while I was still in training. Blood Ops mobilized and sent a team down, but it turned out to be a human problem.

"We have closed the state borders in an abundance of caution," Mary Jane said.

"You closed the boarders?" I asked. "I thought that was Leila, locking us all in."

"Of course we closed the boarders," Mary Jane sniffed at me. "Do you really believe we would allow this to spread to the rest of the country?"

While her makeshift boarder walls contained the spread of Leila, it didn't allow the innocent safe passage either. But I kept that point to myself.

"How long do you think you can keep this pretense up?" I asked instead, wrinkling my nose as the rank air assaulted my nostrils.

"Not much longer," she admitted, her face stoic. If she noticed the peculiar odor, she didn't let on. "We've created television footage of the CDC coming in and treating the afflicted. We've dispatched medical talking heads to go on cable news to confuse everyone with hard science. And we've deployed troops in the Middle East to have a show of boots on the ground."

She flipped her laptop open and began moving her fingers on the touchpad.

"Sounds like you've got it all covered," I said, waving my hand in front of my face. Why didn't anyone else seem bothered by the smell?

"Look," she said, placing the computer on the edge of Bertrand's enormous desk. She tilted it towards us, forcing Bertrand to get up and walk around to see the news footage of some balding guy dressed in doctors' scrubs tossing out impressive sounding medical terms. The anchor woman's head bobbed in agreement, but her hair didn't move. Then images of troops taking mortar fire in some far away desert replaced the dull talking heads.

"Do you smell something?" I whispered to Frankie when an argument broke out between in-studio guests. The air in the office was now thick with the sulfuric smell. I glanced at the airtight windows lining the wall, wishing I could open one.

He nodded. "You do too?" he replied, his voice low. "Bertrand is pissed about something, and he's releasing a wank-load of pheromones. But I thought only vampires could smell it."

"Well, I can too," I said, glancing at Bertrand as he leaned against his desk, arms crossed, staring down Mary Jane. "It's not bothering you?"

"Seven hundred years, love," he said with a wink. "You get used to all manner of foul odors."

I shook my head in disgust at the idea of my olfactory glands working over time for 700 years. One more reason not to want to turn anytime soon. I pulled the collar of my shirt up over my nose like a five-year-old and glanced at my silent grandfather, who eyed me curiously. Mary Jane snapped the laptop shut.

"It looks like you have the situation under control," I said, pulling my shirt back down.

"This is simply a Band-Aid," she said, pulling the computer onto her lap. "And it's starting to peel off. The truthers are unraveling bits of our story. We are going to have to reopen Route 95 to interstate commerce soon. We need this situation dealt with."

Bertrand returned to the chair behind his desk. He steepled his fingers and gave her a curt nod. "What does Secretary Hagel propose we do to contain the situation?"

"He doesn't care what you do," she said, leveling a knowing look at him before picking up her bag. "He said Blood Ops should use whatever means necessary to get this dealt with as quickly as possible."

"Blood Ops is over," I said. "Dr. O is being held hostage, and Secretary Hagel ripped the operation out from our Vegas base. Our operatives are in the wind."

"That's your problem," she said, tucking her computer into the opening in the supple leather.

"Actually, it sounds like it's *your* problem," I said, anger seeping into my voice. Tavio chuckled, but one glare from Bertrand shut him up.

"Not really," Mary Jane said. "We don't want to have to drop a bomb on this state."

"A bomb? You wouldn't..." I started, narrowing my eyes. She didn't look like she was bluffing. "You can't just drop a bomb on your own citizens. You'd have anarchy."

"Cuba could launch a nuclear missile at D.C. or New York and...misjudge."

"You'd wipe out the entire northern coast," Max said, his eyes wide. He was so certain that his employers, the federal government, wouldn't commit mass murder against its citizens. Frankie and I, on the other hand, knew that she wasn't bluffing. Hiding all preternatural species was *that* important to the government.

"Collateral damage," she said before getting to her feet. Man, she was tall. "We don't care how you do it, you just do it. By any means necessary." She strode to the door before turning and facing us one final time. "You have one week to get this under control. Then we reevaluate our options."

"You can't just drop a bomb on innocent people," Max protested.

"I'm not saying that we would. But do you really want to test us?" she asked, turning on her spiky heel and walking out of the room, leaving an uneasy silence in her wake.

"She's bluffing," Max said, his voice betraying his uncertainty. It was more like wishful thinking.

Bertrand cocked an eyebrow. "Are you sure, Agent Deveroux? You're willing to take that chance?"

I glared at him. "What do you care? You can just pull up stakes and find a new city to ruin. There's no shortage of urban wastelands in this country."

"Yes, but I'm rather fond of this urban wasteland," Bertrand said with a lopsided smile. "So, do you have a plan to contain your mother, or are you just going to wing it?" His fingers formed air quotes at the final two words while I shot him a venomous look.

"They're breaking into Steele City," Max said as he tossed me a curt nod.

"Are you psychic, Agent Deveroux?" Bertrand asked. "You know this, how?"

I jumped in. "He was with us when we scoped out the prison."

Max gave me a side-eyed glance. "I was there when you all *blew it* scoping out the prison."

I pressed my fingers along the bridge of my nose. A headache was coming on again.

Frankie dropped a protective arm around my shoulders. "You okay?" he whispered, his lips brushing along my ear.

"I'm fine," I muttered, shrugging his arm away.

The edges of Max's mouth twitched up when Frankie's arm slipped from its perch. Frankie flashed an icy glare in Max's direction.

Gramps emerged from the shadows and relaxed into Mary Jane's abandoned club chair opposite Bertrand, observing the whole exchange with amusement. He leaned back and kicked his Huarache-adorned feet up on Bertrand's expensive desk.

Bertrand's mouth puckered. "So, old friend? We agree to a truce, then? For the greater good?"

"Truce? With this one?" Uncle Tavio asked as he charged forward, his thick Italian accent boomeranging through the room. He shoved Teddy's feet off the desk and stood between his boss and the old witch who'd made himself at home.

"Crawl back to the desert, *lo stregone*," Tavio spat out. Literally. Twice. Then Tavio made a devil horn sign, which was pretty rich coming from a vampire in league with a demon.

Gramps didn't let up. "You can call me whatever the hell you want. Doesn't change the fact that I was right."

"Right about what?" I interrupted.

"The sham marriage between your parents," he said. "Was never meant to be a happily ever after."

Tavio leaned in and gnashed his fangs at Gramps, aching to take a bite. "It was your daughter who killed my brother—"

"Never said who was at fault, now did I?" Gramps asked, kicking his feet back up on Bertrand's desk.

Tavio's teeth snapped dangerously close to my grandfather's neck. "And now you show up to ruin the child too?"

"What child?" I asked.

"What child?" Tavio turned to me, his eyes wild. "You, of course."

"She is no child." Gramps' protest cut off my own. "She is a witch."

"I will stake her before I let that happen," Tavio roared.

I scrambled to my feet, but Frankie was faster. He blocked me with his body. "No one is staking Nina."

"Hey, I'm right here," I said, elbowing my way around Frankie. "I can speak for myself. And I'll stake you right back, uncle or not."

"Enough! All of you," Bertrand barked as the aroma of sulfur whipped through the room again, tipping me off that he was losing his temper. I covered a small cough. "We are nothing if not forgiving. Right, Tavio?"

Tavio withered under Bertrand's glare. He shuffled to the far corner of the room, which also happened to be where the whiskey cart was located. He took the top off a crystal decanter and poured out a finger, downing the amber liquid in one swallow.

Gramps was a different matter. He pulled out a pack of Faros from the pocket of his worn jeans. Once he tapped out the cigarette, he took a matchstick tucked into the pack and struck it against Bertrand's expensive desk. A blue cloud of smoke enveloped his head as he puffed. Bertrand waved at the acrid smoke creeping towards him. Gramps just puffed harder.

The old man's assuredness around the demon was astounding.

Max cleared his throat. "How about we discuss the prison break now?"

"Excellent idea," Bertrand said, clapping his hands together. "Thanks to Ms. Colton, we now have a timeline. And a tight one at that."

My grandfather worked over Max with his eyes. "But first, how did you turn Berserker? Doesn't come naturally, does it?"

Max clenched his jaw, which kicked off a chain of tension through his entire body.

"We really do need to focus on springing Dr. O," I said, snatching a candy bowl from the side table by the couch. Vampire speed kicked in and I had the bowl under the line of ash on Gramps' cigarette before it fell to the plush carpet.

"Berserkers are extinct," Gramps continued, ignoring me. "Who made you this way, boy?"

I slumped into the club chair beside him and balanced the bowl on my knee. He ignored all the vitriol in the room that was building towards him.

Max opened and closed his fists repeatedly, causing veins to pop along his forearms. I licked my lips and watched the veins throb at the buildup and release of pressure. The blood pumped faster as Max's adrenaline spiked. My stomach ached for the blood under those veins. I closed my eyes, ignoring the hunger, but my keen hearing picked up the sound of blood rushing through him.

"Can we get on with the plan?" I snapped, eyes still closed. "I'm starving."

The room went silent so I opened my eyes. My grandfather's stern expression softened.

"I see we don't have much time," he said.

"No, we don't," I agreed, relieved that we were finally focused on the task at hand. "Max, I am not sure how much longer you can keep a lid on the Berserker. And if Leila finds out...." I shuddered.

"You mean she doesn't know?" my grandfather asked.

"No," Max said, running his hands through his mess of overgrown curls, his cheeks taking a ruddy hue. Keeping his Hulk under control made his skin blotchy. One New England winter and his California sun-kissed skin turned to paste.

"How do you keep this from her?" my grandfather asked.

"Because she's not looking for a Berserker," Bertrand said, his voice edged with impatience. "She's focused on something else."

My grandfather nodded. "Of course she is. But you are on the inside with her, correct? You're able to control *la bestia que vive dentro de ti*."

"The what?" Max asked with a shake of his head.

"The beast that lives within you," I translated, much to my surprise. As a general rule, my Spanish sucked.

Frankie gave me an odd look. "Right. Look, there's another reason we need Dr. O out sooner rather than later, as if we needed one. Max isn't going to be able to keep his beast under wraps for long." He gave Max an apologetic nod. "Sorry, but you're a time bomb. Tick, tock. Someone pisses you off enough, you'll blow. Leila will find out. Then checkmate, mate."

"He is much safer if Leila doesn't know," my grandfather agreed. "She likes her science experiments."

My eyes snapped open and I crossed my arms. "What does that matter if the damn Pentagon is going to drop bombs on this state? Leila can't experiment if we've all gone kaboom."

Frankie's homegrown sound effect of a bomb exploding did nothing to lighten the mood.

"No one is getting blown up," Bertrand snapped, raking his hand through his thick silver-tipped hair. "You will go in, spring our good doctor and make the federal government happy. If not, nuclear bombs will be the least of your worries."

Bertrand dispensed the threat with the same matter-of-factness reserved for talking about baseball stats. I opened my mouth to snap back at him, but Max silenced me with a quick shake of his head. So I settled for stewing in silence. My uncle wasn't so cowed.

"So what, then?" Tavio tossed out his spiky question from the relative safety of his far corner of the room. "They just waltz into the jail and spring the doctor? Is this *testa di cazzo* going to spell Nina invisible?"

"No, this dickhead isn't going to spell shit," my grandfather said, grinning at Tavio's surprise at the translated insult. "She's going to spell herself."

Tavio snorted. "You've heard about the weather the past six months? That's not New England. That's all Nina."

"She is a terrible witch," Bertrand said, reinforcing my uncle's criticism. I itched to jump across the desk and rip the smirk off his face. "But she will be an exceptional vampire, when it's her time. I am certain of that."

My grandfather cocked his head. "Exceptional? You sure about that?"

"And you, old friend, will shape her into an exceptional witch," Bertrand said.

Bertrand and Gramps locked eyes on each other and nodded once. Both men grinned in agreement.

I shivered, unsure if my trepidation was because they were wrong or because they were right.

8

"*USTED ES UN IDIOTA*," my grandfather roared. It was my fifth attempt at lighting a piece of paper on fire. The best I came up with was a light smolder. The smoke tickled my nose and produced a sneeze attack. The only thing burning in the kitchen was Gramps' patience.

"You aren't focusing," he grumbled, and pulled out a book of matches to spark up another cigarette. Watching flame ignite that easy was a tease.

"It's hard to focus with a gaping wound in your hand," I lied. Sort of. He'd sliced me pretty deep to get blood for the spell. But the cut had healed over by now.

"So much for your *poder de la vampira*," he smirked, puffing on the cigarette.

"I told you I was hopeless," I said, cracking open the window above the sink to let his cigarette smoke out. "Hell, everyone did."

"Bullshit," he barked. "You are a Martinez. Martinez blood is magic blood. It won't work because you won't let it."

"Like I have a choice," I muttered, pouring out more of my blood, which was collected in his boring brushed nickel chalice. "You know, I think you should bedazzle this thing. Give it some style."

"You don't like it?" he asked, although his tone told me he didn't give a shit. At all.

"Maybe the blood should be fresh?" I offered, although I inwardly cringed at the thought of making another donation. The bow knife he used to cut into my skin looked well used and unwashed. I swear I felt a staph infection sliding into my skin along with the blade. Even not-yet-dead vampires needed antibiotics and tetanus shots.

"This is a baby spell, not big enough to require blood any fresher than this. And you're slow at spelling. Even fresh blood is old by the time you're done."

"Oh," was about all I could muster. My failure at being a witch was beginning to grate. Disappointment was written all over the old man's face.

"So you do it again. With focus this time."

Dog nudged my hand supportively. I gave her a quick scratch behind the ears, then inhaled deep and closed my eyes.

"What are you thinking of, right now?"

My eyes snapped open at Gramps' interruption. "Setting the paper on fire."

"Wrong," he barked, taking another drag on his cigarette.

"No, not wrong," I said. "That's what I'm thinking." I snatched the cigarette out of his mouth, turned on the sink and ran it under the water. Then I tossed the wet butt out the open window. "That shit will give you cancer."

"Bah," he said, his face grim. "Don't blame me because you have the wrong focus."

I watched him tap out another cigarette from his pack. He rolled it between his fingers and stared at me, daring me to try the spell again. I met his steely look with one of my own, and he tucked the cigarette behind his ear.

"How about you tell me what I'm supposed to be thinking?" I asked, my posture retreating into a slump as my inability to do a simple fire spell deflated me.

"Can't," he said. "Magic comes from deep inside. From your soul."

"That's it," I snapped, slamming down the window. "If you're going to turn all New Age guru on me, I'm done."

"This ain't no New Age crap," he said. "But you need to feel this."

"Feel what? I felt that funked up knife cut into my skin and that's about it."

He slammed his hand down on the counter and I jumped back as the dishes in the sink rattled. "See that? That's energy."

I forced my shoulders down from my ears and shook my head. "This sounds awfully new age-y."

"It's science," he corrected. "Matter is made of atoms and underneath atoms are nothing but energy. So what do you think magic is?" I shrugged again. He tossed up his hands. "Magic controls and manipulates all these threads of this energy, linking together different planes of existence."

"If that's all it is, anyone can do it," I said. "What makes witches so special?"

He shook his head. "Only people who are sensitive to their internal energy can force it externally. That's really what happens when that witch blade of your father's slices a witch. And yes, I know about it," he said at my surprised expression. "Who do you think gave Babe that knife? Anyway, that blade is a conduit for the transference of energy."

I pursed my lips and stared at the piece of paper. "Magic as a transference of energy, to only be done by those of us in tune to it. So it's like getting an electric shock from a carpet?"

Gramps guffawed. "What the hell did you think it was?"

"I don't know. It was magic," I said. "Just magic."

"Just magic," he mocked. "That's like saying it's just vampirism."

"Isn't it?" I asked.

"That's magic too," he said with a sigh. "Of a different sort."

"What sort is that?"

"Doesn't matter," he said, gesturing towards the paper. "Now, close your eyes and feel the energy."

Dog lifted her head from where she was lying at my feet, and he shot her a frigid look. She bared her teeth, the hair on her back stood on end. The old man returned her snarl and her throaty growl turned into a whimper.

"Now trust me," he said, seeing my hesitation.

I looked down at my hellhound, who skulked in defeat at my ankles. "Trust you? I don't even know you."

He clucked. "I'm family."

I put both my hands on my hips and stared at him. "Yeah? Look at what family's done for me.".

"I take your point," he said, leaning against the counter. He looked me up and down before giving a low whistle. "Witch and vampire. That's your mom. A witch and a vampire. You think you can beat that combo?"

"We can try," I said, feeling defiance rise in my chest.

"We? Who's we? Your vampire boyfriend? The Berserker? Don't forget, you're down a Druid. And you're down a witch."

"I'm down more than a witch," I said, wrapping my arms around me and driving my hip into the counter. "I'm down Babe."

"And she was a powerful witch," he said, his rheumy eyes touched with sadness. "No one was better to teach you. But Leila is very powerful, too. And she's not afraid to dance with the darkness. So you can't be either."

I rubbed my arms, as if that would take the chill of his words away. "You're here."

He laughed. "You think I'm here to participate in this war? Kid, I'm here to teach you. That's it. I don't get involved."

"Isn't showing up here getting involved?" I argued.

"I'm incognito. Dust. In the wind."

I rolled my eyes. "You're a coward. You're totally cool with the federal government dropping a bomb on the entire state because your daughter's a psycho?"

"Not my fight," he said.

"Then you are okay with Leila killing witches? Killing Babe?" I asked, my voice rising in frustration and anger.

"You have to choose how, and when, and where you fight, kid," he said. "How about I leave the self-righteousness of it all to you."

I returned his steely glare with one of my own. "So you're not only a coward, but a coward who wants to pick the winning side."

"Maybe that makes me smart. A survivor," he grunted. "Did you think of that?"

I wrinkled my nose at him. "Then why show up here at all?"

"That's my business," he said, his pale blue eyes turning a stormy grey. "You want to learn or not? Because I can pack up my shit. Go back to Mexico."

I chewed on my lower lip, weighing the pros and cons of going this alone. The idea of Gramps ditching sat like an anchor in the pit of my stomach. There was no way I could best Leila's magic without Babe to guide me. I needed his help, which meant swallowing my anger. And my pride. "You really think you can teach me?"

"I like a challenge." Gramps grinned, the light catching a gold cap on his left canine tooth. "Now do it again. You're wasting time."

I took a few deep inhales, then closed my eyes and pictured the sheet of paper resting on Babe's well-worn cookie sheet, which was now crusted with black scorch marks from my earlier mistakes. I dropped my shoulders, which had inched their way up to my ears with tension, and began to mumble the incantation. Before I could finish the third syllable, a stab of pain struck my head, just behind my eyes. Sucking in my breath, I focused on the spell even as the pain grew in intensity.

I dribbled my expelled blood from the chalice onto the paper. "Goddess of fire, accept my blood. Torch this paper, turn it to crud."

I cringed at my juvenile rhyme, but it was the best way I had to remember not only the words but the intention. The incantation didn't really matter, Babe always said. It was the intent behind the words that did.

A flash of heat and then a crackle of flame told me that it worked even before Gramps released a triumphant whoop. I cracked open one eye, despite my splitting headache, and watched as flames shot up from the pan, leaving a pile of ash where the paper once rested.

I stumbled my way into a straight-back kitchen chair and rested my head on the cool wood of the table, the pain turning from sharp agony to dull ache.

"That was a stupid incantation," was the only feedback Gramps offered.

"It worked, didn't it?" I snapped, my head still pressed into the cool wood.

"What's wrong with you?" he asked.

There was no way I'd mistake the question for sympathy. "Nothing," I lied.

He yanked my head up off the table by my hair, examining my face. I looked at him through pain-blurred vision. "Head hurts?" he asked. I untangled my hair from his fingers, not responding. "You get those a lot?"

My hair free, I dropped my head back down to the table. "It's stress," I said, my voice muffled.

"Sure, stress," he said, his voice hinting that he didn't believe me. "You should learn to relax. Go meditate or something."

The scrape of a match against the table caught my attention. "Take your cancer stick outside, would you?" I barked without lifting my head.

"Suit yourself," he said.

The smell of marijuana slammed me in the nose. "You've got to be kidding me," I grumbled to his back as he exited to the back porch of Babe's second floor apartment.

"Gramps is a stoner," Casper giggled, and I jumped in my seat at the unexpected voice. With the migraine in full effect, his abrupt arrival in my body barely registered.

"Among other things," I grumbled. "Where the hell have you been? I could have used your help with the spells. The old man just about hexed me for my lousy witch skills."

"Sweetie, I love you but that old man gives me the heebie-jeebies," Casper said.

I felt him settle into my body and shudder. "You mean, what I feel when you body jump into me?" To be honest, it almost wasn't weird anymore. Almost.

"Please, he may look all innocent and feeble and old man-like—"

"He doesn't look innocent or feeble," I interrupted him. "But I'll give you old man-like."

But Casper just barreled right over me. "But that's just an act, you know that right? You have one hardcore *brujo* up in this joint, and that is nothing to mess with."

I sighed and rubbed my temples. "Hardcore *brujo*. Right."

"You talking to that ghost friend again?" Gramps yelled from just outside the door. "Because I can hear you. Both of you."

Casper squealed in terror. "How does he know about me?" the ghost wailed inside my head.

I got up and dragged my body with its aching head to the kitchen cabinet and dug around for the aspirin. "What do you mean both of us?"

"Don't play me, child," Gramps said, his voice holding a hint of a warning. He poked his head through the open door into the kitchen. "That ghost scared of me?"

Casper went still. "Yes," I said, struggling to open the childproof top.

That was all it took to jumpstart Casper again. "Aw, hell," Casper moaned. "Why're you telling him I'm scared of him, Nina?"

"Because you are," I muttered, popping three pills in my mouth and turning the faucet. I didn't bother with a glass and just tipped my mouth into the stream of water.

"But he doesn't need to know that," Casper complained.

I pulled my head up and wiped my mouth with the back of my hand. "So you're scared of him, so what? Everyone's scared of something." I turned to Gramps. "In or out, Gramps. You're skunking up the apartment with that weed."

"That's not skunked," he said before touching the lit end of the joint to his tongue to put it out. I wrinkled my nose.

"See?" Casper asked, whose agitation made me jittery, like I over-dosed on caffeine. "How are you not scared of him?"

Gramps tucked what was left into his cigarette pack and pocketed it. He stepped back inside the kitchen, his eyes never leaving me.

"The ghost is smart to be scared," he said. "He can sense my energy. My power. My force."

"What are you, a Jedi? Your force has nothing to do with it," I said, dumping the ash from the cookie sheet into the sink and running cold water over the pile, just in case it decided to ignite again. "His family is from Mexico and your reputation precedes you."

"Nina," Casper gasped, "stop talking to him about me."

"Oh please," I scoffed. "What's he going to do?"

The old man settled into one of the rickety wooden kitchen chairs that Babe was so fond of and grinned. "Cruz Trejo. How's your *abuelo*? I remember the day he left the village. Owing me."

If a ghost could go white with fear, I was certain Casper was doing so. "Owing you what?" I asked as Casper shrunk into the back of my conscience.

"It was a spell he asked me to cast," Teddy said. "A particularly nasty spell, too, if I recall."

"What? No cash upfront?" I asked, throwing in an eye roll for good measure. "Babe always told me witches shouldn't charge for services. For, you know, spells and such."

He scowled. "It's a donation. Witches gotta eat."

"So he paid his *donation*," I said, putting air quotes around the word. "He owes you nothing."

"That spell brought the damn *federales* down on me," he said, slamming the palm of his hand on the wood, making Casper jump, and me by extension. "I'd say he owes me a hell of a lot more than some token donation."

Casper launched out of my body like a rocket. I gripped the counter, his propulsion taking my breath away, literally.

"Aren't those the chances a witch takes?" I asked once my heart-rate slowed. "Salem, after all." I waved my hand in the general direction of the infamous town in Massachusetts.

"Murder charges are no joke, child. It'd do you good to remember that," he said, pushing himself up from his seat and crossing to stand beside me at the sink. "Now light the damn fire again. No discipline. Babette coddled you."

He slapped a new piece of paper onto the burned cookie sheet.

His vibrant blue eyes receded into their sockets, turning black in the shadow of the cloud that spread over his face. The old man who appeared to be some weird hippie that lived off the grid transformed into something much more sinister. Wind outside whipped past the windows, rattling them, while a storm cloud shaped in the outline of my grandfather's craggy face formed over the apartment. Dog let out a soft whimper and then crawled under the kitchen table at the first crack of thunder.

I turned my focus to the new sheet of paper in front of me. Picking up the filthy bow knife, I cut a jagged line in my arm. When I opened my dry mouth to spell, only a small croak came out. I cleared my throat and tried again.

That horrible rhyme sputtered out but this time the words held no meaning. My mind wandered to the stranger beside me, his power still radiating out, threatening. He grunted out a laugh, amused by my inability to conjure something as simple as fire. I tried again, hissing words out through gritted teeth. Forcing the knife deeper into my skin, blood spurted out from my arm as I pumped my fist, turning the paper crimson.

My halting words became stronger, more sure, as my own anger bubbled to the surface. But my focus wasn't on the sheet of paper. I squinted at the window. A spider web of cracks formed in the glass until it shattered under the force of the wind pushing against it. Splintered glass sprayed across the room as the wind whipped through the gaping hole. The slight sway of the house turned into something that threatened to crumble the solid construction into a pile of toothpicks. The glassware in the kitchen cabinets clinked together. Babe's framed artwork dropped off the walls. Glass shards littered the floor.

Power pushed through me. I spread out my arms and felt the magnetism of the earth hold me firm while the winds strengthened, threatening to lift the house up and send us to Oz, just like Dorothy. A smile cracked through my concentration. This was pure power, and it felt good.

I jumped when a large crack of thunder shook the building. The sky opened and golf ball-sized hail slapped against the roof, threatening to bust through the tar shingles. Car alarms rang out as the ice pummeled the vulnerable vehicles on the street. A slight tremor built to a teeth-rattling 4.1 earthquake. Then, I watched as the road behind our building cracked, causing a sound like a cannon shot to explode through the neighborhood. The jagged gash danced across the sidewalk towards a home built in 1792. The rift in the asphalt caused the house to break apart, and half of it disappeared into a sinkhole.

Oh crap.

I closed my eyes and shifted my focus. I breathed in and out, slowing my heart rate that spiked with the surge of adrenaline. The howling winds slowed and the slam of ice on the hard surfaces subsided. What remained of the 1792 house hung at the edge of an abyss.

My head snapped around at the sound of Gramps' triumphant whoop. He was hanging out of the broken window, an unlit cigarette dangling from his lips.

"Come check out what you did!" he called out.

I shoved my trembling hands into the back pockets of my jeans and edged my way to the window. Glancing outside, I was greeted by smashed windshields and dented car hoods. Gramps' nicotine stained finger pointed at the empty lot on the other side of our building. A small hole poked up from the asphalt pavement and molten lava leaked out of the opening at the top.

Gramps lit up the cigarette and took a deep inhale. "Now *that* is magic."

I turned to respond with a smartass quip but gasped instead. A searing pain ripped through my skull. Vertigo kicked in and I crumbled to the floor, clutching my head. My stomach churned and I crawled towards the bathroom. But by the time I made it to the hallway, I was covered in vomit. I curled up on the floor, exhausted.

My grandfather's firm hand pushed my head away from the puddle of puke. "Damn, child," he muttered. "Your magic is trying to kill you."

Then everything went black.

9

A PAIR of gentle hands slipped my t-shirt over my head. The hands then inched my jeans down past my hips before lifting me into a tub of warm water. I opened my eyes. Once they adjusted to the glare from the overhead bathroom light, Frankie came into focus.

"Hey," he said, working the bar of soap he had in his hand.

"Hey," I murmured, cradling my still aching head in one hand. "What are you doing?"

While the warm water lapped against my skin, it dawned on me that I was nearly naked. My bra and boy-short underpants gave the illusion of modesty, but not much.

"You got sick, passed out," Frankie said, running the soap along my barf-crusted chest. "Do you have any recollection of what happened?"

I nodded and closed my eyes, the pain receding a bit. "I did magic."

"Yes, I saw," Frankie said, sounding impressed. "You managed to topple a house that withstood a few hundred years in less than a minute. Not to mention that nifty little volcanic eruption going in the empty lot out back."

My eyes were still closed but a small smile played on my lips. "Are you saying you're proud of me?"

"Always," he replied, moving the soap over my shoulder.

"Then can you explain why am I naked in the tub?"

"Nearly naked, not *naked* naked," he corrected me. "What kind of friend would I be if I allowed you to fester in your own vomit?"

"How big is the mess?"

"Remember that Vegas strip long weekend we took to unwind after the Florida job?"

I cringed. Vegas involved copious amounts of champagne, several Elvis impersonators and an overripe banana. "That bad?"

"Not quite," he said. "But close." He handed me a loaded toothbrush and a plastic cup. I moved the brush over my teeth while he took the showerhead down and directed the spray away. Then he turned on the tap and waited for the water to heat up.

"Tip your head back," he instructed when it was steaming. I spit my mouthful of toothpaste into the cup, wiped my mouth with the back of my hand and leaned back. A cascade of warm water flowed over me. Once he saturated my hair, he placed the showerhead between my hands. The scent of grapefruit filled my nose as he massaged shampoo into my hair.

"That smells much better," he said, although the sour smell of vomit still lingered in my nose. "Any idea what made you sick?"

"No," I said. "I did the spell, Gramps puffed with pride and then boom! I thought my head was going to explode."

"These headaches keep getting worse," Frankie said, working the shampoo into a lather.

"I don't know if I'd say that. I haven't passed out from it since—"

"Since you first got the wound from the twin of your father's dagger," he finished, taking the showerhead from my grip. "The witch killer."

"What are you saying?" I asked, opening one eye to look at him. I immediately snapped it closed when the soapy water dripped into it. "Ow, that burns!"

"Sorry," Frankie said, wiping soap from my eyes with the edge of a towel. "I wonder if that blade poisoned you somehow. It was called a witch killer, after all."

"I don't think the witch killer label was literal," I said, slipping deeper into the warm water so that it covered my shoulders. "According to the old man, the knife stole Marcello's witchy energy and transferred it to me. If anything, that knife made me more powerful."

"Then maybe that's what's making you sick," he offered, turning off the faucet. "Perhaps your body can't handle it."

"I'm fine," I lied. "Maybe I just need glasses."

Frankie chuckled, and the scent of my conditioner filled the air. "I think you'd look good in them. In a hot-for-school-marm sort of way."

His deft fingers massaged the product at the base of my skull and a small sigh of pleasure escaped my lips. It was silenced when Frankie's soft lips pressed against mine. I stiffened for a moment in surprise, but didn't pull away, enjoying the light caress of his tongue as it played along the edge of my mouth.

"Wait," I mumbled, around his lips. "What are we doing?"

"Testing the water, so to speak," he said.

The tub water splashed a little as I lifted my hand up and pressed it against his chest. "But now?" I hesitated. "I mean, the feds have nukes pointed right at us."

"I think that makes it the perfect time. End of the world, nothing left to lose," Frankie chided. "But I don't think they're pointed exactly at us. Nor do I think there's a finger sitting on the button. Not yet, anyway."

"But we need to—"

"You need to relax," he advised me softly. His eyes danced along my body while his hand continued to massage my scalp, seducing me with each caress.

"What about my grandfather?" I asked, gripping the tub with both hands. my body giving in to him.

His hands inched their way down my neck and along my shoulders. "He's in the bar, scrounging up a bottle."

"But I...I...I...just puked," I stammered. I was running short of excuses, but wondered why I was making them to begin with.

"You brushed your teeth," he reminded me and his mouth covered mine again.

I eased back into the water, mind racing. I was kissing Frankie. I was kissing Frankie. *Oh my god, I was kissing Frankie.* And it felt *really* good.

While one hand cradled my head, the other one slipped a bra strap off my shoulder and his hand found its way into the cup. I press my mouth to his with a bit more urgency as his fingers massaged my breast, teasing my nipple into a rigid peak, making my toes curl with pleasure. His fangs elongated, nicking my lip. With the taste of the warm blood oozing out of the cut, Frankie gripped my hair with more urgency. He moved his mouth to my neck, and when I stilled, so did he. Need filled me as he scraped his sharp teeth along my skin. I reached for him, my fumbling hands pulled at his shirt.

Oh my god, what was I doing? This was Frankie!

Water splashed onto the floor as I pulled his body into the tub with me. I felt his impressive hardness against my pelvis through his wet jeans.

Oh my god, this was Frankie?

I shifted my body up against him and turned my head so my neck teased him. The craving for him to slide his fangs into my neck threatened to overwhelm me, and he did not disappoint. His fangs slipped in like razor blades, betrayed by only a slight twinge of pain, and a new wave of sensations took over me. There was no pretense between us, and that bite stripped away the barriers we used to wall off our feelings. I pushed my fingers into his back, feeling his muscles contract, and allowed myself to give in to this newfound intimacy.

Frankie's pull on my blood combined with his pull on my body sent shivers of need through me. He unhooked my bra with one hand. I pressed my exposed breasts against him, relishing the feel of his skin against mine while my bra floated at the surface of the water. It felt good to give in to him.

A sudden seer of blinding pain in my skull over took me. "Yo,

Nina, we gotta talk." Casper's voice popped into my head. I froze, stuck in the limbo space somewhere between desire and mortification.

"Are you all right?" Frankie asked. He pulled away from me, leaving my chest suddenly very cold and very exposed.

"Oh sheee-iiiii-ttttt!" Casper yelled, causing me to wince in pain. "What the hell is going on up in here?"

"What does it look like?" I muttered.

Water splashed onto the floor again as Frankie scrambled out of the tub. "That bloody ghost."

"Hot damn, girl!" Casper practically yelled.

"I think we need a system," I said out loud.

"What system?" Frankie asked before his look of confusion faded to an expression of annoyance.

"Yeah, we need like a psychic 'do not disturb' sign," Casper chuckled. "Although I gotta admit, girl, I didn't think you'd ever get lucky. You're not exactly the cuddly type."

"Shut up," I grumbled.

"What'd I say?" Frankie asked.

I pointed at my head. "Not you."

"You're more of a wham bam thank you—" Casper continued.

"Enough!" I barked, and Frankie slipped along the soaked tile floor.

Shivering, I watched the water pool at Frankie's feet, feeling very naked. I snatched my floating bra and pressed it against my bare breasts.

"Could you hand me a towel please?" I asked Frankie as I rose out of the water. With my free hand, I took the one he handed me without meeting his eyes, wishing I could disappear into a sinkhole like that historic house. "Could you turn around?"

He obliged. I stared at his slumped back while I ditched the soggy bra and wrapped the towel around me in one quick motion. Red crept up my cheeks when Frankie turned back to face me. I stepped out of the tub and stared at the puddles around my feet.

"We need to talk," Frankie started.

I nodded, but waved him off. "First, I need to see what Casper wants."

"No no no! I don't want to interrupt," the ghost quipped.

"It's a bit late for that," I muttered, sloshing through the water, trying not to slip. "I'll just leave you to dry off. I think there's a spare pair of sweatpants in the guest room."

Frankie winced. "An American jogging suit. Brilliant."

"You can be such a snob about your clothes," I grumped at him as I squeezed around his stiff body and through the door.

"There's more to clothes than cargo pants, t-shirts and aviator jackets, Nina!" he shouted after me as I closed the door on him. I leaned against it to catch my breath. But Casper didn't give me a second to compose myself.

"Girl, you want to tell me what I just walked into?" he asked.

"You didn't walk," I said. "You kind of floated. Or appeared. Or whatever it is that you do when you jump in my damn body. You definitely did not knock."

"So," he prodded, "how was he? He looked ample in the—"

"I do not want to talk about this. At all."

"Oh come off it, Nina. Dish. It's what besties do."

"We are not besties," I corrected him.

"Oh please," he huffed. "If we are not besties, what the hell else are we?"

"You can't categorize what we have," I quipped.

"You can't categorize what you and Frankie have either," he shot back. "Come on, Nina. You know you want to talk about this."

I pressed my lips together. He wasn't wrong. Whatever was going on between me and Frankie had smoldered under the surface for a good long time. But that didn't mean I was ready to examine it in any detail. Especially not with Casper.

"Well, I want to talk about it," he said. "And girl it felt good! You don't have to tell me. I know!"

"Do you mean you—" I cut myself off with a full body shudder, then turned on my heel and marched to the bedroom. "What was so urgent that you barged in on me anyway?"

"Max is on his way over," he said.

"So what," I said, pulling on an oversized Drive by Truckers concert t-shirt over the towel before I shimmied out of it. Frankie be damned about my sartorial choices. "Max comes over all the time."

"Not when you're getting cozy in the tub with Frankie," he said.

I picked through a pile of clean clothes in the laundry basket for underwear. Of course the only one I found was a thong. It just kept getting better and better. "You had no way of knowing that was happening. So what's up?"

"Max swiped ID cards for you and Frankie."

"And you know this how?"

He went quiet, which sent my Spidey senses tingling. "Casper, what did you do?"

"I helped," he said so softly that I had to focus hard to hear the words.

"How the hell could you help Max when you cannot even communicate with him?" I asked, attempting to keep the exasperation out of my voice while I tried to step into the panties without exposing my ass—or worse—to Casper.

"I can communicate," he said, his voice raising. "We did the knock once for yes, two for no!"

"Explain to me how that's even possible."

"When I popped out of here while your grandfather was threatening me—"

"He wasn't threatening you."

"We'll disagree on that," Casper said. "I found Max at Bertrand's—"

"You really should not be at the Biltmore by yourself," I chided, raising my voice.

Casper ignored me. "And Bertrand showed us—"

"Bertrand?" I roared, unable to contain my anger. "You went to Bertrand? What is wrong with you?" *Jesus, this kid...*

"Take it easy," Casper said. My stomach cramped while he danced around my body. "He didn't like do a demon spell or anything, he just showed us a way to get the job done. I owe him nothing, I promise."

"Great," I said, blowing out a frustrated breath. I raked my fingers through my wet hair. They promptly got stuck in a snarl. "So then you went off without any sort of protection and the only way to communicate with him was by knocking. No trial run or anything."

"I kicked off a bonafide haunting," he argued, and I could hear a swell of pride running beneath his defiance. "The guards were scared shitless. They didn't know what was going on."

"You could have been killed," I said, yanking my fingers through the snarl.

"You can't kill a dead guy," he argued. "Unless you're Frankie."

"Exorcised. Don't give me a hard time. You know what I mean. You could have been exorcised, which is like worse than dying."

"The only ones that do the real exorcising are the priests," Casper argued.

I shook my head, marveling at how, even in ghost form, he retained his sense of adolescent invincibility. It was kind of surprising considering Casper died the most gruesome death imaginable, at the hands of psycho Marcello, who was draining witches of their power just so he had enough power to off me.

"Not true," I corrected him, adjusting my tone to be easier on him. "Regular old humans are holding their own exorcism rituals. And some of them actually work. And prison guards? You don't think Leila taught them a trick or two? You're a damn lucky ghost, that's all." I dropped onto the bed and pulled my knees into me, stretching the t-shirt out over them. "Let's hope that luck doesn't run out."

Casper was quiet for a moment, a first for him.

"So, what are you going to do?" he asked, breaking the silence.

"I'd love to ground you or something, but I'm not your mother."

"Not about me, about Frankie."

"Didn't I say we weren't talking about that?" I snapped, grateful for the sharp knock on the door interrupting us. "What?" I yelled.

"Get out here!" my grandfather shouted from behind the door. "You have a way into the prison."

"Max must be here," Casper said. Max's arrival sure did animate him. I suspected it was a relief to be able to communicate with someone else, although given that their form of communication was a knock-knock system and not actual conversation, I wondered what that said about me.

Casper and I left the room, and I padded barefoot down the hallway into the kitchen. I stopped short when I realized Max was not alone. Mary Jane Colton, our new boss, was standing beside him, a little too close.

Max raised his eyebrows at my outfit, the concert t-shirt brushing against the middle of my thigh. Mary Jane didn't even try to hide her once-over, my face reddening as her eyes swept my entire length. She was dressed more casually than when we met in Bertrand's office, but her casual was a smart pair of nice-fitting slacks and a form hugging Oxford shirt. And her form, from what I could see, was perfect. She shook out her straight hair, not a wisp out of place. Even her makeup looked effortless.

I yanked the hem of my oversized t-shirt down a bit, rubbing my calves against each other. How long had it been since I shaved? "Mary Jane," I said, pulling my soggy, unruly hair to my back so that it didn't soak through my chest. The t-shirt was a white base, after all. "I wasn't expecting you. Or Max."

"Clearly," she said, her gaze holding all of the judgment of a posse of middle school mean girls. I scowled and shoved past her to join Frankie in the living room.

Frankie was on the couch, looking uncomfortable in a pair of oversized grey sweatpants and nothing else. I glanced at his bare chest, the first time I'd ever really seen him that exposed. I averted my eyes quickly and masked my surprise to see that it was a field of scarred skin from centuries of getting nicked by blessed weapons. Vampires could heal, sure, but wounds from anything consecrated left a battleground. The realization that Frankie wasn't totally invincible felt heavy. Frankie didn't notice my unease since his focus was on Max, who looked impeccable in a fitted charcoal suit, the shoulders pulling slightly at his bulging muscles.

A smile tugged at the sides of my mouth. Did clothes-horse Frankie feel inferior? That was a first.

"I hope you didn't dress up on our account," Max said, trying to lighten the mood, but his eyes inched along my body. I sensed Mary Jane tense as she noticed that his expression wasn't exactly critical. *Score one for the misfits.*

"Nope," I said, irritated by the Barbie and Ken dolls standing in my kitchen. "I did it for Frankie."

My muscular thighs tensed as Max's eyes continued to rake over me. My fangs protruded slightly, my discomfort level rising as he assessed me like a prize cow at a county fair. Asshole.

Frankie sat up, his hands balled into fists, and his eyes glowed their eerie blue.

"Boys, please." My grandfather stepped in between them. "We have a prison to break into."

My face went hot with embarrassment, and I tugged my t-shirt down lower.

Max averted his eyes and cleared his throat. "I snatched some ID cards that will get you into the prison."

Mary Jane's cool voice chimed in. "It's a computerized swipe system that opens the exterior as well as interior doors."

"All of them?" I asked.

"These particular guards have just about all access," Max explained. "There's one section of the prison off-limits to everyone except Leila and her inner sanctum."

"And that inner sanctum would be?" Frankie asked. His eyes still glowed.

"Kittie, for one," Max said. "And a bodyguard borrowed from Bertrand."

I raised my eyebrows. "Bertrand? He's playing both sides?"

"No," Mary Jane bristled. "Jacko is a plant. He reports everything back to us."

"Leila's not stupid," Gramps interjected. "Why did she allow one of Bertrand's men to be that close?"

Max shrugged. "Can't say."

My grandfather turned to me. "Don't trust that."

I nodded in agreement and then looked at Max. "Hand over the cards."

"Bertrand's not playing both sides," he reiterated, snapping the cards against the palm of his hand. "There is one problem."

He dropped them on the counter and slid the cards towards me. I snatched them up and the faces of two bulky guys stared back at me. "You think? Frankie and I can't pass for these muscle heads."

"And there's facial recognition software running to get into the more sensitive areas of the prison," Mary Jane added, her voice clipped. "And that includes your good doctor's cell."

"So basically, you brought us nothing," I said, sliding the plastic cards back towards her. *Dammit.*

Max pushed them back at me. "Best I could do."

"You can figure out the rest," Mary Jane said, her voice saccharine. "You're clever. We have faith in you."

"Jesus, this is just like talking to Bertrand," I muttered, swallowing down my anger. Blood Ops was operating under the thumb of the demon.

"You're a right git," Frankie said, leaning forward, his elbows on his knees. "How in bloody hell are we supposed to get into a facility with facial recognition scanning?"

I pressed my fingers to my temples. "Maybe Darcy can hack in and trick the cameras?" I tried.

"Darce is good, but that seems a stretch," Frankie said.

"*Pfft* to your technology," Gramps said. "I have a spell that can change your appearance."

I rolled my eyes. "Like that potion from *Harry Potter*?"

"It's no potion," he snapped. "And what's a Harry Potter?"

I shook my head. Mexico wasn't devoid of global pop culture, but Gramps certainly was. "If it's not a potion, what is it then?"

He grinned. "Only the best kind of magic. An illusion."

10

FRANKIE LAUGHED at me for a good three minutes, then continued to chuckle as we bounced around the back of Gramps' old school "shaggin' wagon," a 1970s-era Chevy van tricked out for the psychedelic revolution.

"I could laugh at you, too, you know," I snapped, rubbing the ridiculous high-and-tight haircut I now sported. My patience wore thinner and thinner these days.

"You keep threatening to cut your hair," he teased, his grin lopsided. I crossed my arms and stewed in the backseat.

With a short chant and a wave of his hand, Gramps turned Frankie and me into a pair of steroid-bloated goons to match the ID cards Max pinched. At least my goon had a head of hair. Frankie was the bald one.

Gramps said the spell was an illusion, but I didn't think that the illusion applied to the person he spelled. I wiggled in my shag carpet covered seat and shifted my new pair of balls to the other side.

"How the hell do you guys live with this?" I muttered.

"Quit your bitching," Gramps barked as he pulled the van over. "We're about a half mile out. You two will have to walk the rest of the way."

"And watch how you walk," Max cut in. "These two idiots are so overbuilt they practically waddle."

"Yes, figured on that," Frankie said, his gate awkward as he stepped away from the van to make room for my boxy build to climb out.

"Remember, you have no earpieces, no communication with the outside whatsoever," Max added. "Get in, get the intel, get out."

"Preferably before the enchantment wears off," Frankie added.

"I know the spell," I snapped.

"Steroids make you cranky," he spat back.

I shoved past him. "Speak for yourself."

"Both of you best focus," Gramps warned from the driver's seat. "And that goes double for you, *nieta*. If that spell wears off, you need to be ready to recast it. And fast."

He gunned the engine and peeled away, leaving Frankie and me at the side of the highway just as the sun breached the horizon.

"These blokes go to work bloody early," Frankie grumped as we plodded through the thicket of brush that led to the back of the prison parking lot. This small forest of overgrown shrubs acted as a not-terribly-effective sound barrier from the highway. However, it gave us decent cover to slip into the employee parking lot.

We found our way to the lot and waddled up to the front gate. The half-asleep guard was so involved in his giant yawn that he barely glanced at us as he buzzed us into the prison. Frankie and I schlepped down the dank hallway, the florescent lights flickering above us, their irritating hum cutting in and out. An inhuman scream came from inside the prison walls, setting my teeth on edge.

"Morning, Barry. Ronny," a guard waved as he walked past us towards the door. "You guys picked a crap day to come in early. The natives were restless last night."

Frankie stopped abruptly. "Yeah?" His voice was Bronx nasal. I cringed. The Rhode Island accent had a particular sound, and whatever he just bleated out wasn't it. "What happened?"

"You hear that scream?" the guard asked.

"Who didn't?" Frankie asked, shifting his accent, this time over-doing his Boston twang. I gave him a quick nudge, but he ignored me.

"You okay, Ronny?" the guard asked. Frankie cleared his throat and nodded. The guard shrugged. "It's been like that. Weird screams, all night. And howling."

"Howling?" I blurted out, covering my feminine pitch with a quick cough. The damn illusion spell didn't extend beyond the visual.

"You two getting sick?" the guard asked, making his fingers into a mock cross and wielding it at us. If he only knew. "Keep your distance. I'm out of sick days. Anyhow, it's like there's a pack of dogs behind the walls."

"Any idea where it's coming from?" I asked, forcing my voice deeper.

"No idea. It's all echoes," the guard said. He gave me a funny look. "Say, what's with you guys today?"

"Damn, I hope it's not the flu," Frankie said, developing a sudden hacking cough that he aimed right at the guy.

"Jesus, what did I say? Stay the hell away from me!" Our new friend backed away from us right quick, pulling his shirt up over his mouth as if that would protect him from rogue germs. He waved for us to go through. "Good luck in there today."

We both returned a friendly wave and then headed deeper into the prison.

"Just had to stop for a quick chat, didn't you?" I muttered.

"And what's wrong with that?" he asked. "We just got valuable intel."

"Intel," I scoffed.

"They've got the werewolves," Frankie said. "We didn't know that for sure when we walked in."

"Dogs. They've got dogs."

"You really think they're dogs? This is a prison, not an animal shelter."

"Fine, let's say they have werewolves," I said. "We don't know where they're being kept. And right now, we need locations. In addition to knowing who. Or what."

Four more guards walked past, giving us the requisite head nods. Then we were at our first locked door that required the key card. Frankie pulled out his card and swiped. He leaned against the wall and looked at me, flashing a confident smile.

That's when the alarm screamed.

The look of shock that spread on his face nearly sent me into a fit of laughter. Instead, I bit my lip and pretended to look just as confused as the guards rallied by the commotion.

"What the hell?" shouted the middle-aged guard at the head of the group of seven that raced towards us. Beads of sweat broke out along my forehead.

Frankie bellowed back, "That's what I'm sayin'!"

"Damn thing!" The aging guard swiped his own card in the machine and then punched in several numbers. "If you don't look dead at the damn thing, it goes haywire. Happened to me just the other day. Pain in the ass."

"Giant pain in the ass," Frankie echoed in agreement as the door buzzed open. I darted through it, but Frankie took his sweet ass time, kicking the door jam and muttering about faulty technology.

"Yo, Ronny!" the guard yelled after us. "Your wife didn't pack you a lunch today?"

"My lunch?" Frankie stopped, confounded for a moment by the question.

"Yeah, you know lunch. She usually sends you with a lunch box the size of a suitcase." The guard wheezed out a laugh.

"Nah," Frankie called over his shoulder. "I let her sleep in this morning."

The door slammed shut, but not before I caught the guard's confused expression.

"Can the chitchat, Frankie," I muttered as we lumbered through the labyrinthine hallways, following the shrill screams that echoed down the stone corridors.

"You just don't understand the bro factor," he chided me.

I grabbed his overgrown bicep, bringing both of us to a halt. "Bro factor?"

He gave my shoulder a small shove to keep us moving. "Yes, bro factor. You are not a bro, ergo, you would not understand."

"I am a bro at the moment," I muttered, shifting my newly acquired sacks as they knocked against each other. I finally understood the appeal of tighty whities.

We hit a crossroads, ending our conversation. We were now in the heart of the prison and had to make a decision. More screams travelled down the hallway to our left.

"To the noise, or away?" Frankie asked.

"When have we ever run from screaming?" I asked. "I'm not about to change that. Are you?"

Even through the pudgy face, the grin I got in agreement was pure Frankie.

We went left and hustled down the hallway. At the end was another locked door. This time I swiped with Barry's ID and faced the facial recognition scanner full on. Expecting alarm bells to sound again, I held my breath until I heard the lock slide open.

"Nice one," Frankie mumbled as we stepped into the cellblock.

We entered the wing. The cells were pressed against the walls and ran up two stories, with an expanse of nothing in the middle save for a catwalk. A series of chairs were bolted into the cement floor on the ground level. The seats had clamps at the arms and legs to hold prisoner's wrists and ankles. Judging from the gleam, they were pure silver, perfect to weaken a vampire or werewolf, beings who were strong enough to break through the restraints. Blood spatter covered the painted grey cement floor.

The cells were locked with the exception of one. The prisoner was strapped into the chair, and three guards hovered around him, each slicing into his chest with intricate cuts. I grunted at Frankie and gave a short nod to the scene. I thought the guy in the chair was part of the werewolf pack that once worked for Leila, bringing the Beta-Vamps a tainted blood supply. But making an accurate identification was difficult when the captive was partially obscured and wearing a standard prison jumpsuit. The man's skin hissed and smoked each time the blade carved into it, which told me he was definitely werewolf. The guy was out cold, but suddenly exploded awake with bloodcurdling screams before passing out again. The other prisoners cowered in their cells, pressing themselves as far back as possible in a bid not to be noticed.

Another guard stood apart, holding a sheet of paper and surveying the work. He turned towards us when we walked in. His ID badge had the name Robards.

"Barry, maybe can you figure out these damn glyphs," he grumbled, thrusting the paper at me.

I took a look at the crude drawing in my hand and then glanced at the werewolf strapped to the chair.

"Not working, eh?" Frankie covered for me while I gaped at the paper, my mind processing through the rudimentary sketches, struggling to figure out what the hell they were after.

My own knowledge of runes was minimal at best, but based on the symbols drawn on the paper, they were trying to extract the wolf from the man.

"I'd just as soon kill the freaks, but boss lady wants them carved up first," Robards grumbled. "But I'll be damned if they don't all turn out like that one when we get those symbols on them."

He pointed to the cell to our right, and I caught my breath when my head swerved. A half-formed wolf cowered in the corner. Human-like legs were attached to a furry torso, and her not-quite-transformed face still held human traits. Her body was twisted, bones clearly cracked without having fully formed into a wolf, rendering her practically crippled. A low growl came from her throat and she curled her lips in a snarl, showing impressive teeth, that petered out into a sustained whimper.

I swallowed the gore that rose in my throat and turned my attention to the werewolf in the chair. Coarse animal hair sprouted on the tops of his hands. He struggled to keep the transformation from happening.

"So what do you think, Barry?" Robards asked. "You're skilled at dealing with this oooga-booga shit. What's the problem?"

"Oh, I dunno about skilled," I said, stalling. I was hoping to tease out a bit more information on the guy I was impersonating.

"You shitting me? You pulled the goddamn magic out of one witch and transferred it to a human. I mean, you couldn't do it twice, but that was still some crazy-ass shit."

Pulling the magic out of a witch? Turning a werewolf by force? They had to be working with more than runes to run these sorts of experiments.

Robards looked at me expectantly. "So? Waddaya think?"

An idea hit me. "You take this to the old man yet?"

The guard looked baffled. "The old man?"

"Yeah, you know, old guy, Irish brogue," Frankie chimed in.

"Boss lady lets you talk to him?" Robards asked. His stance shifted and he spread his legs wide, fists on hips, taking up more space. It looked like a giant pissing contest was about to commence. "She gave you clearance to go into his cell block?"

"You don't have clearance?" I asked.

"Maybe you have access and you just don't know," Frankie jumped in. "Have you even tried?"

"Take a break," Robards barked at his subordinates, and then turned on his heel. We followed him out of the cellblock, and I heard the lucky werewolf whimper in relief as we walked past.

The guard walked at a fast clip down the hallway, bringing us back to the crossroads. Instead of heading down the other hallway, he turned to what appeared to be a dead end. A brush of his hand against it revealed a door that was enchanted to look like a stone wall. Robards opened the hidden portal. Sandwiched in the thick stone wall was a spiral staircase. Of course, its only direction was down. Robards pushed his bulk into the narrow passage, and Frankie and I followed, turning our oversized bodies sideways to better fit. Water leaked from the ancient stone as we descended, and a musky damp smell thickened the air. We came to another locked door at the bottom. Robards swiped his ID card and waited for the scanner to recognize his piggish face. My stomach flip-flopped when the door buzzed open.

We walked inside a space flooded with florescent lights. Banks of computers were all around the room. Floor-to-ceiling cabinets flanked one wall, and based on what I saw, they housed enough weapons to arm several platoons, both of the human and supernatural sort. A huge reinforced glass window looked into a cellblock. This one was smaller than the one upstairs, and the people — the missing witches, I assumed — housed in it were all strapped to hospital beds. Three prison guards were glued to computer monitors, barely reacting when we entered.

Frankie stood with his legs wide open, mimicking the stance of most of the guards, taking up as much space as possible. "Where's the Irish bastard?" he asked.

Robards nodded towards the back of the room. There was yet another door, locked with the same computerized mechanism, as well as three additional steel bars barricading it.

Frankie gave a low whistle. "Damn. That's a lot of iron."

"He's a sly old goat," Robards said. "The computer locks couldn't hold him in."

I snickered at the idea that locks could hold an ancient Druid in a cell.

"Something funny, Sheen?" Robards barked.

"Yes, sir," I said. "Just picturing the prisoner as a goat, sir."

Frankie elbowed me in the side. "Stop mucking about," he grumbled.

One of the other guards pulled Robards' attention to a closed-circuit television screen monitoring the room. I rubbed at my nose, feeling a sudden need to sneeze. When I pulled my hand away, I noticed blood on my finger, a finger that was also a hell of a lot smaller and had nails with Goth black glitter polish chipping off.

"Crap," I said, looking at Frankie, whose own disguise melted away right before my eyes. He gaped at my changing appearance, and then turned to face away from the guards as he realized that it was happening to him too.

I muttered the incantation that my grandfather taught me, but the spell didn't take. *Dammit, why did I have to be such a crappy witch?* I watched as Frankie's lanky frame replaced the stocky Ronny. The guards at the computer glanced our way and did a double take. *Oh shit.*

Panicked, I tried the incantation again, my eyes darting around the room, searching for the closest weapon. They swept towards the ceiling and that's when I saw it was reinforced by iron bars, enough of them to snuff out the magic in any witch, especially a mediocre one. We were lucky Gramps' spell didn't melt away the minute we stepped foot in the cell block.

"What the hell?" Robards swore as he watched us finish our transformation from 'roided up prison guards back into our own bodies.

"At least the spell was an illusion, so our clothes still fit," Frankie muttered, pulling on the collar of the poly-blend shirt.

"Get them!" Robards screamed at the three guards, who came out of their stupor and realized that we weren't supposed to be in there.

"It's her!" the towheaded guard furthest away shouted. He scrambled to put more distance between us, pointing.

"What her?" Robards barked back at him.

"The one Leila said to watch out for. The one we can't kill."

"Well that's good news at least," Frankie said under his breath.

"You got a price on your head, girly," Robards sneered.

"How much?" I asked, stalling for time. Robards was blocking the exit and the only way out was through him.

"Enough for an early retirement," he said. "Toss me Bertha, boys."

One of the guards snatched a sawed off shotgun from the weapons cabinet and tossed it to his superior. Robards leveled the gun at us. His face flushed with adrenaline. His eyes became bright and yellow-tinged. Almost wolfish. He bared his canines, like a dog. I squinted when it looked like hair sprouted from his ears.

I glanced at the other three guards, mind racing. Two of them exhibited the same symptoms. One was actually drooling. The third guard either didn't notice, or didn't care, that his coworkers were exhibiting werewolf symptoms.

"Um, Frankie," I muttered.

"I see it," he said, eyes darting around the room, voice low. "They aren't human."

"They aren't werewolves either," I said.

"They're—" Frankie started.

"Mistakes," I finished for him, my voice barely above a whisper.

Frankie took a defensive posture and glared at Robards. "Looks like you enjoy this line of work way too much to retire."

"Great benefits," he retorted. "Now why don't you bring that perky ass my way, girly, and let's not have any trouble."

"You sure Leila's good for the money?" I asked. Hell, she better be. Did they even understand what she'd done to them?

"She's got Bertrand's bankroll," said the towheaded guard, the only one that didn't exhibit lycanthropic symptoms. He didn't look old enough to use the semiautomatic rifle held in his unsteady hands.

"You don't talk, rookie," Robards barked. "Got it?"

Frankie and I glanced at each other. "My mother put a price on my head and Bertrand's fronting the reward money?" I muttered to him. "Nice."

Robards had our exit blocked, and now his lackey guards moved to block the way into the cells, not that we'd be able to get through the locks now with the illusion spell broken. Frankie and I were trapped in a room with loads and loads of firearms and three half-werewolves. Not a big deal for Frankie, but the guns made me skittish. And so did the wolves. My mother didn't want me dead, but she didn't say anything about undead.

Frankie rocked back on his heels. "So what do we do, gentlemen? It appears we are at an impasse."

"What do we do?" Robards scoffed. "We haul her ass in and you...well, you we kill."

A wicked grin crossed Frankie's face and the blue of his irises brightened. "I hoped you'd say that."

The three guards blocking the cell door watched Frankie, and their expressions turned from confusion to horror as his fangs grew out.

"Oh my god, is that a vampire?" cried out the human guard, dropping the rifle. It clattered on the cement floor.

"What the hell are you doing?" one of his compadres cried out.

"The bullets are lead," he admitted. His lower lip trembled as a fanged out grin stretched over Frankie's face.

"Mine aren't," yelled his friend, who immediately sprayed the room with silver bullets from his Glock 41 Gen4. I dropped to the floor, noting that Robards took cover under a desk.

Frankie advanced on the guard, but the guy kept shooting. Frankie's shoulder jerked back and I heard the sizzle of silver against his skin. But it didn't slow him down. Based on the glow coming from his eyes, it pissed him off. He yanked the gun out of the guard's hand and pushed him against the cabinet. The guard lashed out at Frankie with barely formed claws, making a gash along Frankie's cheek. Frankie lifted the hybrid up by the neck as he fought like a feral dog, squirming in Frankie's hand and snapping his teeth at the air. Liquid spread along the front of the man's pants just before Frankie plunged his fangs into his carotid artery.

Out of the corner of my eye, I saw the chubby guard digging through another weapons cabinet. Triumphant, he pulled out a stake and with a warrior cry, rushed at Frankie, ready to plunge it into Frankie's back. I leapt from the floor and tackled him before the wood could make contact. I had him on his back, pressing the hand with the stake against the floor. He was bucking his hips, trying to launch me off of him. While I adjusted my balance, he rolled, pinning me under him. He raised the stake, and a bit of drool hung from his lower lip, slowly making its way towards my body. Gross.

"Not supposed to kill me," I said, a slight lisp creeping in as my fangs shoved through my gums.

His fight-or-flight kicked in and the missive to bring me in alive was forgotten. He lifted the stake above his head, ready to plunge it into me. As he brought it down towards my chest, I grabbed his hand and twisted until I heard the snap of bone. The stake dropped out of his limp grip. I landed a right hook to his jaw and he toppled off me, landing on his back. He snatched up the dropped Glock and took a haphazard shot. The bullet whizzed over my shoulder just as I got to my feet.

"Stop shooting," I said through a clenched jaw. He didn't listen. But his nerves made him one hell of a lousy shot. The next one embedded in the ceiling.

My sensitive ears picked up Robards' grumbling, "You want something done right..." and then the pump of a shotgun — good old Bertha. I had scant time to get the hell out of the way of the pellet of bullets that exploded out of the gun. My left shoulder jerked back, and the burn that sliced through my skin told me that I wasn't fast enough.

"Nina!" Frankie shouted over the loud popping of the gunshots.

I turned to see the guard I'd taken down lunging for me, his broken right hand hanging limp. He must have been a lefty because he snatched me by the neck with ease. He yanked me towards him, his set of sharp teeth coming at my neck. I shifted fast to avoid his bite, but I misjudged the angle and yelped as his teeth sunk into my cheek. Frankie grabbed him from behind and pressed his mouth to the man's jugular. Blood sprayed across my face as Frankie's teeth found the guard's artery.

I pressed the sleeve of my shirt against my face, feeling a chunk of flesh missing. I stumbled a little, on edge from the werewolf toxin in my system. It wouldn't kill me, but it could mess with me. The neurotoxin in a vampire bite relaxed the body, since they preferred to feed on docile humans. A werewolf bite produced anxiety that caused their prey to run. They enjoyed the chase.

Already on edge, the bite had me downright twitchy. Robards was right in front of me, and my eyes narrowed, taking in his wolfy grin and that damn Bertha. "You shot me," I said, baring my own small fangs.

Robards' expression turned from triumphant to troubled. His fingers fumbled as he reloaded the shotgun. He pumped it and another shot blasted out. The pellets hit me in my side, and I yelped in pain as the blessed silver bullets settled into my flesh with a pop and sizzle.

"Son of a bitch!" I yelled as a mix of pain and adrenaline ripped through me. "You shot me again!"

My anxiety reaching fever pitch, I lunged at him, gnashing my fangs as I pushed forward, ignoring the agonizing burn of the bullets that my body was rejecting. Expelling bullets was almost worse than taking them in. He tried to reload the gun again, but the bullets slipped from his shaking hands. He grabbed the weapon by the barrel and held it like a club.

A warrior cry came from the human guard, and the terror of the situation broke him out of his panicked stupor. Brandishing the stake that the chubby guard dropped when I broke his wrist, he jumped on my back and wrapped his arms around me, attempting to stab my chest.

I flipped him over my back and he landed with a thud on the floor in front of me. I stepped on his chest to hold him down, while Robards held the stock of the gun and swung it at me like a baseball bat. With my focus on the man under my boot, the barrel connected with my one good cheek, and blood from a broken tooth sprayed out of my mouth as my head swung from the momentum of the hit. The guard under me clawed at my leg, pulling me off balance while Robards came at me again. I kicked my foot down into the human guard's face, bone cracking. He howled in pain, hands releasing me to put pressure on his broken nose. I landed another kick to his head, knocking him unconscious.

Robards and I faced off. This time he threw the gun at me, taking the opportunity to grab his sidearm while I deflected the shotgun away. He aimed and shot in rapid succession, each bullet slamming into my gut. *How many times was this asshole going to plug me?* I roared in pain as he emptied his chamber, then the gun clicked empty. My fangs fully distended, adrenaline pumping, I leapt on top of him.

I sank my fangs into the tight flesh of his neck. Hot blood poured into my mouth. As soon as I swallowed, I felt energy pulse through my body, filling the hunger that gnawed at me since that damn witch blade cut into my skin and sent my vampire nature into overdrive. I pulled away a chunk of his neck with my teeth. His screams were cut short as blood spurted out of his artery and settled in his open throat, drowning him. I spit out his chunk of flesh on the floor and turned to Frankie, who tossed the guard he just downed onto the floor.

"Do you want to talk about that?" he asked, wiping his blood-crusted mouth and nodding at Robards' limp body.

"I think we better get out of here," I replied, doubled over as my body rejected the bullets that Robards sprayed into my gut. It totally hurt more coming out.

"You okay?" Frankie asked, grabbing me by the shoulder before I fell over. He propped me against the wall and ripped the shirt away from my midriff. "They're almost all out. Give it a minute and you should feel better."

I gritted my teeth and nodded.

"I mean, you've never bit anyone to death before," he said. "Maybe we should to talk about it?"

I pressed my hand against the wound on my stomach, feeling the skin knit itself back together under my fingers. The intolerable pain dulled to uncomfortable. "There's nothing to talk about. He wasn't human. I'm fine."

Frankie nodded, even though he looked like he didn't quite believe me. "Problem," he said. "We are no longer facial recognition software approved."

"We'll take one of them with us," I said, pointing at the guard just under his feet.

"Good on you then," he said, hoisting the human up from the floor. He saw his mangled nose and dropped him back down. "Not that one."

"Grab Robards," I said, rooting in the cabinet for guns. I tossed one to Frankie and then brandished two Glocks for myself.

Frankie caught the piece and shoved it in the small of his back. He nodded at the witches. "What about them?"

"They're too weak to get out on their own. We know where they are, and Dr. O's behind that iron door. We'll come back and get everyone out. Even the wolves." I shuddered as I thought about Leila transferring the werewolf gene into her human guards, screwing up both the humans and lycans in the process.

Frankie checked his bullets. "You think Leila will move Dr. O?"

I glanced at the massive door blocking us from Dr. O and shook my head. "She underestimates us."

"We underestimated her, too," he said, and I knew he was thinking about the failed experiments littered all over the room. "Ready to go out there?"

I bent over Robards' body and searched through his pockets. Once I located the key card, Frankie picked up the dead weight.

"It'd be easier if we took his head and left the rest," I said, still edgy from the wolf toxin working its way through my body.

"Feeling awfully vampy right now, aren't you?" Frankie said. "Come on, let's get on with it. I anticipate we'll be shooting our way out of this place. Right bit of fun, isn't it?"

Frankie grinned, eyes still glowing, fangs still out. With blood all over his face, he looked downright diabolical. It was kind of a sexy look for him.

I pressed the grip of the Glock against my forehead as I followed Frankie, who dragged Robards' body behind him. *It'd be easier if we took his head? Kind of a sexy look for him?* What the hell was I becoming?

11

"LET ME GET THIS RIGHT," Mary Jane fumed. She was pacing the floor of the factory apartment. "You killed....no, not killed. You *massacred* three guards in one prison block—"

"They weren't human," I interrupted.

She ignored me and kept going, "—and then shot up 15 more while you ran out of the place. You ripped the head off one of the top commanding officers in the prison, leaving his body at the top of a flight of stairs. And you shot the deputy warden in the leg on the way out. Did I miss anything?"

"We left the human guard in the cellblock alive," I added.

Mary Jane glared at both of us, her face turning red. "It was a simple job. Go in, get intel, get out."

"We weren't expecting the guards to be part werewolf," I snapped, taking in her beet red face. The perfectly put together woman was rankled. It was kind of nice to see. "We know where Dr. O is being held. Mission accomplished."

"You know they'll probably move him now, right?" Max said, running his palm over his face.

"No way they are moving him," I argued. "They have him in a

magic-tight iron cell. Must have been built at the same time as the prison."

"Without that iron around him, his magic could blow the entire prison," Darcy added, peeking at Mary Jane from behind her laptop screen, eyes wide. It was her first time meeting the new boss, and poor Darce was all about first impressions. So far, this wasn't a good one.

Matty dropped onto the couch beside her and sighed heavily. "This was supposed to be date night."

She gave him a pointed look and tilted her head towards him. "Sorry, babe, but I have to work." She rubbed the inside of his thigh.

I poured out a cup of coffee and sat at the large farmhouse kitchen table. I barely recognized my apartment, housed on the ground floor of an old factory building in a forgotten part of the city. Darcy was working and living out of the place while I crashed in Babe's apartment above the bar. My sparsely furnished apartment was now crammed with work stations and cabinets. It hummed with computers, surveillance cameras and, if my eyes were not mistaken, a couple of drones.

I watched Darcy's hand move back and forth on Matty's leg, and wondered what it was like to be so comfortable with someone that you just touched them without putting any real thought behind it. Just a natural, everyday occurrence. I glanced at Max pacing the room, bloated with anger. When I thought about touching him, my hand recoiled. Living with that Berserker curse was doing something ugly to him.

Meanwhile Frankie was stretched out on the floor, legs crossed at the ankles. His slightly-longer-than-shoulder-length hair was up in a man bun. He opened and closed a switchblade, his fidgeting a nervous tick. "That entire bloody cellblock was filled with iron. Iron shackles, iron doors."

Gramps settled beside me at the table with a mug of coffee. He pulled a bottle of bourbon out of his Baja hoodie and topped off his java. He glanced at Mary Jane. "The iron kills the magic. The more iron, the harder it is for a witch to use magic. Not a lot of witches can work in that environment."

"So the iron is why Nina's magic failed?" Mary Jane asked, her tall legs making short work of the apartment as she paced.

I bristled at her words. I was not the world's worst witch.

"That's it," Gramps said, putting his hand under my chin and tilting my face to get a better look at the bite left by the werewolf. My skin knitted back together while we were escaping the prison, but the bite looked like it was going to scar. "And that's why they have your good doctor Lachlan in an iron box. Druid magic could break through whatever iron's around the cellblock doors, but not if he's surrounded by it on all sides."

Mary Jane stopped pacing to stare at me. "How the hell do I explain what you two just did to those prison guards to my bosses? You just took out a bunch of our own people!"

"Not exactly your people," Frankie said, running the knife under his fingernails. I grimaced, knowing that he was probably cleaning out chunks of prison guard flesh. "They're all working for Leila in there."

"I thought our overlords wanted this done by any means necessary," I said.

"You can't just go in there and massacre staff. Those were government employed people," she griped.

"Some of them weren't people anymore," I snapped, slamming my hands down on the worn wood of my farmhouse table. I glanced at Max, who at least held his rage in check. Mary Jane on the other hand looked like she was ready to blow.

"Literally," Frankie muttered under his breath, then spoke louder. "She's turning these humans into something they are not supposed to be. And they are fighting for the wrong side."

Max took a breath and I watched him mouth a ten count. "There had to be another way. There is always another way."

"You weren't there," Frankie said. "One of them bit Nina. Robards plugged her full of bullets."

I nodded and lifted my shirt, staring straight at Mary Jane, showing off faint pink scars raised against the otherwise smooth skin of my stomach. Then I tilted my head to show off the jagged cut along my cheek. She screwed up her face in disgust, no wounds marring her perfect skin. Not even an acne scar.

"And what did you gain by going in there?" she asked, her tone patronizing. "You still have no idea how to reach Dr. O."

"But now we know that we can't use magic to bust him out," I said. "And we know where they house the witches. And we know that they are experimenting on the werewolves."

"This is a mission to get Dr. O out," Max said, crossing his arms and leaning against the kitchen counter. "The others will have to wait."

"They are doing experiments on them, both the witches and the wolves," I repeated. "In the case of the werewolves, they're separating the human from the wolf. They're physically and psychically ripping them apart. They can't wait."

"And you know this how?" Mary Jane asked, shaking out her hair. "They just explained it all to you while shooting you full of holes?"

"I saw a glyph," I said, sipping my coffee. I ignored her tone.

"A glyph?" Max tossed up his hands. "She saw a glyph."

I turned to Gramps. "They were carving runes into the were-wolves. An upside down protection symbol, then a separation symbol and then the symbol for whole, but that one was slashed through."

"You sure you have the symbols right?" Gramps asked.

"Positive," I said.

"Then Nina's right," he said with a clipped nod. "They are separating human and wolf and then splicing it into human DNA."

"Not the worst thing in the world, if you ask me," Matty said with a sulk. Vampires weren't so fond of werewolves, Beta-Vamps in particular. And the feeling was mutual.

"What's the point of separating them?" Darcy asked.

"Other than to kill them in a slow, painful and humiliating way?" I tossed out.

"The point is experimentation, to try different ways to split super-natural powers," Gramps said, taking a pull from the bottle of bourbon. Apparently, the coffee was watering it down too much. "We know she's splicing the wolf gene into these humans."

"But why bother?" Darcy asked. "Obviously, the human merged with the wolf gene isn't making something powerful enough to stop Nina and Frankie."

Gramps wiped his mouth with the back of his hand. "She wants to fuse the wolf together with another supernatural creature. These humans are just her practice batch. She doesn't give a shit if she has to throw them away."

Mary Jane stopped pacing and looked at Gramps. "To what end?"

"Imagine taking the ability to shapeshift like a werewolf and fusing that with the ability to do magic like a witch. Now add the immortality and bloodlust of a vampire," Gramps said. "You've just built yourself a killing machine."

A familiar ghostly goo oozed into my body and I shivered at the sensation. I squeezed my eyes shut in anticipation of a headache.

"Hello, ghost," my grandfather said, keeping his eyes trained on me.

"That man gives me the damn creeps," Casper said, settling into my body.

"Do I?" Gramps asked. He sipped his coffee and made a face. Then he took another drink straight from the bottle.

Casper recoiled deeper into my body, which led to a stabbing pain behind my left eye. "How did he hear that?"

"Ghosts are not immune to spells," my grandfather warned.

"Who is he talking to?" Matty asked, glancing around the apartment.

"I think he's talking to Casper," Darcy whispered. "This gets weirder by the day."

Frankie gave a low whistle. "It sure does. Say there, Gramps..."

Gramps scowled at him.

Frankie cleared his throat. "Can you see the ghost?"

"Of course not, he's a ghost," my grandfather scoffed. "I could always sense him. Now I can hear him, too."

Casper's trembling shook my body. "Holy. Shit."

"Relax, ghost," my grandfather said. "I'm not going to exorcise you."

"Just be careful what you say around the old man," I said. "And what are you doing out of the bar?"

"I needed to talk to you."

"About what?" I asked.

I felt him fidget. "I don't want to say now."

I pressed my fingers into my temples and stood, pausing to catch my balance while my equilibrium adjusted to the ghost. "I'll go in the hallway." Coffee in hand, I left the apartment to mentally huddle with Casper.

"I've been looking all over for you. Where the hell you been?" Casper lit into me the second I shut the door.

"Take it easy, Casper," I said, stumbling in surprise at his outburst. Coffee sloshed out the side of the mug, and I slurped it up off my hand. "Frankie and I were doing recon at the prison. It took a little longer than I thought."

"Well, I got the drop on something and I want you and Frankie to check it out."

"So why are we out here being all secretive? Let's clue everyone in."

"Because I don't trust your old *abuelo* there," he said.

"Casper, he's the only witch that can teach me to how to defeat Leila."

"You don't think it's weird that he shows up here. Now. After how many years just pretending you don't exist?"

"But he's—" I started.

"And...and...and..." Casper stammered. He was racing around my head and it gave me vertigo. "Didn't he try to kill you when you were a baby?"

I cleared my throat. "Well, technically the entire village was trying to kill me."

He harrumphed. "Doesn't matter. I don't trust the old man."

"Neither do I," I insisted. "Casper, I got this under control."

"Do you?" he asked. "How're your headaches?"

"Fine," I lied.

"What, do you think I'm stupid? Your headaches are getting worse because he's making you do too much magic. You aren't ready for this."

I kicked at the wall with the toe of my boot. "I have no choice. I can't save these people from Leila without magic. I'm not full vampire. So I need to be a full witch."

"Even if it kills you?"

"It's not going to kill me," I said.

"I feel the war between the vampire and the witch inside you, Nina," Casper said. "Vampire is winning."

"That's just until I get my magic under control," I insisted. "So tell me, what do you have the drop on and what do you need me to do?"

"My mom—"

"Jesus, Casper, you went to your mom's again?" I snapped. "Do you *want* to get an amateur exorcism?"

"Shut up," he said. "I found out where they're snatching the witches."

My anger drained right out of me and my body went cold. I closed my eyes and took a breath. "Show me."

"You're not going to like it," he warned.

12

TWO HOURS LATER, Frankie and I were traipsing through a wooded area not far from where the werewolves sold opiate-laced blood to the Beta-Vamps a few months ago in an effort to exterminate them. But there was no deserted country road, no dirt driveway to take us where we needed to go. The trees were so densely packed that even traveling in an ATV was out of the question. With the sun dropping low in the sky, we lost whatever light filtered through the forest. I tripped over a tree root, swearing under my breath as I felt myself falling. Frankie grabbed me by the back of my jacket to keep me upright.

"This is just great," I muttered to Casper, who was flitting around in my head, a ghostly bundle of nervous energy.

"Told you you wouldn't like it," he said.

I growled.

"She's got to have someone on the inside," Frankie said, striding through the brush with infuriating ease. "How else would she know when the circles are happening."

"Because they're drawing their magic," I grumbled.

"Didn't we tell all the coven high priestesses to stop drawing magic?" Frankie asked.

"They're on sacred ground in this wood," Casper said. "The magic should be contained within their circle."

"Maybe they're forgetting to cast a circle," I offered. I took Casper's sudden stillness as exasperation. "Hey, it happens."

"It happens to you," Casper said. "These witches know what they're doing."

"Maybe the circle doesn't contain the magic," I suggested.

"If they're doing a cloaking spell—" Casper started.

"Maybe they forgot to do that."

"No!" Casper's voice ricocheted through me. I stopped walking, surprised by the sharpness of Casper's tone.

"Tell me," I demanded.

"Tell you what?" Frankie asked. "And why have we stopped?"

"According to Casper..." I hesitated, taking in what the ghost was saying. "Are you freaking serious?"

"According to Casper, what? What is he serious about?"

"Apparently this place...it's at a crossroads," I started.

"Like a summoning-the-demon crossroads?" Frankie asked. "Is this how Bertrand ended up here?"

"Good question, but let's save that for later," I said. "According to Casper, this particular one is where two ley lines cross."

Frankie came to an abrupt stop. "Ley lines? Like as in magical fault lines?"

I stumbled around a thicket, taking the opportunity to catch up to him. "Yes, and whenever a witch comes to a ley line crossroads, they pull tremendous power."

"And safety, the crossroads are supposed to offer safety," Casper added. "It was how many of the Salem witches escaped persecution. By practicing on the ley line crossroads."

"Casper said that the crossroad of two ley lines somehow shields magic," I explained to Frankie.

"Is that true?" he asked.

"I don't know," I snapped. "You know I never learned the witchy stuff."

"Of course. Never thought you were going to need it," he said. "Look how well that turned out."

I ignored him. "So the witches think they are safe within the ley lines."

Frankie whistled. "Assuming it's true, that's some right proper power. And you really should've paid attention in Witchcraft 101." I shot him a dirty look but he started walking again, his pace quicker. "So if these ley lines are supposed to shield magic, how the hell is Leila tracking them?"

"Maybe because she knows about the ley lines too," I said. "She is a witch, after all. And my parent's old farmhouse isn't too far away. Bet that's why she made my dad buy it."

The thought unsettled me, and I wondered how long my dad had been her stooge.

"So how do we know when we get to said ley lines?" Frankie, ever the pragmatist, asked, snapping me out of my head.

"I guess I'll feel it?" I suggested.

"There should be witches there," Casper said. "My mom's coven was going to try their circle tonight."

"Your mom's not with them, is she?" I asked, panic rising in my chest. Casper got quiet. "Is she?"

Frankie slowed his pace. "His mum's there?"

I stopped dead. "And that's why you asked us to come?" Casper nodded, causing my own head to bob. "Why didn't you just say so? We'd have done this to keep an eye on your mom."

"I'm positive this is how they are snatching so many witches," Casper said. "It can't just be because the strong witches leak power."

"Like Mia," I said.

"Exactly," he agreed. "I mean, how many crones like Mia are out there? A handful, if that. And how many witches did you see at the prison?" My brain turned this over. The kid was smart.

"Mia? What's Mia have to do with this?" Frankie asked, only catching my end of the conversation.

"Casper's asking how many witches were at the prison and did we think they were all crones, who oozed witchy power by simply existing."

"There's a point," Frankie said. "So they're ambushing witches at the ley line crossroads."

My feet tripped along the uneven forest floor once again. "Then rounding them up, bringing them to the prison and siphoning their power."

"Lovely," Frankie said. "But to what end?"

"Obviously not a good one," I said. "We better keep moving."

We trudged along for another thirty minutes or so, every twig snap and branch groan pulling our attention as we powered through the thick brush. My nose and ears picked up the scent and sound of a crackling bonfire before my eyes made out red-orange flames sparking up around a clearing in the woods.

"Hang back," Casper said. I grabbed Frankie by the arm and yanked him back. He collided into me and I fell against a thick tree trunk, his body pressed against mine. Judging from my own body's response, I rather liked it.

"Sorry," he said, righting himself. I remained against the tree, a little lightheaded from my reaction.

"Damn girl, I wish you two would just do it and get it over with," Casper muttered.

"Shut up," I whispered.

"I hope you're talking to the ghost," Frankie said.

Scowling, I nodded. We crept forward again, keeping well within the shadows cast by the roaring fire. The witches were circled around the blaze, eyes closed, hands clasped. Casper's mom, the high priestess, closed the circle. I felt Casper puff up with pride.

The group of women began chanting, their eyes still closed, hands still clasped together. Their voices carried above the roar of the flame, the Latin humming from them drawing a sort of calm through me that was rooted in the pit of my stomach. The smell of sage wafted towards us as the winds shifted and the witches began a slow dance together, keeping their circle intact.

"Widdershins?" I whispered, surprised to see them moving counter clockwise.

"They're doing a banishment," Casper explained.

"Banishing who?" I asked, sucking in my breath as their heads tipped back at once and Latin spilled out of them in a collective cry. Their hair was wild, and I could see sparks of blue electricity jumping from one hand to the next, connecting the witches with a primal energy as the spell coursed through their bodies.

"Who do you think? Your mom."

"Stop calling her that," I snapped. "Besides, I thought you needed an item from the person being banished. What do they have from Leila?"

"Technically, they don't need an item," Casper explained. "But the spell isn't as potent, so it probably won't work. But trying something is better than not doing anything."

"They aren't going quietly into that good night, are they?" I mused, watching their dance with a renewed respect.

A twig snapped in the distance, and I pulled my attention away from the fire. Before my eyes could adjust to the darkness, a female figure stepped out from behind a tree across the clearing. She hissed out a spell, and the earth rumbled beneath our feet, slapping me against the trunk of the large tree I was hiding behind. The witches stumbled, leaning against each other to keep upright while they maintained their circle. The figure tipped her head back and released her own stream of Latin, the words echoing through the forest. Before the coven could react, an explosive force pushed the ground up, breaking the circle and sending the group of witches sprawling. The woman cackled and stepped into the middle of their broken circle, where her face was illuminated by the fire.

"Kittie," I said, raising my lip in a snarl.

"Your sister?" Casper quipped.

"She's *not* my sister," I snapped.

"She's adopted?" Frankie suggested.

"Bertrand said my mother made her. I've no idea what he meant by that."

"So she's the one doing Leila's dirty work," Frankie said.

I nodded towards the flashlights blazing up the forest behind Kittie. "Looks like she has help."

Five armed men stepped out from behind the trees, rounding up the felled witches and encasing their hands in iron. "Are those cops?" I whispered to Frankie. "They don't look like cops."

"Bloody hell, Nina," Frankie said. "I think they're mercenaries."

"Great," I grumbled. Mercenaries meant ex-military and highly trained. Like pit bulls, mercs don't give up. Our last dalliance with them involved a shit-ton of blood and a trip to the infirmary.

"Think she hopped them up with the werewolf gene?" Frankie asked.

Mercenaries with werewolf DNA spliced in? Even better. "Only one way to find out."

Frankie was all fangs when he smiled at me. "Try to keep up, Nina."

Then he was a blur as he raced into the center of the circle, taking advantage of the element of surprise to down the first mercenary. The guy got off two close-range shots, hitting Frankie in the shoulder.

"The bullets are soaked in holy water!" Frankie yelled out before punching the guy who was shooting at him. It was a perfect right hook, and hard enough to drop the trained assassin immediately.

"But are they werewolves?" I yelled back at him.

Before he could answer, Kittie stepped into the crossroads and tossed out a spell that knocked Frankie back. As she chanted, Frankie dropped to his knees. He ripped off his long leather jacket and tore at his shirt. The bullets lodged in his shoulder were eating away his skin, like acid.

I sprinted towards Frankie, but Casper took over my form and jerked me back behind a tree. "What the hell are you doing?" I said, struggling to regain control of my body.

"She shouldn't be able to do that," Casper said. "The ley lines are giving her more power. You can't just run out there without a plan."

"Plan? You want a plan?" I said through gritted teeth. "Here it is.

We get Frankie away from her and then rip her freaking head off. Ready?"

"You can't run out there like a—" He stopped himself.

"Like a vampire?"

"You know what I mean," he said.

"If she's getting power from the ley lines, we can too right?" I asked. Casper went quiet, so I continued. "I'm not running out there like a vampire. I'm running out there like a witch."

"What spell do you want to throw at her?" Casper asked, his voice animated.

"We can set her on fire," I suggested. It was the only spell I felt fairly confident about, since I'd invested several hours worth of practice with Gramps.

"We should probably bring her in alive," he said.

Frankie groaned in pain. I poked my head around the tree. I could barely bring myself to look at him. The flesh was nearly dissolved from his shoulder and the spell was creeping up his neck.

"Look at what she's doing to Frankie," I said. "And you want her alive?"

"Nina," Casper warned.

"Fine," I mumbled. "Let's drain her magic."

"Drain her magic? How?"

"Gramps explained that spell to me, the one that's in the witch blade."

"He explained it to you?" Casper questioned.

"Theoretically speaking, I can do it," I insisted.

"And you don't have a knife," Casper protested. "There's no way you can do it."

"I've got to do something," I said, desperation rising in my chest.

"But that's dark magic!" Casper shouted.

"This is not the time to argue about dark and light magic."

"It's a complicated spell."

"If you don't want to do it, get out of my body," I ordered.

"No way, you need me to—"

"To do what, Casper? Keep me on the magical straight and

narrow? That's getting too many people killed. You want to come for the ride, fine. But we're going dark."

I felt Casper do a slow bleed out of my body. Guess I got my answer.

Free of the ghost and his conscience, I sprinted into the clearing. The remaining mercenaries were rounding up the frightened witches at gunpoint while Kittie continued to work her spell on Frankie.

The moment I stepped into the ley line crossroads, energy surged through my body. My feet pressed into the ground, soaking up more power. I felt invincible, and I sent a sidekick into Kittie's stomach that sent her sailing out of the circle with a satisfying "oof," releasing Frankie from the spell. He collapsed to the ground, weakened, but his body immediately started to heal.

I dropped into a crouch. Hands pressed against the dirt, I drew power from the earth and allowed it to fill me. The energy from the ley lines was heating up my blood, the vampire part of my body burning up from the pure magic that flowed into me. I stood, bringing the force of the lines up.

"Nina!" Frankie yelled as mercenaries opened fire. A torrent of Holy Water-infused bullets came at me. My body jerked as the bullets slammed into flesh, but with the magic from the lines flowing through my form, I didn't feel a thing.

"I need time to throw the spell!" I yelled at him. *Goddamn, I better not screw this up.* There was no time for do-overs.

A nearly healed Frankie jumped into action and went after the guys with the guns while I prepared to hit Kittie with the spell to drain her magic. Gramps described it to me when I asked how they rigged a knife to steal a witch's essence. But my question was rhetorical, and since it was dark magic, I spent the entire time insisting that I'd never throw a spell like *that* rather than pay close attention. I swallowed, metaphorically eating my words while I prayed that I got the gist of the incantation right.

Fingers twisting, the physical movement helping me focus on my intent, the spell spilled from my lips. I pulled my hands towards my chest and Kittie staggered towards me. *Dammit.* I had control of her body, not her magic. With a swift motion, I shoved her back as I watched her begin to mouth a spell, her tattoo rattlesnake undulating along her skin. My mind raced as I pieced together what I did wrong. Taking a breath, I tried again, readjusting my focus not on Kittie, but on the snake whose rattle was now louder than the shouts of the mercenaries that Frankie was systematically dropping.

With the tattoo as my linchpin, the spell took root. Kittie rubbed at the fading tat, and her face went from hateful to horrified as she realized why it was disappearing from her skin. She dropped to her knees, digging nails into her flesh, as if that could keep the snake inked to her body.

As I pulled the magic out of her, I looked around for a vessel in which to place the energy. Not spotting anything that would work in a pinch, I went numb with panic. There was no spelled knife, and the other witches were bound in iron, rendering their bodies useless to take the magic straight. I was the vessel. There was no other choice.

I had no idea what taking straight magic would do to a body. I braced myself for the onslaught of mystical energy.

"This is gonna hurt," I muttered to myself. I took a deep breath and then drew Kittie's magic into me. My senses went haywire. As I pulled the power in, my hands went numb, the numbness traveling up into my arms before radiating out, like hot, thick liquid flowing under skin. Every nerve ending in my body was on fire. My teeth and jaw ached, and what felt like tiny needles pricked into my conscious. I gasped in pain as my bones felt like they were splintering. A high-pitched noise filled my ears. My heart raced and my breath came out in rapid gasps, like I was in the middle of a marathon running at a sprinter's pace.

With Frankie's attention now on me, the three remaining goons with guns charged, firing their weapons. I released a guttural scream as their bullets pierced my body, the wounds burning. Without thinking, I threw a spell, the foreign incantation spilling out of me as easy as if it were a favorite recipe. The wind picked up, slow at first, but soon hurricane gusts were pushing my attackers towards me. As they crossed into the ley line intersection, my voice carried over the whipping winds. The bullets embedded in my body shot back out. The three gunman dropped to the ground, felled by what they'd dealt out. Then I tossed Kittie's last spell at them. The bullets that hit their bodies exploded and began eating their flesh. Their screams of pain carried over the whipping winds.

I dropped to the ground and, control shattered, my body convulsed. The men's shrieks echoed through the silent woods, ricocheting off the trees. A stink of foul meat permeated the air and their terror turned to weak gurgles as the spell worked its way further into their bodies, attacking their inner organs.

My convulsions stopped and my body stilled as silence spread over the scene. I gasped to fill my lungs, taking in cool, clean air. My head still ached, but I was able to sit up. Frankie sat outside the ley lines, Kittie in his grip. Her face was a stark white, as if in shock. But Frankie, he looked like he'd seen the ghost of Dracula.

"Bloody hell, Nina," he said when he found his voice. "It looked like you were being electrocuted."

"Felt like it too," I said, letting out a shaking breath. He was still staring at me. "What is it?"

"You still look..." He tipped his head first to the right, then to the left. "Charged."

"That's ridiculous," I said. I reached my arm towards him to show there was nothing sparking off of me. Just as I was about to razz him, an arc of white light fired straight out of my fingers. Frankie grabbed Kittie and yanked them both down, the energy just missing the top of their heads as it shot into the distance. There was a huge crack and then we heard a tree slam to the ground.

"Holy shit," I whispered. The mercenaries were littered around the bonfire, their bodies still. I did all this? With magic?

"No shit, holy shit." Casper's incredulous voice echoed in my head as he slammed into my body. But his anger melted as soon as he felt the surge of my magic. "Oh man, this is..."

"Yes, it is," I said, breathless from the power driving through me.

"It feels wrong," he said, although his tone said otherwise.

"But it feels good," I said, admitting what he was afraid to say.

With the excruciating pain over, the magic that flowed through my body felt like a cross between being super high and having an orgasm. Invincibility mixed with sex. Intoxicating.

"How long does this last, do you think?" Casper asked.

"Don't know," I said. I flexed my fingers, enjoying the electricity arcing from them. "But a witch could get used to this."

"Nina, yoo-hoo, over here," Frankie called out. He was waving his hands to get my attention. "You done with the theatrics? We've got to get out of here."

"Where'd the witches go?" I asked.

"Scattered," Frankie said.

"Casper, can you check on them?"

"I'm not ready to go just yet," he said. "Damn, power *is* intoxicating."

"Casper," I said, the tone in my voice a warning. Just as I was about to chide him, his spirit left my body with such force that I staggered back a few paces. "What the hell?"

Casper inched his way back in, cautiously. One foot out the door, so to speak. "Why did you do that?"

"I didn't *do* anything."

"Well, I didn't leave."

"I don't know what happened. I thought something..."

"What did you think?"

"That you needed to get the hell out of my body and find those witches, make sure they—" I didn't even finish the sentence and he catapulted out of my body again. "Damn, I can reject you at will now?" I snorted.

"That's not funny," Casper said, popping back in again. "You know that hurts, right?"

"Go check—" I started, but this time he leapt out of his own accord.

"So, what do you want to do with this one?" Frankie asked. He pushed Kittie, and she stumbled forward. Frankie had bound her hands with one of the iron handcuffs, so her balance was off. Her unzipped jacket fell open, exposing her neck and the top of her chest.

I squinted at her in the dark. My night vision was better than most because of my vampire genetics, but I didn't have Frankie's crack eyesight.

"Do you notice something different about her?" I asked him.

His eyes raked over her. "Looks like our darling Kittie to me."

"Look again," I said.

As I spoke, a rattlesnake rattled close to my ear and I felt a tickle start from the base of my skull, move down my neck, then stretch across my shoulder. I ripped open my jacket and stared down at my chest. A snake tattoo covered my skin, the rattle shivering along the curve of my neck.

"Bullocks, Nina," Frankie said, running his finger along the snake winding across my clavicle. "How'd you snag her tattoo?"

I shrugged. "No idea. The spell was to drain her magic, that's all I know."

"You mean you stole my magic," Kittie spat. "The tattoo was what held it, you halfwit."

"Drain, stole. The point is, I have a lot of magic running through me right now. So don't piss me off."

"Maybe that was your problem doing magic? You didn't have a tattoo?" Frankie suggested.

I gave him a dirty look and clapped my hands together to make sparks.

"Right," Frankie said, shaking his head. "Let's get both of you to your grandfather. He better be able to sort this. You're a blooming Tesla coil right now."

13

GRAMPS POKED at the rattlesnake tattoo, which spent the past hour wending its way around my body. Each contraction of the snake pushed more magic into me. I was practically vibrating.

"Hot damn," Gramps said, raising his eyebrows. Every time the snake's rattle issued a warning, my fingers sparked. "Do you know what this means?"

"That I play a mean static electric shock game?" I joked.

"It means that you stole my magic," Kittie snapped.

She scowled at me from her uncomfortable position on the floor. Frankie had looped her arms around a support pole in the middle of Babe's, hands still in the irons, even though her magic was gone. She sat on the saw-dust covered floor, straddling the beam.

"I thought that only that witch knife stole magic," Frankie said.

Gramps' eyes sparkled. "She did the same spell, but rather than imbuing an object with the power to take the magic, Nina simply took it straight."

I wrapped my arms around my middle and shivered. "So what does it mean?"

Gramps harrumphed. "It means that this is not temporary."

That top-of-the-world feeling turned into something queasier. A quick stabbing pain shot through my temple then disappeared behind my eyes.

"What do you mean 'not temporary?'" Frankie voiced the question that was caught in my throat. "Kittie won't get her magic back?"

"Her magic is now Nina's," he said. The glee in his voice was unnerving.

I shuddered. "I don't understand," I started, forming the words with care. "How will this not revert?"

"You do know dark magic is exactly that, right?" Kittie huffed. "What did you think would happen?"

"You think I want your ugly-ass tattoo on my body?" I snapped, blinking through another bolt of pain. It stabbed through my head, then disappeared. "The spell was supposed to neutralize you, that's it. Not like I wanted this to happen."

I tamped down the feelings of guilt. Taking a witch's magic was like removing an arm or leg, rendering them somehow less than whole. Even I understood that.

She glared at Gramps. "Did you tell her it was temporary?"

"Never said it wasn't," he said.

"Did you know?" I leveled the direct question at him.

"I wasn't sure if you had the power to do it," he said. "The ley line crossroads are powerful. I figured there was a chance."

"So you just sent Nina out there, without any sort of warning," Frankie said. His eyes started to glow, and I heard his fangs gnash.

Gramps clapped his hands together. "Look at her. She radiates power."

"Radiates power my ass," I grumbled, nerves churning through my stomach. My eyes darted around the room, sweeping past the nearly bare shelves behind the bar. I focused on a bottle of Smirnoff Vodka. I took a quieting breath and felt magic whirling through me. With a subtle nod of my head, the bottle flew across the room towards Gramps. His eyes went wide before he jerked his head out of the way just in time. The bottle smashed into the wall behind him. The clear booze streaked down into a shard-filled puddle on the floor. I shut my eyes at the near-blinding pain that charged through my skull.

"Bloody right thing no one likes Smirnoff," Frankie said with a nervous chuckle.

"Can you take these off?" Kittie whined. "It's not like I can do anything. I'm human now."

She formed the word "human" slowly, working it around her mouth until it came out like a curse.

"Nah," I said. "We'll keep you shackled. Just in case."

"What harm can she do?" Gramps asked, his left eyebrow moving up about half an inch.

"No sympathy for the devil," I said.

Kittie cackled. "If you think I'm the devil, you should spend more time with our mother."

That caught my interest, and I tamped down the now blinding pain chewing at my temples.

"*Our* mother?" I said, with a small snicker. "You're no more my sister—"

"Oh we are not bound by blood," she said, rolling her eyes like a petulant teen. "But Leila made me in her image." She looked down at her bound hands and dropped her voice. "Or tried to."

"So you were created?" I asked, my interest piqued. "How?"

"I assume the same way you were," she snapped at me.

I blinked at her, the pain doubling down in my head. "You do know about sex, right?"

"You sound so sure of yourself," she said, a cold grin spreading across her face. "You were awfully quick to cast a dark spell."

"Once," I said through gritted teeth. "And you gave me no choice."

"Once you take a step into darkness, there's no going back. See, we're not that different after all."

Casper slithered into me, jolting me upright. He fidgeted around in my body, which made me feel like I was on the losing end of a boxing match. I slumped in my stool, my back propped up against the hard wood of the bar. "I am not like you," I grumbled.

"What gives, Nina?" Casper asked as he continued his futile attempt to get comfortable in my body.

"We're built the same," Kittie continued, not paying attention to my squirming figure. "You'll see, my darling sister."

"You don't belong here," I hissed.

"What are you talking about?" Kittie and Casper said at the same time. Casper's question was punctuated by a colorful word in Spanish.

"You aren't quite right, Nina," he said. "Something feels off."

Agitation rose in me, and a smell of ginger torched through the air. My nostrils burned.

"What is that?" Frankie asked, his nose upturned at the smell.

My grandfather's voice boomed through the bar. "Enough of this nonsense. We've got spells to cast."

Spells to cast? All I wanted to do was go to sleep. My stomach churned. Was that from Casper? When was the last time I ate?

"I think I need to do something else," I said, forming words that had no meaning together. My mind raced and Casper raced around inside me in a panic. Even though I felt myself grounded by the hard wood of the barstool under my ass, the room was spinning. The smell of ginger grew stronger, and my stomach gurgled in anger. I opened my mouth to say something, anything, but instead of words, bile foamed out.

I heard Frankie swear and the world dropped away. I felt his strong arms surround me. He pulled me off the stool and brought me down to the floor.

"What the hell is going on?" he yelled at my grandfather. "Do something! Why don't you do something?"

The desperation in Frankie's voice was palpable. I wanted to reach out to him, tell him that I was okay, that it was just a terrible headache. But my body refused to listen to me. Instead, it bucked and seized against the wood floor. Frankie threw himself on top of me. Only the weight of his body kept me from levitating.

"She's burning up," he called out, his hands moving behind my sweat soaked neck. "Bloody hell, Gramps. Do something!"

I opened my mouth to say something, but only guttural grunts found their way out. I clawed at my clothes. My body heat was oppressive. When my eyes popped open, Frankie recoiled in horror.

"Her eyes," he whispered as he crawled off of me. What was he talking about? I wanted to ask him what happened to my eyes. But instead, a shock of pain ripped through my body. I bolted upright.

Kittie shrieked when I turned towards her. I heard a hiss expel from my lips and my body crawled towards her of its own accord. I couldn't control myself. As my murderous rage built, more burning ginger assaulted the air, like a pumpkin pie factory was on fire and I was in the core.

Casper hunkered down inside me and started a spell that pinned me to the spot. My body attempted to move towards Kittie but his conjuring foiled every attempt. Fighting against Casper's spell sent my body into convulsions.

"Dammit, Nina," Casper said. "You got the darkness in you now."

"Hold her down!" my grandfather yelled at Frankie. "I have to expel the ghost."

"No!" I pleaded, choking on my own vomit. Casper pushed himself further into my psyche. I felt him recoil against the dark magic each time he dug in deeper. He didn't want to live inside my body anymore, but expelling Casper would exorcise him for good. I wasn't ready to lose another person I cared about, ghost or not, and he wasn't keen on letting me go either.

"You've got to get out," I whispered. "Exorcism is coming."

But he held steady in my body and both of us fought like hell to keep him there as Gramps started his spell. I screamed again. My grandfather's spell slashed through my body like a knife skinning me from the inside. My temperature still burned hot, and more of that ginger scent spiced the air. I sneezed, and blood exploded from my nose.

"Stop fighting this," Gramps hissed. He pressed a medallion against my forehead and pain ripped through my skull. "That ghost is killing you."

"Nina," Casper wheezed. My grandfather's spell was winning. I felt Casper's hold on me weaken with each word my grandfather uttered.

"Noooo!" I yelled as my form seized before going limp. The acute pain disappeared but a nagging ache still settled into my body. Casper wasn't in there anymore. Tears squeezed their way out of my eyes, which I kept clamped shut. If I looked at my grandfather right now, I'd kill him.

Frankie's soft voice broke the silence. "Holy. Crap."

"'Holy crap'? That's all you can say? Not, 'Damn, you're a good looking man'?"

That familiar voice. That intonation. That *sass*.

I sat up. My eyes snapped open. Casper stood over me. I reached for him. He was as three-dimensional as me, or Frankie, but my hand sliced through him. He was formed from vapor.

"Hey, that's getting a little personal," Casper teased, his grin wide. "Check it, I'm here. In the flesh. Sort of. Hey, are you *crying*? Oh snap. You were crying. For me!"

"This happened in your head every time he was in there?" Frankie asked. "No wonder you had headaches."

"You didn't exorcise him?" I said, looking at my grandfather.

"Why would I do that?" he said. "He's a solid witch, in a manner of speaking." We watched as Casper tried to negotiate a seat on a barstool. His transparent body refused to cooperate. "You'll get the hang of it, kid. Just keep working on it."

"Are we the only ones who can see him?" Frankie asked.

"Hell no," Gramps said. "He's visible to anyone."

"But he's still..." I paused and looked at Casper.

"Dead?" Gramps finished for me. Casper winced at his indelicacy. "Of course he's still dead. We aren't necromancers. Terrible business, necromancy."

Kittie snorted at that. I glared at her.

"So why did my body freak out when Casper was in there?" I asked. Gramps shrugged, but I wasn't buying his feigned ignorance.

"That dark magic," Casper said. "I was trying to fight it with my own magic but..."

"But magic wars have cut down many a witch," Gramps finished for him. "There's a long tradition of witch-on-witch violence, on both sides."

"That damn tattoo pushed the dark magic inside me," I said. "We gotta figure out how to get it out."

"Laser removal?" Frankie suggested.

"Oh my god! You can't just laser it off," Kittie exploded, yanking at her bound hands. "You stole my magic. It's part of you now."

"You forced me to do it," I argued. "I had no choice."

"Please," she said. "You were more than willing to take what was mine. You welcome the darkness."

"You really want to see me welcome the darkness?" I threatened.

She sniffed. "You don't have it in you."

The snake tattoo issued a warning rattle, and a flood of words poured from my mouth. It was like I was possessed, watching someone else cast the spell that caused Kittie's eyes to go wide.

"Tell me what Leila is doing," I demanded, my spell forcing Kittie to do my will. Her tongue swelled and lolled out of her mouth, and I drew back, repulsed. "What the hell is happening to her?"

"Oh, ho ho! My daughter's a wily one. Looks like she didn't trust you, Kittie," Gramps said with a chuckle that told me he was impressed. "She put a silencer spell on you."

Kittie's eyes went wide as her tongue continued to enlarge, threatening to cut off her air supply.

"How do we reverse that?" I asked.

"You really want to?" Gramps asked.

"Of course I want to," I said. "She's going to die like this."

"Find it in your little dark heart," he said. His laugh was cold.

Casper's lips turned down. "You are only as dark as your spells. Stealing another witch's magic. That's some dark shit. It's almost as bad as casting a death spell. But what's in your heart, Nina? The dark shit doesn't define you. That's not you."

"So what do I do?" I whispered.

"Dig deep, girlfriend," he said. "You got this."

I wanted to give in to this cruel magic. I wanted to enjoy watching

Kittie in the throes of an agonizing death. But Casper was right, that wasn't me. Kittie didn't have any magic left to defend herself. I'd stolen her only means of protection against Leila. And against me.

Kittie gasped as her engorged tongue continued to block her airway. I thought about Babe, about her light, her kindness, her gentle way of magic.

Taking a breath, I tried a spell. Kittie's face was turning blue from her lack of oxygen.

"It's not working," I cried out to Casper.

"The darkness does not define you," he repeated, surprising me with the strength of his voice. "Do it again, Nina." I looked at him, my eyes pleading for his help. He looked me in the eyes. "You got this."

Under Casper's encouraging eyes, I unleashed a new torrent of words, an incantation that released Kittie from my dark hold. She collapsed against the pillar, panting.

Shaking from the adrenaline pushing out of my body, not to mention the relief that the spell worked, I pulled my knees into me and hugged them. "So I'm the wicked witch now?"

"Nah, not when you do shit like that," Casper said. "Let's just say that you're a little less inhibited with your magic now."

"There's a compromise," Frankie said. His voice was bright but edged with worry.

"Oh the darkness, blah blah blah," Gramps mocked. "You're no innocent. You've killed before. You'll kill again. This one notwithstanding." He gave Kittie a little kick.

"To save lives," I snapped. As my anger rose, my body tingled. "I've killed to save lives."

"No matter," he said. "Taking a life. That's something you can't turn back from."

"It was justified," I said. Energy pulsed into my body and the snake tattoo shook its rattle. This time, I welcomed the magic growing in my body, allowing it to feed me. Gramps had pushed me down a road I didn't want to travel. He tricked me into stealing Kittie's magic. He preyed on my novice skills to trick me into practicing a part of the craft I never wanted to welcome into my life. I allowed my rage to envelope me. My fangs dropped.

I catapulted up from the ground and lunged at my grandfather. My hands gripped him around the arms. I felt the sinew of his muscles, freakishly powerful for a man his age. My fangs snapped as I pulled him into me, laser focused on his jugular, which throbbed faster as adrenaline flooded his body. Fear. I smelled it. It was intoxicating.

Frankie's own powerful hands grabbed me and pulled me back. "Nina, no," he said, wrapping his arms around me from behind. "You'll regret it."

What I regretted, what Frankie regretted, was that we didn't see the talon blade sooner. Gramps' movement was lithe, the blade dropping out from under the long sleeve of his Baja hoodie. In one fluid movement, he drew the blade across my neck before slamming it into my carotid artery.

Warm, sticky blood flooded down my neck, soaking my shirt. Frankie pulled me into him, his hand trying to cover the wound, trying to keep me from bleeding out. A low cry was building from his chest as he whispered my name. I gasped, my fingers ripping at him as I struggled for air. Each labored breath was followed by a gurgle as my lungs filled with fluid. Everything went soft focus, except for Frankie, whose face was close to mine. Tears streamed down his cheeks.

I reached a bloody hand to his face, and touched his cheek. I'd never seen him cry before. A red streak trailed my hand as it dropped and my body went limp.

"Stay with me, Nina," he whispered. "Please stay with me. I love you."

Then, I died.

14

My eyes snapped open. It was pitch black, no crack of light to help my eyes focus. I shifted around and my shoulder bumped into a cushion with something firm behind it. I pushed myself up on my elbows and my head encountered the same barrier. I was enclosed in something.

My fingernails clawed at the cushioned wall above me. Fabric and polyester padding pulled away, revealing a pine surface. I slapped my palm against the bare wood.

"Hello?" I called, my voice horse, my throat sore. I was met with silence from the other side.

I continued to claw at the wood. Splinters embedded under my nails as my fingers worked. My eyes and nose itched from the sawdust that coated my face.

My stomach growled. It wasn't the usual "I skipped lunch" growl. It was full-on, rabid, ravenous, and then some.

Tucking my knees up to my chest, I pressed the soles of my feet and palms of my hands against the lid and pushed. It didn't budge. I put more force behind it, which was hard to do in such an awkward position. Nothing.

I pulled my arm back and sent a forward jab straight up into the spot of exposed pine. A loud crack and then shards of wood rained down on me. Just enough florescent light spilled in through the hole that I was able to see what entombed me.

A coffin. Someone put me in a goddamn coffin.

While I digested that, I heard footsteps above me, then the sounds of someone descending a staircase. I wrinkled my nose. The air that flooded into the coffin carried a slight stench of mold. Voices, muffled at first, became clearer as the footsteps moved closer.

"She's awake," Frankie said.

"Not possible," my grandfather said. "It takes days to turn."

"We don't have days, remember? Not while Mary Jane's running the countdown clock," Frankie said, the irritation in his voice rising. "You didn't consider that, did you?"

"I considered everything," Gramps retorted.

My grandfather? My grandfather. Memories from how long ago? A day? Two? More? They slipped into my mind, and I pressed my hand along my neck. A large raised scar remained where the blade had punctured my neck. I died. I was dead.

Holy crap. I was *undead*.

My mind raced and I tried to remember how fast vampiric dead became not so much anymore. And whose idea was it to put me in the damn coffin? I punched another hole in the wood. I had no strength. I wasn't even as strong as I was when I was human. I wasn't healing fast enough. My empty stomach roiled. I wasn't fully turned yet. But damn I was hungry.

Something landed on the top of the coffin with a thud. Sharp teeth made their way around the hole I punched in the coffin's lid and ripped away at the wood. A heavy paw dropped through the enlarged opening, and pressed against my chest. Dog was digging me out.

"Good girl," I whispered, my vocal chords still frayed from the knife. She whined in response and continued to work her way through the wood and poly-foam material, shredding the faux silk interior. It was pink. Was this coffin Frankie's idea of a laugh?

Once Dog chewed through an opening just large enough for me to fit through, I pulled myself up to a seated position. Dog laid down on the foot end of the coffin, panting. I scratched her ears and recognized the damp stone walls that surrounded me. I was in the very back of the bar's basement, a near-forgotten part that was too damp and too isolated to be used for much of anything. Except storing a coffin, apparently.

Footfalls continued to echo through the low ceilinged keg room as they made their way towards me. The old wooden door creaked open on its rusty hinges. Frankie and Gramps stood in the doorway, both bathed in an eerie blue hue from the florescent overhead lights.

The memory of my grandfather slamming a talon blade into my neck jarred me out of my stupor. His skin undulated from the blood that circulated through his body at five quarts per minute. I licked my dry lips. My fangs, which now replaced my canine teeth, grew longer.

"Nina," Frankie said, his voice cautious as he stepped into the room.

My movements were fluid and fast. Before Dog could jump off the casket, I was past Frankie. With my indescribable hunger growing, I gripped my grandfather by the shoulders and sunk my sharp teeth into his neck. Blood — salty with that hint of cinnamon — flooded into my mouth. It poured down my throat and into my stomach. But the hunger wasn't abating, so I sucked harder, pulling more nourishment into me.

Frankie's strong fingers gripped me around the mouth and pried me off of my grandfather. Gramps staggered backwards, holding onto his bloodied neck, mumbling, "*Sanguinem copia fatiscunt aut quae stirpibus exit corpus meum.*"

Frankie's arms wrapped around my waist as I doubled over from a crushing pain in my belly. Gagging, the contents of my stomach emptied on the cold cement floor. I dropped to my knees, taking Frankie down with me. I leaned back, exhausted, against his hard chest.

"Good on you. You missed his artery," Frankie said, although slight disappointment tinged his voice.

"What's happening to me?" I whispered.

"You're in the middle of the turn," he said. "You need more rest."

"Don't put me back in that thing," I begged.

"It was just temporary. Until we got a room set up. It's all sorted now."

He hoisted me up. Cradled in his arms, Frankie carried me out of the room and away from the shredded coffin. Dog tapped along behind, her nails the only sound in the basement.

My grandfather leaned against the wall, hand still pressed to his neck. Blood from the open wound on his neck oozed between his fingers. My grandfather's eyes followed me.

"You could have killed me, girl," he said.

"And you did kill me, old man," I said. "Eye for an eye. Right?"

Dog whimpered from around Frankie's legs while my grandfather and I exchanged glares of mistrust.

"Leave it," Frankie said, drawing me closer into him. "Your body needs time, needs rest."

I lost consciousness before I could argue with him.

15

WHEN I WOKE UP AGAIN, I was screaming for air. Frankie rubbed my back while I gasped for it. But my lungs had collapsed in on themselves. The futility of breathing only made me more desperate to fill them. How was I alive?

My ears burned from the voices on the other side of the wall. Living. Human. I could feel the heat coming off of their bodies even through several feet of wall plaster. I sniffed a heady mix of witch and human scents, and was struck with a ravenous ache in my belly.

Food.

I shoved Frankie off of me with so much force that he flew across the room, slamming against the far wall, leaving a body-sized dent. I tripped over myself in my rush to get to the door. I flung it open, and sunlight poured into the dark room, blinding me. I screamed when it hit my skin, blisters erupting from the white hot light. Frankie crashed into me, pushing me out of the sun. He slammed the door shut before my arm burst into flames.

"That's not a good idea," he said. He lifted me up and carried me back to the bed. My body hit the mattress and I doubled over in pain. My stomach churned with hunger.

Frankie handed me a glass. I sniffed the contents. Metallic and stale. I wrinkled my nose.

"It's unsatisfying leftovers, but it'll take the ache away," he said, tipping the glass to my lips. I shivered against his body while I choked down the foul contents of the glass. Old blood with the taste of antique silver numbed my tongue. But it was the aftertaste — like meat left on the counter too long on a hot day — that coated my mouth. It was disgusting, but quelled the agonizing pain in my gut.

I shivered. "Why is it so cold?" My voice was hoarse, my throat still strained from the stab wound.

"You'll get used to it," Frankie said, placing the glass on the bedside table. He pulled a quilt up over me and tucked me in, sitting on the edge of the bed.

I gave into my body's tremors as I tried to get warm. "What happened to me?"

"You died, love," he said, resting his arm across my body. "You're turning."

"Still?" I repeated. I tilted my head towards him, his face clear even in the dark room. He wasn't in shadow. Vampire vision. "How long?"

"Everyone's different," he said. "You more so. Witch and all."

"Doesn't the vampire negate that?" I pulled closer into him, the cold so overwhelming and uncomfortable. I curled my arm over my stolen snake tattoo, unnerved by its stillness. The witch died along with the human.

"Your grandfather said—"

My eyes narrowed. "You mean he's not dead yet?"

Frankie played with my hair. "No, I didn't kill him." I glanced at him. "And neither did you."

I knocked his hand away. "What the hell are you waiting for?"

His smile was rueful. "We need him right now, love."

"For what?"

"For making sure you don't die twice. The witch and vampire warred in your body. Now they have to find harmony."

"The witch is dead."

Frankie shook his head. "It lived in your mother after she turned. Why couldn't it live in you?"

I cursed the witch the minute deranged vampire Marcello sliced me with that spelled knife and ignited dormant powers I didn't know I had. For months, I wore the witch like an ill-fitting suit, unable to find myself through all the spell work. But now, without the magic vibrating in my body, I felt foreign, like I had a missing appendage. Like a phantom limb, imagined magic would tickle my nose or dance through my finger tips, but when I touched the source, the magic disappeared.

Or maybe I was getting used to being a vampire.

Snapping myself out of my gothic reverie, I worked my tongue over the sharp fangs that replaced my canines. Anger was more exhilarating than mourning. "Kill him."

"That's the hunger talking."

"I don't feel anything," I lied. In fact, I felt everything. But what I felt about Gramps was just more matter-of-fact. He plunged a knife in my neck and I bled out while choking on my own blood. Family or not, the man needed to die.

"You do, trust me," Frankie said. He dropped his arm back over me, as if to hold me down.

"I'm not going out to kill him now," I pointed out.

"Just in case," he said, giving me a squeeze.

My body tensed around his weight, becoming more aware of his proximity. His scent was a heady mix of rain-soaked soil and molten metal — a mix of earth and blood. I shifted closer to him, his scent surrounding me, grounding me. My fingertips danced along his forearm.

"You need to get more rest, Nina," Frankie said. His lips lingered along my hairline.

"I am done resting," I said, flexing and relaxing my muscles one by one. His body shifted against mine, and my nerves jumped to attention. "It all feels so weird, Frankie."

"I know," he said. He brushed my hair away from my face. "It takes some getting used to."

"Everything feels heightened," I whispered.

"You can hear them in the kitchen, right?"

I nodded, licking my lips. "More than hear them. I can sense them. Smell them. Feel them. I can almost taste them."

He gave a rueful chuckle. "I'd sincerely hoped that you would never feel this way."

"It doesn't feel bad," I said, rolling to my side to face him. "Not as bad as I thought it would."

"That's good, then," he said, sliding his hand over my shoulder and down my arm, setting my nerves on fire with his touch.

His black t-shirt was tight across his body, and I could see the outline of his chest muscles through the fabric. I feathered my finger-tips along the soft cotton, feeling his firm body underneath. "So you think I'm still a witch too?" I asked.

He nodded and closed his eyes as my fingers continued to dance along his t-shirt. "Your grandfather said the magic was killing you. It was slow, but it was happening. Said the headaches you'd been having, the nausea, all of that was triggered when your magic was released. He said absorbing Kittie's magic, the dark magic, pushed the process along faster. He said that death in such a manner would have been excruciating."

I stole a glance at his face. "And you believed that excuse?"

"Why wouldn't I believe it?" he asked, shivering involuntarily as my fingers brushed along the raised scars on his chest. I could feel them under his shirt. He leaned his head back against the headrest and I wondered if his scars were sensitive. "Those headaches kicked in when your witch powers surfaced. Marcello hitting you with that blade made them even worse."

I pressed my nails into him, my frustration rising. "When that knife kick-started all this, Tavio tried to give me a stone, a demon cursed object that he said would stifle the witch. He claimed having both in my body would kill me. I thought he was full of shit."

"Tavio? He knew?"

"And I didn't believe him. And I didn't take the stone—"

"—because it was a demon curse," Frankie finished.

"And I didn't want to lose the witch," I admitted.

Frankie jumped up and paced the room. The nervous energy radiating off of him spiked my bloodlust.

"We still don't know if you're in the clear," Frankie said. "What happens when the turn is complete? Too many questions, too much of a risk. Your grandfather could be the only one who knows how to fix you if your body goes to war with itself. Without Bertrand's inter-ference."

"Dr. O would know," I said, wrapping my arms around my middle and swallowing down the hunger and desire rising in me.

"Dr. O is behind iron bars."

"We're getting him out," I insisted.

"Of course we are. But he's not here right now, and now is crucial. And I won't risk losing you. It's not worth killing that bastard." He stopped pacing the floor and turned to me, fear etched into his face.

"Frankie," I whispered. I lifted a shaking arm towards him, motioning for him to come to me.

He flashed me a sad smile. "That's the vampire talking."

I sat up, unsteady. His eyes glowed, an eerie blue lighting up across the room, tracking my movement. The muscles of his lithe body flexed and relaxed with each shift of his position. Want flooded over me, the sensation almost too much to bear. I pulled my blood stained t-shirt over my head. He took a few tentative steps towards me, stopping at the foot of the bed.

"Nina," he said, touching my bare foot with trepidation, "you're in the midst of turning."

"I know exactly what I am doing," I said, reaching behind me and unsnapping my bra. I shrugged out of it, exposing my small breasts. He licked his lips, eyes on me.

"We can't," he said. Frankie didn't move from the end of the bed but his eyes continued to sweep over my body while his hand brushed along my ankle, inching up my calf.

I scooted to the end of the bed and took his hand from my leg, moving it to my left breast. I pressed it where my heart used to beat.

He closed his eyes and curled his fingers against my skin. "Nina, we can't," he repeated. "We shouldn't."

His hand fell away and I dropped my head so he didn't see my eyes fill with tears. Damn. Vampirism was worse than PMS, and Frankie's rejection smarted. I began to slither away. But before I darted from him in humiliation, his hand caught me behind the neck and he pulled me to him. His mouth hovered just over mine.

"Don't think I don't want this," he said, his voice rough. "I've wanted this for a long time."

"So what's stopping you?" I asked. My physical hunger was sated by the stale blood, but this more primal hunger threatened to consume me. Not enough blood in the world could tamp this down.

"This could be the transition talking, and I don't want you to regret this," he whispered, his mouth just inches from mine. My lower lip trembled as he captured it gently between his teeth. "It changes everything, you know. There is no going back."

"Got it, no going back," I repeated, tugging on his t-shirt, digging my nails into the fabric until it tore away with a satisfying rip. His body exposed, I admired his angular lines. Frankie was long and lean; bulking up was not in his DNA. I stared at the scars that covered his torso. I ran my hands over his cool skin, tracing the raised lines and peaks, the remnants of the deadly job that bound us both.

No longer able to hold back, his mouth crushed mine and my adrenaline spiked. I pulled at the buttons along the fly of his jeans. His hands fumbled along my body, like a 13-year-old kid playing Seven Minutes in the Closet for the first time.

"Sorry," he said, pulling away from me. "I promise I'm better than this."

My emotional pendulum swung the other way, heightened by the vampire DNA that was growing like kudzu through my cellular structure, leaving me feeling physically and mentally exposed. My confidence threatened to bottom out, and I snatched up the quilt and clutched it against my bare chest. "Am I too aggressive?"

"Not at all, love," he said. The tenderness in his eyes told me he wasn't lying. "But I've wanted this for so long that I'm rushing."

"I don't think I can wait either," I said, relief flooding me. My senses heightened, every time Frankie touched me I wanted to scream in pleasure. Control was a hard thing to muster.

"Really?" His smile of relief turned to one of mischief. He tugged at the quilt, exposing my half-naked body. "Let's try this again. But I want to savor you."

The quilt dropped away again and he pressed me down onto the bed. He settled his body between my legs and kissed me again. His tongue teased along my lips before slipping into my mouth, dancing around my newly formed fangs. His right hand cupped my breast and he ran his thumb over my taut nipple. His mouth released mine, and he moved down to my neck, scraping it with his fangs. At the soft spot just under my ear, his tongue teased me and I angled my body up against his. His fangs sank into that sensitive spot, and I moaned and tilted my hips into his pelvis.

"Wait," I whispered as my body stilled. "Do vampires need condoms?" My body was primed and, like a runaway freight train, this was only going in one direction until we ran out of track. Once this got going, it was going to be nearly impossible to stop if we were ill-prepared.

Frankie released his fangs from my neck, sending shivers down my back as the cool air touched the open wound. "They aren't necessary. Nothing to worry about in that department." I guess being undead had its advantages.

He kissed me again. His lips tasted like blood, my blood, which only increased my arousal. My hands swept down his body, and I pushed his unbuttoned jeans down his hips. Then I did the same with my own, kicking them off the rest of the way. I reached for his erection, but he stopped me.

"There's nothing more I want right now," he said. His expression told me he was telling the truth. "But, let's slow it down, love. It's not a race. We can enjoy this."

I growled my disapproval. My impulse control was waning and I needed to release the tension building inside me. But his expert hands traveled down my body and slid between my legs. I closed my eyes and shuddered as his fingers explored me. I wrapped my legs around him and moaned when he found my core.

"Are you certain?" he asked.

"Are you kidding?" I said through gritted teeth. "It's all I want right now."

"Right now?" he repeated. His fingers danced inside of me, and I pressed against them, proof of my interest in doing this *right now*. "I don't want you to regret this."

"Why would I?"

Frankie's cerulean blue eyes dropped to my mouth as I bit on my lip, trying to keep a measure of control. Then his gaze jumped back to meet mine. "There is no going back from this. There is no 'friends with benefits,' as the kids say. I want you. All of you."

"I know," I whispered, closing my own eyes. There was no going back to before. Before I was a novice witch and not-dead-yet vampire. Before my own grandfather bled me out on the floor of my bar. Before Aunt Babe died at my mother's hands. Before Max was just a hot FBI agent stopping into the bar for a beer and a flirt.

Now, I was dead. Well, technically undead. I drank blood. And, at this very moment, I was desperate for craven sex with Frankie, my best friend, work partner and, now, my fellow vampire.

My attention snapped back to Frankie when his fingers probed me deeper, driving me closer to climax before he pulled back again. "Maybe we should stop," he whispered, although his hands said otherwise.

Frustration flashed through me and my eyes lit up the area surrounding us an eerie green. Like a reflex reaction, I pushed Frankie off the bed and against the wall, pinning him to it with an arm stretched across his neck. I ran my tongue over my sharp fangs. "Why should we stop?

Frankie moved fast, flipping me around so I was pinned against the wall. My feet off the ground, only Frankie's arm kept me from falling. His body leaned on mine, the feel of his skin sending shivers through my me. I met his gaze with a look that challenged him to take me. He backed away, dropping me so I landed on my feet with a gentle thud. "This is exactly why. You're not yourself, Nina."

"I'll never be myself again," I pointed out, wrapping my arms over my chest.

"You'll come back to yourself once you learn to control your impulses," he said, looking at me with a mix of desire and disappointment. "*All* of your impulses."

He turned and hunted for his jeans, yanking them on when he located them crumpled on the floor. I stared at his fingers as he buttoned them. "I know exactly what I want."

"Of course," he said. "It's your first impulse. Was mine too, after I fed. When you first turn, your base desires are overwhelming. First you want food, then you want to fuck."

He handed me my filthy shirt. I fingered the fabric caked with dried blood. "You gave me food." I left the final part of that argument unsaid.

"A hungry vampire is a dangerous vampire. A horny vampire will get over it."

I watched him examine the remains of the t-shirt I clawed off of him. His movements were slow and considered, like he was still weighing up the pros and cons of our predicament. A flicker of regret crossed his face. "You really don't want this?" I whispered.

"Of course I want this," he said, giving up on his ruined shirt and tossing it on the bed. "But not this way. Not until I am sure."

"Sure of what?"

He walked to the door and put his hand on the doorknob as he looked back at me. "That you feel the same way. That there will be no regrets."

"I won't have any."

"Maybe I will," he said. When he turned the knob, I clutched my top to my chest and retreated into a dark corner of the room, away from the sunlight. "I'd take a stake for you, Nina."

He slipped out the door so quickly that for the briefest moment a sliver of sunlight was cast in the room.

16

I STARED at the red-tinged hue of the setting sun, creeping around the velveteen blacks that Frankie pinned up around the windows. I wished I could throw open the curtains and absorb its warmth.

I shivered and pulled the blankets tighter around me. The thing about being dead is it's pretty damn cold, the kind of cold that settles into you bones and makes them ache. And it never really goes away.

There was a light tapping on the door.

"Who is it?" I croaked. I knew it was Frankie. No one else visited me in my sick room. No one liked to be around the dying. But I still asked the question, just to be difficult.

Frankie poked his head through the door. "You up for a visitor?"

I buried my head into the pillows, not ready to face him after what had happened between us. "Maybe later."

His eyes glowed at me through the dark room. He pursed his lips. "It's later."

The door creaked open and Frankie pushed a man in the room, shoving the stranger so hard that he face-planted onto the floor.

I inched my way into a sitting position, ignoring the pain ripping down my spine. "What the hell, Frankie? You think I want an audience for this?"

"For what?" Frankie asked. "Dying?"

I wilted back into the mattress and turned my head away from him. "You'd have to stake me to kill me."

"According to your grandfather, it may take more than a stake to take you down," he said.

I turned my head towards him. "What the hell does that mean?"

"Why don't you ask him yourself?"

"Because I will sink my teeth into his fucking heart and bleed him dry."

Frankie clapped his hands together. "That's my girl! But as I mentioned before, we need the old man alive. This git..." He kicked the man, who mistakenly assumed Frankie wasn't paying attention and was crawling towards the exit. "This git is dinner."

"I'm not hungry," I lied. My eyes tracked Frankie. His behavior wasn't the least bit strained. Did I dream our near-hookup last night? If I did, it still felt very real.

"You need to eat something, Nina, or you will waste. And that is much worse than death."

I swallowed. This was the first time I'd smelled a human since starting to turn, and he smelled delicious. "Where'd you get him?"

"Does it matter?" Frankie asked.

My glare told him it did.

"Found him snooping around the alleyway," Frankie continued. "Said your mum sent him."

I sat up again. The aches from the movement stabbed at my body. "Sent him for what?"

"Go on, tell the lady," Frankie said. "What'd Leila send you for?"

"I don't know any Leila," the man said, shrinking away from me.

The way his eyes darted around the room told me he was lying. I crawled from the bed and padded toward him. Each step was agony, but I propelled myself forward, pushing through the pain. I yanked at what was left of his overlong hair on his balding head and pulled him to his feet.

"It's time to tell us why Leila sent you." I said this with a slight lisp, my sprouting fangs impeding my speech.

At the sight of them, the man trembled, his entire body quaking with fear. "Please don't, please don't make me," he said, his voice little more than a squeak. "She said if I told, I'd—" His lips kept moving but noise ceased to vibrate from his vocal chords.

"Goddammit." I shoved his head back, and the force of my push hurtled him backwards. His head slammed into the plaster wall and, with a blank expression, he crumpled to the floor, lips still moving and broken bits of plaster raining down on his head. My fangs itched. "She spelled his ass."

"Can you break it?" Frankie asked, crouching down to look into the man's eyes.

"I'm a vampire now, Frankie," I said. "I can't do shit with spells anymore."

"You don't know that," he replied, looking up at me, his expression hovering between hope and annoyance.

I climbed back onto the bed, my body weary from that small exertion. "Just leave me be."

"Not until you eat," he said, getting to his feet.

"Is that why you brought that useless cretin into my room?" I asked, crawling under my quilt.

"I thought we'd kill two birds. He tells us why Leila has him surveilling the place and then you have a little dinner."

I pulled the blanket over my head. "I'll have a bag later."

I heard Frankie's footfalls coming towards the bed. "No more bags for you."

"Why? Are we out?" I asked from under my blankets.

"Doesn't matter," he said, his voice in close proximity. "You need to feed on fresh blood. Nutrients leech out when it's been sitting."

"Like cooked vegetables?" I asked. "I think you're bullshitting me."

He pulled the quilt off of my head. "You feel like hell, right?"

I buried my face in a pillow, ignoring him.

"Like something's gnawing at your insides? Like your bones are going to shatter?"

I pulled one of the pillows over my head, still ignoring him.

"That's because you aren't getting the fuel your body needs. You need real food. Fresh blood. Not bagged."

My plan was to continue ignoring him. But what I couldn't ignore was the blistering pain that shot through my bones. I curled up in a fetal position, pillow still pressed over my head.

"Still think I'm full of shit?" Frankie asked.

I grunted from under the pillow.

Frankie's footfalls crossed the room, and I peeked out from my hiding place. He grabbed Leila's stooge by the back of his neck and dragged him across the room. Stopping beside the bed, he pushed the man on his knees then angled his head to expose his throat. "Feed."

I closed my eyes. "No," I croaked out.

"Bullocks, Nina," Frankie roared. "Why are you being so bloody difficult about this?

I raised my head and looked at him. "Because I don't think I can stop myself."

He softened his expression. "You're worried about losing control? About killing him?"

I grimaced and dropped my head back to the bed while another wave of pain overtook me. The pain was similar to the migraines, except now it extended through my entire body.

"Well that's daft," Frankie said, giving the guy a shove. "I brought him up here in case you did kill him. You lose control and we lose him? Not exactly a monumental loss for society."

"He's a human," I said, cringing at my breathless voice. "Leila's manipulating him."

"Look at him, Nina," Frankie said. "You think he even cares about that? All he knows is that some woman told him that it was cool to go on a killing rampage and he just shrugged and went along. Is that really a life worth saving?"

"We are not judges," I said, ignoring the hollow feeling gnawing at my gut. "And we are not executioners."

"No?" Frankie asked. "Shall I list our body count?"

"Our body count didn't include innocents."

"I think we've moved beyond those labels, don't you?"

My sigh shook my entire body and I pressed my fingers against my eyes. I felt the weight of Frankie's body settle beside me on the mattress. He kept his hand gripped to the back of the prisoner's neck.

"The pain you feel?" he asked, searching my face. "It's only going to get worse. And you'll snap and feed anyway. When that happens, you won't be in control, you will kill, and you will not discriminate. If you allow it, the guilt will ravage you, and I don't know how to bring you back from that."

"So what are you saying, you want this guy to be like my practice run?"

Frankie nodded. "And if you throw a spanner in the works and kill him, not really humanity's loss."

"You're both freaks," the man spat out. "And I can't wait to put a stake in the two of you."

Frankie's hand was still on the scruff of the guy's neck and he forced the man down until his stomach was flat on the floor. Frankie's boot took the place of his hand. I could feel the vibrations from the man's heart racing, and the sound of his blood flowed like waves thundering against rocks. My stomach seized from hunger, and a bit of saliva slipped from my open mouth.

"Did you hear him? He's going to stake us both," he said. With one foot pinning the guy to the ground, Frankie spread out his arms. "Who's the monster now, Nina?"

I raked my fingers through my hair. I was desperate to feed but was I willing to do it at the expense of my humanity? "How do I do this?"

Frankie smiled and pushed the man's head to the side. "Can you see the artery? It's throbbing just under the skin."

The small pulse from the artery wasn't visible to humans, but to my vampire eyes it looked like the ocean surf surging just under the skin. I licked my lips.

"Without killing him?" I added.

"One thing at a time," Frankie continued, pointing to the pulse. "You slice in with your teeth just there. And then drink."

"That's it?"

"No trick to it. Exactly what it looks like," he said.

"But how do I know when to stop?" I asked.

"The beat slows down, gets fainter. You can feel it. That's when you know he's losing too much blood."

I swallowed, unable to take my eyes off the soft flesh. "You're sure?"

"Promise."

I crawled off the bed and sat on the floor beside the man. He squirmed with fear as I inched closer to him, but Frankie held him firm.

"God, no," the man whispered, as I leaned my head in towards his neck. Hysteria set in and he attempted to rise to his feet, presumably to bolt, but he was no match for Frankie's strength. Just one hand on the neck was all Frankie needed to keep him immobile. Unable to run, the man started yelling, "You sick fucks. You sick fucks!"

The scent of fear poured off of him, sending my adrenaline into overdrive. His hysteria pressed every one of my vampire buttons, and I gripped his arms, driving my nails into his flesh. I was losing control over my hunger.

"Do it, Nina," Frankie said, his eyes vibrant. The man's fear got under Frankie's skin, too. But Frankie had several hundred years on me, so his bloodlust was tempered.

My bloodlust, however, was in full-on go mode and I sank my sharp canines into the man's doughy flesh. Blood touched the tip of my tongue on impact and my body responded immediately, the sharp aches that plagued me for hours dulled with just one swallow of the viscous stuff. I wondered what the guy had for lunch. The usual metallic taste had spicy undertones with a hint of garlic. I pulled harder with my mouth and it was like I opened a spigot. Between my pulling and his now-racing heartbeat, a steady stream of warm blood flowed out.

As my strength grew, Frankie relaxed his grip on the guy's neck. I slipped my hand under his, replacing it. The cervical vertebrae felt delicate under my firm fingers. The more the man thrashed under my grip, the faster the blood flowed, and for a brief moment, I wondered if I could swallow it fast enough. But I kept up. The nourishment coursed through my body, and my excitement rose as my strength and power built.

The thrashing ceased and the man slumped forward. His pulse began to slow and along with it the steady flow. I pulled him closer to me and sucked harder, desperate to swallow every drop of the tangy fluid.

Frankie gave my shoulder a nudge. "Nina?"

Intent of finishing my meal, I ignored him.

"Nina," he repeated, louder.

This time he got a short shake of my head and a grunt.

Frankie tugged on my arm, and I worked my mouth faster, desperate to pull out the last drops. The man shuddered, his lungs rattling as he struggled for breath. Frankie grabbed me by the forehead and pried me off. A chunk of flesh flew off the man's neck when I yanked my teeth out. He flopped to the floor.

"Whoops," I whispered. The man's lifeless eyes stared at me. His death mask expressed his sheer terror.

"That went well," Frankie said, his sardonic tone conveying the "I told you so" that he didn't utter. A twinge of guilt gnawed at me. "Did you feel the heartbeat slow?"

I turned away from the dead body. "I guess."

"You remember, that's your cue to stop. Right?"

I stretched, catlike. For the first time since Gramps stuck a knife in me, my body felt like itself. Only this time it ran on high octane. "Like you said, no great loss to humanity."

My words — and the coldness, the calculation — felt foreign even as I said them. I glanced down at the dead man. Did he have a family? A partner that would miss him? Or was he really just a vessel for hatred, anyone's hatred, not only Leila's?

I sighed. "Frankie, this runs counter to everything I believe — or believed — not even 10 minutes ago."

His voice was gentle. "You've turned, love."

"I turned, what, days ago?" I said, raising my eyes from the limp body at my feet.

"Two days," Frankie said. "But now you'll live, in a manner of speaking." He looked at my confused expression and sighed. He sat at the edge of the bed and stared at his long, elegant fingers. "I didn't think we'd be having this conversation for at least another 50 or 60 years. You died—"

"Was killed," I corrected him.

He nodded. "Right, you were killed. Vampire DNA takes over, you're brought back to life. But you need to feed or you'll waste. Blood bags will get you only so far. You need the nutrients of fresh blood."

"I got that part of it covered," I said, tapping my foot.

Frankie raised his eyebrows. "Right, impatience noted," he said, grabbing my leg to still it. "Anyway, that period of time you spent between rising from the dead and eating this git, you still had a conscience."

"Wait a second," I said. "Are you saying vampires don't have a conscience?"

"You're like a toddler again, Nina, but in an adult body. Some things you have to relearn."

"So why didn't my conscience go the minute I turned?"

"The wasting makes you weak. Almost like you're in a sort of limbo. Taking the blood from a living human bolsters your strength, but your humanity wanes."

"And now?" I asked.

"You'll never question eating again."

I opened my mouth to tell him off but a familiar rise of power churned through my body, my hair lifting slightly as small electric volts jumped around my skin. I touched my tattoo, the snake's rattle beginning to stir.

Frankie dropped the flippant attitude. "Looks like you needed the vampire healthy for the witch to emerge."

"You think I can spell?" I asked, my voice barely above a whisper.

The magic coursed through my body, and my heightened vampire senses felt it blazing through my blood like fire.

"Try it," Frankie suggested. "Try to spell."

I hesitated. Before Leila, I'd never heard of vampire magic and witch magic sharing the same body. But the snake tattoo said both were living inside of me. Ironic that both forces of magic lived while my body was technically dead.

My magic was always strongest when it was tied to the elements, and I wanted to channel my focus outside of the window, no small task since I couldn't draw back the shades because of the sunlight. I scrunched up my face, staring at a bit of yellow sun peeking in from behind the heavy black curtains. Focused on the light, I conjured a quick spell and watched as the darkness encroached on the sun. I didn't dare release my focus until the room went completely black. Then, with a snap of my fingers, the fragment of sunlight came back again.

Frankie's eyes darted from the shimmer of sunlight on the floor back to my face. "Did you just conjure an eclipse?"

"I think so," I said, listening as yells of surprise carried up from the kitchen. "So I can still—"

"Be witchy? That's pretty amazing," Frankie said, reaching for my hands, which were shaking. "Do you realize what this means?"

My elation leaked out of me as I considered what this meant. "It's means I'm dangerous."

"You were always dangerous, Nina. Especially with that wild magic shooting all over god's green earth," Frankie said with a chuckle before sobering. "But this does mean that you have to keep a measure of control."

I nodded and twisted my fingers around his hand. Without a conscience, I'd have a hard enough time keeping control of my vampire abilities, never mind my magic. "Frankie," I said, hesitation danced along the edge of my voice. "You have a conscience. How did you end up with it?"

"Like I said, there are things you have to relearn, including empathy and all the other things that go with having a conscience.

Vampirism alters your brain functions, we can all agree with that, yes?" I nodded. "So welcome to the one percent, Nina. You are now officially a sociopath."

I scowled. "Do you think my grandfather knew this?"

"Of course he knew," Frankie said. "And he probably thinks it easier to be a bit mad for what we need to do."

17

I KILLED the engine about a half a mile from the Massachusetts border — and the headlights a mile before that — so we rolled through the dark suburban streets as stealthily as possible. I dropped my feet and dragged them on the pavement until we came to a complete stop in between a raised ranch and a recently renovated cape. Just like the rest of the neighborhood, both homes were dark. Judging from the kid's Schwinn bikes and Razor scooters haphazardly strewn in the driveways, like lumps of forgotten detritus, the entire community bailed in a hurry.

Darcy dismounted, pulled off her helmet and rubbed her lower back. She hated riding. Casper flew, literally, beside us the entire way. The spring air still held onto the biting edge of winter, giving his ghost-pale cheeks a bit of a flush, although it could have been from his mounting excitement. He was about to haunt a few unsuspecting guards stationed at the border.

Casper decided we needed a girl's night out, so to speak. He was the only one enthusiastic about it.

A night on the town wasn't an easy prospect. There were no safe places in Rhode Island where we could let our hair down and relax, so Casper suggested skipping over the state line into Massachusetts. Easier said than done.

True to her word, Mary Jane had secured with state boarders with a razor wire fence. MPs walked between checkpoints to make sure no one scaled or cut through the barrier.

"So are we doing this?" Darcy asked, pacing in the shadows cast by the streetlights. "Or do you want to go back?" She sounded hopeful at that last part.

Darcy spent a better part of an hour whining about leaving Matty for the night, but Casper convinced her that a night off would do us all a world of good. The way she kept eyeing me as we went over the plan to get around the guard post made me suspect her apprehension about leaving Matty had more to do with my newly formed vampiric nature than with my spoiled cousin. She was afraid I'd eat her.

Not that it wasn't a rational fear. Frankie spent the better part of the day teaching me how to control my cravings. But anyone who's ever tried to kick sugar or caffeine knows controlling cravings is no easy feat. Like being on a diet, the trick was never to let yourself get gnaw-your-arm-off hungry. Also like being on a diet, there was always the danger of "emotional eating." In the case of the vampire, "emotional eating" was a 'roided up version of "hangry." Controlling the urge while on a full-on vamp out took epic will power. The older the vampire, the easier it was to control the urges. I was a newbie, and thus a blood-sucking time bomb.

"Remember, I'll give the signal once I get them far enough away," he said, floating above us.

"You're really going to yell 'Geronimo'?" I asked. Casper had recently discovered old Hollywood westerns.

"When will I ever have the opportunity to yell that again?" he asked. He was practically glowing.

"Let's just do this," Darcy said through her clenched jaw.

"It'll be fun, you'll see," I said, my own teeth gritted into a bad facsimile of a smile while I watched Casper float towards the heavily armed guards. I didn't see any stakes in their arsenal.

Darcy yanked her helmet back on her head and climbed behind

me, ready for Casper's signal. I had my heel set for a fast kick-start as soon as he shrieked the magic word.

"This is so stupid," Darcy said, her voice muffled by the helmet.

"We can't exactly do this in Rhode Island. What choice do we have?"

"We have a choice not to do this at all, in any state," she said. "I mean, girls night out? Now? While the Department of Defense has missiles pointed directly at us?"

"That was exactly what I thought when Casper suggested this. But he insists we need to get out of dodge for a few hours. And maybe he's right," I added. "It's not like they're going to blow us up tomorrow. We have a few days."

"This is suicide," she continued, this time pointing at the guard tower. "Well, not for you. Or Casper. You're both already dead. But I'm not."

"They start shooting, you start wailing," I said, squeezing my hands against the handlebars so hard they threatened to crack.

"I'd rather not," she replied. I twisted to get a look at her face, but all I saw was the bug shape that the helmet made out of her head. "I don't like killing innocent people."

"Innocent isn't the word I'd use," I said, pushing the lesson that Frankie taught me earlier in the day out of my mind.

We watched the guards shine their flashlights into a cluster of pine trees. Casper was rustling the branches.

"People are scared," Darcy said, breaking the uncomfortable silence. "What do you do when it turns out that the monster under the bed is real?"

"You don't blindly follow a psychopath."

Darcy shifted her weight so I had to put my right foot on the pavement to keep the bike balanced. My eyes tracked the guards' movements. Their lights now moved up and down the fence behind them.

"No?" she asked. "Leila promised to protect them from people like—"

"Like me?" I finished for her.

"Like us," Darcy said. "I'm a monster too." I loosened my grip on the throttle. "And I'm not saying that they're right. I'm saying what they did is understandable."

"And if they just got to know us, they wouldn't be afraid of us? They'd love us for who we are?"

"Something like that," she said.

"You were always a glass half-full kind of girl."

I heard a hard sigh and she rested her hands lightly on my waist. She probably fogged up the helmet. "No, I just refuse to believe that people are inherently bad."

"Which is why you don't want to kill them."

"And that's wrong how?"

"They'd stake me in a heartbeat. Frankie, too. Matty..." I said, raising my voice. The guards looked sharp in our direction, but Casper pulled their focus again.

"Matty's harmless."

"Most spiders are harmless. You see what people do to those," I challenged.

She stayed quiet.

"Look, Darce, I get it. And I love that you have so much optimism, particularly about humankind. But they burned Babe at a goddamn stake, right in front of me. And what they were doing in Steele City," I said, with a shudder. "I can't share your same faith in humanity."

"They were under Leila's spell—" she started but Casper's cry of "Geronimo" echoed down the desolate suburban street, cutting her off.

I twisted the throttle twice and dropped my foot on the starter. The bike rumbled to life. I pressed the clutch, kicked it into gear. The back wheel screamed against the pavement, spinning. Darcy grabbed my waist as the bike lurched forward and we raced towards the abandoned checkpoint.

I took a second to appreciate the purr of the Triumph's motor vibrating through me. The Bonneville was customized by Frankie. Black-on-black, low to the ground and stripped of all unessential hardware, the bike was built for stealth. I loved it.

"Shit!" I yelled, adrenaline pumping hard as the engine revved.

There was a third guard, one we didn't notice, in the makeshift guard hut. The sound of the bike's loud pipes dragged him out of the glorified shed, waving his Colt CAR-15 carbine.

Then, he started shooting.

He was clearly new and not well trained, which made him almost more dangerous. A spray of bullets flew towards us, pinging against the metal frame of my bike and bouncing off the asphalt. Darcy squeezed my midsection tighter and buried her helmet into my back. A feeling of déjà vu ripped through me. I'd taken this ride before, but it was Mia on the back of my bike. That didn't end so well.

I doubled down and accelerated, aiming straight for him.

"What are you doing?!" Between the noise of the bike and the rat-a-tat-tat explosions coming from the gun, Darcy's yell sounded more like a whimper.

I shook my head and squeezed my thighs tight against the gas tank as the speedometer rose. I wasn't losing Darcy. No way.

I aimed the bike right for the guard, playing the ultimate game of chicken. Motorcycle vs. automatic weapon. Even as the distance between us closed rapidly, I felt like I was moving in slow motion. I was close enough to watch his face fall from determined to confused. The "oh shit" expression happened when I was close enough to see the whites of his eyes.

"Oh my goddess, you're going to hit him!" Darcy screamed.

"Hang on!" was my response. It was more for me than for Darcy, but she did as she was told and tightened her arms around my waist. I dropped my head and braced myself, ready to absorb the impact of the bike smashing into his body.

At the last minute, the rent-a-cop jumped out of the path of my bike, rolling into the manicured shrubbery in front of an abandoned faux-Victorian home.

Darcy and I sped over the state line. A cowboy "yeee haaaaw" made me spare a glance over my shoulder, and I saw Casper chasing behind us. He took this cowboy thing seriously.

I slowed the bike, giving him a chance to catch up. We moved at a steady pace through the new development. Cookie cutter homes set back from the street by a large expanse of lawn. Unease swept over me again. Suburbia creeped me out.

After about a half a mile of well-appointed curb appeal, I turned onto the main drag and eased into traffic, the first we'd seen for at least 30 minutes. Casper moved along the curb, dodging streetlights. He wasn't invisible but he was ethereal enough that he could appear as a trick of someone's imagination.

We traveled for about 15 minutes. The neighborhoods of expensive new developments gave way to older communities whose homes looked a little rough around the edges. Once we passed a housing authority apartment block, a small strip mall came into view. A hand-painted sign, "MOOSE CABIN," was illuminated by spotlights. A Budweiser neon sign blinked through a narrow window. I pulled into the lot and parked my bike in between a rusty pickup truck and a dented minivan.

Girls' night out had officially begun.

18

"SEE? ISN'T THIS FUN?!" Casper yelled over "Bad to the Bone," which was blaring from the jukebox.

I expected Moose Cabin to be a crappy dive bar, but it turned out to be a little too "sports bar" for my taste. We managed to commandeer a table in the corner, away from the multicolored lights of the soundless TVs and Keno screens.

While Casper looked three-dimensional enough to pass for human, he was as ethereal as air. So while I was busy rising from the dead, Casper had practiced sitting on solid objects. By the end of the few days it took me to turn, he was adept at keeping himself from falling through chairs. He beamed when he took his seat. Small victories.

What he didn't learn to do was pick up a drink. Still, even if he had been able to lift the glass to his mouth, he couldn't ingest the drink. Instead, it would puddle on the floor. So he ordered a Sidecar, and, once Darcy set it in front of him, he stared at it. Darcy had a gin and tonic. Kentucky Bourbon was my jam.

"So how about those border guards," Darcy said with a giggle. The adrenaline from the trip gave her pale cheeks a flush. She raised her glass. "Cheers."

I nodded at her. Since Casper couldn't lift his glass, I didn't want him to feel left out of a toast. "And to Casper, for doing some seriously good spooking."

The ghost beamed at the praise.

"Take a sip of mine," Casper said, nodding at his drink. "Tell me if it's good."

"Nope," Darcy said with a slight shudder. "Cognac is nasty."

I made a face. "I have to agree with Darcy on that."

While Casper complained about our lack of supportiveness for his predicament, my nose twitched. I sniffed the air. The pungent smell of wet dog hit my nose. Casper continued his treatise while my eyes swept the joint.

Maybe the Salem Witch Trials had taught them a thing or two, but Massachusetts didn't seem too concerned about the supernatural entities just on the other side of their gates. Maybe they believed the lie the federal government fed them. But based on the rowdy group of werewolves downing beers at the bar, this state had their own supernats living amongst them, and out in the open. So why wasn't this state in the throws of the apocalypse? I brought up the question with my besties.

"You think we'll have a problem with them?" Darcy asked.

"Between the three of us?" Casper said with a snort. "Girl, please. We can take them."

"That's not the point," I whispered. "I wonder why Massachusetts isn't freaking out and burning their population at the stake."

"Maybe they don't know?" Casper suggested.

"Razor wire and border guards just to cross over for a coffee milk? You think they're buying the official government line of dosed drinking water?"

Casper considered it. "I'd crawl through razor wire for that." I shot him a dirty look. "What? That shit's delicious."

I sipped my bourbon. "Point missed, again."

"Maybe we should ask," Darcy said. She lifted her chin towards the group of werewolves.

"You don't think that's asking for a fight?"

"Well, Casper's right, we can take them," she said. "Now that you're dead—" She watched my face fall and laid a gentle hand on my arm. "Sorry, honey, but you are, there's no sugarcoating that one. Anyway, now that you're dead, I can take them all out with one wail, and I don't have to worry about *that* killing you."

"You can wail on command?" Casper asked, eyes wide. "Amazing."

"She cannot wail on command," I said. "Can you?"

"Maybe? I've been working on it," she said. "But if one of them hits me hard enough, I'll definitely wail."

"Listen to us," I said. "We sound ridiculous."

"This is supposed to be our down time, our night out," Casper said. "No talking about work." An awkward silence spread amongst us. Chatty Casper broke it. "So what's the deal with you and Frankie?"

Even. More. Awkward.

I crossed my arms and stared at my drink. "That's none of your business."

"Come on," Casper coaxed. "You have to tell us."

"She doesn't have to," Darcy corrected him before she turned to me. "Really you don't have to. But if you *want* to, we're all ears."

I slumped down in my chair. "There's nothing to tell, really."

"That's a lie!" Casper got so excited he slipped through his seat. He righted himself before anyone noticed. "Frankie came out of that room shirtless and sulky. And he's pretty easy on the eyes without the shirt."

"It's no secret the guy is crazy about you," Darcy added, dunking the lime slice in her drink with her swizzle stick. "Did you at least let him down easy?"

I slumped further into my chair, as if I could become part of the furniture. "I don't want to talk about this."

Casper pursed his lips. "Did *he* turn *you* down?" His posture stiffened. "Oh my god, he turned you down!"

Darcy spit her drink back into the glass. "What?"

"You made a play for Frankie and he... Did he? No!" Casper was buoyant from excitement.

"Sit down, you're hovering. Like literally," I said, my voice low, eyes darting around the bar. Everyone's eyes were on the screens.

"This is so exciting!" he squealed.

I glared at him. "What's so exciting about that scenario?"

He rolled his eyes. "It's romantic. He wanted to wait until you were...well, more yourself."

"I don't know how to be more myself," I said. I sipped my drink, the bourbon burning a warm path down my throat.

"You're still you," Darcy said. "Just without a pulse."

"And a taste for blood," Casper added.

"She always had that," Darcy said, flipping her platinum tresses over her shoulder. "Ultra rare steaks and burgers that were pretty bloody. Now she's just off of the solids."

I let out a massive sigh, thinking about how I'd never eat a burger again. "But I liked the solids. A lot."

"I can't eat solids either," Casper said, giving me conspiratorial sad face. "I miss my mother's carne asada."

I snarled. "So we should start our own 12-step program?"

"Okay, what's with you?" Darcy asked. "You're like PMS on steroids."

"What do you think it is?" I said, my edginess evident in my voice. "I'm a goddamn vampire."

"You were always a vampire," Darcy pointed out.

"No, I was never dead. So technically not a vampire."

"You gotta make your peace with that," Casper said. "That shit will tear you up inside."

"What do you know about it?"

"Hellooooo! Ghost. I had to learn to live with that," Casper said.

One of my newly formed fangs pressed into my lower lip while I took in his astute point. I always knew that someday I'd go full-on Dracula. But what 18-year-old kid thinks he's going to spend the rest of eternity Swayzed out?

Casper puffed his chest out with pride. "And look at me now."

"And every bit as handsome," Darcy said. She raised her glass and winked at him.

Casper blushed. "So back to Frankie."

I shrugged. "Maybe he's just not that into me."

"Frankie not that into you?" Darcy snorted. "That's not even possible."

"Maybe he was into me before the turn, but after? Dead people are not that appealing."

Casper yelled "hey" while Darcy cleared her throat. "In case you didn't notice, I find a vampire hot."

"But that's different," I said.

"You're prejudiced!" Casper said. He clapped his hands together — or rather tried to.

"I am not."

Darcy sipped her gin and tonic through the tiny straw. "Honey, you are going to have to come to terms with this predicament."

"Seriously, no one likes self-loathing. Unless you're going to go all out gothic vamp, maybe then you can get away with that," Casper said.

The image of a gothed-out me hit us all at the same time and we burst out laughing. Between being in a state that wasn't gunning for supernatural creatures, the Kentucky bourbon and time with my two best friends, the stiffness in my body waned. For the first time in days, I relaxed.

Darcy studied the change in my posture. "So. You ready to dish now?"

I looked back and forth between them. Both of them had bright eyes, like kids anxious for a bedtime story. "Yes, we almost hooked up. And yes, he stopped it before anything serious happened."

"By serious, you mean...?" Casper prodded.

"Exactly," I said with a nod.

Darcy released the breath that she held. "Wow. I cannot believe you and Frankie almost. And that he didn't!"

I tapped my pinky nail against my glass. "What do you think it means?" I asked. Relief flooded into me as I unburdened myself to Casper and Darcy. My self-esteem had taken a serious hit when Frankie turned me down.

"He respects you," she said. "Definitely."

Casper nodded his agreement. "He wants to make sure you're ready. That it's not your vampire talking."

Darcy sat back in her chair, a big smile spreading across her face. "He loves you."

"Hang on a sec," I said. "Let's not get ahead of ourselves. I mean, we haven't even had a date."

Casper's face lit up. "That's a fabulous idea!"

I rolled my eyes. "How the hell can anyone go on a date? Things being the way they are."

"Leave it to me," Casper said. "I'll figure something out."

"Maybe you guys can cross the border," Darcy suggested. She glanced around the bar. "This place isn't half-bad."

"I'm not sure I'm completely comfortable with the element," I said, jerking my head towards the guys at the bar. A few drinks in and the tension in the place ratcheted up a notch.

"The werewolves?" Casper asked.

"Yup," I said, trying not to stare at them. Whatever happened in that bar was not my problem. Unless they had a territorial beef with us, which they shouldn't. With Blood Ops in disarray, the country's supernatural problems were no longer mine. No matter what Mary Jane thought.

Darcy lowered her voice. "Why do you think they're out in the open?"

"Maybe they're passing for human," I said. Werewolves, like witches, blended easily into the human community. Werewolves were the outdoorsy types, the ones that loved camping, hiking and lake swimming. You generally didn't find them in urban areas.

Darkness spread over Casper's face. "Maybe Massholes don't have a problem their supernatural folks."

"When you think about tourism dollars," I said, "Salem is a cash cow. Could be like New Orleans."

The supernatural was such a financial boon to New Orleans that they protected them like humans, preferring to deal with their rogue elements in their own way. It was the one city where Blood Ops was forbidden to operate.

"We ever get a call in Mass?" Darcy asked. The way her face was screwed up told me that she was doing a mental rundown of the various states we had been deployed over the years.

"I think once, we were sent to Springfield, maybe?" I said. "Basketball Hall of Fame?"

Darcy snickered. "Haunted basketballs."

Casper looked between us. "Basketballs cannot be haunted."

"Nothing was haunted," I said. "Turned out to be a prank."

"Then we were never called into the state for an authentic supernatural incident."

"Still, surprised we didn't know Mass was off-limits," I said. Casper's annoyed expression told me that he felt left out from our Blood Ops shorthand. I explained. "It wasn't a secret that we were not allowed to operate in New Orleans. In fact, it was drilled into us that if we harmed any supernatural being within city limits, we would be charged as if we harmed a human."

Darcy sipped her drink. "But worse. There was a hidden law in the books that said that the voodoo clans would dispense their own justice."

"So maybe it's the same here," Casper said, slipping in his seat again. "Should we mull a move to Mass?"

"Damn," Darcy whispered, glancing towards the bar. "I think they noticed that." She nodded at Casper, who was righting himself.

"What makes you say that?" I asked.

"I don't know," she quipped. "Maybe because they're staring?"

The werewolves' rowdy conversation also ceased. The other conversations around us hummed along until they also realized that the loud mouths were quiet.

My fingernails tapped out a rhythm against my glass of bourbon. I heard the men slam their pint glasses against the wood of the bar, then footfalls made their way over. Their hulking presence loomed above us before they uttered a word.

"You three lost?" one asked. He looked like a former high school line-backer who stopped his daily exercise 10 years ago but hadn't adjusted his snacking habits. He ran his hand through his overgrown sandy hair and then across his scruffy beard while he waited for our answer.

"Just came in for a drink," Darcy said, shooting all of them a 1000-watt smile. In addition to being deadly, banshees were sexy as hell. Think about that combination.

The tall skinny one with pockmarked cheeks sniffed the air. "You're welcome here," he said, leering in Darcy's direction. "You two, however..." His lips lifted in a snarl as his eyes skimmed over me and Casper.

"Not natural," the one with slick backed, silver hair muttered. He nodded at Casper. "You're definitely not natural."

My fangs itched and my stomach growled, and I wondered what werewolf tasted like. Darcy kicked me under the table. My attention refocused from snacking on the werewolves to diffusing the situation.

"Like my friend said," I said, talking around my fangs, "we're just stopping in for a quiet drink. Not interested in anything else tonight."

Former football player sniffed the air over me. "Bloodsucker?"

"Now that's just rude," Casper said, his peevish expression matching his voice.

"Agreed," the silver-haired one said. "That was rude. You apologize."

The beefy guy muttered a half-assed "I'm sorry," which elicited a rough shove from the elder werewolf, who I assumed was the alpha. The alpha dropped into the empty seat at our table. "Just trying to look out for our own. You can appreciate that."

I gave him a short nod. "I can."

"So, considering that, what are you doing over the border?"

"Just needed a place to relax," I said, not an untruth. "We want no trouble."

He cocked his head. "They don't have bars where you're from?"

I shook my head. "Not when there's a curfew in effect."

"Ah, Rhode Island," he said. "How's the state detox program

going?" He barked out a laugh. They knew the cover story was bullshit.

Darcy glanced around, her patience out. "Why aren't you guys running for the hills?"

"Keep to ourselves. No need to run."

"The state just lets you guys be?" she asked, her tone hinting at her disbelief.

He shrugged. "We all work together."

"Meaning?"

"The vampires compel the humans when necessary, the werewolves are security, the witches lay down protection for all of us."

Casper looked impressed. "Y'all work together like that?"

"Always," the man said. "Have to. If we didn't, we'd be like Rhode Island." That made him guffaw.

He slid a business card across the table to me. The name on it was Lincoln Davis, and it included a cellphone number. "Next time you come into town, we'd like to know about it before you cross the border. Just a consideration."

"You guys are like your own little supernatural vigilante group," I said. "How cute."

He grinned, and I caught sight of his sharp canine teeth. He was definitely the alpha. "Now Ms....?"

"Martinez," I offered.

He cocked an eyebrow. "Martinez?" he asked.

I nodded.

"You wouldn't happen to have had a run in with a pack in Connecticut a few months back?"

Darcy and Casper both exchanged glances before leveling their stares at me. I took a breath, mostly out of habit since I didn't technically breathe anymore. Honesty was probably the best policy with this guy.

But I kept it short and sweet. "Yes."

"Hm," he said. He leaned back in his chair and took a long pull on his bottle of Bud, his eyes never leaving my own. "That's my cousin's crew."

I nodded, sipped at my own drink, and kept my mouth shut.

"He's a real son-a-bitch. Asked us to come down and help control the vampire population." He gave that a little snort. "Seems you had an infestation."

"Beta-Vamps," I said. "Harmless creatures, just want to be left to themselves."

"I told him that," he said, chuckling. "Then you handed him his ass."

"Well, I wouldn't quite characterize it as that," I said. "He got in bed with the wrong lady, is all."

Leila had his cousin by the balls. She spelled his little girl to turn wolf before she went through puberty. Turning into a werewolf is bone-breaking work, literally. A small child can't handle that sort of trauma. Leila essentially held this little girl hostage so that the pack would feed the Beta-Vamps a bad blood supply, effectively decimating the vampire population using the undead equivalent of HIV.

"Your mother," he said. My poker face melted away, revealing my surprise. "Yup, I know that women running the show over there is your mother."

"She gave birth to me, but she's not my mother," I said, swallowing the remainder of my drink. The burn of the liquor took away the sting of the word mother.

"Fair enough," he said. "And I agree, he did get in bed with the wrong lady. Should've got into bed with you."

I ignored the wolfish grins coming from his pack members. "You talk to your cousin lately?"

"Nope," he said. "We don't get along that great. He's still pissed I wasn't willing to help him out with your ma's diabolical plan. Why would I?"

"Indeed," Darcy chimed in. "Sounds like you have a good thing going here. Why complicate that?"

"It'd only call attention, right?" I added.

He nodded. "I like the way you ladies think." He glanced over at Casper again. "But I still can't figure out what the hell you are."

"I like being mysterious," Casper said, casting his sad eyes at his untouched drink. Knocking it back would have added a touch of drama.

"Ain't that the truth," Darcy mumbled.

"So," I said a little too loud. His pair of lackeys turned their heads towards us to make sure we were still behaving. I needed Lincoln's undivided attention. "Has your cousin's pack gone missing?"

Lincoln narrowed his eyes. "What do you mean 'missing'?"

Darcy kicked me under the table again. I ignored her.

"Exactly that," I said. I pointed to the cellphone case attached to his belt buckle. "You may want to call his wife, assuming they didn't snatch her up, too."

Lincoln pushed himself up from the table, glaring at me while he pulled out his phone. He crossed the room in three long strides, phone in one ear, finger in the other.

"What are you doing?" Darcy hissed. "You're going to piss them off."

"They have an air of simmering anger," Casper agreed. "What if this boils it?"

I rolled my eyes. "A risk we've got to take. If we want to liberate the supernats from Steele City — wolves included — it couldn't hurt to have a pack on our side."

"Okay, but let's reverse the roles for a second," Darcy said. "Would they help us?'

"Normally? No," I said.

"Why not?" Casper asked.

"Wolves are pack animals," I explained. "They keep to themselves, lived in remote areas, and keep as much of their business as they can within their pack. They would never liberate any non-werewolf caught up in any penal system, fair or otherwise. They look out for their own."

"So why are we even talking to them?" Darcy asked.

"That behavior may have saved them in the past, but now it's a huge liability for the entire supernatural community to close ranks. The fact that this alpha found a way to work with witches, vampires and whomever else tells me that he recognizes this. This guy's asshole cousin not withstanding, he's someone I want on our side."

"Fair enough," said Darcy. "Just tread carefully please."

While we waited for Lincoln to return, Casper and Darcy continued to press me for details on the Frankie incident. Their questions were met with one-word answers and I squirmed in my seat even giving those. By the time he got back, I wished I could ghost out like Casper.

"You nailed it, lady," he said, settling back down into his seat, a new bottle of Bud in hand. "Cousin's gone missing, plus a bunch from his crew. You got any idea where his ass is holed up?"

I prepared to explain the situation at Steele City when Lincoln pushed his chair back and leapt to his feet. "Charlie!"

Lincoln sprinted across to the room to his two fellow pack members. The chubby one, Charlie, took a knife in the gut, the silver hilt still stuck in his torso as the blood spread across his flannel shirt. The alpha and the pockmarked one were surrounded by four humans who held various silver-coated weapons. I assumed the sawed-off shotgun that one guy pulled from under his duster was loaded with silver shells.

"Crap," I muttered. So much for a night off. I nodded at Casper to get behind Darcy, silently wishing he was still invisible. Then I got to my feet and shielded both of them.

"Boys, you are in the wrong state for this shit," Lincoln growled. I took a second to marvel at the control he had over his body. His nails grew out razor sharp, and his canine teeth gleamed in the bar neon. It wasn't a full moon, so an all out turn wasn't in the cards, but I was impressed that he controlled his deadliest parts.

"You're harboring fugitives from our state," one of the men responded, jerking his head in our direction. "We just came to take what's ours."

"By stabbing one of my boys?" Lincoln asked. He flexed his fingers, itching to lash out.

"You were awfully hospitable to them," one of the lackeys said. He spit on the floor for good measure.

"Kurt!" Charlie cried out, leaving a bloody handprint on the pock-marked werewolf's shoulder. "It burns. It burns, man!" The smell of charred flesh seared my nose. The knife was doused in holy water.

"So who's next?" the one with the shotgun asked. A grin spread across his face. He leveled the gun at me. "Whatcha gonna do about it, witch?"

This time, it was my turn to smile. No one knew I was no longer living, so they didn't bother bringing a stake to the party. I looked at Lincoln. At his nod, we both dove into action.

I went after the one with the gun first. My teeth sank into his flesh and blood rushed into my mouth, overwhelming me briefly before I found my rhythm. Warm and salty, the blood didn't sate my hunger. To the contrary, it made me crave more. I drew on his neck harder, draining the life out of him as I reached the 10-pint mark in seconds. I tossed the limp body aside and moved to the next man, who was now scrambling to get away from me and Lincoln, whose claws were in the man who knifed Charlie. Lincoln ripped out an internal organ.

I took a second to appreciate skinny Kurt, who was knocking some serious sense into guy number three. With Kurt fighting like a professional bantamweight, I turned to my attention to the fourth guy, who brandished a straight edge blade. Before I could lunge for him, he snatched Darcy and held it to her throat.

"Don't come any closer!" he shouted. The tremble in his voice betrayed his fear. I wiped the blood off my mouth with the back of my hand and stalked around him.

"I can see your blood moving under your skin," I said, licking my lips.

He pressed the blade to her throat. "I mean it, I'll cut her. You come any closer."

Casper slipped behind me like a wisp. "Nina, he'll kill Darcy."

I stopped and blinked a few times, staring at Darcy's panicked face. All she needed to do was wail to end this. But with living were-wolves in the room, she wouldn't risk it. I forced myself to ignore my hunger. The man relaxed his grip on the blade. I tamped my hunger down, which was not easy. And now we were in a pickle.

"Tell your friend to stop, too" he ordered. I nodded at Kurt, who let the guy he was fighting sink to the floor.

But instead of relaxing, he pressed the blade back into Darcy's neck. "The other one, too," he said, panic rising in his voice.

A quick glance behind me told me that Lincoln was stalking toward the man like he was prey.

"Lincoln," I said, shocked at how normal I sounded, "let this guy be."

"You kidding me?" he asked, his voice throaty and canine.

Leila's henchman yanked Darcy toward the door. "You're letting us walk out of here." He pointed the blade at me before turning it back on Darcy. "And you're coming with us. No funny stuff or your friend here..." He grinned.

Right. There was no way I was letting them go. Leila had no idea I turned. The element of surprise was on my side. Or it was. Until I ate one of her guys. And I didn't want these fools tattling.

Darcy cleared her throat. "Let's go, Nina," she said. "Now." Her long eyelashes fluttered as she blinked in quick succession. A single tear slipped down her cheek. Oh. Shit. She was going for it.

"Yup, right now," I said.

"But—" Lincoln started.

"It was great to meet you," I said, snatching my leather jacket off the back of the chair. "I'll be in touch."

"You'll be in prison," he said. He glared at the guy holding Darcy hostage.

I winked at him. "You'll be my one phone call."

"Just be sure to turn up the music after we go," Darcy said, leveling a serious look at Lincoln. "Real loud, okay?"

The thug with the blade to Darcy's throat dragged her to the door. I raised my hands in mock surrender as Kurt's victim, his face bloody and eyes puffing up, got to his feet. He gave me a weak shove and then, still unsteady from the beatdown, held onto me for balance. I practically carried him out the door.

A dark blue van was parked just outside. Darcy was shoved in the back, and I followed behind her.

The guys jumped in the front seats and slammed their doors. While they were high fiving each other for a job more or less well done, "Sweet Home Alabama" cranked up on the bar's sound system. Darcy's sniffles turned into a sob.

"Goddammit," one of them swore. "Are we going have to listen to her boo-hoo all the way back to Providence?"

"Knock her ass out," the other one said.

Just as he turned to do exactly that, Darcy burst into her wail. I pressed my fingers into my ears while her high-pitched sobs threatened to shatter my eardrums.

Since there was always a threat of death, I'd never heard Darcy wail before. The cry was more musical than I imagined, almost beautiful in a haunting way. Regardless of her melodic harmonies, the ear-piercing shrieks were deadly.

The two men moved in slow motion as the dire circumstances of their situation dawned on them. One tried to dial up assistance on his cellphone, a perilous mistake for whoever was on the receiving end of the call. Both men's eyes widened and blood oozed out of their ears, dripping onto their shoulders. Their own cries of agony were no match for Darcy's lethal ones.

When their twitching stopped, Darcy shut her scream off, just like cutting out the radio. She looked up at me, her mascara formed raccoon circles under her eyes, which she wiped at with the back of her hand.

"Well done," I said, surveying the dead bodies slumped the front seats. The sudden quiet felt strange.

She sniffled. "Thanks. Not bad for the first time on command."

"You've been working on it?"

She nodded. "With Matty."

"That practice paid off."

Casper floated through the closed door of the bar. If the werewolves didn't figure out he was a ghost before, they did now.

I pushed the van door open and climbed out. "How's Charlie?"

Casper peered into the front seat. "Doing better than these two meatheads."

"That's a relief," Darcy said, jumping on to the pavement.

"So we like werewolves now?" Casper asked. I crossed my arms and shot him my best disappointed-in-you look. "What? It's hard to keep track!"

"Lincoln's a good man," I said. "And it's all about the alpha."

"Ain't that the truth," Darcy said.

Lincoln barreled through the door and stopped abruptly when he saw the three of us outside of the van. He looked into the front and gave a low whistle. "I heard y'all were good," he said. "But this is some next level shit."

"You guys have a way of disappearing bodies?" I asked. He nodded. "You comfortable with me owing you one?"

"We might be able to work something out," he said, crossing his arms. "How about you explain what happened to my kin?"

"She's got them all."

"What do you mean, got them?" he asked.

While I explained what we saw in the prison, his anger rose. His pupils dilated and his eye color changed from brown to yellow. I told him about the experiments, the way she was attempting to separate the wolf from the human, and a low growl shook his entire body.

"You going in to get your people out?" he asked, after I explained that she was doing the same to the witches, and Dr. O.

"I'm planning on getting all of them out," I said. "Witches, wolves and my boss."

"You call on us when you're ready," he said. "And all the better if it can happen on the full moon."

My hand was dwarfed by his enormous one when we shook on it. Energy flowed from his palm into mine, driving its way into my body. The strength of it bolstered my confidence. Werewolves storming the barricades with us? Leila wouldn't know what hit her.

19

"YOU MADE A DEAL WITH WEREWOLVES?"

Someone wasn't exactly thrilled about our girls-and-ghost night out.

"And somehow that's worse than *killing me*?" I asked Gramps, grinding my teeth together to keep from biting him. "You killed me. You. Killed. Me. That's *so* not okay."

"Had to, I told you," he said, running a hand through his silver hair.

"I still don't get it," Darcy chimed in.

"Let me make it simple for you," Gramps said, shaking his head. "The witch and the bloodsucker were at war in her body. Once she learned dark magic, and to control it, it was a death sentence. Rather than make her suffer through it, I did the humane thing..."

"And shoved a knife into my throat," I said with an involuntary shudder. "Between you and Leila, Christmas is gonna be a blast this year." Busy in the kitchen creating some sort of potion, he ignored me, so I continued. "You could have at least warned me. Or let me make up my own damn mind on how to deal with it."

He slammed his knife down on the butcher block. The herbs he was chopping flew up and spread all over the counter and the floor.

"What would you have done? Die an unspeakable death? What was happening to you was akin to the worst kind of cancer, that kind that kills you slow and painful like. I put you out of your misery. Quick and easy."

"You call getting your throat cut and bleeding out quick and easy?"

He turned back to his herbs. "What's done is done."

"Well, he's right about that," Darcy said around a yawn. Now that she was keeping Matty's hours, it was getting close to her bedtime. "What's done is done. You're a vampire now."

"And a witch," Gramps added.

I crossed my arms and glared. "Like I want to throw another spell after all this?"

"You have no choice," he said. "You want to beat Leila, you have to work both your magic and your...you know. The other part."

The urge to kill that rooted in my belly as soon as I became a full-fledged member of the bloodsucker team spread through my body as my anger rose. I stared at my grandfather's skin, watching the blood move in near-microscopic waves through it. "Vampire," I said, digging my nails into my arms to keep from vamping out. "You turned me, so you say it. Vampire. V-A-M-P-I-R-E."

Frankie stormed into the kitchen from the backdoor, dragging a skinny dude by the neck. Before he slammed the door, I caught sight of the red-yellow glow of dawn growing along the skyline.

"Found this skulking around the trash bins," he said, tossing him into the living room. The man slammed against the wall and then sunk to the floor, his expression of fear mixed with defiance.

"I know what you are," the stranger said. "I can see past whatever it is you're pretending to be. I know that your bar's not burned. I see it. I can see."

"How's that possible?" Darcy asked Gramps, her voice on edge. "This building was supposed to be spelled. Is it wearing off?"

"Pfftt, wearing off," Gramps said. "Of course it's not wearing off." He turned towards the skinny man, who cowered at Gramps' death stare. "Boy's a witch."

"I'm no witch!" The young man mustered the courage to respond, although he tacked on a hasty "sir" at the end.

Gramps left the kitchen to hover over the cowering man. He bent over and sniffed. "That's the stench of a nervous witch," he said, straightening up.

"I'm no witch," the skinny guy repeated, louder. "And I'm going to tell the authorities about you. All of you."

His brown eyes turned green for just less than a split second. If I was still human, that quick flicker of color wouldn't have registered. But my heightened senses caught him in his lie. Green eyes are witch eyes, and while the gene may be recessive in some witches, heightened emotions can change iris color, even if only for a brief moment. He was a witch and he was lying about it.

"Why'd she send you?" I asked, watching his Adam's apple wobble in his throat as he swallowed.

A sheen of sweat covered his body. "Who?"

"She let you out, released you," I said, stalking the witch in a semicircle. My nostrils flared while I scented him like my grandfather, a ginger odor growing stronger as his fear rose. "Why? What did you promise?"

"Nina," Darcy issued a warning.

"I don't know what you're talking about," he said. His eyes darted around the room. He was looking for a way out.

I lunged and wrapped one hand around his throat. I lifted him up and pressed him against the wall. "Why did she send you? How does it feel to sell out your own kind?" I dipped my head towards him and flashed my razor sharp fangs.

His eyes widened. "Oh shit. They didn't tell me you're a vampire too," he squeaked, his eyes wide.

And there it was, caught in a lie. He knew exactly who I was, and Leila obviously sent him. My simmering anger turned to a boil. Betrayed, by my own kind. Again. My eyes focused on his pulse moving in his neck, while my ears followed its beat. His heart rate changed from an anxiety raised 102 beats per minute to a fear-boosted 147 when my rattlesnake tattoo issued its warning. Then, I struck. Like the venomous snake that wrapped me in my magic, my fangs sunk into his skin and the warm blood, with its rich spicy flavor, sated my hunger.

The man's heart rate slowed. When he went limp, Frankie pulled me off him. "Enough, Nina. You need to learn to feed without killing." I wiped my mouth and watched him carry my snack to the couch. "You can't leave a pile of bodies in your wake."

"And we can't risk him running to Leila and telling him her secret," Gramps said. He was back at the counter, grinding his herbs. "Let her finish her meal."

"I should get going," Darcy said. She had already pulled on her jacket.

"What's the rush?" I asked. "Curfew's not lifted yet."

Darcy didn't meet my eyes. Between that and her pallid complexion, I knew exactly why the rush. My feeding grossed her out. As a Beta-Vamp, Matty couldn't feed on living people. Their fangs weren't sharp enough to break through skin. Not only physically unable to feast, they also lacked the predator drive. So she only watched Matty get sustenance from a blood bag. That was the vampire equivalent of running through the drive-through versus actually hunting your meal.

"It's getting light," Frankie said. "She should be fine."

He eyed the glow from behind the window treatments. This part of the apartment wasn't light-proofed. I know he wanted to get me in the bedroom, but not for any fun reasons. With the thick black drapes hung to keep out the sunlight, the bedroom looked like we hired a goth teen as our interior decorator. All that was missing was a Vlad the Impaler poster covered with hearts.

I hated it, but the precaution was necessary. Unlike Frankie, I didn't have the benefit of a demon curse that allowed me to walk in the daylight. The space was better than the coffin hidden behind the keg room in our musty basement.

Darcy waved her goodbyes and fled out the door that led to the bar to keep more sunlight from filtering into the room.

I nodded at snitch-witch on the couch. He was still unconscious from blood loss. "What are we going to do with that one?"

"Finish him off," Gramps said, using a mortar and pestle to grind down coriander.

"I'll compel him once he comes to," Frankie said.

"She'll see through the compulsion," Gramps warned. "You think she didn't plan for such basic trickery?"

"Fine," Frankie said. I lunged towards the couch, aching to drain the last of his blood. But Frankie beat me to the body, and in one quick move he twisted the man's neck until a clean snap broke the silence in the room.

"What the hell did you do that for?" I snapped. "You said I could kill him."

"No one ever said that," Frankie corrected me. "You need to learn control. Letting you drink him dry would give into your bloodlust."

I opened my mouth to curse him out, but Gramps talked right over me. "We need to discuss what happens next."

"Nina needs to get into the bedroom before any more sunlight leaks in here," Frankie said.

"This will take just a moment," the old man said. "Kittie shared some valuable information about the prison while you were out petting the rabies brigade."

I traced the snake tattoo's path along my arm. "You actually trust what comes out of that woman's mouth?"

"She has no reason to lie," he said. "Leila made her what she was and then refused to save her. She feels betrayed. We can use that."

"She feels betrayed?" I scoffed. "The only one betrayed was us. Me."

"Let's leave this until tomorrow," Frankie warned.

I ignored him. "I think it's curious that you make me steal her magic and then plunge a knife in my throat. You want to talk about that too?"

The old man sighed. "I will not apologize for not allowing you to suffer."

"None of this happened in a void," I said. As my temper flared, my hunger did as well. I eyed the dead body on the couch. Would it be gross to drink postmortem? I shook my head and refocused. "If I didn't steal Kittie's magic, I would not have gotten sick. Hence, no need to..." I drew my hand across my throat.

"As your magic grew stronger, you were getting sicker. The headaches, they became more frequent as you came into your own as a witch, right?"

I turned to Frankie, but he just shrugged. "Sorry, Love. I noticed it."

I leaned against the wall, my arms crossed. "And what do you mean Leila made Kittie? Seriously, she's not my sister, right?"

Gramps chuckled. "No, she's not your sister by blood. But your mother gave Kittie that ink. She worked spells on that poor girl to replace you." Gramps must have caught my expression softening. "Not like she missed you, let's not fool ourselves here. Leila is a selfish woman. No, she was trying to replicate you, and the power that you'd grow into as a hybrid."

"But Kittie's not a vampire," I said.

"Exactly," he said. "Didn't work, now did it?"

"Why didn't she just bonk Marcello then?"

"Because she turned, remember?" Frankie said. "Vampires can't...procreate."

"My father was a vampire, so that shoots your theory full of holes."

Gramps tossed his spelling tools into the sink. I noticed he didn't worry about mixing the food knives with the potion prep. "Your father had a little help."

I looked at Frankie. "Seriously?"

"Nina, we are dead. Dead people cannot create life. There was a spell or two involved to make this happen."

"Bertrand?"

Frankie nodded. "And I suppose he refused to replicate the process for Leila after everything went south. The demon is a bastard, but he was a friend to your dad."

"Bertrand doesn't have friends," I said. Sunlight was bleeding into the apartment now and heat blisters bubbled up on my exposed skin.

"Nina, you've got to get into the room," Frankie warned. "Like *now*."

He didn't have to tell me twice. The blisters itched like crazy.

Frankie followed me into the bedroom and closed the door behind us. "What are you doing?" I asked. "If you think you're getting lucky, that ship capsized." I opened the dresser and rooted through it for pajamas.

"Did it now?" he asked, stretching out on the bed. I slapped his boot-covered foot off the blanket on my way to turn on a lamp at the side table. We both could see in the dark, but the night vision took some getting used to.

"Go home," I said.

He grimaced. "I don't have one of those, remember? Darcy and Matty took over the whole bloody factory."

"Stay upstairs in my apartment. You don't need the vampire lair."

"You've seen the apartment right? It's nothing but computers and monitors and walkie-talkies and all these other technological gizmos. It's her own personal Radio Shack."

"Well, you can't stay here," I said.

"Why not?" he asked. "The ship, as you said, capsized."

"Go on the couch."

He wrinkled his nose. "With Gramps out there? No thank you. The man's witchy ways makes my skin crawl. What do you think he was concocting?"

"You're awfully chatty tonight," I said, yanking my t-shirt over my head. If Frankie wasn't going to leave the room, I'd make it damn uncomfortable for him to stay.

"You think that's wise?"

"Capsized."

"Right," he said, looking away from me. I kicked my jeans off and they landed in his lap. He shoved them onto the floor.

"If you're in the mood to talk, let's talk about the prison break," I said, slipping under the covers in a tank top and panties. "You can look now."

Frankie cleared his throat and shifted towards the edge of the bed, away from me. "What about it?"

I squinted, annoyed that he moved away. "How are we getting in? The iron will render any spells useless. And after our recon mission disaster, they're probably expecting us."

"We need to incapacitate the guards. Clearly," Frankie said.

"You think the two of us and a werewolf pack can handle that?"

"What are you, a nutter?" he asked. "And like you said, she's probably boosted patrols and has them armed to the teeth."

"Drive a truck through the stone walls? They're old. Could crumble, right?"

"You're daft," he said. "We're not getting in with magic or with muscle. Not unless we raise an army."

Frankie and I were a ragtag army of two, plus four werewolves. Leila had a prison full of trained guards at her disposal. She had us beat on sheer volume. Unless...

I gave Frankie a devious smile. "What if her army goes turncoat?"

"Are you trying to kill me again?" Frankie asked when I scrambled out of bed and hunted around for my cellphone. "I mean, good lord, Nina. Can you at least throw on a bathrobe?"

"I'll be two seconds," I said. "If you're getting too hot and bothered by my walking corpse, close your damn eyes." I pulled my phone out of the back pocket of my jeans and held it up in triumph.

"Who the hell are you calling at this hour?" he asked.

I made a big point of crawling back under the covers. I settled back against the pillows and then swiped through my address book. "I'm calling Bobby."

"Bobby? Who the hell is Bobby?"

"Start spreading the news..." I sang — out of tune — to jog his memory.

Frankie's expression went from puzzled to disgusted. "Not that vampire we fished out of the Gowanus Canal?"

"The very one."

"Are you mental? He must be radioactive by now," Frankie said with a shudder. "All bloated from that water. And whatever was stagnating in it."

"He's fine," I said.

"And you know this how?"

I shrugged. "We've kept in touch."

"With Bobby, the gangster vampire? How could he possibly be of any use in all this?"

"He knows someone who could help."

"Help with what?"

"Help us raise an army."

"You know I was joking, right?" Frankie said. "We can't raise an army."

I found the number for Lady Elaine's tea shop and hit the call button. ""Nope, but his friend can."

A mellifluous voice picked up the phone on the fifth ring. The tone and timbre relaxed me immediately. Lady Elaine was the most popular tea leaf reader in New Orleans, but it wasn't because of her skill divining the future. It was because she possessed an uncanny ability to con any person that heard her voice. Drawn in by her musical notes, humans were too weak to resist any of her requests, which were mainly of the financial variety. She was running a solid con, but that's what happens in the front-facing, tourist-friendly part of the French Quarter.

I needed Bobby for the spells that happened behind that front-facing façade, in the dark corners of the city, stretching out to Louisiana's bayous.

"Lady Elaine, it's Nina," I said, hoping she remembered me. Now that I was vampire, I was immune to her dulcet tones, sort of. I could feel my psychic armor chipping away with each syllable she uttered. It wasn't happening as fast as it did when I had human ears, but it was happening.

"Nina, Nina, Nina..." she said, elongating the vowel at the end of my name. "Of course, Nina! The living dead girl."

"Except now I am dead dead," I said.

She sucked in a breath. "You mean, you...turned?"

"Didn't you get the prayer card?" I asked.

"No," she said, my joke going so far over her head I heard it splash in the Mississippi. "But I saw it in the tea leaves and it wasn't supposed to be this soon."

I rolled my eyes at her lie. She was a good reader but that thing about me dying? All humans were going to die someday, right?

"So to what do we owe the pleasure of your call?" she asked. "I assume it's not to announce your recent demise?"

"I was wondering if Bobby was around."

I heard a bell jingle in the background and she cooed hello to a customer before calling for Bobby to pick up the phone. "Hope you don't mind, but I have to dash, Nina. Bobby'll pick up in a minute. Good to talk to you."

And with that, the phone dropped on a hard surface. After about a minute, footfalls plodded towards it. For a vampire, poor Bobby wasn't exactly light on his feet.

"Nina, as I live and breathe..." He chuckled at his own joke. I wasted the prayer card line on Elaine. Clearly.

"Bobby, good to hear your voice. How are things in the Crescent City?"

"Can't complain," he said in his heavy New York accent. "You still running with that stuck-up Brit?"

"Hey!" Frankie protested.

"Hey yourself, you friggin' aristocrat," Bobby said. "So what's up, Nina? You comin' down for a visit?"

"Actually," I said, "I hoped you would do me a favor."

"Anything for the pretty lady that pulled my ass out of the Gowanus," he said. "Waddaya need, girl?"

"Bobby," I said, putting on my best Southern drawl, "we need some serious voodoo up in here."

20

"DID YOU FEEL THAT?" Casper asked, his eyes flitting around the bar.

"Feel what?" I replied, barely glancing up. I was armpit deep into a box of inventory the Clown Shoes Beer distributors sent over, courtesy of my new werewolf buddies in Massachusetts. They sent 50 cases of beer plus three kegs and an assortment of hard liquor. None of it was top-shelf, but it would make what few customers remained happy for the next few weeks.

I liked Lincoln and his pack even more now.

"That," Casper said. He was faux sitting at the table close to the door. "Like someone breezing past."

"You're probably catching a draft," I said. "If you're getting cold, come sit over here." I jerked my head towards one of the empty barstools.

Frankie came up from hauling kegs into the keg room in the basement. We both examined Casper while he slipped across the wood floor. He didn't walk, exactly. He glided, his feet hovering centimeters above the ground. Without *terra firma* to stand on, he had an awkward gate, not unlike a limp, barely perceptible to human eyes, but barely was the key word. Any human paying close attention could catch it. Any non-human too.

His sitting was splendid, though. My vampire eyes didn't discern any difference between the way his ass angled onto the barstool and a corporeal one.

"You're getting there with the walking, mate," Frankie said. "Keep practicing."

"What was wrong with it now?" the teenaged ghost whined.

"I know you're frustrated," I said. I gave his hand a sympathetic pat, but my own just dropped straight through it. "It just looked like there was nothing solid underfoot." His face drooped, so I was quick to add, "Regular people won't notice a thing though."

That seemed to cheer Casper for now. "So who's the guy coming up from the Big Easy?"

"Don't call it that," I said.

"What? Why can't I call New Orleans the Big Easy? Everyone else does."

"Everyone who doesn't know any better," I retorted. "Call it NOLA. Call it the Crescent City. But do not call it the Big Easy."

Frankie chuckled. "We had a run near there once, so we took a few nights off and played tourist."

"We did not play tourist," I corrected him. "We crashed with a vampire we know, and he took us to all the haunts."

"And she means haunts literally," Frankie added. "And that's also where she learned that the locals knew they were in the presence of an outlier if said outlier called their city the Big Easy. She's had a bug up her bum hole about that term ever since."

"And I don't know who our friend is sending up," I said. "We never met him while we were down there, but Bobby said he's exactly the help we need."

"When is this Southern gothic mystery supposed to arrive, anyway?" Frankie asked.

I glanced at the face of my phone: 8:03 p.m. "Any minute now."

"How's he getting here?" Casper asked.

"Yeah, one can't exactly fly into the airport these days," Frankie said, surveying the liquor bottles lined up on the bar. "I hope he brought some good bourbon with him."

"I mentioned that to Bobby but he said this guy had his ways around it."

Casper shivered. "Damn, I just felt it again. You need to fix the insulation up in this place."

"There's nothing wrong with the insulation," I said. "You're dead. Dead people get cold. That's the problem."

"Actually..." Frankie started. He reconsidered when he looked at my face. "Never mind."

Casper jerked, wedging his body halfway through the wooden bar. "There! There, right there! Tell me you didn't feel that."

"Feel what?" Gramps asked, kicking the front door closed.

Casper shook his head at me. "Oh no, that's not the draft I'm talking about."

"Let me guess," I said. "It was a different draft." I pushed a glass of water in front of him. "Practice your grip."

"Come on, Nina, you're worse than my mother," he whined.

"It's like physical therapy," I said, cracking open a bottle of Clown Shoes' Tramp Stamp. I took a long pull and savored the hoppy flavor. They did make a solid brew. "You've got to keep working your muscles."

Casper wrapped his hand around the glass, trying to keep it from slipping through. "Really? If I try hard enough?"

"Oh honey, I have no idea," I admitted, wanting to hug the kid when I saw his crestfallen face. "I've never been around a ghost with a body. But we'll figure it out. I promise."

Casper nodded, resumed his attempts to defy physics. I put my bottle of beer down on the bar and began shelving the liquor bottles. Gramps dropped himself into Al's usual spot at the end of the bar.

"You got a tequila for an old man?" he called down to me.

"Nope," I said without looking up from my work.

"Whiskey then. How about a whiskey."

"Not that either."

He drummed his fingers on the wood. "I see a bottle right there, in your hand."

"No idea when I'll get more inventory. I can't squander it."

"Right," he said. "Look at all your customers."

Sarcasm noted.

Frankie slipped onto a barstool and propped his chin in his hands. I bet he'd ask for popcorn if we had any.

I took out a shot glass and poured out a measure. I looked down to my grandfather, lifted the glass and drained it in one swallow. I wiped my mouth with the back of my hand.

"You're a cold woman," he said.

"And you're a murdering asshole. What are you doing here?"

"I heard a magic man from the Big Easy was coming into town."

I opened my mouth to say something, but Frankie gave me a quick head shake. I chewed on my lip instead.

"So," Gramps asked, "you call in some voodoo jokester?"

"And if I did?"

"What can some old Creole do that I can't?" he boasted. "I'm the biggest brujo in Catemaco, the only city in the world dedicated to witches. Did you know I slept with Marie Laveau? You bed a woman like that, she tells you a secret or two."

Frankie burst into a fit of laughter. "That would make you well over 150 years old. Unless you had relations with her corpse."

"Laugh all you want," Gramps said. "We made love on the spirit plane."

I shuddered at the thought of Gramps getting it on with an elderly voodoo queen on any plane, never mind the spirit one. "So you tell me, what can this Creole do?"

A burst of air swept up the bar, pushing my beer bottle over and overturning Casper's glass of water.

"Dammit," I muttered. Beer was in short supply and I couldn't afford spills. I snatched up a bar towel and began mopping up the mess.

"This Creole can hear every word you said, old man. And this Creole is insulted."

"Wow," I whispered as a man shimmered into view beside Casper.

His skin was a deep cocoa brown, a striking contrast to his vibrant emerald green eyes. Chiseled cheekbones met a strong jaw and an aquiline nose. He shook out his thick dreadlocks, which weaved their way down to the middle of his shoulder blades. He crossed his arms in front of his broad chest, biceps bulging.

A smoking hot man just appeared in my bar. Why didn't a magic trick like this happen on sorority night? We'd have cleaned up.

I snapped my gaping mouth shut when Frankie cleared his throat.

"How did you do that?" I asked, shaking my head to clear out the cobwebs.

Frankie's back stiffened. "I take it you're the bloke Bobby sent."

"Weh," he said. His gem-colored eyes raked over my body, sending delicious shivers down my spine. I giggled.

"Weh?" Frankie spat out. "What in bloody hell does 'weh' mean?"

"Yes," I said. The word came out breathless. I shook the cobwebs out of my head and continued. "'Weh' means yes in Creole. Bobby definitely sent him."

"Right," Frankie said, sizing him up.

"I'm Nina," I said, sticking my hand out to shake his. "Welcome to Providence." He took my hand and laid a delicate kiss on top.

"I didn't know vampires could blush," Casper squealed.

I yanked my hand back, rubbing it with the other. "The ghost is Casper. That's Frankie." I jerked my head towards the sulking vampire.

"I'm Leon," he said. "Pleasure to meet you. Bobby is a big fan of yours."

"What about me?" Gramps yelled from the end of the bar. "You going to introduce me."

Leon turned to Gramps. "You're a man who needs no introduction. You're Catemaco's most infamous *brujo*." He gave a small bow and flourished his hand.

"Yeah, well, you be sure to remember the *brujo* part," Gramps said, his whiskey-soaked voice sounding gruffer than usual. "I ain't no witchdoctor. That's more your bag of tricks."

Leon laughed, showing off a set of perfect teeth, not a fang in sight. "Maybe we teach each other a few things."

"That was a pretty neat trick," Casper said. "Was that some sort of invisibility spell?"

"Weh and no," Leon said. "But I don't disappear, I just blend."

"Like a chameleon?" I asked. He nodded. "Wicked."

"Can you disguise yourself as prison bars then?" Frankie asked, the corner of his lip curling into a snarl. "Because if that's all you're good for, may as well head on back to the bayou."

"Oh my friend," Leon said with a disarming grin, "that's not all I have in my bag of tricks. What you need?"

"We need to break a few people out of a prison," I said, leaning against the bar.

A slow smile spread on his face. He placed his elbows on the bar and leaned into me. "But first you need to break in."

"Exactly," I said, shifting my own weight towards him. If I still had a heartbeat, it would be pounding right now. "We're in good hands, here. See, Frankie? Good hands." I slipped my hand into Leon's calloused one. "Ohh, you must grind a lot of herbs."

"Steady on, Nina. Stop taking the piss," Frankie barked.

"Who's taking the piss?" I asked. My eyelashes fluttered a bit.

"You! You're taking the piss. Act normal."

I laughed. "Normal? I am normal."

"For fuck's sake, you just giggled. That's not normal. You're not normal." Frankie turned to Leon. "Sir, kindly turn off whatever it is your doing. This doesn't help our cause."

Leon smirked. "What's the magic word?"

"Gris-gris, I suspect," Frankie said, referring to voodoo's magic talisman.

Leon conjured a small gris-gris bag from under the barstool. He dropped it in the liquid that remained in Casper's glass, causing the flat water to hiss and bubble. My schoolgirl-crush stupor lifted. Leon was still hot, but now his hotness didn't consume me like a 15-year-old with raging hormones.

I yanked my hand away from his. "What the hell did you spell me for?"

"Sorry," he said. "Bobby told me I should do something like that.

Said you were a bit of a hard-ass chick, and I should try to loosen you up a little. No hard feelings." He at least had the good sense to look sheepish.

"You're playing with fire there, boy," Gramps chimed in. "Lucky she didn't chew out your throat with that spell. And you." Gramps turned to me. "You had no idea you got whammied?"

"It was completely painless, I assure you," I said. I snatched up the bar rag and rubbed at an invisible stain on the counter.

Changing the subject, Leon nodded at Casper, who went dead quiet (pun intended) once the gris-gris hit the water. "So who's the ghost?"

Gramps cocked an eyebrow. "What gave him away? Is he floating again?"

Leon snickered and leaned towards Casper. "His aura."

"Ghosts have an aura?" Casper asked, clamping his mouth shut immediately. He shrunk away from Leon, going silent once more. I peered at him from my spot behind the bar. He refused to look anywhere except at the worn wood in front of him.

Gramps broke the silence, barking down the bar at Leon. "You a priest?"

"Naw," Leon drawled. "Just a simple root man."

"This friend of yours, Bobby?" Gramps pulled out a cigarette and rolled it along his lips. "He sends a gris-gris guy when you need a priest? This is no job for a novice."

"He didn't look all that novice to me," I said. Gramps conjured a flame on one of Babe's old Veladoras. He turned the candle face toward me and, like a schoolyard taunt, I saw it was the Resurrection candle. As he brought it towards his Faros cigarette, I worked a fast spell in my head and expelled a small puff of air, extinguishing the fire before he sparked up his smoke.

Gramps gave a grudging snort but didn't remove the cigarette from his mouth. "Still."

"You want help, I'm here," he said. "You don't want help, I go home. Ain't no thing. Means I won't miss French Quarter Fest. And the cold up here," Leon shivered. "My bones don't like this."

"I think he's exactly what we need," I said, taking a minute to admire the man's form.

Frankie moved into a wide stance and crossed his arms across his expanded chest. "You just remember who was here first."

Gramps guffawed. "A jealous vampire is a dangerous one. You remember that gris-gris man."

"Didn't mean nothing by that spell," Leon said, extending his hand towards Frankie as a gesture of peace. "Bobby didn't tell me she was spoken for, my friend."

Frankie clasped Leon's hand just as Max swept into the bar, a blast of rain-soaked April air following him in. His hulking frame filled the door way and water rolled off his anorak and onto the floor. "Who's spoken for?"

"Nina, apparently," Gramps said, his voice strained. He was stretched across the bar, reaching for a bottle of cheap vodka that the distributor sent over.

"No one is spoken for," I said, snatching the bottle before he could get his paws on it. I shelved the vodka where it belonged.

"You putting me on some sort of health program?" Gramps asked.

I ignored him.

Max shook out of his wet jacket and strode towards Leon. His bulbous muscles strained against his thin cotton t-shirt, still sweat-streaked from the gym. Constant workouts were part of his anger management prescription, but it looked like the Berserker behaved like steroids on his human body. He squared off in front of Leon. "Who the hell are you?"

Leon stood his ground and simply smiled. "Leon Rusé." He extended his hand to Max.

Max just stared at him. "What's your business here, Mr. Rusé?" He trilled the "r" as a mocking gesture.

"I was invited," Leon said. His emerald eyes darted between me, Frankie and Max. "By Nina."

I twisted the towel around my hands. "Sort of. I mean, I never met him before. He's a friend of a friend. An old vampire I know...we know — me and Frankie — lives in New Orleans and he owed me a favor."

Max's eyes swept along the array of bottles still lined up on the bar. "This old friend send a shipment up too?"

"No," I said. "A werewolf pack in Mass hooked me up."

"Calling in a lot of favors, aren't you?" Max pushed past Leon and sat in the stool next to Casper, glancing over at him. Max's mouth dropped open as he recognized the ghost. "Wait, aren't you...?"

Casper offered a thin smile. "In the flesh, so to speak."

Max was on the scene when Casper was murdered, so he knew the ghost in his old physical form.

"I don't even want to know," Max said with a shake of his head. He reached for a bottle of tequila. He twisted the cap and the sharp smell of fermented agave hit my sensitive nose. I pushed a rocks glass over to him. "What else did I miss?"

Pretty much everything, I mused silently.

I resumed putting away the bottles to keep myself busy. Max missed Casper's transformation from possessing my body to getting his own back, with some alterations, of course. And he missed my transformation to the bastard child of Dracula and the Wicked Witch of the West.

"Oh come on, kid," Gramps moaned from his seat. He motioned for me to pour him a glass of what Max was drinking. I pushed the bottle down his way. He pulled out a flask and proceeded to fill it.

Frankie broke the awkward silence. "Did you check the new keg?"

I put a beer mug under the tap and pulled the handle. Air and a bit of foam sputtered out, then the amber liquid poured from the tap. I filled the glass and slid it in front of Frankie.

Max's arrival felt like a large lead weight dropped on the bar. Casper slumped miserably over a fresh glass of water. Leon shifted around the bar, staring intently at the blue cobalt bottles that lined the upper shelves. Frankie hovered close to him, his sullen mood stereotypical brooding vampire. Gramps sniffed his unlit cigarette and expelled a series of loud sighs from his perch at the bar. Now that he had his booze, he wanted a smoke, too.

"Any idea what's in them?" Leon asked, pointing at the bottles. His voice infused the space with a touch of levity at least.

I shrugged. "Potions stirred by my aunt, most likely. But I have no idea what they do."

"Your aunt was a witch?" he asked, eyebrows lifting. "That makes you?"

"Witch," Gramps said gruffly. "And vampire. Both."

Leon raised an eyebrow and then whistled appreciatively. "Never thought that was possible. You got some power in you then, woman."

"That's the rumor," I said vaguely, examining my nails. I picked at a ragged cuticle.

"Can you take that one down?" Leon asked, smartly not pushing for the story behind my dual nature. I followed his finger, which pointed to an average-size bottle about halfway up the wall.

"They may not be potions," Frankie said. "Babe made a mean moonshine. Her still was on the back patio until the cops took notice."

"That was my recipe," Gramps said. His chest puffed up with pride. "The secret's in the mash."

I glanced up to the shelves. "Frankie, would you mind?"

Frankie puzzled at me. "You can't make that jump?"

I jerked my head towards Max. As far as I knew, he wasn't privy to my vampire turn. Being Bertrand's lackey and playing both sides with Leila meant he wasn't around us much. Not only did I not feel like getting him up to speed, but I didn't trust that he could keep my situation a secret from those two.

Frankie narrowed his eyes at me, but vaulted the bar anyway. He did a straight jump up six feet and hovered midair to grab the bottle before coming back to earth and landing with the weight of a feather. Impressive.

He handed the bottle to me. I uncorked it and gave the content a quick sniff. A rotting scent assaulted my nose. But I realized too late that whatever was in the bottle wasn't liquid. It was a powder, and some of it went right up my nose. I expelled the stuff in a huge sneeze. I replaced the cork swiftly, but the offensive scent traveled into my taste buds. I worked my tongue around, trying to get the foulness out of my mouth.

I rubbed my nose and passed the bottle to Leon. "Definitely not moonshine."

Max gestured to Leon, grump swirling around him like a tornado. "So, why is he here again?"

"Vacation," I lied.

"A vacation here? Now?"

"A modern-day witch hunt? Better than Disney World," Leon said without missing a beat.

Max squeezed his glass and the veins popped in his hand. "Stop bullshitting me."

I sighed. "We needed an extra hand, that's all."

"For what?" he asked. He narrowed his eyes at me. "You aren't even considering going back into Steele City? Are you?" I gave him a weak smile. He turned to Frankie. "Is she?"

"You know Nina. When she gets an idea in her head..." Frankie pressed his finger tips to his temples and pushed them out, arcing his hands away from his body. He included the homemade sound effect of a bomb explosion.

"Thank you for your support," I deadpanned.

"You are out of your minds, all of you." Max's face began to take on a red hue. "You both barely got out of there alive last time."

"Well, technically..." Frankie began.

"Yeah, you're dead, I get it. Invincible," Max said. "But she's not. It's like she has some sort of death wish. Do you have a death wish?"

I swallowed and gave a short shake of my head.

"Well, the three of you go in there—"

"Four," Casper interjected in a small voice.

Max threw up his hands. "Even better. The four of you. I told you before, you need an army."

"What are our choices?" I asked. "You figure out another way to bust out Dr. O?"

"I'm working on it."

"Yeah? What are you working on?" Gramps shouted from the other end of the bar. He took a pull from his flask.

"Diplomacy," Max said. "Maybe you've heard of it. It's that thing that doesn't require kicking doors in or running around half-cocked."

"Who's the diplomat? You?" I asked.

"Bertrand."

I laughed. "Bertrand? He's negotiating with Leila? What's he trading? We've got nothing she wants."

"You've got Kittie," Max said.

"Kittie's dead to her," Gramps said.

Before Max could respond, I pulled the collar of my shirt off my shoulder, exposing the head of the rattlesnake. The serpent's tongue flicked in and out while it undulated just under my skin.

Max shivered. "How the hell did that happen?"

"An accident," Gramps said.

"Like hell," I snapped. "The point is, Kittie's got no magic left. She's tapped out."

"What are you saying? You have it?" he asked.

I nodded. "How's that diplomacy looking now?"

Max stood. "I've got to relay this to Bertrand."

"What's your rush?" I asked, wariness creeping through me. Max was downright punchy today.

"My rush is that he thinks she wants Kittie back. She's playing him for a fool."

"Ami Bertrand is no fool," Gramps said. "I promise you, he knows about Kittie."

"How's that?" Max asked.

"I told him."

Max's face clouded. Mine did too.

"You trading secrets with Bertrand now, too?" I asked, tossing up my hands in frustration. "Christ, old man. Don't you think you should maybe tell me these things?"

"Tell you what?" he asked. "Aren't we all on the same side here?"

"For now," I said. "Doesn't mean you should trust him."

Gramps blew out his lips and expelled a sound of annoyance.

"Listen to your grandfather," Max said. He may have agreed with Gramps, but his expression betrayed his simmering resentment.

"We're on your side and don't want to see you slaughtered. You go into that prison, you won't come out. We'll get Dr. O out. And even if we can't, he's safe. Leila knows better than to hurt him."

"I thought the federal government didn't negotiate with terrorists," I said, annoyance rising as he mansplained.

"You're out of your depth, Nina."

"You do know what she's doing in there, right?" I asked. I shoved my hands in my pockets, worried if I waved them around I'd inadvertently let loose a spell. And given the rise of my anger, it'd be a doozy. "She's experimenting. On the weres. On the witches. She's separating the wolf from the human. She's syphoning magic out of the witches. She's the freaking Karl Gebhardt of the supernatural world."

Frankie huffed in agreement. But judging from Max's expression, he was downright scandalized. "You just compared your mother to a Nazi medical doctor," he said incredulously.

"I thought it was an apt comparison," I said. "Gebhardt was a monster. He did horrific experiments on innocent prisoners. You see the similarities, right?"

Max conceded with a curt nod, but he wasn't giving up just yet. "So now what," he challenged. "You and your new friend here are just going to walk into the place and free everyone? On what planet does that even constitute a plan?"

"Trust, Mr. FBI man, we have a plan," Leon said, turning to face Max.

"Want to fill me in?" he asked.

Leon glanced at me. "Nah, I don't think so."

I turned my head towards him. "He's cool, Leon. Grumpy and argumentative, but he's part of the team."

"You say you trust him?" Leon looked at me, puzzled. I didn't meet his eyes. How much did I trust Max really? I didn't trust him enough to tell him that I turned.

Leon continued. "He'll know exactly what he needs to know to set the plan in motion. Nothing more. Nothing Less."

Max opened his mouth to object, but Frankie cut in. "Might I point out that *we* don't even know the plan?" he said, his lips pursed like he sucked on a sour candy. "Is that what you mean by less?"

"You'll know your part, too," Leon said.

Frankie sucked on his teeth. "I hope that means we'll know more than Max, since we're the ones walking into the building."

"Of course he has to tell us the plan, Frankie," I snapped. His petty jealousy of Leon was grating. "Don't be ridiculous."

"Ridiculous?" Frankie raised his voice and his eyes lit up like LED Christmas lights. He lisped through the "s" as his fangs stretched into place. "Maybe trusting him is ridiculous, did you consider that?"

"Shit's about to get real in here," Casper muttered. He stared at his feet and did his forward moonwalk past me to the other side of the bar. He took shelter behind Gramps.

I crossed my arms and pressed my nails into my skin, forcing myself to calm down before I vamped out in front of Max. Leon wasn't the only one keeping secrets.

"Let me see the bottle," Gramps said, interrupting the brewing argument. The four of us turned and looked at him.

"What you need, old man?" Leon asked, holding the bottle closer to his body.

Gramps pointed at it. "That bottle. It's the devil's shoestring, isn't it?"

A slow smile spread over Leon's handsome face. "You know the hoodoo?"

"I know some," he said.

"You're clever for an old *brujo*," Leon said. "You know what's in here." Leon shook the bottle.

"You laying a trick?"

Leon shook his head. "No sir. But you aren't too far off."

"What the hell is laying a trick?" Max asked.

"I think they mean prostitute, mate," Frankie quipped.

Leon laughed. "Ain't no hookers laying this trick, friend."

Max pushed himself off the barstool and stood to his full six feet. I was dwarfed by the added bulk of the muscle he'd gained. I shrank back a bit under his shadow. But it wasn't his size that caused unease to rise. His features were masked with a darkness that I didn't think I'd ever see in him. He stalked around the edge of the room, shaking his arms and legs every few steps, like his limbs were falling asleep and he was shaking out the pins and needles.

Leon's eyes tracked Max. "You all right, man?"

Max's body twitched. "Yeah, fine. Why?"

"You just don't look so good," Leon said, giving Max wide berth as he returned to the bar.

Max stepped in front of me. "Pour out another, would you?"

"You sure about that?" I asked. Even though there was a thick slab of wood between us, I instinctively took a step back.

"It was a rough day," he said, his voice gruff. "Pour out another."

I picked up the bottle of vodka, but instead of pouring it, I tucked it into my body. "Yeah, what happened today?"

His face went even darker, something I didn't think possible. "I watched her kill a witch."

My head spun as I took in what he was saying. "What witch?" I managed to blurt out. I glanced at Casper, who looked green with fear.

Max shook his head. "Didn't know her. But still."

"How'd she do it?" Leon asked.

"It was like an accident," Max said, his hard expression softened. "She was syphoning the magic—"

"Syphoning magic?" Leon asked. "What does that mean?"

"It means exactly that," Frankie said. "She's taking their magic."

"It's how she killed Babe," I said softly, remembering that awful moment when she plunged a spelled knife into my aunt's stomach. "The blade she used pulled the magic out of the body and into her."

"So she does mean to kill them," Leon said.

"Not this time," Max said. "She's trying to take the magic and keep them alive."

"And how's that working out?" I asked.

Max slumped his shoulders in response.

"Why bother?" Leon asked.

Max pushed his barstool back and stood. "Why bother what?" He began pacing the length of the bar.

"Hang on, did you just ask why bother keeping people—keeping witches—alive?" I asked, my voice raising with each syllable.

"If she didn't care about keeping them alive before..." Leon started.

"Why start now?" Frankie finished for him. "It's the right question to ask. I mean, your mum is off her onion, but I think she has no qualms about slaughtering anyone."

Max stopped and faced me. "She thinks magic rejuvenates."

"An endless supply of power," Gramps said, drumming his fingers on the bar. "Damn clever idea. If she can syphon and keep them alive, she'll never run out of it. She'll be able to enhance her power by stealing theirs."

"I guess she'd run through witches pretty quickly the other way," Leon agreed. He let out a low whistle. "Y'all got some bad juju up in this place."

"I told Bobby the situation was fucked," I said, tension creeping into my shoulders.

I poured out a measure of alcohol for Max and walked it to the end of the bar. He took it with a nod of thanks and swallowed the drink in one go.

"It's not something I want to see again," he said. "She suffered. I'm sure of it." He handed back the shot glass. "So what's in the bottle?" Max asked, changing the subject.

"Payback," Leon said. His grin turned malicious. "Inside this bottle is payback. And she's a nasty little bitch."

21

My back pressed against the cold, damp rocks of the prison wall. I was flanked between Frankie and Leon. We inched towards the front door, stopping every few feet as spotlights made the sweep of the grounds. Dressed in commando blacks, we blended into the shadows cast by the overpowering lights. We were about to take over the prison.

Leon glanced over at me. "Ready?"

Frankie gave his yes with a squeeze of my arm. I nodded in the affirmative.

Leon whispered a few words in Creole French, and the automatic doors slipped open without us standing in front. We hung back at the edge of the building, waiting for someone to notice that something wasn't quite right.

Darcy's sigh was loud in my ear. "Are you in yet?" she asked over the headset.

"Not quite," I muttered, keeping my voice low.

"Don't forget, you need to let me know as soon as you get in there—"

"We bloody well know the plan," Frankie snapped at her through his comms unit. "We came up with the damn thing."

I considered shushing him, but decided against it. Both Frankie and I were on edge. We were about to walk into the prison with a New Orleans witch we barely knew. Just the three of us, taking on an unknown — but no doubt large — number of trained guards.

This was a stupid idea.

It didn't take long for the guard standing sentry in the first room to wander into the dark. His back to us, he examined the doorframe and pulled on the mechanism, trying to force it closed. Leon's knee twisted from his own impatience waiting for the man to come all the way out of the building. Just one more step and Leon's Creole drawl stunned the man. The guard turned and faced the witch, who blew a handful of white powder at the man. The guard dropped to the ground, becoming nothing but a lump in the darkness.

Frankie pushed on my back, nudging me forward. Leon had already disappeared through the door. I remained still, listening for the sound of boots stomping on the hard floors in the sally port.

Leon promised he could rally an army to our side once we entered the building. The problem was, our plan relied on Leon's hoodoo magic, and he didn't share exactly what that entailed. That was an awful lot of trust to give one hoodoo priest.

Leon poked his head around the corner and flashed us a lopsided grin. "You coming or what?"

I stepped through the door, Frankie close behind, and I felt a soft puff against my back as the door slid closed. Leon raised an arm to keep both of us from stepping all the way into the room.

He nodded at the floor. "Watch your step." There was a coating of black dust sprinkled all over the cement.

"How can we avoid that?" I asked. The dust was everywhere.

"You can't," he said. "We wait."

"Wait for what?" Frankie asked. Based on his tone, my fellow vampire's patience was wearing thin.

"This," Leon said as eight guards plowed through a set of locked doors. He jerked his head towards the closed-circuit camera.

"Kill the video, Darce," I said into my mic.

"Killing in three...two..." Darcy paused for an unnerving moment, probably because I was slow in telling her to end the video. I'd never really witnessed hoodoo magic before, and it was pretty showy and a bit of a distraction. "One. Okay, I have a visual of an empty lobby on loop. Working my way into their security system now."

I registered what Darcy was saying but I didn't quite take it in. I was too busy watching the eight guards kick up the black dust on the floor as they stomped their way towards us. Each step became less aggressive until they stood in front of a smiling Leon.

"You *are* building an army," I whispered when the eight of them raised a hand in salute to Leon like he was their general. "How?"

Leon swept his arm towards the floor. "Thanks to your beautiful aunt."

"What was in that bottle?" Frankie asked. He waved his hands in front of the guards' faces. Ignoring him, they stood stoically in full salute. "It's like the goddamn queen's guard."

"The main ingredient I needed for the foot track magic," Leon said. "Once they step on it, they owe allegiance to me. In other words, I'm the boss."

"So what now, boss?" I asked.

"We track more magic," he said with a grin.

"So we have to get through the next set of doors," I said.

"I'll send my boys in to dust the place," he said, pulling several bottles of the magic powder out of his backpack. He tossed one to each of the eight guards who had been standing at attention. At Leon's brief command, his soldiers went into the prison, the secure doors opening easily since the facial recognition software recognized their clearance. I caught a quick glance of our new allies sprinkling the powder onto the ground before the doors closed behind them, the lock sliding into place.

"Hey Darce," I said into my mic. "Get ready to hack into the doors."

"Got it," Darcy said. I heard the swift clicks of computer keys as Darcy's deft fingers worked on cracking the security system. The lock slid and the door popped open again.

I shook my head. Our first prison break in would have gone so much smoother this way. Of course, they would have detected the security breech, making this attempt in that much more difficult. Right?

"Ladies first," Leon said, bowing slightly as I slipped through the door.

A small giggle at his gallant gesture caught in my throat.

Frankie snatched my arm and yanked me back towards him. He glared at the rootman. "How about Leon go first, love. Just in case his hoodoo army didn't get the spell right."

"With pleasure," Leon said with a smirk. He stepped gamely into the interior of the prison and motioned for us to follow. Frankie slipped in behind Leon, his movement more cautious. He stopped just inside the entryway, probably on purpose, leaving me in limbo just outside the door, craning my neck to see around him and Leon.

I tapped his shoulder. "Come on, Frankie, move."

"Just making sure it's okay," he said.

"Are you serious?" I muttered. Now that we were in the thick of a mission, he treated me differently. He treated me like I couldn't be trusted not to give into my bloodlust. Like I was fragile, ready to break down. I gave him a hard shove and, losing his balance, he stumbled through the door.

I muscled my way through. "Don't do that again."

"Do what?" He feigned stupidity.

"You know exactly... Whoa."

Telling off Frankie was interrupted by the unbelievable sight that greeted us in the prison. Guards flanked the walls of the hallway, all in formation, saluting Leon as he walked past. There had to be a few dozen of them, giving us a medium-sized platoon.

"That's it for the powder," Leon said, shaking the detritus from an empty container.

"This is our army?" I asked, my eyes sweeping over the lines, surveying the them. More than a few had potbellies that spilled over the belts of their ill-fitting uniforms. I counted seven pimply boys who looked barely 18.

"Bit ragtag, don't you think?" Frankie said, tempering the insult.

"They are fearless," Leon said. "That counts more than skill."

"How about ability?" I asked, hands on hips. I caught the eye of a diminutive woman—the sole female—at the end of the line. She didn't have much height but her body was thick with muscle. She probably wasn't agile, but her brute strength would get us through a few doors. Plus she had a warrior's face. I was betting on her. "She leads."

"Good choice," Leon said, ordering a Creole command. The line of guards turned and faced the long hallway, ready to move out.

"Still getting the werewolves first?" Leon asked.

I nodded. "The ones that are strong enough will be assets if they join us."

"That's a big if," Frankie said.

"Worth the risk," I said.

"Which way?" Leon asked.

"Left," I said.

Leon barked a command and we followed the formation of the guards barreling their way down the hall.

"Darcy, get ready to open the werewolf cellblock," I said.

"No problem," she said. I heard her crack her knuckles.

The hallway was long, but I worried that we'd be stuck at the end, boxed in, waiting for the locks to pop. Leon's hoodoo army moved fast for the majority of out-of-shape guards that filled its ranks.

"How's it coming, Darce?" I asked, my tone tepid. I didn't want to put pressure on her but we had less than a football field to go before we hit the locked doors.

"Easy-peasy," she said.

She muttered to someone else, her hand over the microphone so I couldn't make out what she said.

Gramps' gruff voice came over my headset. "Anyone see Max?"

"He's getting the box truck," I said.

"You sure about that?"

Frankie glared at enormous iron doors that loomed in front of us. "Bloody hell, just tell us what's going on. We're about to get in the thick of this shit. Better we know now if we need to change our exit plans."

"Don't get your knickers in a knot, English," Gramps complained. "We got a call from your werewolf friends in Massachusetts. They said Max never showed to meet them at the truck."

"Have Al drive the damn truck," I said, distracted. The formation of guards was slowing to a stop. We reached the end of the line and the door was still bolted.

"He won't get through the checkpoint at the guard house with the truck. They don't know him."

The three of us had scaled the barbed wire fence to get to the building, but a box truck couldn't be that stealthy. In a pinch, Al could just plow the vehicle through the front gates, but we were relying heavily on the element of surprise for this mission. A box truck barreling through the front gates of a prison wasn't subtle.

"What about the spell you gave me and Frankie?" I pressed my hand against the damp stone wall, using the natural rock under my hand to ground me. As my frustration rose, so did my hunger. Our hoodoo army started to look yummy.

"No time for transformation. We don't have a picture of a guard to transform him into."

"Transform him into Max," Frankie suggested.

"What if he's—"

"Just bloody well deal with it!" Frankie snapped.

I glanced at Frankie. His hair was wild and his eyes glowed green. I knew he was ready to rage. Only his advanced age kept his blood-lust from taking control. His lithe body held its tension, every muscle at the ready. I licked my lips. Frankie had never looked sexier.

The sound of the locks shifting inside the massive iron doors echoed against the hard stone surface of the hallway. Darcy got through the firewall. Her exclamation about the hack being like taking blood from a Beta-Vamp drowned out Gramps' protests.

"Spell Al to look like Max and give Darcy back her headset. We need to communicate with her now," I said, my focus on Leon hustling to the front of his platoon, ready to give the command for his troops to charge in.

At Frankie's short nod, he ordered four men to pull open the heavy doors. Once the opening was wide enough, a stream of grey uniforms flooded into the anteroom of the werewolf holding pen.

We followed the mass of zombified humans into the cellblock. Batons out, they were beating the un-spelled guards, who were in shock, into submission. Human shouts mixed with the already turned werewolves—some barked with excitement and others whimpered. But behind the bulletproof glass that looked into the block, the cells looked empty. I imagined the weres cowering in their cells in fear.

I shoved my way to the control booth while the guards attacked each other, pressing on various buttons to try to open the doors to the cells. The computer just chirped out sounds of failure. "Can you hack into the control panel?" I yelled into the mic, over the noise of the melee happening all around me. I ducked a baton that one of the zombie guards wielded as he missed his actual target.

With a frustrated sigh, I snatched the weapon and leveled it at the zombie's original target, beaning him in the head. He crumpled to the ground.

"That's how you do it," I snarled at the zombie guard. His dead eyes stared at me, mouth gaped open. He took his baton back when I handed it to him. Mindless warriors. We wanted them, we got them.

"Tell me about the control panel," Darcy said, returning my attention to the smorgasbord of buttons in front of me. "This one has some serious security. It could take me hours to break in. You're going to have to figure out how to override it."

"Crap," I said, staring at the computer, a cursor blinking at me from a blank screen. "Can you tell me what I'll need to do to get in?"

"Is it asking for a password?"

"The screen is just blank."

"Is the computer asleep?"

Darcy sounded exasperated, like when you call IT support because you forgot to plug in your computer.

"There's no keyboard to press."

"So that means no typed password," she muttered. "Dammit. I bet it's facial recognition, like the doors. Do you see a scanner or a camera?"

"Negative," I said, seeing nothing but a flat plastic border above it.

"Maybe it's inlaid in the monitor itself?"

I leaned my head to the side, trying to look past the dark screen. As I twisted my head, a small, boxlike device under the glass caught my attention. It looked like a camera.

"I see it, " I said, the coursing adrenaline leaving me a little breathless. "Now what?"

"Now nothing," she said, her voice flat. "Because your face won't work."

I dropped my eyes to the guard I clobbered, still unconscious at my feet. I bent over and shoved my hands under each his armpits.

"Up you go," I muttered as I pulled the man to a standing position. Propping him up against the panel, I yanked on his hair, angling his head so that it directly faced the camera. "Say cheese."

I stood there for a second, waiting. But nothing happened. I dropped the guard's head and it lolled against my shoulder. "Dammit, Darcy. Nothing's happening. What else can I try?"

The wolves' howling got more frantic, competing with the panicked shouts from the werewolves who were still in human form. Bones cracked all around me as Frankie took out guard after guard. I heard Leon barking commands at our zombie army to hold off the rush of Leila's guards descending on the room.

"What did you just do?" she asked.

"I tried a guard's head."

"Was it still attached to his body?"

"Yes," I said bitterly. They were not going to let Frankie and me live down the last prison break.

"Crap," she said, her breath quick. "Okay, it may be retina scanning. Can you pry open one of his eyes?"

I juggled his flopping limbs, trying to keep him propped up and wedge his eye open.

A zombie guard pushed against us and we stumbled closer to the monitor. I lurched forward and my hip slammed into the panel. Holding the awkward position, I pried open an eye while the computer beeped its way to life. A red light darted out from the camera embedded into the monitor and scanned the unconscious guard's eyeball. The orange lights on the panel turned green. I shoved the dead weight of the guard off of me and slapped at all the buttons. Adrenaline coursed through my veins. We were so close to releasing these wolves.

The door buzzed and the locks slid, and I pushed towards the door through the chaos surrounding me. Our spelled army was relentless, going in for the attack against a group of guards who seemed almost uncomfortable hurting their comrades. The humans tried to subdue the spelled guards with nonlethal force.

My blood craving surged but I forced myself to stay under control. I could hear the rattle from the snake tattoo and my fingers itched to throw a spell, but my unwieldy magic in such a confined space was asking for trouble. These guards were uncomfortable hurting humans, even these humans trying to bludgeon the non-spelled guards. But they'd have no problem removing my head, or Frankie's, or any supernatural being's. They shot Mia in the back of the head at close range simply for being a witch. And we were the ones they called monsters.

Frankie muddled his way through the arms and legs of the fighting guards towards the now unlocked barrier between us and the werewolves. Since I was closer to the door, I beat him to it. He mouthed "wait" at me, but I was sick of him treating me like some Living Dead doll. I itched to get the wolves released so we could keep going and get to Dr. O. Besides, our hoodoo guards were being subdued one by one. We could use some angry werewolves to bolster our thinning ranks.

Before Frankie could shout at me to stop, I yanked open the heavy-looking door, although its weight felt quite normal to my vampire strength. I expected a flood of angry werewolves, in both human and wolf form, to storm through the doors, but instead, the doorway was empty. I paused, the hair on the back of my neck standing on end and my vampire senses keyed to high alert. My unease didn't stop me from stepping over the threshold.

A heavy iron net dropped from the ceiling onto me, sending me to the ground.

So much for a sixth sense. I didn't even have five. A heavily armed crew of prison guards charged out of the door, stepping over me as I struggled my way out of the tangled mesh.

"Crap!" I yelled, still trying to make my way out of the net. "It was a ruse, Darcy. A ruse! Let everyone know they moved the wolves."

"What are you talking about?" Darcy asked, the tone of her voice just south of panic.

"I'm in the cellblock," I said, grunting as a guard landed a swift kick to my ribs. "It's a trap. There are no wolves in here. Just guards. I have no magic."

Three guards pulled the iron mesh around me and I didn't fight them. The tighter they wrapped it, the easier it would be for me to break out through the metal mesh. They were compensating for a strong witch, not a full-on vampire.

Frankie was barking orders into the headset, but I wasn't paying attention. Instead, I scratched out at one of my attackers, drawing blood from his forearm. A fist flew into the side of my head, but I licked my lips and relished an early meal. My arms strained against the iron. Its jagged edges cut into my skin as I readied my dramatic breakout. I was starving.

Gramps' voice snapped me out of my cannibalistic thoughts. "Nina, don't let them know you've turned."

"I can take them," I growled, saliva dripping from my mouth as I stared at the blood leaking from the guard's arm into neat droplets on the cement floor.

"You have the element of surprise," Gramps warned. "You need that."

Frankie's howls drowned out whatever Gramps was saying. I turned, twisting in the iron net that rendered my magic null. Four guards had Frankie pinned while a fifth sprayed him with a fire extinguisher. From the burn mark erupting on Frankie's body, the chemicals for putting out fires were swapped with holy water. I started to rip through the iron that bound me but Frankie's weakened voice came through my earpiece.

"He's right. You have the upper hand. And you're our only way in. Do not vamp out."

"But—"

"I'll be fine," he said, and I watched his teeth grit from across the room as they hit him with more of the spray. "Holy water's for amateurs."

No it wasn't. Amateur vampires probably wouldn't survive the waterboarding Frankie was getting. Amateurs like me. I recoiled from the water puddling on the floor. An acid bath would tip them off faster than a vampire at a blood drive.

Frankie gave me a quick wink before he stopped thrashing long enough for them to turn the hoses off. His playing possum told me he didn't want me to get splashed by the spray.

The guards pulled the iron mesh tighter around me while Frankie went limp and slumped against the wall. I cringed at the welts that erupted on his exposed skin. My shock was released in an audible gasp when he turned his blister-covered face towards me.

"Don't like seeing your bloodsucker boyfriend all beat up?" a guard hissed at me.

I shuddered as his hot breath brushed against the back of my neck. I almost wished for a splash of holy water to burn off the lingering sensation.

Leon and his zombie army refused to quit, and they ripped through the cellblock, Leon encased in a swirl of dust and spell work. I watched as the small but solid female guard sent her steel toe-booted foot straight into the balls of my captor. He toppled with an ear splitting shriek of pain, releasing his grip on my iron chains so he could shove his hands against his throbbing crotch. I fought with the netting to extricate myself. A second guard rushed to secure me but my zombie savior stepped in with a solid right hook. The cracking sound told me she shattered the man's jaw. A third guard who started forward thought the better of it and raised his hands as he backed away. I whooped in joy until a shot rang out. The mood of the entire room went from manic to subdued in a matter of seconds, and my lady ass-kicker cleared the cobwebs from her head with a shake. When she raised her eyes to me, confusion spread along her face.

"Crap," I muttered twisting my head around. The shot that rang out snapped our zombie army out of their stupor. Before I even looked at Leon, I knew the reason why. So I wasn't surprised when I turned to see a trickle of blood slip from the corner of his mouth, his eyes staring into the void, he crumpled to the floor. When the witch dies, the magic dies with him.

With the hot foot spell toothless, the guards came out of their zombie stupor. Blank expressions turned confused then horrified as they took in the mayhem surrounding them. The cellblock went eerily quiet as the moaning zombies returned to human.

They shook their heads, unable to make sense of the carnage soaked into their uniforms, splayed across their face and lodged underneath their fingernails.

The female guard yanked her gun from its holster and leveled it at Frankie. She blasted him with a barrage of bullets, and Frankie's body jerked against the wall from the force of their torques. I almost snickered at her stupidity — bullets didn't kill vamps — until I saw Frankie fall to the floor into convulsions.

I clawed at the iron net. "What the hell did you do to him?"

"Hollow point bullets filled with ash," a guard said, trying to pin my arms down.

I fought against his grip, careful to keep my strength in check so as not to give me away. "Ash?"

"Like the kind you get at church during Ash Wednesday," the female guard chirped, eyeing me intently. She brought her gun up, and I swallowed. Did she figure me out? I braced myself for the hail of palm ash-filled bullets but instead she brought the butt of the gun down into the side of my head.

Starbursts filled my line of vision, and then the room spun. I felt my body thud to the hard cement floor before everything went black.

22

Ice cold water soaked my front while strange voices muttered unintelligibly around me. My eyes blinked open, adjusting to the stark light. I was in the cellblock with the witches, sitting in a chair with iron shackles binding my wrists and ankles. The bright light left me in near blindness, but my ears picked up the quick breathing patterns that came only with fear. Tension edged along my body and mixed with relief. At least some of the witches were still alive.

"The witch is awake," a gruff voice said from my left. I glared in his direction, my adrenaline pumping through my body, lengthened fangs hidden behind my lips, which pressed into a thin line. I squeezed my fingers into fists, struggling to keep my inner vampire hidden. But it was itching for release and my control was waning.

"Where's Frankie?" I managed to get out through gritted teeth.

There was a snicker. "She wants to know where her vampire is," said the deep voice that went along with it.

"The vampire is alive, if that answers your question," Leila's voice thrilled through the air. I suppressed a shiver.

"Where is he?" I repeated. Ash-filled bullets were no joke and the holy waterboarding weakened him substantially. But I was also fairly certain that Leila was the only other vamp in the facility besides me and Frankie. The witches were contained by their iron cells. The werewolves were chained up with them. As usual, the humans underestimated us.

"A trade," Leila responded, her cool voice sending chills into me. "Where's my daughter?"

"I'm right here, *Mom*," I spat out, my lip raised into a snarl.

"I mean the one I like," she said. "Kittie."

Hurt stabbed into me for a split second while I absorbed her words. Of course she didn't think of me as a daughter. She killed my father, faked her own death for decades and came back just in time to murder the woman that raised me. The only thing Leila and I shared was commingled witch and vampire DNA. But I was born into my vampire. Leila was bitten.

"Little sis was neutered," I said, unable to keep a measure of gloat out of my voice. I willed the snake tattoo to rattle, and even underneath all of the iron binding my powers, it gave off a little shake, strong enough for me to feel a surge of power dance through my body.

"How did you do that?" Leila hissed, suddenly in my face with vampire speed. She reached towards the tattoo peeking out from my shirt, retracting her hand as the snake rattled again. "You stole her magic? How?"

"I had a good teacher," I said, refusing to look away from my mother's piercing glare. Predators sensed weakness.

Leila eyed the iron binding me before turning away. Fists clenched, she began to pace, her human guards shrinking back each time she passed by them. I watched her irritation build with each silent step. Was Leila afraid? Of me?

She turned to face me again, her face contorted in rage. "You ruined everything. Again."

Her fangs were visible as she curled her lips in anger.

My adrenaline kicked in. I pressed my lips against each other, keeping my mouth shut, my own fangs itching with anticipation. My self-control was waning.

There was a buzz followed by the click of metal locks and the door to the cellblock opened. My eyes, still blinded by the spotlight in my face, made out a large muscular shadow moving towards me. I braced myself as it came closer, stepping in front of the aggressive brightness. My eyes blinked rapidly as they adjusted to the dimmer light. Max loomed over me, shoulders back, fists balled. He flashed me a tight smile and I stiffened.

Max was a rogue operator. He blew off the box truck pickup, the one that was supposed to drive the werewolves, witches, Dr. O and the rest of us away from this supernatural death camp. He couldn't be trusted. I tracked his movements, his body taut under his jeans, biceps bulging around his t-shirt.

"Max," Leila purred. "Any other intruders found on the sweep?"

"It was just the three," he said, turning his head towards me to share a fast wink. "Two now. The witch is dead."

"Dingdong, as the song goes," I muttered.

The back of Leila's hand met my cheek, and I made a show of pain, my head lolling to the side.

"He was not a local witch. Where did you find him?" she asked.

When I didn't respond, she slapped me again. There was more force behind it, stabbing my left fang into my cheek. I spit out a gob of blood then worked my jaw to make sure it wasn't broken.

"Not local," Max said. "Driver's license said Louisiana. Some town I'd never heard of."

"A backwater bayou witch?" Leila turned to me, gloating. "You *are* getting desperate."

I twisted my wrists in the bindings. I masked it as a nervous tick, but each subtle twist loosened the bolts from the wood chair. I was careful not to pop free. "He got us in, didn't he? Not so backwater. Now where is Frankie?" My glare rested on Max this time.

"Yes, where is Frankie?" Leila repeated, her question framed more as a threat.

"He got away," Max said.

Relief flooded me, but I stilled at Max's matter-of-fact tone. Leila's minions cowered in fear. Max didn't even break a sweat.

Leila bared her fangs. "What do you mean he got away?"

"We took him out of the cellblock and he bolted," he said, taking a step back from her and her sharp incisors. "It's just as well. The prison's not equipped to hold vamps."

"Not yet," she said pointedly.

"I thought you only needed her," Max said, nodding at me like I was some specimen under glass, not someone he sort-of-kind-of had a thing with. His refusal to say my name rankled, and I gave the bindings a violent twist.

Leila pressed her hands to her temples, her frustration clear, dangerously so. She raised her head and flashed him an icy smile. "Yes, I only need her and the old man. But I don't trust that vampire won't do anything stupid."

"He was soaked in holy water and riddled with palm ash bullets," Max said. "He's hurting."

"He was well enough to get away."

"I think he wasn't well enough to stay and fight. He'd never abandon her." Again, he nodded at me and refused to say my name.

"No?" Leila snorted. "What is this, true love?"

"Yup," Max said, pursing his lips. "That vampire would die for her."

"But you wouldn't?" Leila's cackle coated me with ice. I gave an involuntary shiver.

"Let's just say she wasn't my type."

I scowled. Sure, I was stupid for thinking I could date someone who was human...well, human at the time. But even after he was turned Berserker by Bertrand, his unease with our kind was palpable. But hearing an ex say it out loud—even a one-date-only ex—that still stung.

"If that vampire would die for her, he should have stuck around," Leila said, dripping cruelty with every word. "After all, look at what your daddy did for me."

My rage roiled inside me. "Where's Dr. O?"

"Oh? You miss your daddy figure, too?" she taunted, not missing a beat. She snapped her fingers and I heard footsteps shuffle behind me. The sharp smell of stale blood flowed into my nostrils, and a bit of saliva leaked out of the corner of my mouth at the pungent scent. I willed myself to tame my hunger. The sound of feet dragging along the floor followed. Her goons tossed a limp and bloodied Dr. O on the floor in front of me.

"What did you do?" I gasped at the sight of his bruised face, arms marked with all manner of glyphs and needle marks. He raised his head at the sound of my voice and relief flooded into me. He was still alive. Weak, but he was still alive.

"Let's see," Leila said, as she paced in front of me, counting on her fingers. "First I took your daddy. Then I took your aunty. Now..." She grinned, her fangs glinting in the fluorescent light.

"You won't be taking him," I said, my voice thick.

"No," she said. "Not yet anyway. I need him to stir one little spell for me."

"What spell is that?" I asked, tempering my anger. The bolt holding the wrist restraints was loosened enough that if I raised my arms, it would simply pop out.

"Why, the spell that made you, of course," she said.

I froze. "What do you mean?"

"Leila, please," Dr. O said, his voice barely above a whisper. "Leave her out of this."

A cold smile broke across her face. "Our little witch doesn't know?"

"Know what?" I asked. Panic mingled with curiosity, filling my stomach with a tight ball of tension.

She snorted. "I really need to explain the birds and the bees? At your age?" She heaved a dramatic sigh. "Vampires are dead. They can't have children."

"My very existence proves that false," I interrupted.

"But did you ever stop to think why?" she asked, her eyes glowing their eerie green as her excitement grew. I wondered if I looked like that when I was vamping out, because it was creepy as hell. "Of course you didn't. You weren't a miracle, Nina. You're not special. You were conjured."

"What do you—" I started, looking down at Dr. O as he reached for Leila's shoe, his mouth forming the word "no." She kicked him in the face before he could get the word out and he went down with a thud. I yanked towards Dr. O's slack body, but strain of the bolts kept me in check, reminding me to settle back down.

"I mean, we created you. Me, your father..." She turned to me, her eyes vibrant. "...and your well regarded mayor." She laughed as my expression turned from defiance to dumbfounded. So Gramps wasn't bullshitting me. "You don't think a centuries dead vamp can father a child without a little demonic intervention?"

Max's hand clamped down on my shoulder, giving me a small squeeze. Was this a protective gesture? I glanced up at him, his face contorting as he tried to contain his anger and keep the Berserker chained in his body. Bertrand made me a monster. Just like he made Max.

Max's anger channeled into me through his hand. I wasn't there when Max asked the demon for a favor, but I was sure the outcome wasn't what Max had in mind. The outcome never is where demons are involved. That's why it's best to avoid dealing with them at all.

Leila reached her hands to her knees and squatted in front of me to get a better look at my face. "Bertrand is your daddy too," she taunted.

"Leila, don't," Dr. O pleaded from where he was heaped on the floor, his own magic neutered by iron binding.

"Don't what, old man?" she said, turning her attention to him. She straightened and stalked to him, circling his spent body. She prodded his midsection with the toe of her high-heeled black boot. "Don't tell my daughter the truth? That we had a little demonic fertility help? Keep her in the dark like you've done for decades? It's time she learned that she was a mistake, an error. But damn it all if she wasn't the closest we got."

"I thought you did it for love?" he whispered.

"Love?" she scoffed. "Love! You are all so damn sentimental, aren't you? It was an experiment."

"An experiment for what?" I asked, digging my nails into the arms of the chair. I cast my eyes down, worried that they were glowing as my anger built, giving my vampire away. Not yet. It wasn't time yet. Not when I was finally getting a sliver of truth out of this woman.

She turned to me, her copper-colored hair so much like my own flowing around her. "To build the perfect weapon."

"To fight who?" I asked, my voice edging higher as my control waned.

"Everyone," she said.

"There's a good answer," Max quipped.

She glared at him. "You'd do well to remember your place, human."

"But I wasn't a perfect weapon," I interrupted.

"You weren't meant to be the weapon," she said. "You weren't meant to live, child. The charm was meant for me."

"But you weren't an immortal at the time," I said, realization settling in. "If Bertrand's charm didn't work, you'd be dead."

"And your father was a willing participant, with all his talk of love. He thought we were creating a baby."

"But really you were checking to see if the demon charm would kill me?" I said.

"Not kill you, create you," Dr. O interrupted, his voice weak. "Genetically speaking, if the embryo created from the coupling of a vampire and a witch survived, there would be reason to believe that whatever allowed the genetic mix to pair could be applied to an already living witch. It would give that witch the strength to carry both vampire and witch magic. Without that charm, the strength of the two combined would be disastrous to the host body."

"So you knew?" I asked.

"What's a little alchemy between friends?" Leila taunted.

"I knew that there was magic involved, of course," Dr. O said, closing his eyes. "I didn't know that it was for anything other than starting a family."

"So Bertrand's charm is how you're able to hold witch power, even after you turned," I said, not adding that it was how I was able to as well. "So what do you want from me?"

"Your demon mayor has been unable to replicate his charm," she said, surveying me. "Or perhaps he's been unwilling?" Leila met my gaze. The right corner of her lip curled up in amusement. "Either way, I need to do it without him. We can analyze your blood. We can kill you, watch you turn, figure out what he did to create you. And maybe replicate his spell. My experiment on Kittie gave me a good idea of how to do it." Annoyance flashed over her face. "But then you didn't need a tattoo to ignite your power. All you needed was a nick from a spelled knife."

That infernal knife triggered the entire chain of events. It was like the safety of a gun, needing to be released in order for the trigger to work. It was also a death sentence for me, with the vamp and witch waging war within my body.

"So what did you need the werewolves for?" I asked. I wanted her to keep talking. As long as she was talking, no one was dying.

"She won't stop at one genetic experiment," Dr. O said, curling in on himself. I hiccupped to hide the surge of power that coursed through my body as Dr. O shifted his position. The iron wasn't completely blocking his magic either. He was too powerful for that.

Leila glared at him, telling me she felt it too. "Please, lose the horrified expression. It's called progress."

"It's called murder," I said. Max squeezed my shoulder harder, and I felt my clavicle shift under the pressure.

Leila slinked, cat-like, towards Dr. O, pulling her blade out from where it was sheathed at the small of her back. Her mouth twitched up in a grin that made my blood colder than it already ran. I gasped as I realized what she had been doing. He was covered in blood from countless stab wounds. Leila didn't slice into him deep enough to kill him, but only enough to syphon his magic.

As powerful as Dr. O was, he was weak from enduring the iron and untold number of wounds. I wasn't sure he had enough magic to keep himself alive, never mind a plunge of that infernal blade.

We were out of time. The cavalry in the box truck hadn't arrived. My vampire beast was barely in check. Dr. O couldn't withstand anymore blood loss. It was do-or-die, and I was ready to die doing.

I yanked my arms lose of the bindings while I jerked my feet forward, popping the bolts that held iron clamps around my ankles. Shrapnel from the hardware went flying, kicking off a sort of duck-and-cover confusion among Leila's human army that I used to my advantage.

Hurling myself out of the chair, I raced towards Dr. O. Without my team of werewolves in the box truck, I was on my own. Vampire and witch or not, there were a lot of heavily magically armed humans standing between me and our exit, and Dr. O was my priority. I'd figure out how to get the rest of the witches and werewolves out some other way.

A burst of electricity hit me, and it felt like I was running through molasses. Even though my body moved at vampire-speed, I barely inched closer to Dr. O. Another jolt slammed into me, and the distance between us stretched out like a Bugs Bunny cartoon. I glared at Leila, her hands and lips moving as she tossed spells at me, hindering my progress. Shit. With the iron bounds released, my own magic — shitty as it was — would have to counteract her spells.

I closed my eyes, pushing my focus inward. I imagined breaking her spell; imagined what my speed would feel like; imagined the air tickling my skin as I zoomed through it towards Dr. O.

"*Mobilitas*," I blurted out, the Latin word for speed exploding off my tongue with all the delicacy of a freight train. My body hesitated, leaving me hanging in a midair leap. "Damn it all," I muttered, my mind racing over the countless ways that I probably blew the spell. Just as I was about to give the spell a go in English, my body lurched forward, breaking through the magical barrier that held me back.

"Grab her!" Leila shrieked, flashing a mouth of full fangs as she barked orders at her minions. Her eyes brightened, and, with no blood running in her veins, her skin's translucence was magnified. Her anger must have kicked her bloodsucker into full force. With the vampire dominant, her magic was slower, weaker. That's how I was able to break through her spell. I finally had an advantage.

A pack of guards stepped between me and Dr. O, and it was my turn to let my freak flag fly. My body shifted into an ungainly gait, jerking forward like an out of control NASCAR Sprint Cup. I barreled through the first row of guards, riot shields at the ready, like a set of bowling pins. Face to face with the next layer, I bared my fangs and reached towards one of the officers, his face pale with shock at the site of my vamped out body.

"She's a... she's a..." was all he managed to choke out as I grasped him by the front of his neck and squeezed. His eyeballs bulged and he flapped his arms, searching for his sidearm. The stink of desperation flowed off of him, causing me to gag. It was just enough of a distraction that allowed him to yank his sidearm from its holster and pull the trigger. I felt the lead burn through my abdomen, rip apart my intestines and then slice out of my back. Max laid down a string of expletives.

"Crap," I said, Max's salty language told me where the bullet landed. That'd piss him off for sure.

I tossed the guard, who was now unconscious, into the path of more security advancing on me from the left. His limp body slammed into the group, all four henchmen hitting the ground.

Another spell drove into me. Leila had enough mojo going to hit me with something, but whatever it was didn't seem to have any effect. I pushed forward as three more guards advanced and powered through them with a few well-placed punches, knocking each one out cold. Easy-peasy, as Darcy would say.

Somersaulting over the bodies heaped on the floor, I headed towards Dr. O. But as soon as my feet hit the ground, my knees buckled and vision blurred. Then what felt like a weight dropped into my head, threatening to split it open. Teeth gritted, I pressed my knuckles into my temples, unable to concentrate on anything but the pain ripping through me. Leila had gotten her mojo back.

While Leila's magic held me captive, I was an easy target for her hopped up humans. Lucky for me, they had to bring me down alive, although that was all relative. How alive did I have to be, really? Through my distorted vision, a group of guards, lead by the lone female, advanced towards me, but their movements were cautious, hesitant. They still weren't sure what I was, but they knew it was more than witch. And whatever Leila knew about me, she wasn't sharing. Yet.

I sensed the iron before the mega-shackle clomped onto my wrist. Given the weight of the metal, and my ability to sense it from at least a foot away, they were leaning towards the witch on steroids. The advantage was still mine; they didn't know I turned. Before they could chain my other wrist, I lashed out, striking a blow to the unlucky shackler, sending him across the room. Just as I was about to round on the next one, a force of electricity jolted through my body. I toppled to the floor, my body jerking from one side to the other, setting my nerves on fire. As I thrashed around, I watched the female guard press a cattle prod into my thigh, singeing the fabric of my pants. My focus trained on her gleeful face before a larger jolt killed my concentration again. My fangs extended while I clawed at the cement under my body, searching for some way to ground myself against the feral electricity. I wrinkled my nose as the smell of charred flesh assaulted my vamp-tuned senses.

I felt the vibration of the boom before I heard it, and the woman wielding the cattle prod landed on the floor in a heap, her nearly severed head landing just inches from my own. The flow of electricity that burned through my body mercilessly ceased, but the relief was short-lived. Blood gushed from the woman's open neck, spilling onto the floor and creating a viscous red river that flowed towards me. I licked my lips when the metallic scent hit my nostrils, and I was suddenly very aware of the ache forming in the pit of my stomach. Another heavy boom vibrated the walls, jarring my head up just in time to see a Hulked out Max remove another guard's head with simply the swipe of his hand.

I forced myself to my feet, away from the appetizing stream that pooled beside me. Leila had a momentary moratorium on magic, her eyes as wide as saucers, mouth twitching into a gleeful smile, as she witnessed a Berserker attack. The supernatural creatures had died with the Vikings until Max and Bertrand teamed up to bring them out of extinction.

Max was systematically wiping out each of Leila's guards. Blood spray hit the walls and puddled on the floor along with chunks of flesh and bone that he tore away with his bare hands. Max moved through the ranks, each human cowering before him, their pleas unnoticed by his Berserker-blind rage.

The problem with Berserker-blind rage is that it doesn't always point to the right targets. So once he felled Leila's minions, Dr. O was directly in his path.

The giant loomed over the tiny man still crumpled on the floor. With both his body and his magic so weakened, Dr. O was as good as dead.

I launched myself between Max and Dr. O, not caring that my preternatural swiftness was on full display. Max looked at me, lost in the fog of war, his eyes not registering any recognition. Now in close proximity to him, I caught the pungent scent of adrenaline mixed with sweat. His fury manifested in his heart, the muscle pounding so hard that I could see the taut skin over his chest constrict and relax, working to pump an unnatural amount of blood around his freakishly large body. Between the gore soaked room and the sound of his blood pulsing through his body, my hunger trolled just below the surface. I felt my control slipping away as Max continued to advance on me, threatening me, his jugular vein a tantalizing reminder of the damage I, too, could inflict on the living, no matter what size.

Max raised his hand and landed a punishing blow to my jaw, my bones shattering on impact. I raised my bowed head, my jawbone healing as fast as he mangled it. I massaged its hinges and took in his expression of surprise, probably because my head was still attached to my body. His disbelief short-lived, he snatched me by my neck, lifting me off the floor. His hands threatened to crush my trachea, not that I needed it.

My un-manicured nails sprouted into claws, and I slashed at him until he lost his grip. I dropped back to my feet. Leila stalked behind Max, hesitating as she looked between the two of us.

She motioned to the guards behind her, eyes bright. "Take them both down. Keep them alive."

The guards advanced with a glacial pace. I smelled their unease

— attacking the Hulk and a Living Dead Witch at the same time was a definite cause for consideration. A guard up front decided he didn't want to be in the line of fire and pulled out a Taser, shooting its tendrils at Max while maintaining a safe distance. The probes landed on his chest, and I felt the force of the electricity jolt his body. But, rather than bring the big man down, it only served to piss him off even more.

Max came at me with renewed ferocity. I dropped into a crouch as he reached for my neck again, coming back up to drive an uppercut into his stomach. Every knuckle in my fist cracked as it collided with a wall of muscle. I grunted, but Max didn't even flinch. Instead, he raised the back of his backhand and slammed it into my cheek. The force of his punch sent me flying several feet and I landed against the wall, some of the stones crumbling on impact. Shaking the cobwebs from my head, I scrambled out of the concave dent that held the shape of my body as Max advanced towards me. He reached for me and I ducked to get out of his grip. But with my brain still foggy, I misjudged the space between us and he caught me by my hair, yanking on my braid and pulling my head back. I raised my leg and landed my booted heel straight into his kneecap. A satisfying crack was heard just below his bellow of rage and pain. But instead of releasing my hair, he twisted the plait around his hand and then slammed my face back into the crumbling wall.

I raked my razor sharp claws through my hair, slicing the braid until it dangled in his hand, freed from my scalp. Before he could snatch me again, I sprang onto him. He held steady, and I climbed him like a mountain, finding his neck and sinking my fangs into him. Warm blood exploded into my mouth, and as I pulled, I felt my own strength blossom as his receded.

I glanced up to see Leila's henchmen advancing on both of us, a mix of Tasers, guns and iron chains all at the ready. A metal link slammed into the side of my head. Hands groped at me, trying to pull me off of Max's mountain of a body. My teeth slipped easily out of his neck as he slumped against the wall, his body slowly returning to human form. The chain came at me again. This time I caught it in mid-swing, yanking the chain hard and bringing the man on the other end towards me. I wrapped the chain around his neck and pulled him to my chest, using him as a shield as I turned my body out towards the other guards. Bullets sprayed into both of us, his body jerking at their impact. Throwing his limp body aside, I powered through the wall of humans. They fell on me like rabid animals. Not one of them had the sense to get the hell away from the vampire supped up on Berserker blood.

Vampires have superhuman strength, but a vampire on Berserker blood? I felt invincible. I *was* invincible.

I powered through at least a dozen guards and didn't even break a sweat. Then I came face to face with Leila. A sick smile spread on her face.

There were no more secrets in the room now. There was no doubt that I walked among the undead. No doubt that Max was a Berserker.

"Interesting," she said, her voice barely a whisper. I felt the wheels of her bioengineering brain turn in every subtle shift of movement that my vamp-enhanced senses picked up.

I shifted my body so that I was between her and Max, who had gone from Berserker to blood-drained human passed out on the floor. With Max's blood coursing through me, I shivered and tingled, telling me that I wasn't only borrowing his physical strength. My fingers itched to throw a spell, see if Berserker blood affected my magic too. But Leila was already looking at the two of us like a science project.

Her eyes shifted to Dr. O, who was still heaped on the floor, his battered, bloody body barely hanging on. She still had the blade, and Dr. O still had Druid magic to syphon. I shifted my form to block her view of him, but she just turned her attention to Max again. Crap.

"So many choices," she cooed, lips twitching up into a cold smile, showing her fangs. "Who shall I choose?" She eeny, meeny, miny, moed with the knife.

There was only one way to end this. I dove towards her, pulling back at the last minute as she swept the blade across my middle. A long slice ripped through my clothes and into my skin, drawing blood. A small jolt of magic jumped from my body into the knife. The power was visible, moving like blue lightning, as it climbed up the hilt and into in her hand. Her eyes went wide.

I football tackled her just as she made her move towards Max, knocking the knife out of her hands. I heard the metal skitter along the floor and I hoped it was out of her reach. With both hands free, her fingers twisted and her lips moved, throwing a silent curse at me. The hint of Berserker power behind it sent me reeling back as a stabbing pain ripped through my skull. I pressed my fingers into my head and tossed off what was either a half-assed healing charm or a spell to boil water. Either the pain would disappear or my brain would boil like a ham hock.

Instead, nothing happened. But my racing metabolism diluted her spell enough to pull me out of my stupor. I charged her again, this time plunging my sharp claws into her side. I flung Leila aside, away from Max, a chunk of her flesh ripping off as momentum severed her skin from my razor-sharp nails.

She pressed her hand to her side and removed it. The skin around her abdomen was raw, but it healed over instantly. Another curse hit me, and I was slammed against the wall behind Max by invisible arms. With the ache in my head subsiding, my focus was better. I countered her curse with my own spell.

"*Solutus!*" I cried. The word was barely off my lips when I was dropped on my ass, surprised that it actually worked.

Leila scowled as I scrambled to my feet. "Well, aren't you a right little monster."

"Apple doesn't fall far, does it?" I shot back while we circled each other

"You make Mommy proud," she said, her luminous eyes flashing venom.

Her hands began working as she prepped another spell to throw at me. Against her, my novice magic was practically useless in the iron-covered room. I needed to take Leila down the vampire way.

I hauled my body towards her and shoved my arm into Leila's mouth before she could finish the spell. Her fangs sunk into my forearm and I felt her voice box vibrate as she tried to finish the incantation around a mouthful of my flesh. I closed my free hand around her throat, cutting off the sound before she could utter it. But it was too late. Her spell hit me right in the gut, sending me flying across the room. I landed with a splat against the wall, then slid down, stunned.

Through my brain fog, I saw Leila move for the witch blade. I hurled myself forward, tackling her at the knees. She nailed a solid donkey kick to the side of my face before she sprawled on the ground. I snatched her by the leg as her forward momentum continued towards the knife. Her fingertips tickled the hilt as I hauled her back towards me. I heard her mutter another spell and her leg turned to molten lava. I yelped in pain and dropped it, watching the third degree burn blisters bubble up on my bare hands before my vamp healing kicked in.

The curse gave Leila just enough time to reach the knife. I sprinted towards her, chasing her down before she could snatch it, but she was too close. There was no way I'd reach the blade before she did. Instead, I dove past Leila and wrapped my body around Dr. O just as she plunged the knife at him, shielding him with my body. The blade burned as it entered my lower back, and I gasped as I felt a rush of power spill out of me. The knife vibrated so hard it picked up a tone. Leila's sharp intake of breath told me that my magic was flowing into her.

"I hope it hurts you like a bitch, too," I muttered under my own pain.

Before she could respond, the room was rocked with an explosion, and the few guards that remained were tossed from their station by the cellblock's door. Glass shattered, followed by stone, sheetrock and metal tumbling from the far wall. The room filled with a fine, grey dust. Several long, low honks echoed through the room.

"Nina?!" Al's voice bellowed through the mayhem. "Where the hell you hiding?"

I squinted, a pair of headlights beaming into my eyes and the shape of the box truck coming into focus. I burst out laughing, choking on the acrid dust as it settled around us.

Leila swore and twisted the knife in deeper. The snake tattoo rattled and hissed, writhing under my skin as it held onto my mojo. A sticky wetness covered my back but the original rush of power from my body slowed to a trickle.

How the hell was I beating the blade?

The sound of the truck's backdoor sliding open was followed by footfalls landing hard on the cement floor. An almost unrecognizable Lincoln, the large Alpha from Moose Cabin, fought his way through the wreckage, tossing the large boulders that made up the old walls like they were nothing more than stone. I cringed at his half-turned appearance — a wolf-like torso with human appendages, a human mouth with large, yellow wolf teeth, a bulging forehead, and mix fur and human skin quilting its way around his body.

It wasn't a full moon, so their transformation to wolf was limited. They almost looked more frightening this way.

"Go find the wolves!" I yelled at him, which turned into a groan as a new stab of pain lurched through my back.

Leila forced the knife in deeper, as if that would kick-start the flow of magic. The snake undulated on my skin and my magic didn't budge. Leila shrieked in frustration and yanked the knife out of me. I winced again. The blade clattered to the floor and I saw that it was charred black and rendered useless. I panted, eyes tracking Leila, while my body knitted itself together. She turned in a circle, surveying the damage. She grinned at me, and I shivered.

"Quite the mess you've made," she said, her eyes glowing. Standing straighter, the air crackled around her. I tensed up, hoping I'd have enough time to deflect whatever spell she was readying.

"Hello, daughter." Gramps' voice came from behind the truck. Then he stepped through the path that Lincoln had cleared through the rubble. "I thought you were dead."

"Daddy," she cooed. Her smile chilled everything in the room. "I thought I smelled that backwoods magic of yours."

"You're using an awful lot of that backwoods magic yourself," he said, barely cocking an eyebrow.

"You taught her well," she said, giving me a brief nod. "But not well enough."

"You murdered my daughter," he said. His voice went soft and the lines on his face looked deeper and more drawn as he remembered Babe.

"She didn't like you," Leila hissed.

"She was afraid of the dark magic," he said. "And was right to be. You could have used a little of that fear yourself."

Leila cackled. "Fear it? Please. I wield it. It does my bidding."

"Hmmm," he said, moving his head in a slow nod. "You don't respect it, child. To respect it, you need to fear it. And not respecting its danger? That's your undoing."

She glared at him as her small hands began to turn in on themselves, her deft fingers working around a complicated spell. Her hair began to lift from the electricity running through her body while her lips formed a silent curse. Gramps was at the ready with his own spell, quicker with experience at throwing it. Whatever he tossed at her, she took it right in the gut, doubling over at the force of the magic. Her breath was ragged as she stuttered out a reversal spell. When she raised her head, her lips were a faint blue. Damn. Gramps threw a death spell at her. It only failed because the iron was taming his considerable power. The witch was not playing.

But neither was Leila. Her voice shrilled through the room as she landed her own spell. Gramps suddenly dropped to one knee, a wrinkled hand clutching at his chest. Gore rose in my throat as the old man's face went from beet red to a grey pallor. While she didn't get all of it, she was still juiced on some of my magic, and her constant chanting made the spell hard for him to break.

"Who's undoing is it now, old man?" she crowed as he gasped for air.

I snatched a piece of rebar poking through the smashed wall. It still had a hunk of cement attached to one end. Holding it like a baseball bat, I swung it at Leila. Between the weight of the makeshift weapon and the vamped up velocity of my swing, the rebar flew from my hands and headed directly towards her. She dropped to the ground at the last minute, the rebar just missing her and embedding itself into the far wall. But the distraction meant that she released her magical grip on Gramps. He slumped to the floor, unconscious. Bounding towards her, I took a leap just as she brought herself up from her knees. We both went tumbling to the ground, arms and legs twisting as we rolled from impact.

I heard her faint voice, barely a whisper, and knew she was spelling. Untangling myself from her limbs, I sent a sloppy punch that landed across her cheek just as I tumbled backwards. She scrambled up from the floor, pitching her body at me before I could stand. Leila pressed her knees into my chest.

I looked up at my biological mother into eyes exactly like mine. Same shape, same vibrant green color. My snake tattoo rattled a warning as Leila pushed out another spell. I reached my right arm up and gripped my hand around her neck. Squeezing, I pushed my body up while she tried to maintain her balance on my chest. Whatever spell she wanted to hit me with was temporarily squashed.

Her knees still balanced on my chest, I dropped my back to the floor, then levered up my legs, using momentum to push me upright and send Leila off of me. The element of surprise meant I landed on my feet while she was left sprawled on her ass. My triumph was short-lived, however, as she started to spell again.

"Can't this woman stop with the damn spelling?" I grumbled. The energy she raised pricked at the hairs along the back of my neck. I kicked out at her, my frustration landing in her solar plexus. She snatched my ankle and yanked me down. I twisted as I fell, taking the impact with my hip rather than my tailbone. I released a string of curses — salty language, not spells — at a maneuver I should have evaded. Even though Leila's real source of power was her magic, she was still a vampire. And my rising frustration made me sloppy.

I didn't have the right gear to fell a vampire, so I had to knock her ass out. Vamps were much easier to kill than drop. Add the witchy stuff into it, and I understood why Leila created the hybrid in the first place. Getting both under control was damn hard. I had to shut off her ability to spell, but so far I was only successful in interrupting the onslaught.

I pulled myself into a crouch. I wasn't going to beat her as a witch, but with the Berserker blood coursing through me, I could take her down as a vampire. Leila was spelling again, and this time I allowed the force of her magic to slam into me. I felt it light my insides on fire. The burning started in the pit of my stomach and radiated out from there, through my very soul. A hiccup escaped me and a puff of smoke slipped from my lips. I choked on the scent of my own entrails burning. I gritted my teeth, more from disgust than pain, and hoped that the burn wounds festered only briefly before my Berserker-enhanced speed healing kicked in. Because that was just gross.

Once I felt my body begin to heal, I exploded out of my crouched position and rushed her like a defensive end. The sound of her "oomph" on impact was satisfying. I knocked Leila off-balance and carried her body ten feet until I slammed her back into a wall. Her eyes bugged out at me, and I smiled, smoke still trickling out of my mouth in sporadic intervals. I pressed my right forearm against her throat, pinning her against the wall. I blew a smoke ring in her face, and smiled.

"Nina, catch!" Gramps shouted, tossing me Leila's charred witch blade. I snatched it, one handed, from the air. The weapon was useless to syphon her power, but it was still sharp enough to send into her heart.

I pressed the blade's tip against her chest. Saliva dripped from the corners of my mouth. I waited, not sure for what. For her to tremble in fear? For her to apologize for being a shitty mom? For her to bring Babe back from the dead? Instead, her lips twisted into a smile.

"What the hell are you waiting for?!" Gramps yelled. "Stick her with the damn knife!"

I pulled the knife back but hesitated again when she lifted her chin in defiance. Realization threatened to overpower me. She didn't think I could do it.

My body surged with power as my anger rose. Without hesitation, I slammed the knife into her heart. She let out a surprised squeak from the force of the blow. I pressed my forehead against hers and stared at her eyes as life began to bleed out.

"The storm's coming." Her whisper was followed by a small throaty chuckle. The blood pooled in her mouth, dripped down her lower lip. "And it's going to break you. It's going to break all of you."

Her head fell to the side and she closed her eyes. I yanked out the blade, hoping it was sharp enough to take off her head. But Max's strong hand grabbed my forearm just as I swung the first hack at her neck. To be truly dead, her head had to come off. Then she'd turn into a pile of dust and ash.

"What are you doing?" I seethed. "I have to finish this."

He shook his head and tried to pry the knife from my grip. "We need her alive."

"Alive?" I repeated, strengthening my grip on the knife. "What kind of sick game are you playing?"

"She's gonna wake up," Gramps warned from behind us.

"It's not a game," Max said, his voice even. I noticed he was wearing part of a bloodied guard uniform. The pants hung low on his hips, shirt unbuttoned, showing off an impressive set of abs. "Colton needs her alive."

"Mary Jane?" I asked. What they hell did the U.S. government want with Leila?

"And where are we supposed to put her?" Frankie's voice echoed through the now quiet room as he climbed over the mess of concrete, stone and rebar. "Sorry I'm late, love. Good god, what the hell did they do to him?" He dropped to his knees beside an unnaturally still Dr. O.

Tears warmed my eyes as I watched Frankie cradle Dr. O's limp body. I turned to Max. "You can't hold her. She can magic or vamp her way out of this prison."

"Bertrand said he had a place to contain her," Max said. "She can't get out."

"What's the point of keeping her alive, Max?" I ask, itching to bite someone, anyone, as my frustration grew. His was the closest neck.

"We can't trust Bertrand. Or Colton," I added, glancing at Leila's face when I thought I saw her eyes flutter.

"Put that damn knife back in her heart," Gramps hollered. He saw it too. "Goddamn amateurs."

I knocked my elbow into Max's face, hitting his eye, and then stuck the knife back into Leila's heart.

"Thank you," Max said, blinking a few times. He clamped iron manacles on Leila's wrists.

"Those won't completely neuter her magic. She's too good a witch for that," I warned, thinking about her strong spell crafting in a room surrounded by the metal. Her magic was too strong to rely on the usual safety measures. "And if you pull that blade out, you'll have the vampire to contend with."

"Leila's not as good with the vampire," Max said. "She's not as comfortable with brute force as you."

I scowled. "But she's still a vampire. Don't underestimate her, Max. And don't let Bertrand get cocky."

Frankie lifted Dr. O up off the floor. "We've got to get him out, love. He needs medical attention."

"Where are the wolves?" I asked, turning my back to Leila and Max. She was his problem now.

"They're in the truck," Gramps said. "That Masshole werewolf shuttled them into the back while you were beating my daughter's human sheep senseless."

I nodded at him. "Can the witches ride with them? Or have the werewolves turned?" I suppressed a nervous giggle at the irony of breaking the witches out of certain death only to lose them because we stupidly housed them with a bunch of turned werewolves.

"The ones that are turned are in no shape to kill anyone," Lincoln said, coming around the back of the truck. "They're barely alive themselves."

Gramps shuffled around the bodies piled on the floor, liberating a set of keys clipped to a bloodied guard's belt loop. "I'll go free the witches."

"You make sure those wolves don't snack on our people," I said to

Lincoln. "I doubt the witches have enough magic left in them to fight off a rabid dog."

He gave me a curt nod before disappearing behind the truck again. I walked away from Leila, leaving Max to deal with her, and made my way over to Frankie. He looked at me, pain etched in the slight lines around his eyes. "I don't know if he's going to make it," he said, his voice barely above a whisper. "He's lost a lot of magic, and that's what kept him alive for almost as long as me."

I blinked back tears and looked at the old man's noble face. "If he must, at least he'll die with the people who love him, and not alone on a cold slab of iron."

Frankie's jaw tensed at my words but he kept silent, and I understood his pain, born of grief. Mortality bothered vampires more than it bothered humans. Vampires literally lusted after life, and before I engaged with my dormant witch, I found the idea of death almost unbearable. But with the witch serving as a grounding force, death didn't strike me as so permanent anymore.

Besides, look at Casper. Sometimes the dead come back to haunt us.

23

I SHOVED Darcy's tangled mess of chords and electrical equipment onto the floor to give Frankie a place to lay out Dr. O. Gramps hovered behind both of us, cracking his knuckles, impatient to do the spell. Dog slipped under the table and growled when he got close.

"We can't do the spell yet," I muttered, wishing Gramps would cool his jets someplace else while we waited. The spell relied on timing, and we had to get it just right.

"I don't like this," Frankie said, his body a blur as he rushed into the apartment. He slid Dr. O onto the hard wood of the table. Dog nuzzled the old Druid's hand as it hung off the table. "This spell will kill you, Nina."

"We have the entire plan mapped out," I said, feigning confidence in my voice. "All I have to do is get from the kitchen into the hallway. Piece of cake."

"Not when the sunlight is streaming in," he grumbled, narrowing his eyes at me.

The spell that Gramps said would help Dr. O survive needed two witches and a dose of sunlight for it to work.

"Darcy and Matty are taking care of it," I said, adding a bright smile to take the edge off.

Darcy and Matty were tacking blackout paper on all the windows in the hallway. Then they were going to install a makeshift heavy drape over the door that theoretically would keep the sunlight out of the hallway when I busted through.

There was a soft knock at the door and I wondered where the hell Darcy and Matty fucked off to. They were supposed to be making sure the hallway didn't leak sunlight, but they probably were hunkered down in Matty's sunlight sealed lair. They couldn't keep their hands off each other, end-of-the-world be damned. My eyeball twitched as I slipped past Frankie to get to the door. Dog padded down the hall behind me.

Father Dougherty stood on the other side of the threshold, shifting on his feet. He glanced down the stairs at his left, moaning sounds coming up from the darkness at bottom, confirming my suspicions. His glance moved to Dog, who sat on her haunches beside me, her soulful eyes watching him. He tugged at his priest's collar and continued to move his weight from foot to foot. The decision between walking past a hellhound or listening to sex between a banshee and a Beta-Vamp played out on his face.

"Sorry," I said, opening the door wider to let him in, my face hot. He paused once more to look between the basement and my sullen hound before giving me a curt nod and crossing the threshold. Once he slipped past me and Dog, I poked my head into the hallway and looked towards the front door. At least they got the blackout paper up. All that was left to install was the draping, which was stored in the basement. Getting the thick dark cloth out clearly led to their unsanctioned work break.

I closed the door, leaving it unlocked so the two lovebirds could let themselves in when they were finished. Ambling back into the kitchen, Dog at my heels, I gaped at the sight of Father Dougherty standing over his old friend and administering last rights.

"What are you doing?" I asked, barreling between him and Dr. O, the cross in his hand burning my skin when my arm hit it.

Frankie grabbed me from behind, keeping me away from the priest. "Dr. O wants it done, Nina. He requested it."

"He's awake?" I asked, touching the old man's craggy face. He looked every bit his age now, his pale visage nearly translucent.

"He was," Frankie said. "Just enough to tell Dougherty to do it."

Tears stabbed at my eyes and I slumped into the oversized couch, grateful that the open loft allowed me full view of Dr. O from anywhere in the oversized room. I glanced at the heavy curtains on the windows, willing the sun to rise faster. Once it did, we'd do the spell, open the curtains and, with a little luck and vampire speed, Dr. O would live and I wouldn't be burnt to a crisp.

"Where are you going?" I asked Frankie, my voice sharp as I caught him heading toward the door.

"To get you a blood bag," he said. "You need food in you to outrun the sun."

I relaxed my shoulders and settled back into the couch cushions, closing my eyes. I heard Dog grunt into a prone position at my feet and a small smile quaked at my lips. Frankie would have to go into Matty's room to borrow a blood bag. "You may want to knock before entering."

"Having a go again?" Frankie muttered, his footsteps heavy with annoyance as he clumped down the hall. "Those two are bloody rabbits." Frankie slammed the door behind him, and his voice slipped through the heavy steel as he shouted a warning for the lovebirds to get dressed.

Father Dougherty picked up last rites again, and my jaw clenched as his words of faith echoed through the apartment. I wanted to blame recoiling from the prayer on my vampire, but I knew it was because I was losing someone else. Someone I loved. Someone who loved me. Dr. O took on my weirdness and molded me into a human first, monster second.

I sighed, willing myself to remember that point when the vampire in me threatened to wipe out my conscience. My stomach clenched again, and I squeezed my eyes tighter as my mind wandered to Frankie and the blood bag. Did we have enough time for me to go out and get some real food instead of the microwave dinner he was bringing up from the basement? The stress was making me hungry, which meant hangry loomed close behind.

The cushion beside me shifted as Gramps joined me on the couch. I popped opened one eye and looked at him, not entirely trusting that he wouldn't toss a spell at me while I was trying to keep myself from losing it. "What do you want?"

"I'm sorry about the old man," he said, rising his chin towards Dr. O. "But you need to know there's a good chance the spell won't work."

"But there's still a chance that it will."

He sighed. "I don't think that we should risk your exposure to sunlight."

Sitting up, I opened my other eye and leaned towards him, opening my mouth to show my fangs as I shifted closer. "Says the man who drove a knife into my jugular and watched me bleed out."

"There was a reason why I did that," he said, leaning in towards me in a show of bravery. Or stupidity, since my hunger was beginning to gnaw at me. "Besides, you aren't truly dead."

"No, now I'm undead," I said, clicking my fangs against my teeth. Where the hell was Frankie with that bag? I needed to take the edge off.

"But not *dead* dead," he said, leaning back and folding his arms into a self-satisfied posture.

My reflexes took over, and in a swift movement, I had him pinned to his end of the couch. I opened my mouth, scenting him with both my nose and taste buds. "I wonder," I said, my voice low, "if I drained a witch, would I get your power too?"

"You can only hold the power from my blood until you metabolize it," he said, his voice steady. A light sheen of sweat broke out over his forehead. It was the only evidence of his fear.

Father Dougherty cleared his throat. "Nina?" His voice cracked when he said my name. When I looked up at him, he stepped around the table, putting the solid wood between us. "Lachlan is asking for you."

I retreated to the other side of the couch, averting my eyes when I saw that Dr. O was watching me through his rheumy blue ones. After a final nasty look in my grandfather's direction, I stood and walked to Dr. O's makeshift hospital bed, eyes lowered.

"I'm here, Dr. O," I said, my voice low.

The dying Druid reached for my hand and squeezed. A jolt of magic shot up my arm. My body responded with a small jump at the shock. Dr. O chuckled.

"So you can feel my magic now," he said. "That's good. That's good."

"Is it?" I asked, biting my lip. The snake writhed under my skin as it took in Dr. O's power, and I squirmed under the sensation. Feeling magic didn't feel terribly good.

Dr. O took a large breath, as if taking in my apprehension. "Your body has been battling two kinds of magic since you were stuck with that infernal knife. Your survival depended on turning."

Gramps' harrumph from the couch served as an "I-told-you-so."

"I had hoped, however," Dr. O continued, his weak voice growing louder and more resonant, "that you would not turn quite so soon. Learning to control both newly acquired witch magic and vampire power is going to be a difficult task."

"Some would say impossible," Father Dougherty interrupted. Though his face was kind, his voice carried a hint of disapproval.

"Stop being so damn Catholic, Dougherty," Dr. O snapped. "That's always been your problem." The priest crossed his arms and looked sufficiently chagrined. Dr. O winked at me and I gave his hand a small squeeze. "But, Nina, I agree with your grandfather. This is not a spell you should attempt."

I started to protest when I heard Darcy, Matty and Frankie come in through the door, their loud chatter carrying through the apartment. The three were arguing about how best to put up the draping. Frankie sauntered in, his smile widening when he saw that Dr. O was awake. He tossed me the blood bag, which I caught with one hand, and came over to give Dr. O a careful hug.

"Won't be long now," Frankie said as he straightened, nodding towards the windows. I imagined the pitch black outside transitioning to a deep shade of grey. My body went numb as I thought about my arm burning from a sliver of sunlight that came into my room after I turned. But I was newly undead then. Butterflies danced in my empty stomach. *I can do this.*

I bit open the blood bag and pounded the stuff in one shot. Frankie raised one eyebrow but kept his mouth shut.

Dr. O cleared his throat. "Nina, don't do the spell. There's no reason to do the spell."

I made a face and wiped my mouth with the back of my hand. "I'd say keeping you alive is a big reason."

His chuckle was wheezy. "I'm old, Nina. I may be older than Frankie, if you can imagine. I've had my time on this earth."

I leaned my hip against the table and stared down at him, willing myself not to cry. "But I haven't had enough time with you."

He squeezed my hand again. My fingers felt small, being crushed in his. "Learning how to let go is part of growing."

"I've grown quite enough over the past few months," I said, a tear running down my cheek as I thought of Babe.

"Yes, you did. So did I," he said, sadness blanketing his face. "But the blessing is we had her to begin with. Babe...Me...we served our purpose on this earth. We watched you grow into the woman you are right now. Vampire and all." His eyes twinkled, and he motioned me to come close to him.

I bent over him, my ear near his mouth.

His soft breath tickled my ear as he whispered, "And now you have the love of a good vampire. That's more than enough."

My face flushed and I straightened. Avoiding Frankie's eyes, I forced a smile only to keep the ugly-cry at bay. Back stiff, I turned to look at the draping over the windows. The edges looked lighter, spring's grey morning breaking fast.

I released Dr. O's hand and crossed to the kitchen counter where Gramps placed a box of spell supplies. I began to pick through the candles, choosing a red one for vitality. Gramps sidled up beside me and busied himself with some herbs. My shoulders eased down from my ears while I used Gramps' ceremonial knife to carve runes into the wax, grateful that I didn't have to do this spell alone. It was complicated, and required me to run like hell out of the apartment before I resembled barbecue.

"You're not listening to him," Father Dougherty said, his eyes wide.

I barely glanced up at him. "If I have a chance to save him, I'm doing it."

"But that will upset the natural balance," he said, his voice edged with steely resolve.

"Leave the natural balance to us witches, Padre," Gramps said, patting at his pockets in search of a cigarette.

"No smoking in my apartment," I warned.

He loosed a string of Spanish swears that turned Father Dougherty's ears beet red.

"I don't agree with this," the priest said. "This is not the natural order."

I slammed an open palm down on the counter. "Leila is the one who messed with the natural order! If she didn't syphon out his magic, he'd be fine. We are righting her wrong!"

"The whole thing is madness," Father Dougherty continued as though I didn't say anything. "We are not meant to live forever."

"Tell that to Frankie," I said. "You're going on what? Seven hundred years, give or take a few decades?"

"Maybe humans aren't meant to," Frankie added. "But we're not human, none of us."

"My oldest friend, you shunned our magic...," Dr. O explained.

"Silence, Lachlan, please," the priest said.

"...and joined the clergy to try to atone for it," Dr. O continued, ignoring the priest's protests.

"You're not well," Farther Dougherty insisted. "You're speaking nonsense."

"I speak truth," Dr. O said. His rising voice resonated through the room. "You fear your magic and that's why you hate it."

I raised my eyes to look between the two old friends. The priest looked stunned, like Dr. O slapped him. And, in a way, he did.

Dr. O turned his head towards me. "This is your cautionary tale,

Nina. We all have both magic and monsters inside us, just like you. The trick is to fear neither. Only then you learn to wield it with benevolence. Even the dark parts." He nodded at Gramps, who tilted his head towards Dr. O in deference.

I cleared my throat. "Then I'm doing this spell so I don't fear it."

"Nina," he started, "don't fear the darkness, yes, but remember there is a natural order."

"To hell with the natural order," Gramps barked. "The sun's coming up. We need to do this. Now."

He lit the rune-carved candle then held out his hand to me. I clasped onto him, the energy from his body moving from his fingers into my hand, jolting through my body.

"Sacred fire, give him strength..." Gramps began the spell, using his free to hand to pepper herbs into the flame.

"Sacred earth, give him spirit," I continued, picking up the herbs with my fingertips and spreading them over the candle, the flame sparking up. The air filled with the thick scent of incense.

Gramps and I alternated the spellcasting, and my stomach fluttered as we closed in on the denouement. Magic was quite theatrical, I realized, turning over the next steps of the spell in my mind. Frankie would swing the thick drapes back, allowing sunlight to stream into the room. The idea was that the light energy from the sun would heal Dr. O's psychic wounds and restore his magic. The physical wounds needed medical attention but that would come later — he lost more magic than blood. The spell was a gamble. Dr. O's magic was ancient magic, and this spell was decidedly not. But we hoped the runes carved into the candle would make up for it.

Dr. O reached out and grabbed Father Dougherty's hand just as we uttered the final line, "Sacred sun, give him life." I bounced on my toes, ready to run. Frankie pulled on the drape. Sunlight spilled from the top of the window, and my skin immediately prickled as blisters began to erupt.

Dammit, I hesitated, and now I had less than milliseconds to get the hell out. My body jerked into motion. I was too young to have the grace and fluidity of someone like Frankie and my herky-jerky moves were an affront to the vampire mythology. Just as I dove for the black draping around the door, Dr. O's voice boomed out, speaking in ancient Celtic. Stopping short, I slammed into the wall to kill my momentum and got a mouthful of brick dust as my impact crushed the red clay. The sky went pitch black and the air in the apartment crackled, the electricity going out. The candle flickered and then extinguished.

I turned to Dr. O. His silhouette told me he was sitting up on the table. Father Dougherty stood beside him, shoulders hunched and hands on the edge of the table, his breath coming in ragged, uneven gasps.

Frankie's voice broke through the shocked silence. "That wasn't the spell, was it?"

"That was definitely not our spell," I said, my voice cracked in surprise. "What the hell just happened?"

"I'll be dammed," Gramps said, chuckling. "You clever old coot." There was a sound of liquid sloshing as Gramps pulled his flask out of a pocket. The smell of tequila hit my nose.

"I don't understand," I said, brushing crumbled brick off my clothes as I moved towards the lumps their bodies made. My eyes were fighting to find some sliver of light to grasp onto, which was how our night vision worked. But the darkness was total.

Dr. O forced an eclipse.

"Put the draping back up, Frankie," Dr. O said. "The sun will come back soon."

"What just happened?" I repeated, shuffling forward, following their voices. I caught a sliver of sunlight returning just as Frankie pulled the draping back over the window. The kitchen lights flickered back on. Whatever Dr. O did was strong enough to cut the power.

"You son of a bitch!"

My eyes went wide at Father Dougherty's rough language. The normally sedate priest looked like he was ready to commit murder. My eyes tracked to his target, Dr. O, whose shoulders slumped over, the wrinkles that cut into his face even more defined. His skin was dry and had a crepe-y appearance. Was Dr. O aging?

He lifted his head and saw my searching expression. "Yes, Nina, I am simply an old man now."

"I don't understand—" I started.

Father Dougherty interrupted, his hands balled into fists. "You selfish son of a bitch. I didn't want your magic!"

"I had no choice, old friend," Dr. O said, his face drooped with regret. "I know it's not what you wished, but it's what is necessary."

"You held the magic just fine," the priest said, eyes welling with tears.

"I held the bulk of your magic for too long," Dr. O said quietly. "It was time for you to take the burden."

The younger-by-not-much priest dropped his chin towards his chest in deference.

"I didn't think you could do that," I said, realization washing over me.

"Do what?" Frankie asked. He started the question from across the room, but was by my side when he finished it.

"Dr. O took the bulk of Father Dougherty's magic on himself," I started.

"Why?" Frankie asked the miserable-looking priest.

The priest sighed. "I was a reluctant Druid. I didn't want to live with the magic. It felt unclean."

"So you simply took his magic on along with your own?" Frankie asked Dr. O, who simply nodded.

"What a spell," Gramps said, his eyes dancing with excitement. "Best bit of magic I've ever witnessed. And you must be one tough-assed Druid to carry the magic of two people around. For how long?"

Dr. O shared a small smile. Father Dougherty moved an arm around Dr. O and helped him off the table. Frankie grabbed the other side and they maneuvered the exhausted man onto the couch.

"I had left just enough magic in him to keep him alive," Dr. O said, as he settled against the cushions with a grunt. "He doesn't age as slowly as me, but it was enough to cheat death many times over."

"But now your—" I stared, my voice cracking before I could finish.

Dr. O nodded. "Now I'm human, of a sort. I will live in my old age, all the aches and pains that come with the wisdom of years. I will eventually move on." He smiled, his wrinkles prominent. "When, you want to know, don't you?"

I nodded.

"That remains a great mystery. One of the few mysteries I have left, and I refuse to spoil it."

A knock on the door pulled my eyes away from him. I tried to take a breath but no air filled my lungs.

"Dammit, Darce," I groused as I stomped down the hallway. I pushed open the door. "You missed the entire—"

Special Envoy Mary Jane Colton stared at me, her icy gaze sending a chill down my spine. "We missed what, agent?"

"Agent?" I asked, turning to look behind me.

"She means you," Max said. He stood just behind her, stance wide.

"Just call me Nina," I said, stepping to the side to let them in. His arm made a protective barrier between her and me as they stepped into the apartment. "You can stand down, Max. There's no more of my magic flying around."

"Your magic is the least of our worries," he muttered.

I closed the door and sagged against it, watching Mary Jane's sharp heels dig into my old wood floors. I had a feeling I wasn't going to like why they were here.

"We have a problem!" Mary Jane called out to me from my kitchen.

"Why am I not surprised?" I muttered, tracing her steps into my apartment. She and Max hovered in my living room, looking warily between Father Dougherty and Dr. O. "Father Dougherty and Dr. O, this is Special Envoy Mary Jane Colton. The new head of Blood Ops."

She extended her hand. "Doctor, it's a pleasure to meet you. I am happy to see you back, safe and sound."

Dr. O nodded deferentially but ignored her hand. "Indeed."

Mary Jane gave him a forced smile and straightened, smoothing her perfect white Oxford shirt with the palm of her rejected hand.

"So what's this problem?" Frankie asked. His eyes danced in amusement at the power play filling up the room.

Max glanced at Mary Jane as she cleared her throat.

"You lost her, didn't you?" I asked, crossing my arms over my chest.

Gramps clapped his hands together and plopped into kitchen chair. He leaned back, balancing the chair on its back legs. All he needed was some popcorn.

Mary Jane pushed her shoulders back. "She got a spell off—"

"Of course she did," I said, my temper rising. I pressed my nails into the skin of my arms, feeling them sharpen as I tried to keep my vampire under control. Vamping out on your boss was not a good idea, no matter how much she deserved it.

"I thought you contained her," Frankie said. His voice was controlled, but his eyes flashed a bright cobalt, telling me his vampire was rising to the surface as well.

"She slipped through our containment," Max said.

"How?!" I barked.

Mary Jane whipped her head around to give me a sharp look, which I matched.

"You took the knife out, didn't you?" I asked.

"We thought we could hold her..." Mary Jane started.

"But you misjudged," I finished for her, my anger stoking my bloodlust, boss be damned. I grabbed at her, pinning her against the wall, my forearm pressed into her chest while I nosed at her neck, scenting her. Mary Jane's accelerated heartbeat sent tremors through her body as saliva dripped off my fang and drew a wet line against her skin.

"Nina," Frankie said, turning my name with a heavy warning.

"I got it under control," I lied, as my mind tried to force my impulses to behave. I swallowed and released my arm from her chest. Her feet landed on the floor with a thud. I didn't realize I lifted her up. "You people want to run Blood Ops but you behave like a bunch of inept humans."

Mary Jane, her breathing shallow, rubbed the wetness off of her neck. "We are human."

"Maybe that's the problem," Frankie quipped.

"Bertrand already chewed our asses out. We don't need it from the both of you," Max said. His arm went protectively around Mary Jane while he examined her neck.

"I didn't touch her," I said, scowling at both of them. "Let me guess. Now you want us to clean it up."

"It's what you do, right?" Mary Jane said.

"You did this yourself," I said. "Max, we told you keeping her alive was a mistake."

Mary Jane pressed a manicured hand to Max's chest before he could respond. "We needed her alive."

"What for?"

"We have our reasons," she said.

"Are you mad?" Frankie fumed. A shiver of recognition went through me as I noticed he was dangerously close to vamping out too. Damn, that meant Frankie was beyond pissed. "She's in the wind. She has no ties here."

"She has Nina," Mary Jane said. "She won't leave this state until she's done with her."

"Done with me?" I said. "You mean kill me."

Mary Jane just smiled. Great boss, right?

"Forget it," I said, seething. "It's your turn to bring her in. We did our part. Too bad you failed at yours."

Mary Jane shook her head and made a clucking noise. "Remember our deal. She's still out there, and this state is still a tinder box."

"So you're saying your missiles are still pointing this way," I said, drawing my lip up in a sneer. I stared at her neck, her skin above her carotid artery moving in subtle waves. My fangs itched. That blood bag wasn't enough.

"Missiles?" Dr. O asked, his movements pained as he struggled to stand up. Father Dougherty took his arm and eased him back down to the couch.

"Yes, missiles," Frankie said. "These gits are going to clear out Leila with a bunch of bombs."

"And yet you wanted her taken alive," I said, narrowing my eyes.

"It wasn't our original intention to take her alive," Mary Jane said, her impatience rising to the surface. "But it was a courtesy extended to Bertrand when he asked."

"You blew it and now we have to clean up your mess because of a courtesy to Bertrand," I said, my anger bubbling up. "That's just brilliant."

"Where do you think we'll even find her?" Frankie added. "The prison was easy. Not so much now."

"Locator spell, perhaps," Mary Jane said, her right eyebrow rising. "I thought there were powerful witches in this room."

Gramps snorted. "Lady, like Nina said, you blew it." He dropped the chair down to all four legs. "I'm hightailing it back home to Mexico, and if you all are smart, you'll do the same."

My cell-phone chirped out the tune to "Sunday Bloody Sunday," and I glared at Frankie, who shrugged. It's the end of the damn world and he's messing with my ringtones?

I snatched it up from the kitchen counter and checked the caller ID. "I don't think a locator spell is going to be necessary," I said, before swiping. "What's up, Chuck?"

But I knew exactly what the Beta-Vamp was going to tell me before his panicked voice burst through the phone. Leila had found her way to the old farmhouse.

24

"I DON'T THINK I've told you that I love your new look," Frankie snarked at me, his grin wide. He held up a pair of kitchen scissors and opened and closed them, eyebrow raised.

I yanked my hand through my shower-wet hair, which now stopped halfway between the nape of my neck and my shoulders. The ends were ragged from being sheared by my sharp vampire talons, not a professional with top notch scissor skills. "Maybe I can look up a spell or something to fix it."

He chuckled. "How about calling a hair salon? Some have evening hours, you know."

I gave a noncommittal shrug. I wasn't one for spa days.

"In the meantime, do you want me to clean it up for you?"

"You know how to cut hair too?" I asked dryly. I pulled the belt of my fluffy robe tighter and tapped my foot lightly, glancing at the shuddered windows. Nervous energy and adrenaline still spindled through my body.

The sun was still up, so the shades were drawn tight to keep out the daylight. The one thing Leila couldn't do was walk in the sun, so she was contained in the basement of the farmhouse until dusk.

Since she wasn't a threat with the sun out, everyone but Frankie cleared out. Matty and Darcy were holed up in Matty's basement. Father Dougherty took Dr. O to the church rectory. Gramps went straight to the bar. Max and Mary Jane...well, they could go to hell for all I cared. I suspected they went running back to Bertrand's, so close enough. Everyone was reconvening here just before nightfall. But that was about as far as we got with any sort of plan.

"I had her Frankie," I said, my voice barely above a whisper. "I just had to take her head, and this whole mess would be done. Over."

"Nina, we've been over this a million times," Frankie said, thunking the scissors down on the counter. He looked exhausted. "Come on." He patted the top of the kitchen table. "Let's get that haircut cleaned up. Did I ever tell you about the time I worked for Vidal Sassoon?"

The edges of my frown twerked up. "You are such a liar."

He held up his hand. "Swear on my Aunt Fanny."

I gave a small jump, planted my ass on the table and crossed my legs demurely, pulling the ends of the robe down my legs. I put my hands over the choppy ends of my hair. "What'd you do at Vidal Sassoon? Clean the toilets?"

"Give me a little credit," he bristled. "I was the shampoo boy."

I cleared my throat to keep from laughing. "You?"

"It was the '70s," he said, his tone of protest raising my suspicions.

"The '70s you say?" I prodded while he tried to pry my fingers off the ends. "And what makes you think that you can cut hair when all you've done is shampoo?"

He sighed, dropping his hands from my hair. "I'm observant, you know that. I picked up a few tricks. This is a simple cleanup, just even out the ends." I gripped my hair tighter, pulling on my scalp. "Can anything I do make it look worse?"

That was a good point. My shoulders dropped along with my hands. "Have at it," I said, wincing when I saw him pick up the scissors out of the corner of my eye. He ignored me and shifted my shoulders so that I was sitting straight. "What do the '70s have to do with the haircut?"

"Nothing," he said, a bit too fast. I felt a light tug on my hair followed by the sound of a scissor snip. I raised my hand to block my hair again, and he sighed. "I had to wear a certain uniform."

"And?"

"Doesn't that explain it all?" he asked, annoyance edging his voice. The next snip was a little sharp.

"What, were you on roller skates?" I teased. "Wearing gold lamé?"

He cleared his throat. "Yes."

I burst out laughing.

He slapped the scissors on the counter. "I told you it was the '70s. Everyone wore gold lamé!"

I was laughing so hard, I was tearing up. "You must have looked ridiculous," I said, wiping my eyes.

"You done?" he quipped, picking the scissors back up when I nodded. He started in on my hair again while the image of Frankie the Shampoo Boy in gold lamé kept dancing through my mind. I still quaked with laughter. Frankie paused his trim and sighed. "It wasn't very comfortable either. The fabric doesn't breathe. Now stop mucking about or I'll poke you in the neck."

I smirked at the bad joke. "Too late."

Frankie hacked at my hair and a comfortable silence settled in between us. We had shared similar small moments like this for years: reading books, watching TV, me oiling my knives while Frankie whittled stakes.

Scissors down, Frankie fussed with my hair, attempting to style it. I reached my own hands up and laced them into his fingers.

"Want to take a look?" he asked.

I shook my head. "I trust you, Mr. Vidal Sassoon."

"That may well be your undoing," he said. While he was teasing, I knew a nugget of truth was buried inside. For both of us.

"Wait, don't move," he said. A slight breeze brushed across my skin as he speeded from the kitchen down the hallway. Before I could yell after him, he was back beside me, holding up a hand mirror.

"Come on then, take a look."

I wrinkled my nose and shook my head.

"What, are you afraid you no longer have a reflection?" he teased. "Come on Nina, marvel at my brilliance."

I sighed and took the mirror from him, and held it up to examine my new do. My face softened as I took in his masterful work. He turned my jagged ends into a pixie-ish bob that still managed to hold edgy appeal. I looked...pretty.

"I want you to see yourself through my eyes, love," he said, his voice quiet. "You're beautiful."

He pulled my hair and tipped my head back, gentle but with an undercurrent of demand. He dropped his head and his mouth found mine.

His kiss was unexpectedly gentle, almost tentative. The trepidation was mutual. My heightened senses triggered heightened emotions, and I wasn't sure what was real anymore. Was this attraction to Frankie a result of the vampire turning me lusty? Or did we really share something deeper and more meaningful, something nurtured by time, friendship and our unique partnership. The couple that dies together, stays together.

Frankie pulled me into his arms and lifted me off the table. My weak moan of protest went unnoticed as he carried me to the bed, his lips never leaving mine. He settled himself on top of me, putting his weight on one arm while he worked at the knot in my belt with the other. I felt the fabric give, and he pushed the robe open. My skin prickled from the exposure to both the cool air and Frankie's glowing eyes, his desire bringing the vampire forth. My own passion ignited as his fingers brushed along my exposed skin, his eyes tracking the path from my neck, between my breasts, then brushing lightly down my stomach. I shuddered in anticipation of where they were headed next.

He dropped his head into the crook of my neck. "You are beautiful," he whispered, his tongue tracing a tantalizing line from just under my ear down my neck. I gasped when his teeth brushed the sensitive spot, which turned into a moan as his razor-sharp fangs slipped just below the surface of my skin. I pressed my pelvis up to meet the rough fabric of his jeans, raw desire flooding me as his teeth dropped deeper, the pain turning to pleasure and then the pleasure turning into pain, an intoxicating yin and yang that had me close to climax.

Frankie's slid his teeth slowly out of my skin, keeping me from tipping over the edge. My fingers pulled at his pants, loosening the fabric with a satisfying pop of each button. I pushed them down his legs while he pulled his t-shirt over his head.

"Bite me," he whispered. He shifted his body to move his chest over my mouth, my lips feeling his creviced skin from his raised scars. "Right there. But careful not to pull blood, just bite. You think you can?" He stilled, my mouth touching a scar just to the right of his heart.

My body quaked at the promise of feeling his skin between my teeth. "Bite, don't pull," I said with a nod.

I gingerly raked my fangs along the hardened surface of the scar tissue. His response shot through his body, encouraging me to push through the surface. We moaned together as my teeth forced themselves deeper. I pressed into him again, fully feeling the depth of his desire with nothing between our bodies, the tightness of the tough scar tissue around my fangs arousing both of us. My teeth sank deeper still, and my lips caressed his skin. I lost myself in passion, teeth ripping into the tight scar tissue as lust propelled me. I took a deep pull against his chest, my body aching for blood and sex.

Frankie pulled himself away from me. His speed had him at the bottom of the bed before I realized he was gone. I shifted onto my elbows and pulled my robe closed. "Did I do something?" I asked, keeping my eyes lowered while I tugged on my hem.

"No, no, not at all," he said, slinking his way back up the bed. He peppered small kisses along my face. "But you started to pull blood from me. My blood would make you ill."

"Your blood?"

"Well, any vampire blood, since you're one of us, now," he said, weaving his fingers into mine. "Since we are technically dead, our blood is stagnant. Drink stagnant blood, get sick."

I brought my hand to my mouth. "Sick like how?"

He raised his eyebrows. "Remember how sick I was from the opioid laced blood supply?"

"Another thing that can kill us?" I asked, and he nodded. I flopped back into the pillows. "Vampires sure are good at keeping what kills them a secret."

"It does help cull the necrophiliacs," he said, settling in beside me. "We can still bite, just don't pull."

I closed my eyes and turned my head, the mood broken by my newbie vampire bungle. The thought of the next 24 hours closed in on me like a coffin.

"Frankie," I said, sitting up. I raked my fingers through my damp hair, feeling its even ends. He did a good job. "Look, Frankie. This stuff with Leila, turning vamp...everything. I think it's all clouding my judgment."

He smirked. "Clouding your judgment?"

"Yeah, you know," I said, not meeting his eyes. "I haven't had any real time to process what's happened. To me, I mean."

"Fair enough," he said, running the tips of his fingers along the fabric of my robe. I touched my neck where his teeth had been and a shiver of pleasure slipped through me.

"I mean, my emotions," I stammered, trying to ignore the tingling feeling that dropped into my lower body. "Everything is just so heightened right now." My focus waned as his fingers slipped under the belt of my robe.

"You will get used to that," Frankie said as he pushed the robe off my shoulders. I closed my eyes and dipped my head towards him, mouth open to scent his musk.

He moved his hand to the back of my neck, tilting my head towards him. His lips moved to mine, a tentative press before he unwound his fingers from my hair.

I grabbed his shoulders and pulled him to me. My uncertainty disappeared in a new cascade of vampire-enhanced hormones. He wrapped his arm around me, his mouth tentative even as his soft lips pressed on mine. I ran my tongue over his fangs, feeling their deadly point. Frankie shuddered in pleasure, and then his own tongue swept along mine and control slipped from me, my hunger for him growing. Our fangs were an erogenous zone?

"Nina, wait," Frankie said, holding me at arms length.

"I can't wait any longer," I panted. Desire overwhelmed me. My need to feel his touch boarded on obsessive. While my pragmatic mind attempted to reign itself in, my emotions overruled logic. " We need to do this. I need to do this."

"Why?" he whispered, pulling me to him, wrapping his arms around me in a tight hug.

"Because it's the only time I feel human," I whispered.

His body relaxed into me. "I'm sorry, love. I wanted you to be human for a good long time."

"I'm not human anymore," I said, driving my nails into the mattress.

"No, you're not," he said, regret dimpling his face. "And your human life was cut short, and I am so sorry that I couldn't do anything to stop it."

His expression withered, and he pulled me to him. Our bodies were held together without the violent, desperate force of vampire. Instead, he molded his body around me and placed his mouth on mine. Frankie was my rock. He was my best friend. He was my conscience. He was, indeed, my soul.

Frankie's usually sharp moves were languid as he settled me against the mattress and stretched his body out beside me, our lips never separating. His hand moved under my robe, circling the skin on my stomach with light strokes. My own fingers wrapped into his overgrown black hair, slipping like silk against my hand. I leaned into Frankie and hooked my leg to his while his fingers inched up my body, sending small jolts of anticipation through me. My body relaxed into the mattress. I'd forgotten how comfortable it was after spending months at Babe's apartment above the bar. Now that I needed the vampire security of the factory, I'd be moving back.

"Nina? You okay?" Frankie asked, aware that my mind had wandered.

"Yes, I am okay," I said, voice shaking.

He levered up on one elbow while one hand remained a warm comfort on my belly. "Then why do you sound like you're about to go all weepy then?"

I pressed my head into his chest so he wouldn't see how close to weepy I really was. "Because this is the most human I've felt in a long time," I said, my voice quiet.

His mouth covered mine again, but the hunger was gone. Instead, his hand gentled along my skin, moving in languid strokes down my belly. His hands found my center and, gentler still, his deft fingers teased me. This time I opened to him, took all of him into me. No arguments, no Casper dropping in. Just us.

I brought my hips to meet his, our bodies in synch. I pressed my fingers into his back as he brought me closer to climax with each thrust. Frankie groaned as we reached the precipice, and I pressed against him, pushing him deeper into me, allowing him into the deepest recesses of my body, trusting that he would always do right by me. Always care about me. Always stay with me.

Frankie's movements became more urgent. His fangs pressed into my neck, the small nips at my skin driving me over the edge. With a final shudder, we both collapsed in a relieved heap, our bodies still intertwined.

Frankie pressed his lips to the top of my head. "You are safe, love," he whispered. "You are."

25

I STARED into the dark woods from the side window as we drove the dark and twisty roads out to the farm. The waning moon didn't throw much light, and the headlights on Max's SUV were killed. Although Leila would hear us coming, we hoped the lack of light would dampen her night vision. Of course, it meant our eyesight wasn't on point either. The trees blended with the darkness to create indecipherable misshapen lumps.

Frankie kept shifting in his seat behind me, the sound of his clothes rustling against the leather of the oversized SUV's interior. The quiet interior of the car filled with his worry and more than a hint of frustration. My own nerves played along with his. Even Max kept his eyes on the road with his lips pressed thin.

"I'll be fine," I whispered, more to myself than to either one of them. We were going in without much of a plan. Some potion concoction Gramps handed me before we hit the road was my only witchy weapon. I wasn't even really sure what it did. Gramps called it Plan B. Not terribly helpful when Plan A wasn't exactly sorted, but Frankie and I were stocked up with all manner of sharp objects. Plan A it was!

Max took a sharp right and inched up the long dirt driveway. The first floor of the old farmhouse glowed with candlelight in the distance. The greying, dilapidated wood missing in some spots wasn't so obvious in the darkness. The faint orange glow from candles made the property look almost charming.

"May as well turn on the headlights," I said, slumping against the seat. "She knows we're coming."

Max killed the engine and we stared at the house about a quarter mile up a gently graded slope. "How can you be so sure?" Max's voice broke the eerie silence.

"Candlelight," Frankie said. He stared at the house, his gaze weary. "It feels like she put out the welcome mat."

"This is the first place we'd look for her, with or without Chuck's tip off," I agreed. "And she knows it."

Frankie reached behind him, checking the stakes nestled in the small of his back. "You ready?"

I nodded. "As I'll ever be."

I reached for the door handle but Max stretched his arm across the passenger seat, pinning me to my spot. "Wait a minute."

Frankie went motionless behind Max, like a predator stalking prey. "What do you think you're doing?"

"You cannot go in there without your grandfather," Max explained, craning his neck to keep an eye on Frankie.

"We don't have time for Gramps," I said. I shoved at his arm and flashed a fang, a slow simmer of anger threatening to turn to a rolling boil. "She's in there now. And we can't risk her taking off."

Gramps was finessing a spell to put a temporary damper on Leila's magic. The one thing the battle at the prison told us was that she was more lethal as a witch than a vamp. Without her juiced up mojo, she'd be just another vampire to bring down. But it was a complicated potion, and Gramps was still working on it when we left, Mary Jane's missile clock ticking.

Max relaxed back into his own seat but he didn't ease up. "So you're just going to go in there and do what exactly? How will you bring her down?"

"Drive a stake in her," I said, narrowing my eyes.

He crossed his arms and smirked at me. "You have to bring her in alive," he reminded me.

"Because that worked out so well the last time," I shot back before pushing the door open.

"You can't fail, Nina," he said, settling a hand on my arm, to keep me from leaving. "Mary Jane's not bluffing. She will give the order to fire those missiles if it comes to that."

"If it comes to that," Frankie said. "The missiles will be a mercy."

"That is exactly why we need to go in now," I said, shaking Max's hand off my arm. "What if Gramps doesn't make it in time? This is the last shot we have, and we're taking it."

I climbed down from the raised cab of the SUV before Max could argue. Frankie and I had a failsafe, and it centered around ripping out Leila's heart. Max wasn't going to like that. Or rather, Mary Jane wasn't going to like that. But Max, intent on keeping the boss lady happy, would make us wait for Gramps and his spell. What if the spell didn't arrive in time? What if it didn't work? Taking her down while her magic was flowing was not a simple task. It would take time that Mary Jane wasn't giving us.

Frankie jumped out the backseat and followed me up the dirt drive. I pulled out my cellphone and texted Chuck to know we arrived and were setting the wheels into motion. It was a courtesy more than anything, and a reminder for him and his nest to stay hidden in their bunker. The last thing I needed to worry about was Leila taking out a nest of Betas who had no defenses against humans, never mind the vampire-witch hybrid superpowers that she possessed.

"You good?" Frankie asked, matching my slowing pace as the front porch loomed just ahead.

"We don't really have a plan," I admitted, slipping my fingers into the cuffs of my leather biker jacket, double-checking that my blades were spring loaded and ready to go.

"When have our plans ever really worked to our advantage anyway?" he asked, flashing me a sexy grin that rippled through my entire body.

I stopped at the bottom of the steps leading up to the porch and turned towards him. I pressed my hand against his cheek. "After this is over, let's try a date night."

"And there's my incentive to not die twice," he said, taking my hand and giving it a fast squeeze. We started up the stairs in tandem. I hadn't been in the house since Leila's psychotic boyfriend nearly killed me here a few months ago. Frankie had to bind me to him so that his vampire immortality could keep me alive. My sense memory recalled every creak in the wood, as well as the rotting floorboard on the fourth step.

Frankie paused in front of the door, and a sense of unease sliced through me. He reached for the door handle, turning the nob easily. A chill shivered up and down my spine and I gave my head a curt shake. This didn't feel right.

Frankie gave me a one shoulder shrug. There was nothing we could do but open the door. If we walked away, Mary Jane would rain hellfire on the entire state, taking out humans and nonhumans alike. For a split second, I considered the ramifications of walking away. We were close enough to the state line and could cross into Connecticut in a matter of minutes.

"We're better than that love," Frankie whispered, as if reading my mind and becoming my conscience. "We've got a job to do, so let's get on with it." He reached for me with his free arm and pulled me to him. "I'm with you, always," he said before his lips pressed on mine, leaving a soft, sweet promise that he would stay by my side and see me through this fight, no matter what.

He pushed the door open and I cringed when its rusty hinges screamed our arrival. We both paused at the threshold, seeing a line of wilted carnations littering the floor, their stems pointing the way towards the kitchen. I wrinkled my nose at their moldy perfume.

"Finally!" Leila's voice called out from that direction. "The guest of honor has arrived."

I placed one foot into the house, hesitating when my snake tattoo gave a small rattle of warning before the energy of Leila's magic prickled my skin.

"Spelled," I mouthed to Frankie, jumping quickly through the ward on the door. Frankie tried to follow, but was snapped back by an invisible barrier.

"Won't work," Leila called from the kitchen. "That ward keeps out anyone non-witchy."

I brought my gaze to the doorway, focusing on the center, remembering what Gramps said about magic and energy. The molecules dancing together had to be there, I just needed to learn how to see them. My peripheral vision dimmed as I stared intently into the open space, willing myself to see what wasn't obvious. I stepped back into it, pausing at the threshold to allow the magic to wash over me. I closed my eyes and felt its thrumming, over and around my body, the snake following its patterns of movement. In my mind's eye, I imagined seeing the energy that crawled over my skin, my nerves on fire. When I didn't think I could hold onto the magic any longer, I stepped out of the ward and snapped my eyes open. I gasped, watching black-tinted undulations moving like sound waves across the door. I pulled my arms around my middle, gaping at the once empty doorway in shock. It worked. I actually saw the magic.

"Nina?" Frankie's low voice brought me back to myself. Shaking off my shock, I examined the waves for a hole, some spot in the ward that had a weakness we could exploit, but the spell was tight. There was no way I'd be able to take it down.

"Call Gramps," I mouthed to Frankie. If he was more than 15 minutes behind us, I was screwed.

"I don't like this," he mouthed back, giving me a desperate look as he inched back down the stairs.

I flashed him what I hoped was a reassuring grin, though it felt more like a grimace than a smile. I closed the door on him, my way of telling him to go back to the car until Gramps could deal with the ward. He didn't need to listen to Leila massacre me if that's what it came down to. I was on my own.

Even though my feet were light on the wood, the aged boards creaked under my weight. I sidestepped a gaping hole in the floor, shifting towards the leaded glass windows, giving me a limited view of the kitchen. Ice ran down my spine when I saw that Leila was not alone in there. I reached into my jacket, fingers brushing the stakes nestled into holsters. I felt the outline of the runes Frankie carved into one, the etched magic once saving my ass from a demon. Sparks lit my fingertips, the fire sending small jolts through my neurons, telling me that this was the weapon that was supposed to work on witches. Good thing, since it was the last etched stake I had. The other three were plain old Hawthorne wood.

Tilting my chin up, I strode into the kitchen, hoping my faux confidence would turn into the real thing. But it drained when I saw four witches seated at the Formica kitchen table. "Crap," I muttered, my heart sinking when I saw that Casper's mom was among the group.

She opened her eyes wide as she recognized me, and I returned it with a quick headshake. Leila had snatched part of the coven, but she had no idea that she'd captured the mother of my favorite ghost. No point in alerting her to that.

"There you are, darling," she said, her voice dripping the saccharine to match her smile. A lopsided cake covered by birthday candles and haphazardly applied white frosting sat in the center of the table. The candles flared up at every shift in the air as Leila flitted around the table, dropping paper plates in front of the witches. They tracked her with their eyes and, given their stillness, it was a good bet that she spelled them immobile. Their arms and legs remained unbound. "I feel terrible that I missed so many of your birthdays," she continued. "So I thought we could make up for all of them."

She stopped moving and the candles settled down to a flicker. "I have a confession to make," she said, dropping her voice to a whisper. "I'm not the best baker. But I can cook up a storm." She cocked her head, surveying my response to that. "Nothing? No?"

Babe always said that you could always tell if a witch was good with magic through how good she was as a cook. Spelling was a metaphorical mix of textures and flavors, and witches who understood the magic of cooking would understand to the magic of spell crafting.

"At least you tried," I said coolly, refusing to let her rattle me. I moved around the perimeter of the room, my eyes moving between the cake, Leila, and the four witches immobile in their chairs, the only outlet for their terror through their eyes.

"The birthday girl cuts the cake," she said, snatching a knife from the counter.

"I'm not hungry," I said, watching her fidget with the sharp blade.

She swiped the knife in a circular motion, coming dangerously close to one of the witches, who shut her eyes tight in response.

"What are you doing with these witches?" I asked.

"Aren't these witches part of your coven?" she asked, eyes widening in mock surprise. "You mean you don't have a coven? How very sad for you. And dangerous." She drew out the last syllable; the snake-like sound caused my tattoo to shake its rattle in warning. She pressed the knife against the neck of Mariana, Casper's mom. "So what you're saying is we don't need them anymore."

Gramps' warning about remaining coven-less ricocheted through my head. Sending an anxious glance over to Casper's mom, I rocked onto the balls of my feet. I was ready to pounce, my eyes tracking on the knife. "What good will killing them do? That's not a spelled knife. It can't steal their power."

"No it won't, darling," she said. "But killing them sure would be fun."

She plunged the knife into the cake and the candles extinguished in the whoosh of air from the movement. She hacked into the cake on the other side and pulled out a sloppy slice, plopping it onto a paper plate. She pushed it towards me, and I glanced at the white cake.

"Funfetti would have been fine," I said, blinking at the dry, white cake. It looked like there were maggots writhing in the pastry. I suppressed a shudder. "Thanks, Leila, but I'm on a liquid diet these days."

"Call me Mom," she said, her green eyes—so much like mine it was like looking in a mirror—were as cold as marbles.

"I don't think so," I said. My eyes darted back to the knife as she flicked it. A blob of frosting landed on the table in front of Mariana. I had to figure out how to break the spell Leila had on the witches. If they could channel magic with me, we could defeat her.

"You called my sister 'aunt,' didn't you?" she asked.

"It takes more than blood to make a family, lady," I responded, glaring at her.

The witches' eyes tracked Leila as she stalked around the table. I followed in her wake, keeping a good deal of space between us. Her eyes went brighter, fangs peeking out from under her lip. Her copper hair, so much like mine, shifted in a wind as she began to draw on her power. *Was she going to throw a spell or bite?*

Vampire speed kicking in, Leila snatched the nearest witch. Before I could react, she brought the knife straight across her throat. Mariana's scream over seeing her sister slain punctured the eerie silence, breaking me out of my shock. I rushed to the witch, still frozen by Leila's spell, her eyes trapped in a silent scream as blood poured out of the wound. I pressed my hand over it, a futile effort to staunch the gush of blood.

Dammit. My mind raced for a counter-spell, and my worry rose as she methodically moved to the next witch. Warding off a repeat attack, I scrambled onto the table. Pushing my body between Leila and the witch, I shielded my heart and braced myself for the knife to slice into me. I yelped in surprise a pair of sharp fangs punctured my neck instead of a blade.

Leila released my neck almost as quick as she bit into it. She scrambled backwards. "You little bitch," she cried, spitting blood from her mouth. "So it is true."

I smiled. "Surprised?"

She wiped her mouth with the back of her hand. "Who did it?"

"Gramps," I said, my smile broadening as her own face twisted in rage. She loosed a bellow that shook the entire house. Anger made people sloppy, vamps and witches included, and Leila was already unhinged to begin with.

"That man, that man, that son of a bitch man!" she muttered, pacing the kitchen, aged floorboards groaning under her weight. "He loved my sister. But me, he treated me like a disease all because I married a vampire. Didn't even want to marry a goddamn corpse. Forced my hand. That son of a bitch. Forced. My. Hand."

She slammed the knife into the kitchen table, just barely missing my leg. The surviving witches, still stuck in their positions, shrieked as the table rattled.

"You didn't want to marry my father?" I whispered, backing off the table slowly. Leila looked at me, her face wet with tears. She shook her head. "So why did you?"

"Why don't you ask Bertrand?" she snapped. Turning her wrath towards the witch to her left, she twisted the woman's neck in one swift move.

"Bertrand?" I breathed, staring at the slumped over witch, her head lolling at her chest. Dammit, I had to break her spell on these witches, but she kept pulling my focus. And where the hell was Gramps? I changed tactics. "Come on, Mommy Dearest, you know that's not the witch you want to kill."

I scrambled back, focusing on the undulations of my snake tattoo, allowing its feral magic to work its way into my body. My fingers went numb, the telltale sign that they were about to shoot sparks. But I didn't want sparks. I wanted fire. I focused my energy on building the sparks into something more lethal, but my hands had other ideas. My hands reached towards the witches who were still alive and Leila's spell oozed out of them, my hands like a set of magical magnets. The spell manifested itself in my hands as a ball of goo, and, once the witches snapped forward in release, I chucked the ball of energy at Leila.

She shrieked as the magic hit her, freezing her in a rather unflattering position, her face twisted in anger.

"Run!" I yelled at the dumbfounded witches, snatching up Casper's mom and pulling her towards the door. I heard Leila muttering Latin and knew that the spell wasn't going to hold. I wanted these witches out of the house before she was free.

Just as Mariana scrambled for the threshold, I felt the heat of a fireball behind me. I gave Mariana a shove to the floor and dove after her, the spell splatting into the wall. The old, dry wood was like kindling and fire engulfed it on impact.

"Get out," I screamed at Mariana and the other witch who clutched onto each other, frozen in terror. They stared at me, wide-eyed, and for a split second, I wondered if Leila's spell on them didn't break. Then Mariana screamed, and I ducked and summersaulted towards them in one fluid move, narrowly avoiding a fire-engulfed ceiling beam as it crashed to the floor. I snatched them both by their armpits and gave them a shove through the doorway into the living room. Another fireball narrowly missed my head, and I leapt onto the witches' backs to drop them to the floor before it pegged one of them. The spell landed at the far end of the room, but the rising odor of singed hair told me that it was a near-miss.

I scrambled to my feet and started dragging the fear-frozen women to the door. I kicked at the old door, its wood splintering under the force of my boot. I pushed both witches through the jagged hole. I tried to step over the threshold to the not-yet-torched porch, but my foot landed against an unseen barrier with a thud. I tried again, this time shoulder first, and bounced back as if something solid was there.

I turned and watched Leila emerge from the kitchen, the fire licking at her back, her copper hair wild. Her lips moved in some unheard incantation, and a line of yellow-orange flames streamed across the ceiling like an ocean wave. I shook my left arm and a blade released and dropped out from the cuff of my jacket. I reached behind me with my right and pulled the etched stake out from the holster nestled in the small of my back. She had bested me as a witch, but I was the better vampire. Right now, I had to be.

I pushed off the balls of my feet and flew a good seven feet off the ground. As I came down for a landing, I brought the sharp blade down towards her chest. She angled away, her own vampire speed a match for mine. I missed my target but sliced her across the face with the holy water imbued blade. She scuttered backwards, the pungent smell of her burning flesh hitting my nose through the acrid smoke of the burning house. She dropped the green ball of oozing magic that she was forming. She pressed her hand to touch the gash along her cheek as the skin around it erupted in angry, red bubbles. I smiled, my sharp fangs showing. She wasn't used to getting hit with consecrated items. They wouldn't kill her, but they would slow her down. And I was supposed to bring her in alive.

Leila's hand launched out and grabbed the arm that held the stake. She shoved a spell into me. I shrieked and fell to my knees and she dropped down with me, refusing to release my arm as magic surged into my body. I heated up rapidly, my stagnant blood beginning to boil. Waves of nausea overtook me as I tried to rip myself away from her. Hand firm on my wrist, Leila turned the stake towards me and pressed it against my chest. I panted as her magic burned into me, the realization slowly coming over me that she was probably doing magic outside of a protection circle. I focused on the energy flow coming into me, cringing as I felt my core temperature spike even further. My scream of "*novis*" shook through my body and she dropped my wrist fast, giving me a split second of opportunity to reverse the stake and plunge it into her stomach.

Leila loosed a bloodcurdling scream. She put her own hand over mine, trying to pull the stake out while I continued to push in. She drove another pulse of magic into me, and this time the energy clamped at my dormant heart, threatening to force it to beat again. But I only clutched the stake harder, refusing to release my grip. Leila sent another wave of electricity into me. Each time she fried me, my brain went fuzzy and the room went black, only to come back to myself as the voltage pulled out of me. She was trying to restart my heart by pulling electricity through me. But her ability to draw an unending arc of energy was stymied by the rune-etched stake leaching her magic away. If she succeeded in jumpstarting my heart, there was a good chance I'd come back brain dead.

She cried out as she pushed a huge force of energy into me. I felt a flutter in my chest and then my heart surged. I tipped my head back and opened my eyes, staring at the fire licking at the ceiling above me. I struggled to turn Leila's spell back at her again, but my eyesight was rimmed in black as my brain began to fail. I took a gasping breath, my first since my grandfather took my human life from me, and my lungs filled with acrid smoke, choking me. My body weakened, and I felt myself slipping away.

"*Mortis eius reversus,*" a feminine voice shouted above the roar of the fire that engulfed the house.

I came to, blinking rapidly as my eyes readjusted to their vampire vision. I braced myself as I felt another surge of electricity, but this time it beat a path out of me and into Leila's hand. My benefactor, whoever it was, reversed the spell so it flowed into Leila.

"*Deus habitat in medio eius,*" a deeper voice cried out. The spell called on a higher power to enter my body, and a sense of grace drove through my psyche before it turned in on me. I matched my shriek to Leila's as my body became a holy weapon and waged war against the vampire in both of us. Leila dropped my hand and careened backwards, sending me sprawling to the floor.

"*Deus dimittere illam.*"

The pain of consecration lifted and I turned to see Mariana and Gramps standing in the threshold, hands clasped together, waging a magical battle together.

"You okay, kid?" Gramps called out, and I nodded, ducking as Leila regained her composure enough to throw another ball of fire towards us. Her aim was sloppy, but the attack still caught Gramps in the arm, smoke wafting up his colorful Baja hoodie as he slapped the flame out with his hand.

Mariana gave Gramps a sideways look as he muttered what I recognized as a dark spell, but she held onto his hand and the potency of their paired up magic sent Leila backwards. She careened towards the impenetrable flames leaking out of the kitchen.

"We can't hold this long," Mariana warned as the ceiling behind me partially collapsed. Leila was on her hands and knees on the floor, flames shooting around her as she lifted her head. Vengeance was etched on her face as she pulled herself up, magic rising, snuffing out the fire in her path as she stalked towards me.

"This ends now!" she cried out, her low voice shaking the house, more of the ceiling coming down from the vibrations. Her fingers twisted and she muttered a spell, then in a fast motion, she pushed her hands out. A wave of energy blew through the room and I hit the deck. Gramps and Mariana weren't so lucky. Pushed backwards by the force of the curse, it lifted them off of their feet, pushing them out of the house and onto the dirt driveway.

"Nina, catch!" Frankie called out, throwing me a stake. He was still stuck on the porch, the ward around the door holding strong. I stretched out my hand and the wood smacked into my palm. I twisted the sharp point as Leila came driving at me. My arm arced down, ready to plunge, but she dove at the last minute, tackling me at the knees just as I sank the stake into her. Both of us splayed out on the floor. I twisted my legs around her neck, tightening the grip. I flung her over my shoulders as I rolled onto my back then used the momentum to jump to my feet.

I turned in time to see Leila's face screwed up in pain as she pulled the stake out of her side. Panting, she palmed it and shouted a spell. The impact of the magic coated me, causing me to move like molasses. I struggled to push through the spell as she came at me, the point of the stake headed straight for my chest. Still moving in slow-mo, I arched my spin and collapsed into a back bend, the stake sailing an inch above me. I snapped back up once Leila and the stake cleared, the spell broken once she passed me. She pivoted around before I turned, and I howled when she embedded the stake in my shoulder blade.

I felt the energy drain into the wood, like a slow leak in a tire, as the rune in the stake dampened my magic. I stretched my arm around to pull it out, but I couldn't reach it. I was in a world of shit without my magic. And judging from the cat-that-ate-the-canary smile that spread across her face, Leila knew it too.

She looked wild, the room almost completely engulfed in fire, the flames tickling at my skin as I watched her mouth move in a silent spell that promised to knock me on my ass. The house beams moaned and crackled as more of the ceiling leaked down in streams of hot ash and flame. Leila was standing between me and the door, and the house was collapsing in on us.

The roar of the fire silenced her words, and I braced myself for whatever she was throwing at me. But instead of slamming into me, I felt her curse slip around my body like an ice cube barely brushing against my skin. Casper stepped through the flames and materialized beside me.

"How'd you like that for a counter-curse?" he shouted over the road crackling fire.

"What are you doing here?" I responded, glancing between him and my mother.

"Saving your ass," he said.

"Thanks for that," I said, eyeing Leila as she worked a new incantation. She looked pissed. "So what now?"

Casper's hand took mine and gripped it firmly. *When the hell did he learn to grip something?* His energy shot through my fingers and up my arm, popping the magic dampening stake out of my shoulder with its force. The energy reversed its course back into Casper. He muttered a bunch of Latin and squeezed my hand hard as Leila stepped towards us with no hesitation.

The fire burning on the ceiling pulled down towards Leila as if it were in a vortex. The flames covered her body, churning and swirling in an angry, red-yellow sea. The control Casper had on the fire was awesome, changing its size and shape with the flick of a wrist, as if he were conducting an orchestra.

Leila roared and shook as she wailed out a counter-curse, the fire finally extinguishing. She emerged from the lingering smoke without even a first-degree burn.

"Damn," he muttered. "Now I know why you can take this inferno."

I nodded, understanding washing over me. Leila was immune to fire. It was how she survived the fire that we thought killed her and my dad. And since the flames shooting at me didn't seem to have any effect, I probably was too.

Leila licked her fingers, as if tasting the spell. "This one tastes like something my father made." She raised her eyebrows. "You're not just a witch. You're a ghost too."

She kept creeping towards us. I watched her mouth move, trying to decipher her unheard chanting. *What the hell spell was she pulling?*

"Hang on!" I yelled at Casper as I felt his grip weaken. Shit, Leila wasn't spelling us, she was exorcising him. His opaque body became effervescent. I clutched his wrist with my other hand, as if that alone could keep his soul here on Earth.

"Nina," Casper called out to me, panic rising in his voice. "You're going to have to do a summoning spell to keep me here."

"Is that safe?" I asked.

"It's better than a banishment," he yelled back. He doubled over from pain as bits of his skin began to tear away from his body. I searched my brain for a spell that called the dead.

A faded memory popped into my head. When I was in Blood Ops training, an instructor tried to call a spirit without the use of a spirit board. The memory of the spell lingered even though no ghost appeared. I had to trust it would work.

"You who lived yesterday, come into the light," I started. "Step out of the shadows and remain linked to our lives."

Casper sucked in a breath, and I watched his magic rip through his body like a Tesla coil. But instead of entering mine, our energies merged where our hands touched.

"Do it again," he said, his voice sounding stronger.

I repeated the spell, and this time Casper joined me, his own voice lilting above the din of the inferno swirling around us. I felt another surge of power shoot through me.

"Again!" Casper yelped, and I felt his grip get tighter. We launched into another round, and as his spirit grounded itself onto the earth, I heard a new chorus of voices behind us, chanting the spell.

"Do you hear that?" I asked Casper when we finished the spell.

He gave me a quick nod. "We'll worry about them later."

"Them?" I asked.

Casper's face screwed up with worry. He simply stared at Leila, who was glaring at the wall behind us, her forward march towards us finally halted. I shot a quick glance over my shoulder and my stomach dropped. There were all manner of spirits, most dressed in

1800s garb and in varying stages of decay, stepping through the back wall and into the burning house. The spell didn't only keep Casper bound to the earth, but it also raised the restless spirits in the graveyard behind the house. *Double damn.*

"What the hell did we just do?!" I yelled to Casper.

"Whatever we did, we can't undo it right now!" he replied, ever the pragmatist.

Leila didn't look happy to see the ghost militia at our back. Frankly, it unnerved me too. But like Casper said, that was a problem for another day.

Leila was today's — and yesterday's — problem and she was making her way to the exit. The woman was going to cut and run, and if we lost her again, Rhode Island would face an atomic Armageddon.

Desperation licked at the back of my neck along with the graveyard ghosts. I released Casper's hand. "Get the hell out of here," I called out to him, snatching the bloody stake off the floor before I rushed forward. I slammed my head into Leila's solar plexus like a football linebacker, propelling us both outside. She sprawled under me on the dirt as the house collapsed in on itself, and the night air filled with ghostly shrieks and moans. I raised the stake in my right hand, ready to bring it down into her.

"Don't kill her!" Max shouted as he sprinted up the drive from the car. "Do! Not! Kill! Her!"

I paused, the stake hovering just above Leila's heart. Her white tooth grin stood out in sharp relief from her soot-smeared face, giving her a clownish, macabre appearance. She chuckled again. My eyes went wide as I felt her take in a bundle of power.

I glanced around, trying to figure out where she was pulling so much power from, and I realized that we were sprawled on the ground that once held the barn that burned to the ground some 30 odd years ago, supposedly killing her. There was something magical under us that she was drawing power from, and I felt her body swell with energy against my own.

I closed my eyes as the magic pushed out from her like a force, but instead of letting it streak through me, threatening to fry my synapses, I focused on welcoming it instead, opening my body to its raw power. It set my teeth on edge, leaving a metallic taste on the tip of my tongue as energy vibrated through me, filling my body with a relentless pulse of power that threatened to consume me. When I couldn't take it any longer, I pushed it out, shoving sorcery into the night sky where it manifested as bolts of lightning that crackled just above the tree line. Then I slammed the stake down into her heart, its force ten times greater than anything I'd ever thrown, and her eyes went wide.

"Stupid girl. Now you'll never know the truth of what you are," she said, a small giggle escaping her lips before her body went limp, her energy sinking out of me and dropping into the ground.

I rolled off of her and knelt beside her body, the murderous glee on her face frozen in a death mask. It was the same expression she wore when she dropped a torch into the pile of kindling and burned Babe on the stake.

I shook my blade loose from its holster and before I could think it through, I brought it down across her neck, severing her head in one fast move.

"What the hell did you do!" Max shouted, his footsteps heavy on the ground behind me. He dropped to his knees just as Leila's body ignited and turned to ash. The wind picked up to carry it across the dirt. "What the hell did you do?" he asked again. This time his voice was barely above a whisper.

I spit out thick soot from the fire that still burned bright, the wood still cracking and splintered behind me. "No choice," I said with a shrug. I won. And winning meant that I killed my mother. And I had to wear that fact like an ill-fitting suit for the rest of my immortal life.

I stood and strode down the dirt drive, gravel crushing under my feet. Away from Max. Away from the burning house. Away from Gramps and Mariana, who enveloped her corporeal son in a massive hug, her back shuddering in sobs of joy to finally be able to touch the child she thought she'd lost. I even strode away from Frankie.

A cool rain started, each drop cleansing the sludge of the battle off of me as I stumbled my way towards home.

26

"HEY, NINA, ANOTHER ROUND DOWN HERE," Al called to me from the perch on his bar. His shit-eating grin told me that this round was on one of the poor college students that he bamboozled using Eva's divination skills. I sighed, pulling on the tap to pour three more beers. Goddamn grifters were going to scare away my best customers — college kids who liked cheep beer and the dive bar ambiance.

There was a loud crash from the table area and I climbed onto the bar to get a better look over the half-wall. "What do you think you're doing?" I yelled at Matty. My idiot cousin turned over two tables in an attempt to lay down a ridiculous looking throw carpet. There was a microphone stand and an amp on the floor.

"Matty needs some practice time," Darcy explained from her stool next to Al, a stack of boxes between them. She was cross checking the orders with the most recent shipment. She slapped Al's hand away as he reached for a not-yet unaccounted for bottle of something. Cutty Sark, maybe? *Who the hell ordered that?* I had to sort out my daylight issue if everyone kept going off list with the orders.

"So why can't he rent out a practice room or something?" I grumped. I crossed my arms and narrowed my eyes at my clueless cousin as he ordered around my paying customers to set his gear. "Like maybe get a garage or something."

Darcy rolled her eyes at me. "Killing Hannah is *not* a garage band."

I raised my hands in apology and jumped back behind the bar to fill a few pints for Matty's *helpers*. I was putting it on his tab, too.

"Besides, he needs some spending cash."

I slapped a half-filled pint glass down on the bar. "I am not paying him to play—"

"No, no, no," Darcy said. "He's going to put out a tip bucket."

I raised my eyebrows. My egomaniac rocks star cousin playing Babe's for tips? "I still don't see how this helps him. Or Babe's."

"This is really about him honing a new, acoustic solo show," Darcy explained, lowering her voice. "He needs to go out on tour, Nina. He's dead broke."

"He's dead something," I muttered. "And how the hell is he broke? Tavio's got to have something squirreled away." Compound interest was an immortal's best friend. My dad left me with several pieces of investment property and a very healthy bank account. Frankie had been quite comfortable over the past few centuries.

"It's a cash flow issue," Darcy explained. "And it's not like he can compel a good record deal."

"Tavio can," I reminded her. Beta-Vamps didn't have any of the benefits of being a vampire and all of the drawbacks. But his dad was a full vampire and could do the dirty work. Unless he was too busy doing Bertrand's.

"Tavio's pissed that Matty keeps blowing through his money, so he cut him off," Darcy admitted. I closed my eyes and shook my head. "Please, Nina? It'll be great for business, you'll see! The lead singer from Killing Hayley, playing stripped down solo sets at Babe's? You'll make a killing." I raised my eyebrows at her choice of works. "In a manner of speaking."

I scowled at the thought of Matty hanging around the bar even more. If he was here for a reason, it was harder for me to toss his ass out when I got sick of his whining. But one look at my best friend's pleading, hopeful face and I softened. We can't help who we fall in love with, right?

"Fine," I said. "We try it for one week. But he gives me any shit, acts surly or he makes me lose customers, he's done. Deal?"

Darcy's smile lit up the room. "Deal," she said with a little squeal. She leaned over the bar and gave me a fast kiss on the cheek. "And they said the vampire made you grumpy," she whispered before scurrying into the other room to get a front row seat at Matty's first solo gig.

"Who said that?" I called after her as the first chord from Matty's guitar filtered through the room. He warbled a bit into the mic and, I had to admit, sounded pretty good.

The front door opened and a passel of college kids stomped in. The girls in the loose group squealed in delight when they saw Matty in the side room, strumming his guitar. They rushed into the space. "I didn't know Babe's had live music," I heard one of them say.

Al was throwing eyeball daggers at me. "What?" I said with a shrug. "I can't tell Darcy no."

"That's why she was the one that asked," he groused. "Good lord, acoustic sets at Babe's? Now the weepy emo little shits will never leave."

"Oh shut it, Al," Eva squeaked. "You think anyone wants to hang out with grumpy old men?" She dropped her voice. "Or vampires?"

"Who's saying that?" I asked again, this time my voice edging up. I wasn't a grumpy vampire, *dammit.*

"'Ello, gorgeous," came from behind me and I turned at the sound of Frankie's voice. One hip leaned into the bar, and his arms were folded across his chest. His sly grin made me wonder if he was spreading the grumpy vampire rumors, but, caught up in his ocean blue eyes, my exasperation melted away. I snagged a bottle of Clown Shoes from the fridge and cracked it open. He wrapped his hand around mine and the bottle, pulling me towards him.

"I think you owe me something," he said into my ear, his voice a sexy growl.

"Do I?" I asked, a smile tugging up my lips.

"You do," he whispered, "And I intend to collect before sunrise."

I allowed myself a brief, sweet moment as the promise of pleasure pressed through my body. We had battled Leila and came out the other side all right.

"A promise is a—" I started, my flirting cut off by the motion of a pissed off Mary Jane stalking towards us from the door. Max trailed in her wake.

I released Frankie's hand and busied myself cleaning the bar glasses in the sink, one eye on Mary Jane as she maneuvered through the crush of college kids.

"Did you check everyone's ID?" she snapped, her linen suit rumpled from the press of bodies she'd just pushed through.

"I didn't know you were ATF," was my cool response. She may be my boss in Blood Ops, but I was boss of this bar.

Max cleared his throat and adjusted his button-down shirt so his badge was showing. I flicked my hands, spattering both of them with water. A small grunt of satisfaction slipped from me when not one of my young barflies cared that there was a fed in the building.

"We're off the clock," Frankie reminded them. He raised his eyebrows at me before taking a long pull from his beer.

"We didn't come in for a debriefing," Mary Jane said, wiping at the sudsy water that had hit her expensive linen. I didn't bother covering up my smirk. Childish, I know, but this woman irked me. And it looked like I was starting to ruffle her pristine feathers.

"This is serious," Max said. "Things are different now. You can't be so...rebellious."

"Rebellious?" I asked, eyes wide in mock surprise. "You mean a secret government operative snuffing out supernatural creatures should be more...orthodox?"

One of the college kids turned to us. "You're talking about X-Men, right?"

"Absolutely," Frankie said. "Go listen to the music. I'll give you ten quid if you request 'Free Bird.'"

"We do things by the book," Mary Jane continued, this time keeping her voice low. "We have some pressing things to deal with."

"We're taking a few days off," I lied. Well, not really, but a few days off sounded pretty good. I hated to shut down the bar again, but maybe Darcy would cover. I did agree to let Matty launch his solo career from here, after all.

"I need the team for something else," she said, but my eyes were on Max, who looked warily around the room.

"Where's Casper?" he asked.

"He's with his mom," I said, tacking on a dramatic sigh at the end. "Can you two just get to the damn point? I was hoping for a bit of downtime."

"It's about Bertrand," Max began.

Okay, now they had my attention. "What about him?"

Mary Jane tucked her silky hair behind her ears. "We don't trust him."

"Well duh," I said and went back to washing out the glasses. I should have known better than to get my hopes up.

"You're close to him," she said.

"Me? What about Max? He trusts Max way more than me."

"That's why I need you to get closer," she said.

"No way," Frankie said. "She's not facing a demon on her own."

"She will have the full support of the agency," she continued.

"That's a relief," I said mockingly. "Look, Mary Jane, I need a break, okay? It's been one crisis after the next. Dr. O is—"

"Human," Frankie interrupted.

"Human," I agreed. "And alive. Leila is dead."

"Twice," Frankie chimed in again.

"Yes, and she wasn't supposed to be," Mary Jane reminded me.

I plunked another pint glass into the soapy water and bubbles wafted into the air. "It's safer for everyone this way."

"Look, I'm trying to give you both a way out. But you insist on doing it the hard way," Mary Jane huffed. "Fine. We are sanctioning you both for not follow direct orders to keep Leila Martinez alive."

I paused, my hands still under water. Frankie and I looked at each other and burst out laughing.

"Haven't had the time to talk to HR, have you?" Frankie asked.

"Take a day or two and give our files a good going over. How many times have we been sanctioned, Nina?"

"I think I lost count at around 57," I said.

"You don't seem to understand," she said, a cold smile spreading across her face. "Your complete disregard of authority has jeopardized an ongoing undercover investigation."

"What ongoing investigation?" I asked, bringing my hand up out of the water. Soap plopped on the bar counter.

"That information is above your security clearance," she snorted.

My vampire reflexes kicked in and I grabbed her wrist with my soapy hand, soaking her expensive linen shirt with cheap dish detergent. I yanked her close. "Lady, you don't even know half the shit we've seen. Nothing is that classified."

I released her arm, shoving her away.

"What the hell is this racket?" Gramps' voice boomed through the bar as he shuffled from the door going up to the apartment.

"Your staying above a bar," Al bickered back at him. "What the hell'd you expect?"

"I'm talking about that sad-sack singer," Gramps retorted. "Makes me want to cry in my beer." He looked from me to the beer taps then back to me again. "I have no beer to cry in. See the issue now?"

At Gramps' entrance, Mary Jane backed off, wiping at her shirt with a cocktail napkin. I poured Gramps a 'Gansett as he raised his eyebrows at me. "Impressing the new boss?"

I chuckled. "Apparently."

"You two take your vacation time," he said, nodding at Frankie. "I think you need some, what's it called, alone time?" He followed that up with kissy noises, and Al burst out laughing.

"Yeah, yeah," I said, vaulting over the bar to bring some free beers over to the tables that Matty disturbed to set up his stage. It gave me an excuse to escape their razzing, which continued until I got into the other room.

"On the house," I said with a smile, putting the beers down in front of the happy patrons.

I stopped to watch Darcy, sitting front row and positively smitten with Matty as he serenaded her with a love song, like she was the only person in the room.

Frankie came up behind me and wrapped his arms around me. "Maybe retirement isn't such a bad idea," he whispered into my ear as we both watched Matty command the little makeshift stage. "Settle down here, run the bar."

"No more staking vampires," I murmured.

"Or accelerating global warming," he teased, referring to my uncontrolled magic.

"Hey," I protested. "I've gotten better."

"Sod it, Nina. We've got Dr. O safe, and Leila's out of the picture."

"But Bertrand—" I cut myself off, remembering what Leila said about Bertrand making me, like Max.

"Bertrand, what, love?" Frankie asked.

"He's still running things," I said, turning my head to watch Max. He and Mary Jane were standing by the door, heads tipped together. Max looked comfortable with her, touching her arm as they spoke. Did Max's interest in keeping Blood Ops together have to do with his Berserker curse? If we were both made, did he think I could help unmake us? Did I even want to?

Max and Mary Jane snuck a glance my way, and I wondered what they were plotting. I sighed and turned back to watch Matty work some magic on an intricate guitar chord. This was not my problem. I told Max not to make a deal with a demon.

"So let him," Frankie continued. "Bertrand didn't interfere with Leila. He let us handle it. Let's allow him to handle Providence."

"He didn't exactly help, either," I said. "I still don't trust him."

"Nor do I," he said. "But do we have to fix everything?"

"I guess not," I said with a shrug.

I thought about the years of sacrifice that Frankie and I both made, and the people we'd lost along the way. I thought about Babe, almost hearing her loud laughter coming from behind the bar, her presence etched into the old wooden boards and polished brass. I thought about Casper, struck down at 18 by Leila's serial killer lover. He was still with us, but for how long? The ghosts in the Biltmore withered with each passing year, turning into angry poltergeists as they refused to leave our plane. How much time did Casper have before we had to force him to pass over?

Then I thought about me, and I mourned for the human that I once was. And the humans, the people we fought to protect from the criminally minded freaks like us, well... They weren't great at separating the good guys from the hoodlums.

"Besides, do we really want to work with an organization who responds to a crisis by dropping bombs on its own people?" Frankie continued.

"Can we afford not to?" I wondered aloud.

He chuckled. "It's rather pompous to think the human race cannot get on without us, don't you think?"

I sighed and leaned into him, the strength of his muscled body against my own lifting my melancholia. His fingers intertwined with mine, and he brought my hand up to his lips, pressing a soft kiss into my palm.

Darcy beamed from her seat in front of Matty, whose voice, I had to admit, was angelic. He had the entire room hypnotized by his charisma. I snuggled against Frankie, contentment settling over me like a warm bowl of soup. Well, I guess a warm bowl of blood now.

Maybe we were going to be all right, Frankie and me. Maybe, we were going to be all right.

ABOUT THE AUTHOR

Karen Greco is originally from Rhode Island and loves hot wieners from New York System, but can't stand coffee milk. She studied playwriting in college (and won an award or two). After not writing plays for a long time, a life-long obsession with exorcists and Dracula drew her to urban fantasy, where she decapitates characters with impunity. *Steele City Blues* is the third book in the *Hell's Belle* series, after *Hell's Belle* (the first) and *Tainted Blood* (number two). She writes contemporary romance for a small press under the pen-name Jillian Sterling, and has a day job in entertainment publicity. She does not speak in the third person all that often. Really.

Stay up-to-date with the *Hell's Belle* series and other books by joining the newsletter.

www.karengrecoauthor.com

ALSO BY KAREN GRECO

Hell's Belle (Book 1 in the Hell's Belle Series)

Tainted Blood (Book 2 in the Hell's Belle Series)

WRITING AS JILLIAN STERLING

Billionaire Bait

The Forbidden Beat

ACKNOWLEDGMENTS

A huge thanks to my friends and family that slog through early, typo-riddled manuscripts with such enthusiasm.

Thank you to one of my oldest, dearest friends, Lizz, for always jumping on board for the early read. Your support means the world to me. And to my cousins Lia and Lynn, who read Every. Single. Word. and find errant typos. You guys are amazing.

I owe a huge debt of gratitude to my editing team, Rakia Clark and Clarence Haynes. You both make me sound like I know what I am doing.

Finally, to my readers. Thank you for reaching out via Facebook, my website, or wherever you find me. You guys have no idea how much it means to hear from you. You keep me going.

The rocking cover designs for the *Hell's Belle* series are by Robin Ludwig.

www.ingramcontent.com/pod-product-compliance
Lightning Source LLC
Chambersburg PA
CBHW071247170626
46809CB00001B/102